Rewriting the Story

Emily Tudor

Book Cover by Hannah Nguyen

Illustrations by Hannah Nguyen

Edited by Alexa at The Fiction Fix

For the friendships formed through books, and more specifically, all the female friendships in my life. You all have healed something in me you never broke. I hope we can be girls together forever.

And for Lexi & Hannah—my own version of the Grand Mountain Book Club.

Recommended Reading Order

For the best possible reading experience, it is recommended to read The Grand Mountain Series in publishing order. While they can be read as standalones, if you want the full found family vibe from the book club girls, read in the order below. As always, thank you for picking up my stories. It always means the world.

<u>Reading Order:</u>

Replaying the Game

Redefining the Rules

Reconsidering the Facts

Reconciling With the Rival

Rewriting the Story

Content Warnings

This book features on page descriptions of mental health struggles, sexually explicit content, and mentions of a car accident (off page).

Playlist

First Time by Hozier
The Bolter by Taylor Swift
I Wanna Get Better by Bleachers
Getting Older by Billie Eilish
Sidelines by Phoebe Bridgers
Night Changes by One Direction
Older by Lizzy McAlpine
Farsighted by The Band CAMINO
Used To Be Friends by Searows
Best by Gracie Abrams
Warm by Ariana Grande
The Elevator by Lizzy McAlpine
Growing Sideways by Noah Kahan
From the Dining Table by Harry Styles
Luna Moth by Maya Hawke
How Sweet It Is (To Be Loved By You) by James Taylor
That's What I Get by Wallows
All I Know by asiris
Speyside by Bon Iver
I Met You Too Soon by asiris

I Told You Things by Gracie Abrams
So Real by Jeff Buckley
As It Was by Harry Styles
Amelia by Mimi Webb
Feels Like by Gracie Abrams
Ghostin by Ariana Grande
Miles to Go by Gregory Alan Isakov
Ordinary People by John Legend
All I Need To Hear by The 1975
Martingale by Searows
Ribs by Lorde
When We Are Together by The 1975
True Blue by boygenius
Walking in the Wind by One Direction
The Manuscript by Taylor Swift

"I wish there was a way to know you're in the good old days before you've actually left them."

—— **Andy Bernard, THE OFFICE**

"I hope that either all of us or none of us are judged by the actions of our weakest moments, but rather, by the strength we show when and if we're ever given a second chance."

— **Ted Lasso**

Prologue

Then — Senior Year

First Time by Hozier

WAKING UP NEXT TO my boyfriend on a sunny Sunday morning and hearing the birds chirp outside is my favorite feeling in the world.

Well, second to his arms around me, his head nestled in the crook of my neck like it is now.

I never thought I'd wake up feeling as much happiness as I have the past few weeks. Henry and I have been staying over at one another's apartments while we're back on campus, and I never knew waking up next to someone could be so therapeutic.

My sleep schedule has always been chaotic, almost non-existent, but thanks to Henry and the routine we have going, I've been getting more sleep than I have in pretty much my entire life. Most nights, Henry and I eat dinner together while we play music in the background, and then he either writes while I sit beside him on the couch reading, our legs intertwined, or we study together. It's only been a month, and this semester seems to be flying by faster than we expected.

I feel like I just got him, and soon enough, graduation is going to be around the corner. We're going to have to decide what our lives are going to look like outside of this place surrounded by our friends.

"Mills, your heart is beating so fast right now," he says as he stirs awake, his hand coming to my face as he adjusts how he's sitting. "What has you all up in arms so early in the morning?"

"Nothing now that you're awake," I say. "Everything is fine, Hen."

He cranes his neck up at me, not saying a word as he waits for me to explain.

"Graduation," is all I need to say; we've had this conversation before.

"I thought I told you not to worry about that right now," he reminds me. "We'll figure it out when the time comes. Let's just enjoy this time together while we have it."

"I know, I know," I say as I sit up.

"Well, if you know, then why do you keep worrying about it?"

I roll my eyes. I can't help it.

"Exactly. You know I'm right, and now you're going full silent treatment because you loathe when I'm right."

"I do not." *I totally do.* Another head tilt, and I break underneath his stare. "Fine, but I get to pick the playlist this morning while we make breakfast."

"Anything you want, Mills," he says as he presses a kiss to my forehead. "As long as you're here with me, that's all I need. You know that."

I can't help my smile. I still don't understand how all this adorable relationship shit doesn't make me nauseous like it used to when I watched my friends fall in love.

For some reason, when it's him complimenting me or saying any of the other thousand adorable things he's always doing, my body just gets...warm. It's the weirdest thing.

And I don't hate it. Where Henry is concerned, everything he does is perfect. He gets my humor like nobody else. He doesn't mind my stupid quips. He loves *me*.

"On second thought," I say as he starts to get up, "maybe we should just stay in bed all morning and forget about the outside world."

He laughs, the sound filtering through my ears as if I just turned on my favorite song.

"That's the same thing you said last night when I wanted to study."

I shrug. "Well, what we ended up doing was better, unless you don't like—"

"Amelia Ellis," he says before pinning me to the mattress. "Get that thought out of your mind."

"I'm just saying..." I trail off, suddenly only able to focus on the fact that he's shirtless and our breathing matches. He presses a long, languid kiss to my lips before he pulls back and we're both out of breath.

"I love you," he tells me. "But let's get some coffee in you before you threaten to stab my eyes out."

That earns him another eye roll. "Whatever you say."

He all but drags me to the kitchen, and just as I'm about to start the coffee maker, he grabs my waist and sets me on top of the counter.

"Put some music on while I dote on you, baby," he smiles as he takes over.

God, I can't believe this man is even real. I never saw him coming.

We met at a concert, of all places, and I almost didn't even go. It was an impulsive decision. Maybe Henry and I would have met otherwise, but who knows? I'm not a big believer in fate, but the stars really did align that day.

One of the bands I love was playing near Grand Mountain over the summer, and since I was by myself on campus taking summer classes, I bought a ticket and went. I didn't know they were playing until the day before, and I'm really glad I saw the post online about it.

It's strange how different my life could look if I hadn't gone to that concert. Henry was a person I never even knew I needed, but now that I have him, I can't imagine not knowing him. I can't imagine being strangers. I don't really ever want to be.

I tend to mess things up—relationships and life in general. I'm not a person most people would call organized, but I haven't fucked this up yet. Henry seems to still love being around me, so I'm clearly doing something right .

"Oh, I love this song," he says as he starts to whistle along with it. "I swear, your playlists are always perfect, Mills."

"That is the highest compliment you could give someone like me, Hen," I say. I hop off the counter and wrap my arms around him as he flips one of the pancakes he made.

"And I mean it," he says as he sets the spatula down, spinning to face me. "Can you pour me some coffee?"

"Of course," I say, knowing just how he likes it—some cream and sugar. I take a sip out of my own mug, taking a deep breath as I peruse Henry's shelves in his living area. I swear, I could stare at his books forever. They're organized in his very own way, and most nights, I'm pulling something down to read or skim while he writes.

My mornings never used to be like this, especially when I was a kid. My family and I were never that close, and as I grew up, having meals together became scattered because either Steven had some sort of sporting event, or my parents were busy working—even on the weekends.

I'm not blaming them, but as I've grown up, I've realized how much I appreciate slow mornings and really taking my time to wake up. With my weird sleep schedule, mornings have always been difficult, and I appreciate how Henry doesn't mind having these slow starts with me. He's more of a get up and go kind of person, but ever since I told him how I like my mornings to look, he's been making Sunday's our go-to day for slowly rising with the sun and taking our time getting up.

"Pancakes are ready," he tells me as he sets the pancakes on the table, pulling my chair out for me.

The two of us eat, the music filtering through his apartment and filling the spaces between our stares and smirks. Henry keeps glancing at the necklace he bought me hanging from my neck.

"You're staring again," I tell him as I take another bite.

"You're telling me I can't be in awe at my beautiful girlfriend whenever I want?" Henry jokes. "Then what are we even doing here?"

"Oh, I can leave if you want," I joke as I start to stand and head for the door. Just before I'm about to reach for the handle, he grabs me, carrying me over his shoulder and throwing me gently onto his couch.

"Amelia."

"Henry?" I question, noting the look on his face.

"You know if you run, I'll chase you." He smirks down at me. "That was a valiant effort, but it looks like you're stuck with me."

I sigh, not saying a word as he continues to stare at me, his smirk now a full smile. I cross my arms, pretending to be annoyed but secretly loving how he chases after me. It's always been known I'm a runner from most things—feelings, relationships, and all that jazz—but Henry has never been afraid of that part of me. He is always the one to remind me I could never run from him—not fully, at least.

I'm stubborn and set in my ways, but he's never tried to change who I am. He accepts me, flaws and all, and even plays into my stupid jokes.

"You make me really happy, you know," I beam up at him.

That earns me a head tilt. "What are you saying that for?" he asks as he puts a hand against my forehead. "Are you feeling okay?"

I smack his hand away with a laugh. "I just wanted you to know that, despite all my stupid jokes, I really do love you, Hen. I love these mornings we spend together, and I love stealing books off your shelves at night. I love that you talk my ear off about all the stories you want to write. I love *you*. Forgive me if I don't say enough how happy I am to be with you."

I slide up to sit on the couch as he throws his arms around me, flipping me around so I'm in his lap.

He doesn't say a word; rather, he tucks a brown curl behind my ear, his hand coming to my neck before he presses a kiss to my mouth. His other hand grips my hip as he tries to pull me closer.

"We're not even done with breakfast, Hen," I say in between kisses.

"Let me enjoy kissing you while I have you like this."

"Like what?"

"Your walls are down, and I'm going to take advantage of this time. If you want to say a bunch of other really kind things, then—"

"Shut up." I push on his chest.

"Ah, there's my girl."

For the rest of the morning, Henry and I enjoy one another's company before we host everybody at his apartment for game night. It's a fairly normal day, but it reminds me of what's really important in life.

1

Then — The Day After Graduation

"It was the end and none of us knew what to do. We knew we were surrounded by reality, but none of us wanted to admit the end was near." — *In A Room With Death,* Henry Hayes

I CONSIDER TELLING PAIGE to flip the car over; it would be a whole lot better than where we're headed.

Today is the day Amelia leaves for London. I wish we had more time, but it has officially run out.

When she told me she got her dream job in London working for National Geographic, my heart stopped. I knew that was her goal, but I also assumed it would be something a little closer to home.

She never even told me she applied to the London office, and the wind was knocked out of me when I found out.

But this is what she wants, and the two of us agreed to make long distance work.

I'm simultaneously excited for her and disappointed in what this means for us. I know she's always felt this itch to leave, but some days, it feels like I'm going to miss her more than she'll miss me. I know that's not true. I know she'll miss me; she's just not very good at showing it.

It's going to be fine.

"Paige, turn this song up! We need to have one more car performance before you leave, Ames," Ella says from in front of me.

We're all tightly packed into Paige's Jeep as we head to the airport. By all of us, I mean, the book club girls—Hads, Paige, Ella, and Amelia...or Mills or Ames. There's no shortage of nicknames with these women. Paige and Oliver take up the front row while Grant and Hads sit in the middle. Her head rests on his shoulder, and I fight the jealousy that they get to continue their relationship like this, that Hads isn't flying across the world away from Grant.

I'm the third boyfriend inaugurated into this circle of girls who became friends over books, and I wear my title with honor.

These four are something special; anyone can see that. Books may have brought them together, but that has morphed into something much stronger, and I know this transition is going to be tough. With Amelia in London for who knows how long, she's going to miss book club every Wednesday. I assume she'll still call to discuss with them, but I know it won't be the same. I have to keep reminding myself she is leaving *all* of us. It's not going to be easy, but I feel lucky to be surrounded by people who will feel the same way I do.

"Ella, I'm not in the mood to perform," Paige says, her voice breaking. Paige already cried twice today, and my heart breaks for her.

Amelia and Paige have been glued to one another since freshman year, when they randomly got assigned as roommates. They've lived together for the past four years, and I've never seen two people so opposite from one another who fit so well.

Our group has been through hell and back this year, and I'm excited to finally be starting life with them all by my side.

Amelia won't be with me, but she'll still be here in spirit.

She's been a little too quiet on the drive to the airport. I don't think she's rethinking her decision—once she makes up her mind, it's hard to change it—but something is wrong.

Instead of pressing her on it, I slip my hand into hers and softly squeeze.

"Paigey, come on." Grant pokes his head through the center console. "I know for a fact you'll feel better after the chorus."

"He's absolutely right! And I need someone to duet with. Everyone knows Grant can't sing that high."

He throws his hands up. "Ells, as your go-to karaoke partner, I'm hurt but—"

"But as a human, you understand. Hearing you sing octaves higher than your voice when you don't actually know the words is like hearing a chicken's neck get snapped," Oliver says. A little harsh, but he is right.

"Oliver, be nice." Hads grabs his seatbelt, stretches it out, then lets go of it. A loud *thwack* rings through the car.

"What the fuck?"

She only shrugs at her brother. "I don't have my ruler. I had to be creative."

I see Amelia's mouth lift, and even though she's smiling at Oliver's misery, I'm glad to see it on her face.

"That's my girl," Grant says as he presses a kiss to Hads' head. She leans into him ever so slightly.

It's hard to believe those two ever hated one another, but according to Amelia, it was a whole thing—Hads and Grant not getting along. I wasn't around back then, but Mills told me the entire story of their relationship in PowerPoint format.

I was around when Paige and Oliver got together; it was obvious to me they liked one another before they got together. They even solved a murder case on campus. It was adorable—if you're into that sort of thing. Everyone in our group still thinks they're both insane, but it worked out okay in the end.

Paige drives slowly, but we somehow end up parking a few minutes and a silent car ride later. I thought we all had more time with each other. This is the moment I've been dreading since Ames told me the news.

My throat has been tight all morning, but I'm not going to cry—not in front of Amelia. She doesn't do emotions very well, and even though I'm not much of a crier, I'm going to miss her.

A lot.

We all sit silently, suspended in time. It's almost as if each of us knows that the moment we get out, reality will crash in and, in order to keep it at bay for a little longer, everyone hesitates.

A few seconds later, Oliver opens his door, and I should have known he would be the first to get out. He keeps joking about throwing a party after Amelia leaves, but I think deep down, he's going to miss her.

Ella, Grant, and Hads slide out next, and Grant folds his seat forward so Mills and I can get out. All of us stand outside Paige's car in a circle, staring at one another. Awkward is an understatement, but the boys and I know this goodbye is more for the girls than us. It's the end of an era, of them all being in the same place.

Paige hasn't even gotten out of the driver's seat yet. Oliver steps up to the door and opens it for her, but she doesn't move to get out.

"Come on, love."

"I can't, Ol."

"Yes, you can. You'll see her again. This isn't goodbye."

I see him reach over and wipe her eyes before she slides out of her car, her shoulders slumped and her head hanging low.

She looks exactly how I feel.

"Let's give them a second," Oliver says as the three of us guys shift to the back of the car to grab Amelia's suitcase. She had most of her stuff flown ahead of her, so it should already be at her place in London, courtesy of Ella's friend Alissa, who is visiting her family over there.

"Hen, how are you feeling?" Grant asks as he pats my back.

"As expected. I knew it would be tough, but I can't shake the feeling that something is wrong."

"You're probably adjusting to the air after dealing with Amelia for so long. Welcome back to Earth, buddy," Oliver says as he drags her carry-on from the trunk.

"Ignore him. He's going to miss her—"

Oliver cuts Grant off. "I'm sure as hell not going to miss her climbing into Paige's bed every morning to debrief. She shoved me clean off my own girlfriend's bed and then claimed she didn't know I was there."

I stifle a laugh. "I remember Paige doing the same thing a few times, but I was allowed to listen in. Ames didn't do that for you?"

Oliver rolls his eyes. "No. She only gave me bruises from pushing me off Paige's bed. I sure as hell won't be missing that."

Fifteen minutes and lots of tears from the girls later, it's my turn to say goodbye to her before she gets on the elevator and heads up to security.

"I'll miss you guys. I promise not to fully disappear on you. I know I always joke about that, but I won't," she says, a few tears falling from her eyes.

"We're a phone call away, Amelia. That's all." A stray tear falls from Hads' eyes.

"I know," she says before looking over at me, a strange but sorrowful look on her face. "Can we talk?"

"We'll be in the car," Grant says as he shoves them all away.

"Wait!" Paige shouts, even though she's fifteen feet from us. She runs over to Amelia and hugs her one last time, almost knocking them both over. "Please call me when you land. And don't forget about me while you're across the pond."

"I could never forget you, P. You know that."

"Okay, sorry," Paige says as she slips from Amelia's hold. "I'll be in the car."

Oliver opens the passenger door for her, knowing she won't be able to drive through her tears, before he shuts it and jogs to the driver's side.

The door shuts, and I look at my girlfriend's beautiful face, her eyes filled with tears.

"Don't cry, Mills. It's going to be fine."

One tear falls from her eye before she speaks. "Henry, I can't do this."

"Yes, you can. You're going to get on that plane, and you're—"

"You misunderstand me. I can't get on that plane as your girlfriend."

What? "Wait, wh—"

"I'm breaking up with you."

Five words, and my heart shatters. Five fucking words is all it takes. I know how powerful words are, and those five strung together in succession are some of the most painful I've ever heard. She has to be joking, right? Amelia makes some weird jokes sometimes—her humor isn't for everyone. This seems cruel, too cruel for her to joke about.

"W-what?" I reach out to grab her hand, but she pulls it away, grabbing her suitcase instead. "Amelia," I whisper, shocked at her sudden coldness.

"I don't want you to be here waiting for me, Henry. I don't want you to wait for me when I don't know if I'll ever be back here again. You need to move on and find someone who can love you, create a family with you, and that's not me."

I've never heard her so devoid of emotion before.

"What are you even saying right now?" I don't even recognize my own voice. "You're breaking up with me? You're serious about this?"

"Yes. I can't give you what you want, and it's for the best—"

I take a step back from her, her words punching me in the chest, my body recoiling at her tone. "We can make this work. We talked about this, and you were on board with doing long distance. What happened? Why are you doing this to us?"

I need answers, but she stands there silently, not giving me any. Is she really going to throw all this away? Why? Is she scared about the long distance? There has to be something. As far as I'm concerned, this came out of left field, and I need answers if she's serious.

My heart needs to know why she would do this to us—to me.

"I love you, Amelia. I *love* you."

"I warned you, Henry. I told you not to fall for me, and you did anyway."

"Because it was so easy to fall, Ames. You made it so easy to love you," I whisper. I'm staring into her eyes, trying to find any sign of life for us, but I can't see anything.

I used to be able to read her like a book, like song lyrics spelled out across her forehead, but now, I don't see a thing. Her eyes are devoid of emotion, only tears filling them.

"Forget about me and find a girl who will love you, because I can't, Henry. I told you in the beginning that if you fell, it would only end badly. I'm sorry it came to this, but—"

"You don't get to break my heart and then apologize, Amelia. You knew what you were doing when you agreed to make this work." I shake my head, my emotions and thoughts running rampant. I'm normally a cool headed person, but as she breaks us, I can't think straight. "I love you," I repeat, as if that will do anything.

"I don't love you," she says, but I know she's lying. Her words say one thing, but her actions from the past year say otherwise. So she didn't mean she loved me when we first said it to one another in that parking lot? She didn't love me when I gave her every piece of myself? She didn't love me when we passed our headphones between one another? What about when we traded our favorite books? What happened to every whispered *I love you* before we fell asleep and woke up tangled with one another?

God, I feel sick.

"It's over, Henry," she says with finality before she looks down at her phone. "I have to go, or I'm going to miss my flight."

"Amelia—" I say, but she only grabs her suitcase and looks at me one more time, as if she's stopping to memorize me.

Don't go. Don't leave me here and run like you always do. You're better than this. I know you, and I know you don't actually want to break us. You're scared of something, but I don't know what.

We can fix this. We can make it work. Please, come back to me.

But she still turns around and walks away, leaving me stuck where I stand, the weight of our conversation making it hard to move.

I feel a pair of arms around me, and when I look down, Paige is giving me a hug. *Did she know? Did she know the whole time that this was her plan?*

"Get off, please," I say, the words coming out strangled.

Paige lets go, and the moment she looks at me, her face falls. "What's wrong?"

"We're all upset, but—" Grant stops abruptly when he sees my face. "Hen?"

"She—" I can't say it out loud. I can't admit it because it doesn't feel real. I feel like I could wake up any moment to find Amelia curled into my side in her bed, and all would be okay.

I just need to wake up. *Why can't I wake up from this nightmare?* Surely, it's a nightmare. This can't be how Amelia and I end.

"What happened?" Ella asks, concern lacing her voice.

"She broke up with me. It's over."

Surprise crosses all their expressions, and nobody says a thing.

I make a split second decision, and before I know it, I'm moving. I head for the elevator, buy the cheapest ticket I can to get through security, and run through the Virginia airport.

I have to see her. I have to talk to her one more time before she gets on that plane and leaves.

Part of me still believes I can change her mind, that maybe if I convince her we can get through the distance, it'll be okay.

We have to be okay.

I love her, and I won't lose her like this. If she's afraid of this, of us, I'll show her we can survive anything.

Her plane is already boarding, and I see her scanning her ticket at the desk.

"Amelia! Ames!" I shout, but she doesn't turn around. "Mills!"

She doesn't spare me a single glance as she gets on the plane, taking a piece of my heart with her.

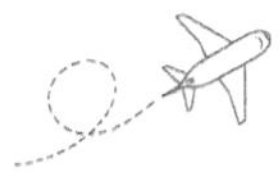

The Bolter by Taylor Swift

One Hour Later

HOW DO YOU LEAVE a place you've become so familiar with?

I thought it would be easier. I thought it would be like leaving home and going to college.

But it's not. It's different.

When I left home and moved around the corner to Grand Mountain, there was no ache. There was nothing physically or mentally screaming at me that I was making the wrong decision. It's the surest thing I've done—leaving home. I knew I had to do it. It felt right deep in my bones.

But this...this has all my alarm bells going off, even though yesterday, I was adamant this was the right move. This feeling will go away, I'm sure of it. As soon as the plane lands, I'm sure the excitement will kick in, and all these feelings will fade.

I know I broke his heart. I know I crushed him where he stood, and when I said those five words, I knew I couldn't take them back.

I'm breaking up with you.

The look on his face? I almost dropped dead, but it was for the best, for me and for him. How does a plant grow new roots when they already have them? They can't. He needs to move on with someone better than me, and I need to focus on the next part of my life. It was what's best. I'm sure of it.

It's not just about him, either. It's about everything I'm leaving behind—the memories, the girls, Grant. They won't be close to me anymore, and all I'll have with them are phone calls and video chats instead of sitting around in that same classroom, talking about the books we've been reading.

I'm going to miss the closeness, but at least phones exist. At least I still have them in the only way I can.

As I stare out of the window, I think about who I was four years ago when I got to Grand Mountain. I wasn't shy, but I was quiet. I was determined to make it through college on my own, knowing that switching my major would make my parents withdraw their help.

"You're destined to be alone, Amelia."

Those were the last words my mom said to me before I left. I didn't bother sticking around to ask what she meant by that, but I'm sure my relationship with my family will only become more strained now.

I'm nervous, I'm scared, but this was the right move. This opportunity was too good to pass up. Part of me wants to rub it in my parents' faces, because they were wrong about me. They were wrong about me being a lazy, unmotivated kid. They were wrong about me when they said changing my major was a waste of time, that I'd always be behind in life.

But I got this job right out of college. I'm moving to an entirely different country because of it. Despite my parents not believing in me, I did this all myself. I'm proving them wrong, and I've been proving them wrong the entire time.

This decision might have been a little impulsive, but everything fell into place after I accepted the offer at the London office. I felt good about it. I still feel that way; I guess I'm just a little unsure of what my life is going to look like going forward. These feelings are normal, I'm sure of it. This is one of those scary, life-changing moments some songs talk about when you finally grow up and head into the real world.

As I look out onto the clouds in the sky, I take a big deep breath, hoping the air will fill my lungs up and I'll be able to breathe again.

Goodbye for now, Grand Mountain.

2

Now — September 2025

I Wanna Get Better by Bleachers

I'VE ALWAYS THOUGHT FLIGHTS were the perfect place to think.

The last time I was on one was after I went to visit my friends. I remember that trip as if it was yesterday, but the memories hit me square in the gut this time instead of being warm and fuzzy.

I adjust my headphones, looking at the dark and depressing clouds outside the window that match my choice of music for the plane ride home.

Home.

It's odd I used to think of it as such. England has been my home for two years, two long years that, when I think back on them, feel never ending. But now, I'm headed back to the place I'm from—Virginia.

I pull the sleeves of my hoodie down, doing my best to shrivel into a ball in my window seat. I learned a lot about myself over these past two years—not all good or bad things. It's been a bit of a mixed bag, but I'm headed back to Virginia, determined for a do-over.

Not only did I grow up in Virginia, but I went to college close to my house. All my life, I had been in this little bubble of my hometown. I started feeling jittery during junior and senior year of college. It always happens like that. I'll be content for a while, and I'll finally get into a routine, only for my mind and body to feel restless when that odd feeling hits my stomach.

Maybe I don't belong here. Maybe I don't belong with these people.

It always comes. It happened to me when I was younger, so I begged my parents to switch schools, and thankfully, they let me. In high school, I had this group of close friends, but I never felt like anyone's best friend or first choice. The jitters lasted until we all graduated and went our separate ways. I never talked to any of them again after we all went to college. My entire life, I've been on the outside looking in, and being alone has been the only thing that has ever made sense to me.

I feel the same way when I think of my family. I've always felt so disconnected from them; none of us ever talked about feelings or anything deep. Everything was surface level, and I never wanted to tell them when I was having a hard time, which was almost always, especially when I was younger. I was always called a distraction to my classmates because I could never sit still. My mind was constantly wandering to a million different things because I couldn't focus, and I was not the best student.

My older brother is the golden child, and I always felt like I was just...around. Steven is perfect. He's smart, athletic. He got a thousand scholarships and excellent grades because he's just so fucking perfect.

I, of course, had to be the one to disappoint them. It took me an entire year to figure out that becoming a doctor was not for me. I didn't enjoy it at all; not only were the classes hard, but another profession began calling to me throughout my sophomore year. I was distracted, getting terrible grades, and even though I knew they would disapprove, I switched my major to journalism when I was a sophomore.

I know they're disappointed in what I've chosen to do with my life, I know they're disappointed in *me*, but I wouldn't have survived medical school. I could barely survive undergrad in the major I started in. So, I took it upon myself to create my own path separate from what they always wanted.

Do I regret it? Maybe. I've found myself reflecting a lot over the past few months about the decisions I've made, and looking back, I can't tell if it was me actually making the choices I did, or if it was my stupid chemically imbalanced brain.

My decision to start seeing my therapist was one that only could have come from hitting rock bottom, which happened when I was in England. Things were dark for a while, and when I finally couldn't find the space to crawl out of it, I realized I needed help.

Which isn't a bad thing, I've come to realize. Normally, asking anybody for help with anything, especially concerning my own feelings, makes me want to run the opposite direction. But as soon as I hit rock bottom, it was the only path I thought could have helped, and to my surprise, it did.

I've gone my entire life, all twenty-five years of it, without being properly diagnosed with Attention-Deficit/Hyperactivity Disorder, or ADHD. It explains a lot, looking back on my childhood and who I grew up to be. I can't believe it took this long to realize something was chemically wrong with my brain, rather than just thinking I was wired this way on purpose.

Obviously, this doesn't excuse all the stupid decisions I've made, but it's helped me make better sense of them. I've been working with Dr. Elyse since the beginning of the year, and the new routine and medication she has me on has worked wonders.

It took a lot of work to get to who I am now, but I'm thankful I didn't give up on myself how I wanted to so many times.

Turbulence jerks me around in my seat, and I grab the handle, my nerves taking over. I'm good at flying, but I'm far more nervous about the landing than I am being up here.

I'm going back to Virginia for good. I'm going back to fix what I broke with the people I love. This is the beginning of my fresh start—if I can even call it that. When I left, I was determined to climb the ladder at my job and find success. I thought that would solve all my problems—by proving my parents wrong and showing them I can be successful.

The only thing that really happened in England was the wake up call I got when I realized my life was going nowhere. I left everything good and beautiful back here, breaking the hearts of everyone I loved.

But Dr. Elyse keeps reminding me part of the reason that happened was because I went so long undiagnosed. It threw me for a loop when she told me I have ADHD, and now that I'm medicated, I feel a lot more in control of my choices. The voice is still in the back of my mind, but for the first time in my life, I feel like I'm making conscious decisions, not impulsive ones.

My parents used to call me unmotivated. Lazy was thrown around more times than I can count, but it turns out, that's the exact opposite of who I am. My brain is just a little different, and Dr. Elyse and I spent a lot of time drilling the word lazy out of my brain.

My decision to come to London was impulsive. I was doing what I always did—running when things got too overwhelming. I tend to bolt when people get close to me, and I thought that was just who I was as a person. I thought I was the daughter destined to watch my family from afar, needing to be away to be able to breathe.

That's not the case at all. Even though my relationship with my family is still strained, maybe one day, if I choose to reconnect with them, I can explain all of this. That's not in the cards for me right now, though. Now, I have friendships to mend and actions to take accountability for.

I doubt my parents would be open to a conversation like that anyway. My family was never one to talk about emotions, and I think the same would go for topics like my mental health. I didn't realize it at the time, but the way my family went about deeper conversations made me suppress my emotions. I was never encouraged to talk about the things that haunted me in the middle of the night, or that I could never turn my brain off when I tried to sleep. I could never tell them I'm not lazy; in fact, I always felt like I was trying ten times harder than classmates to do the same work.

My parents taught me how to give just enough and never too much in that regard, and I've spent the past few months trying to undo years of suppressing my emotions.

Paired with the fact that nobody ever really tried to get to know me, so I never let them, my friendships fizzled out most of the time. I was called flaky by more than one person growing up. The signs were always there, but my parents, teachers, and me specifically didn't read them.

In a way, I get it. I always presented as odd to most people. I laugh at things I shouldn't laugh at, and most of the time, when I leave a room, it's with some weird anecdote that doesn't make sense. I always thought nobody ever really understood my sense of humor, understood *me*.

Until I met Paige.

Paige, my randomly assigned freshman year roommate. Paige, the girl who broke down every wall I built up. I remember that night as if it were yesterday. Sometimes, I wish I could live in the memories and nostalgia, but part of life is about growth, and I can't discount what I've been working on while in London. That wouldn't be fair to past me, who wondered if there was something rotten inside her.

Paige had a panic attack the first night we were at school. We barely knew each other, despite having gone to most of the freshman activities that day together. I've never slept properly—something I once thought was just a quirk, but instead turned out to be because of my brain—and she had a bad nightmare I woke her out of. She was disoriented and terrified, her hands curled around herself, as if she was afraid someone was going to get her.

She told me all about her nightmares that night. It was two in the morning, and neither of us wanted to sleep, so we spent the entire night talking, and for the first time, I felt like I had found someone who understood me. She would tell a story, and I would listen, and then the craziest thing would happen. Whenever it was my turn to tell a story, she would *actually* listen to me. I don't know how I could tell, but just by the look in her eyes, I knew she actually cared about what I was saying. I had never had that in someone before. I had never had someone who wanted to hear about the silly thoughts I thought I had. Eventually, I started giving her small bits of the thoughts that often kept me up at night, and she would listen to those too, telling me it was okay to feel how I was.

She was the first person who ever wanted to actually hear those thoughts, and she never judged me. She just listened. From that night on, we were inseparable. I kept giving her pieces of myself, Ella too, and eventually, when Hads joined our group, it got easier to open up. Not fully, but more than I ever had before.

Those three girls knew me. Better yet, they knew me and they accepted me. They didn't mind that I would disappear sometimes, my thoughts often so overwhelming that I had to take breaks from the world and realign myself. They always knew I would come back. They trusted me, loved me when nobody else would, and accepted every flawed and cracked part of me.

And in return, I ruined it, but that's the entire reason I'm coming back. I'm going to fix what I ruined and prove to the people I love that I'm not going to run again. I'm not going to let my stupid brain ruin some of the best relationships I've ever had just because it operates a bit differently.

I'm headed back for good, not just for Paige's wedding. Nobody knows I'll be back permanently, and I intend to keep it that way until I can prove to the people I love I'm serious about staying.

I have a lot of hard conversations coming—I know that. I'm as prepared as I can be for this, and while I am nervous about telling them about my diagnosis, I want to make it clear I'm not just blaming that for what I did to them.

It was still me, but it also didn't help the decisions I made when I did. I'm still at fault, but I'm also taking the proper steps to fix what I broke.

That's growth if I've ever seen it.

I'm sure the girls are assuming I'll be back for this two-week wedding celebration and then I'll ghost and never speak to them again, but that's not the case.

I'm coming back to prove I can stick around.

I don't regret the time I spent in London. In fact, I'll always look back on it as a decision that helped me in the long run. Not only did I discover so much about myself, but it also drove me to finally reach a place where I feel okay about myself and the life I've lived.

London was merely a chapter of the overall story of my life, and though struggles came with it, I will always be grateful for it.

Coming back to Virginia does have me a bit on edge, like I knew it would. It's going to be terrifying seeing these girls again, knowing how they feel about me. I'm surprised the save the date for Paige's wedding even showed up in January when I was spiraling. I didn't answer that one—I had bigger things to worry about. When the invitation showed up in July, I spent an entire session talking to Dr. Elyse about the pros and cons of going back. Not only would it be a major disruption to my routine, but I didn't want to repeat the same behaviors.

Moving back for good felt like the only option. Plus, I had nothing keeping me in London besides my job, and I can be employed anywhere. Though leaving the job I originally left the States for was *another* topic I went in circles about, my therapist reminded me that though the opportunity was great, it wasn't worth it if I wasn't the best version of myself.

I had barely moved up the ladder over the two years I was in London. The decision to leave it all behind was difficult, but ultimately, it felt like the best option.

Though, nothing is the same. I know it's not going to be. I know it's going to be awkward, confusing, and uncomfortable, my routine in London all out of whack. But I can't spend the rest of my life afraid to fix my mistakes, and I can't keep missing out on these huge moments of my friends' lives, only able to see some of it through social media.

I feel like a stranger coming back to this place I used to know like the back of my hand. Only, it didn't change; I did. The first time I was truly on my own—everything I had thought I needed—and my entire life crumbled. Now, I'm running back to my friends.

I wonder if they missed me how I've missed them in the hard moments. I wonder if they think I'm coming to this wedding just to bolt again after. I wonder if Paige is the only one who still believes in me, or if the invitation was a last ditch effort she thought wouldn't work. I wonder if I'm a person still worth missing.

I wonder if he misses me.

The thought pops into my head before I can stop it. Not wanting to relive the memories of him that echo in my mind, I turn my music up as loud as it can go.

Another wave of turbulence hits, and I'm sure this plane ride is a metaphor for my life—violent jerks of discomfort followed by a steady motion.

I sigh heavily as the next song on my playlist comes on before checking how much longer I have up in the air. Only four more hours to go, and I'm sure in that time, I'll be trying and failing to come up with things to say about my diagnosis and how fucking sorry I am for leaving them all behind.

The consequences of my own actions have once again decided to punch me in the face, and I'm going to sit here and own it for once.

I fucked up, and I have to fix it.

No. I'm *going* to fix it—even if it kills me.

3

"If I can't write, then who am I? Is all I'll ever be an artist with no medium to pour my scars into?" — *Untitled Henry Hayes Manuscript*

BEING A WRITER WHO can't write is arguably the worst career move of all time.

What does it mean when the words just stop flowing? Does that mean it's over? Will I ever be able to string more than three mediocre words together on a blank page? Will any of the words I attempt to write even make sense?

Anything I type immediately gets deleted, and no matter how hard I try, I can't seem to get anything worth a damn down. I wish I could do something other than be delusional for a living, but it's what I love. I chose to sit down one day and write the book for a reason. That's the one thing I've always believed about life: everything happens for a reason.

Those five words have been my motto since I was young. My father always said it to me, and after his accident that almost took him from us, he reminded us of it every single day. He's fine now, but when I was young, it terrified me thinking my dad was going to die and I wouldn't get a chance to say goodbye.

I like to think writing makes me feel better, but in reality, I think it makes me feel worse. Because sometimes, I don't want to look on the bright side of things. Sometimes, I want to complain, cry, scream, and rage like everyone else. I've only ever done that once in my life, and that's not a memory I want to revisit.

But that isn't who I am anymore. I'm more of a suffering in silence type of guy, which is why I have no friends—according to my younger sister and only friend, Mitch. I'm twenty-five years old, and my best friend is someone I met through work. He is quite literally all I have besides my family.

As I stare at the email from my publisher, reading every word over again, I start to question if I can even write in the first place. How is it that they're this excited to see the pages I haven't written yet? I know I'm a little behind, but I swear, every time I open my email, I have something else from them reminding me how excited they are for my draft to be submitted.

I'm well aware first drafts are supposed to suck, but out of the thirty chapters I have outlined, none of them are complete. I don't even think I could call them chapters, just scarcely written words on random pages floating throughout my manuscript.

I don't know why I can't get words down on the page. This has never happened to me before, and you'd think with all the success I had with my first two books, the third would flow out of me.

That's not the case, though. Book three has been the biggest climb yet, and I've barely started up this mountain. Something is keeping my legs from moving.

I reread the email for the twentieth time before my phone rings, and I pick it up, welcoming the distraction when I see Mitch's name flash across the screen.

"Hello?"

"Are you out of breath? Why are you out of breath? Is everything okay?" he says across the line. I guess I'd call him my best friend, even if he is my *only* friend. We try to talk every day, even if it's for a short conversation.

One time, I missed his call by like two minutes, and he freaked out on me. Mitch is almost too nice of a guy. He's always worried about something, whether it be his deadline, his sales, his friends, his family. He's probably worried every second of every day, and I don't know how he manages to get anything done. All I do is worry about getting this manuscript done, and it hasn't helped me push it along.

"I'm fine, dude. Just rereading the email from Literary Nook," I tell him. Mitch knows everything about me, including the stuff I don't mention; he knows it all. He knows about my writing issues, about how I feel when I wake up every morning, and he even knows about her.

The girl who shredded my heart and gave me no reason as to why.

I was able to turn that heartbreak into a novel that sold well and made lists I used to dream about. Then, my second novel somehow surpassed the first one, and more and more opportunities started to knock on my door. It was great. My life was seemingly perfect to the people around me. I was no longer a child who dreamed about being an author. I was officially published with one of the best publishing houses in the country.

I've never been more miserable.

"Hen, you have to stop looking at that. It's going to drive you crazy."

"It already is driving me crazy," I remind him, thinking back to our conversation yesterday, when one random question made me spiral. If I can't get words down, then it's looking next to impossible to have this be my career until I die.

"Yeah, so stop looking at it," he says as I hear him typing across the line. "How is your word count today, or are we not mentioning that again?"

As I highlight the small paragraph I wrote and see the number come up, all I can do is palm my forehead and slump against my desk.

"That bad, huh?"

"Yeah, it is," I sigh heavily. "I'm at about three hundred words for today, and I don't even know if I like them all."

"Well, that's three hundred more than yesterday," he says, trying to lift my spirits. "If it makes you feel better, I only wrote five hundred words yesterday."

Huh, that actually does make me feel better. "For which project?"

He only laughs. Mitch is the type of guy to have more than one story in his brain, and even though I'm also like that, he tends to act on it. Whereas I usually stick to one manuscript at a time, he's always jumping between documents, as if it was a game of leapfrog. I admire him a lot, though. I don't know how he keeps it all sorted.

He did show me his spreadsheet one time, but I can't imagine how confusing it still gets.

"For the one I'm on an actual deadline for. The other two are just passion projects for right now. I don't know if I'll even end up pitching them to my agent."

"Well, if you ever need an extra set of eyes, I'm always here."

"Thanks, man," he says, and I hear another question coming in his pause. "Have you given any thought to the messages you received a few weeks ago? Maybe that has something to do with you not being able to write. I know I hate when I have to decide something. It always weighs my body down until I figure out what to do."

I know he's trying to help, but I've been trying to get that off my mind. I'm pretty sure I'm going to decline the invitation sitting in that group chat.

I hate to admit he's probably right. The invite has been looming over my head like a dark cloud for weeks, and I still haven't made a decision. It definitely hasn't helped my writer's block, but this aversion to writing has been going on since I got home from my last book tour.

I don't know what happened. The tour was great. I met readers from all over the country and got to chat with some other amazing authors I look up to. While I was catching flights and traveling, I was fine.

Then, I got home, and it all crashed on top of me. I realized I had nobody to come with me on these things, nobody to look out into the crowd to be able to celebrate my wins with. It punched me in the face—the fact that I've spent all this time alone and am just now realizing it.

I don't mind being alone. It just made my stomach drop when guilt overtook my body. I had so much to be thankful for. Here I am, living out my dream, but at the same time, I also want something more.

How greedy and unworthy I am to feel the way I do—but I can't help it. Some people would kill to be following their dreams like I am, and here I am, complaining about it.

"I don't know what to do, Mitch. I still have some time, but I can't think about..." I trail off, unsure of what to say. "I just can't."

"Well, if you ever want to talk it out, I'll be here. I know how tough it is since she'll probably—"

"Exactly. That's why I haven't even entertained the idea of going."

He clears his throat from across the line. "Just think about it."

"I will," I tell him, even though I might be lying.

"I have a meeting to get to, but I'll call you tomorrow?"

"Sounds good. Have fun and get those words in," I say.

He smiles back at me. "Get those words in. You can do this. Don't think, just write, okay?"

"I'll try," I say as I hang up the phone.

I stare at my computer for five more minutes, trying to figure out how to reply to the email. I can't seem to write that either, so I turn my computer off, take a deep breath, and head to the kitchen to make a cup of tea.

Tea has always been my go-to beverage to try and help the brain fog clear. I know this one cup isn't going to magically fix all my problems, but maybe it will get something going.

Maybe, maybe, maybe.

Deep down, I know the words are unlikely to come. If I can't even write a simple email, then how can I expect myself to write a whole novel again?

4

Getting Older by Billie Eilish

As I GET THROUGH customs and see all the people embracing, part of my heart lurches.

I wish I had people here to greet me. I wish I had that, but I'm the reason I don't.

Which is why you're back, Ames, I remind myself, trying to keep my head up. I grab my phone out of my pocket as I head to baggage claim.

Amelia: Landed safely. I had a lot of time to think on the plane.

Dr. Elyse: What were you thinking about?

Amelia: How terrifying this is.

Dr. Elyse: It's a disruption to your routine, so that is normal. Remember to breathe and remind yourself once you're settled, we're going to figure out a routine that works for you in Virginia.

Amelia: I'll try my best.

Dr. Elyse: That's all you can do, Amelia.

Dr. Elyse: And your best is enough. Don't forget that.

Part of me wishes I could jump a few months into the future, to when I'll hopefully have all the missing pieces of my life figured out. Not only did I quit my job in England, but I also left everything I didn't think I would need. I'd say I left some friends behind, but I didn't get close to anyone over there. Besides the people I worked with, I had no real friends. Nobody. I didn't do anything on the weekends. I barely left my place after work. I didn't have a life.

I'm moving back here with two suitcases and that's it. I've left my curated routine behind, and now I have to spend the next few months trying to figure out what's going to work best for me over here.

I've quite literally decided to give myself another fresh start. I don't know if you would call it a fresh start, considering this is where I grew up, but that's what I've decided to name it. A fresh start for the girl I've become over the last year.

I could call my parents or my brother to pick me up and take me to my new apartment, but I don't have the energy to face them quite yet. We've barely kept in touch the past two years, and mending my relationship with them was never on the top of my list. My first priority is my girls. They were more of a support system when I didn't ask them to be, and that alone speaks volumes.

I'll talk to them in a few days after I'm settled. The wedding festivities don't start until after the weekend, and I want to get adjusted to the time zone before I try and explain myself to them.

And my therapist always says it's best to give myself a few days of adjustment, since this entire trip back is a wrench in my routine. If I was unmedicated, I would be flying off the rails while doing this, but now, I feel settled—to the best of my ability. Once upon a time, I probably wouldn't have even gotten on the plane. I would have stayed stagnant because it was easier.

That's not who I am anymore. I mean, I'm still terrified, but those emotions are normal to feel after this big life change I'm going through—again.

I assume the girls think I'm only coming back for the wedding festivities, which consist of an entire week-long, bachelorette-style trip to the resort the wedding is at. Apparently, the boys are doing the same thing close by, Grant spearheading the activities for the guys. Hads is Paige's maid of honor, so she planned all this ahead of time.

I was surprised I was invited early for this, since I'm not in the wedding, but I assume the girls want to clear the air and not make the wedding awkward. It's going to be difficult having to talk to them about what's happened, and I still have to figure out how I'm going to describe the time I spent in England. It's hard for me to find the words to describe what I went through, and part of me is worried that once I open my mouth, it's all going to come out wrong.

Obviously, I'm not going to throw the blame onto my recent diagnosis, but it does explain some of my behaviors. Underneath all of that, I'm still the culprit. It's still me making the decisions I did, and I'm owning that.

While I did cut most of my ties in England when I left, I hung on to one. My boss gave me a glowing recommendation letter, which will be useful when I figure out what the hell I'm going to do with my life here. Once I get settled and have a solid routine again, that's when I'll figure out my employment status. The wedding and all its activities are going to take two weeks, and once I've hopefully begun to fix things, I can figure out all the logistics.

I'm twenty-five years old, and my life has felt like a constant stream of mistakes. I can only recall three good decisions: choosing to go to Grand Mountain College, going to therapy, and something that keeps me up at night. While I made the right decision at first, I still smashed it to pieces when it was over.

Regret follows me like a companion, tapping me on the back when I start to think I'm doing okay. Not wanting to think about that, I turn my music up as I grab my bags off the carousel and call a car to take me to my new apartment.

I'VE BEEN AT MY new apartment for three hours, and all I've done is sit on the floor.

Granted, I have no furniture, but I underestimated how odd it would feel to sit in my apartment with nothing besides my two suitcases, music playing softly from my speaker as I take in my new home.

I turned it on to try and distract me from the fact that my medication hasn't kicked in yet. Since I was traveling back to the States, I arrived earlier in the day, and I want my medication schedule to be the same as it was when I was in London.

I take a deep breath before I grab some cleaner from the bag sitting next to me. I stopped at the store before I came here; I wanted to be able to clean before the movers came with a few essential things I bought ahead of time.

I'll go furniture shopping at some point, but for now, all I ordered was a bed frame, a small nightstand, a mattress, and a closet organizer. I have a beanbag coming for the living room as a placeholder for a couch. My tiny one-bedroom apartment is the perfect place for me to end up after the craziness of the last few years. There's a small kitchen, perfect for floor-sitting if need be, and I can fit a table in this open space that envelops the living room and the kitchen.

It's perfect for me, and that's all that matters.

Since I'll only be here for a few days before heading out for the bachelorette stuff, I figured I'd furnish the rest of my apartment when I got back and actually settled.

All I'm focusing on right now are the next few days. One of these nights when I can't sleep, I'm going to figure out how to talk about the past year with these girls.

We were close once. When we were all in college, I can't remember a day I went without texting, calling, or physically seeing one or all of them. Wednesday was always our favorite night of the week, but I was quite fond of all the moments in between. Moments like Paige and I sitting on our kitchen floor, eating snacks when we couldn't sleep, laughing as loud as we could because our apartment was home for the two of us. Moments like studying with Hads and Grant, Hads slapping him with her ruler like she used to. Or still does. I'm not quite sure. I miss when Ella would take care of us all.

Sometimes, I wish none of this happened. I wish there wasn't space between us all that I caused. But if that hadn't happened, I wouldn't have hit rock bottom. If that hadn't happened, I'd still be walking around wondering why I can't seem to get myself out of this haze.

Life is so mysterious that way. One thing leads into another, and eventually, you have the answer you've needed your entire life right in front of you. Instead of living my life thinking I was just a girl who seemed to mess up more than she could keep track of, I've realized I'm better than I thought I was.

I'm not quite a good person yet, but I'm trying to be. I'm on my way to becoming a better version of myself, and right now, that's all I need to do—try.

As I start to lazily clean the floors, one of my favorite songs from recently floats through my speakers.

Music is the longest, most genuine relationship I've ever had. Ever since I was young and found my parents CD player, I was practically attached to that thing. Most of my chore money—when I completed them, that is—went to buying my own CDs.

Since my head is often running with a thousand different thoughts, music was the only thing that helped to turn those off, my mind wandering to focus on the music instead of other things. I can't really do anything in the quiet, or I drive myself crazy with the thoughts that race through my mind, but as soon as my favorite songs filter through my ears, it all quiets.

It's the only thing I've ever really run toward for a consistent amount of time. I used to venture to the beach by my house, and I'd bring my journal while I listened to new albums from my favorite artists. I'd rank on the first listen, then on the lyrics. I had a whole system for it, and I still do the same thing when new ones come out.

My parents never understood why I always had my headphones on, and I was often criticized for never listening to them, but it was hard to share that the world was too loud and this was the only way it quieted.

Halfway through mopping, my doorbell rings, and as I brush past my kitchen and head for my front door. I open it to two delivery guys and a huge box, my mattress vacuum sealed behind them. I smile.

My first piece of furniture in my new place.

"Where would you like this, ma'am?" one of them asks me.

"You can just put that in the bedroom, please," I say as I point to the door. "It's there on the left."

"Sure thing," the other one says to me before I move aside and let them work. I'm well aware my luggage is still sprawled all over the room, but I don't really care. I have no food in my fridge and the stuff I have in my apartment is a mess, but at least I have a bed, right?

This place isn't quite a home yet, but maybe it will be once I furnish it. Maybe when I put sprinkles of my shitty personality in here, it will start to feel more like the place I'm meant to be.

For now, it's an empty playlist I have yet to create. I'm not sure of the vibe I want yet, but maybe the more I settle in, the easier it will be.

I'm done running. I'm done being alone.

I want the life I crave, and I want it with the people I left behind all those years ago when I thought I was making the right decision for my future.

I just have to hope they can forgive me first.

One day at a time, Ames.

5

Then — January 2025

Sidelines by Phoebe Bridgers

TODAY HAS BEEN THE biggest mix of chaos and confusion I have ever experienced.

Not only did I wake up late, but I rushed to the office like a chicken with my head cut off because I thought I had an important meeting about the next issue we were planning this morning. It turns out, I rushed for nothing, because when the conference room was empty this morning, my desk neighbor, Dan, reminded me it was scheduled for next week.

I don't know what's been going on with me lately, but my memory has been getting worse. When I'm in the office, I feel like I can't focus, or someone is always distracting me with something else they need me to do.

And what's worse is the reason I woke up late: I stayed up way too late attempting to clean my apartment, only to have fallen asleep before I had a chance to get anything done.

Last weekend, I decided to try a new hobby—making trinkets out of clay I bought online. It's been super fun so far, but I made a huge mess of my apartment that I haven't been wanting to clean. Last night, I had enough of coming home to my living space always looking like a tornado blew through it. I should be proud of myself that I even tried to clean up, but I've been beating myself up all day about not actually doing it.

My life lately has felt like a constant inner battle of me trying to do everything right and failing miserably, and I don't know what to do to get out of this weird cycle.

"Amelia, are you ready for our budget meeting?" another colleague of mine, Jessica, peeks her head over my desk.

Shit. "I thought that was tomorrow afternoon?"

"Angie moved it. Didn't you see the email about it?"

"No," I sigh—another thing I didn't pay attention to. I really am not doing this whole adult with a full-time office job thing well lately. I check my inbox, and it's the first thing I see. The second thing is an email directly from Angie, and she blocked off a meeting for just the two of us beforehand.

Fuck.

"It looks like I have another meeting before then with Angie, but I'll see you at the budget meeting, okay?"

She smiles at me as I grab random things off my desk before I bolt to her office, not wanting to be late. I take a few deep breaths as I get closer to her door. My mind is suddenly racing, and every bad thought about what this meeting could be won't leave my head.

Am I going to get fired? Have I accidentally embezzled from the company and I'm going to get arrested?

This is not at all how I wanted today to go, and as soon as I stop the spiral in my brain and knock on Angie's door, I throw my best poker face on and smile as she beckons me in.

"Amelia, I'm so glad you're here," she tells me.

Okay, that feels like a good start. "Thanks, Angie. I have to admit, seeing this one-on-one was kind of stressing me out." *For the last five minutes, since I just noticed it.*

"I didn't mean to do that." She smirks as she closes her planner, giving me her full, undivided attention. "How are you doing lately, Amelia?"

Her question catches me off guard. "Uh, I've been fine. Just going through the motions with work. You know how it is." I mean, I broke up with my short-term boyfriend the other day. Our relationship wasn't going anywhere. It was a means to an end, and I think we both knew that. He barely said a word, and it wasn't anything difficult, since we lived separately and barely stayed over at one another's places. There was no awkward clothing exchange, no feelings muddling us up. It was amicable, the easiest breakup I've ever been through.

To be fair, every breakup is easy when the only one I have to compare it to ripped me to shreds.

She nods. "Look, I'll cut right to the chase. I was originally going to have this meeting be about your yearly review, but when I sat down and started going over it with Ken, we were both a little concerned."

I reach for my necklace. "Concerned?"

Another nod. "Yes. So, I wanted to bring you in here and ask how everything is going. I know the transition was tough for you at the beginning, but I'm starting to really worry about you, as your boss and a friend."

I wouldn't necessarily call us friends, but she is someone I see five days a week. Since I don't really have any other friends over here besides my coworkers, I guess she counts as one.

Come to think of it, I don't really have any friends over here. The only people I would consider as such are the people at the office, but even then, I don't go out with them after work, and I don't make an effort to know much about them. I don't ask much about their lives other than what they give me, and I don't tell them anything about me because, well, there is nothing to tell.

"You're worried about me?"

"Amelia, the past few months, I've never seen you so distracted. You're messing up in meetings, you're forgetting to turn things in on time, and you don't seem like you're present. I've only just noticed it, but when I look back, I realize it's been happening for a while."

"I-I'm sorry, Angie. Really, I don't know what's been going on with me lately. I thought it was just happening today, but I can admit, I've been distracted when I'm here." This is so fucking embarrassing. I cannot believe my boss has called me into her office and is asking me if I'm okay. "I promise, I'll focus on getting back on track. Now, if that's all—"

"It's not." She holds her hand up. "I think you need some time to recharge, and since you have the most accrued vacation hours I've ever seen, I think it would be good if you took the entire month of January off and reset."

"W-What?"

"I know this is a shock, but this will be good for you, Amelia. Take some time and really focus on you. Not only do you work too much, but when you're here, you're not focused. It's okay to admit you might need a reset, mentally and physically."

"Angie, really, I'm fine. I just—"

"I know this can seem scary and like it's not the right time, but this is for the best." She reaches out and grabs my arm with a soft pat. "This is for your own good."

"This isn't you firing me then?"

She shakes her head. "Your job will be here waiting for you when you're back and refreshed, Amelia. I promise, this isn't leading to you being let go. Sometimes, we work ourselves too hard and need a break, and sometimes, someone else has to let us know when we need that break."

"And that's what you're doing?"

"Yes. Now, why don't you head home. As soon as you walk out this door, I want you to not think about this place or anything to do with work until you come back. Does that sound okay?"

"I-I guess," I say, my voice low and defeated. This job has been the only thing really getting me out of bed in the morning, so I'm a little nervous about what the next month is going to look like.

"Good," she says before she opens her office door for me. "This will be good for you, Amelia."

I nod, unable to speak before I pack up my things and head for my place, not wanting any of my coworkers to see the tears falling down my face as I leave.

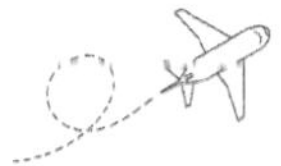

It's been one week since I left work on a forced paid vacation, and to say I've done a lot of self-reflecting during this time would be an understatement.

Not only was Angie right, but I haven't really felt like myself these past few months, and that could be for any number of reasons. I stopped talking to my best friends from back home. I threw myself into my work to distract my brain, though it didn't work, because look at where I'm at now. When I really sat with my decision to come over here in the first place, I realized I'm still stuck in the same place I was when I arrived here.

I haven't been moving forward. I've been stagnant for months, and I only just noticed it this week. Now, I'm on paid leave from my job, I have no close friends over here, no boyfriend. I'm completely alone, and that realization has punched me in the gut.

I thought I was doing okay. I thought I was staying afloat and going through the motions, but I'm not. I'm actually not even close to doing that. In fact, I'm pretty sure I've hit rock bottom, because I haven't felt this horrible...well, ever.

It's an odd feeling, realizing you're not where you thought you would be. I know I have a few weeks to get back on my feet, since I don't have to work, but I still don't feel whole. When this fog used to come about, it used to only take me a few days to recharge before I felt okay again.

The fog hasn't lifted in months, and I have no idea how to get it to go away. I've tried the usual things, and none of them have worked. I tried a new hobby—oil painting—and that only lasted a few days before I got bored. I tried to listen to new music and analyze the lyrics, and I could barely focus enough to listen to an album front to back. I tried getting out of my place and going for a walk, or to my favorite coffee shop or bookstore, and I was so in my head, I thought the world was caving in as soon as I got outside. What's worse is that I still can't sleep. My mind will not stop running about a thousand different things, and I'm not sure how to quiet it down before it drives me to insanity.

Part of me is terrified something is really wrong with me. I don't know how to fix it this time. I don't know how to make my mind stop spinning. I don't know how to get better. I don't know how to feel more like who I used to be.

I've barely been sleeping. Eating feels like the hardest task I don't want to approach, because the thought of having to make three full meals a day and make those three meals different is difficult. Even when I have been eating something, it tastes flat and horrible.

I wish I could find out what's wrong with me so I could cut it out. I wish it were that easy, but I know it's not that simple. Nothing ever seems to be easy with me.

I'm not okay, and I think this is the first time I'm really admitting that to myself. I'm afraid. I'm terrified I won't get better because I don't have any motivation to do so.

But when I look around at my life, nothing is really *that* bad. Most people have it worse. I'm living my dream in another country, working for an organization I've loved for as long as I can remember. I should be happy. I should be living my dream and excited to be doing so, but I'm not.

Everything feels difficult. Sleeping doesn't come often, and when it does, it's not restful. I haven't answered my messages or emails in the last few weeks, and now they stop coming all together because I've fallen out of touch with everyone I love. It's too hard for me to admit it's difficult to pick up the phone and answer. It's too hard to admit I'm falling apart, and it took my boss forcing me on leave to realize it.

I take a deep breath before I head out of my place to the appointment I made on a whim yesterday while I was crying into a bowl of cereal. Today, I'm taking a big step. It's one I never thought I would willingly take, but the conversation with my boss opened my eyes.

I'm not doing well. Everything around me is falling apart.

I need to talk to someone, because if I don't, I worry what might come of it. I'm not saying I would do anything drastic, but I know I can't keep living in this fog with no way to get out. It's too much. It's too hard, and if I keep going like this, I'm going to fall even deeper into this hole, if that's even possible.

I'm finally open to sitting across from a trained professional and dissecting my entire life. If it makes me feel less alone, or better in general, it will be worth it—the awkwardness of spilling my guts to a total stranger.

Therapy is not the answer to all my problems, but it seems like a good start.

6

Now — September 2025

Night Changes by One Direction

Ella: Are you still coming or what?

Paige: What she means is, what is the best address we can pick you up from?

Amelia: I'll share my location with you guys.

> **Hads: Wow, it really is that easy, huh.**

> **Ella: That was the fastest response I've ever gotten from you, Amelia.**

> **Paige: See! Things are looking up already!**

> **Amelia: I'll see you guys soon?**

> **Paige: Ella is picking you up last, but I'll message when we're headed to you.**

> **Amelia liked a message.**

I DON'T KNOW IF I can remember how to breathe properly, but I definitely do not want to choke on air when I see my friends for the first time since I left.

I can't make a fool of myself. I already know it's going to be awkward and tense. My stomach is tied into a million knots, and my mind is going a thousand miles per hour, despite having taken my medication this morning. I've been fidgeting, the anxiety of seeing them today hitting me like a truck. I keep fiddling with my rings, my therapist calling them my own version of a fidget toy. I've repacked my suitcase a few times, triple-checking I had everything I might need while away.

I've become way too attached to making lists for every small thing I need to do, whether it be chores to get done around my apartment, things I need to remember to do while running errands, or work.

My therapist suggested keeping my notebook by me at all times, especially while at work, since my brain gets so distracted. It's hard for me to remember things I want to talk about. Before my journal was attached to my hip, I was forgetful, but now, I've found a way to jog my memory when forty thoughts intersect the original thought I had and had since forgotten.

And here I go again, diverting my brain to a topic that doesn't even matter. *Calm down, Ames. Back to the matter at hand*, I remind myself.

I grab my suitcase, zipping it up for the last time before I move it by my front door, placing my small backpack on top of it. Being in a tense car for two hours is probably not the best way to start this trip out, but I'll also be in the same suite for the entire two weeks. We're all going to be in some sort of forced proximity together. What better way to fix all I broke than to be in the same room with the three people I hurt most?

In hindsight, I could have called a car to take me to the hotel myself, but if I'm going to be serious about repairing my relationships, I can't chicken out on the trip down there. I'm throwing myself into the deep end to prove that even though this is going to be insanely uncomfortable, I'm serious about showing up for them.

I know I have to have some tough conversations, and I need to take full accountability for my behavior, but I can't do it all at once while we're in the same vehicle. It would be too much at once. My plan is to talk to each of them individually, then all at once to fully clear the air. I talked it over with my therapist, and this seemed like the best course of action. I hurt them all individually and as a group. It just makes sense to apologize in a similar manner.

I also don't want to ruin this for Paige. She's getting married, for fuck's sake. *Married.* She deserves the happiest celebration possible without me ruining it by saying or doing something stupid.

The hardest part is going to be looking them in the eye and seeing how disappointed they are in me. I'm sure I've given myself worse stares in my mirror trying to pep talk my way out of feeling like garbage, but it's still going to be hard. I also worry they're going to see me differently when I tell them about being diagnosed. As soon as I tell them I'm in therapy, I think they'll be surprised. I think Paige has told me more than once that I should see someone.

I throw my front door open before I give myself more time to reorganize the bean bag and singular lamp in my apartment. I head for the lobby of my building and hear three honks. I take a small peak outside, nerves coating my body when I see Ella opening her trunk for me. Hads and Paige climb out of the vehicle, and I start to touch the necklace that still sits around my neck, my nervous tick that's lasted me a few years.

God, I am so fucking jittery. Thoughts are racing through my head, most of them bad ones as I think about what I've done to the three girls who probably assume I'm not going to actually come out and face them.

Before them, I felt like I was going to be alone forever. Then, they came along, and suddenly, that theory was proven wrong.

Then, I fucked all of that up thinking I was making the right decision for me and my career. Things got dark, and I couldn't find a way out, their light that used to come easily an ocean away where I left them.

Wash, rinse, repeat. The story of my entire life before I gained the courage to start seeing Dr. Elyse.

I take a deep breath before I open the door to my building and trip over my own two feet. My suitcase falls in front of me as the three of them stare at me.

It's like we're all trapped in some sort of trance we can't get out of. I'm looking at them; they're staring at me, probably trying to make sure I really exist and I'm not just a figment of their imagination.

I take this moment to really take them in. They look so familiar, but they're different at the same time. Paige's blonde hair got a little longer. She looks comfortable in a white sweatsuit that says bride on the front in sparkly letters. I'm sure Ella bought that for her. Ella's hair is still curly and long, but she looks lighter. Her shoulders aren't as tight as they used to be, and her golden skin looks flush with something I can't place. It's probably annoyance, and that's understandable. Hads is leaning against the car, as if she needs it to hold her up as she takes me in. Her short, black bob is blown by the wind, her eyes piercing me before she looks away.

"Uh, hi," comes out of my mouth before I even realize I'm the one speaking. My throat is so dry, but I still haven't moved to get my water bottle out of my backpack. I'm almost frozen waiting for one of them to say something.

"I almost forgot what you looked like," Ella says, clearly mad, and I can't even blame her.

"Hello, Amelia," is all Hads says.

"It's good to see you guys," I say, the truth spilling out.

"It's good to actually *see* you." Ella rolls her eyes at me.

"Agreed," Hads says. "I really thought you were going to bail at the last minute in typical Amelia fashion."

I deserved that one. "I know I've been gone for a while and I have a lot of explaining to do. Your anger is completely valid, and if we want to start out on this note, that's fine, but I'm assuming you invited me as a last ditch effort to see if I would come back. Well, I'm here. So, take all the jabs at me you want, but I feel good about being here simply because it means you guys still have room in your hearts for me. I'm grateful for that, really, I am." I grab my suitcase and wheel it to the trunk, putting it inside before Ella just about shuts my hand in the door.

"The room I have is very little, Amelia. If it were up to me, you wouldn't have been invited at all, but Paige seems to think otherwise." Her voice is tense and direct. I've seen Ella curse people out before, but being on the receiving end of it is the most terrifying thing I've experienced in a while. "If you fuck this up again, consider my heart closed for your business."

I nod, feeling uneasy but trying to remind myself they don't know this version of me yet. They didn't get to watch me change and grow. They only know the girl that left them and cut off contact for a whole year.

They didn't see me struggle through figuring out a routine that would work for my fucked up brain. They didn't see me grapple with having to take forced time off of work during the worst mental time of my entire life. They didn't see it because they weren't around and they weren't around because of my actions. But now, they will see this version of me who's trying her fucking hardset to mend what she broke.

They're going to see a completely different person from the girl who left them, and part of me is worried they're not going to like this version. I know that worry is all my insecurities projecting onto them, but I can't help it. I hated myself when I was in London. I couldn't figure out what was wrong with me or why I couldn't get better, so of course, they would hate me too. All I need is for them to see how hard I'm trying to fix all of this so I can be in their orbit again, but that isn't going to happen five minutes in.

"Amelia?" Hads says to me. "Did you hear what I said?"

"Sorry, no." I twist my ring on my finger. "Can you repeat it?"

She sighs heavily. "Typical," she says before saying nothing and then getting into the car. Ella seems to have already shuffled to the driver's seat, and as I sneak around the back of the car, Paige and I lock eyes on the passenger side.

I can tell by the look in her eyes that she still has hope for me. I can tell she's the only one out of all of them who seems up for giving me this chance. I don't even know if I could call it a second one, because I had so many chances before this that I never took. She's the entire reason I'm here right now, and beside all the sadness I see in her eyes when she looks at me, I can see a tiny sliver of hope.

"I'm still upset with you," she says to me, her voice quiet as she opens her door. "But I am glad you showed up."

"I'm glad I came to my senses enough to come back," I tell her as I get in the car. Ella almost speeds off without me, and I take a deep breath as the tension fills the car. In about two hours, we'll be in Virginia Beach at the hotel Paige and Oliver booked for the wedding. They're getting married on the beach, and I couldn't think of a more perfect location for them to tie the knot.

I try not to think about all the pieces of their lives I missed, but it's hard not to. We've all grown and changed so much, but we weren't around one another to see it. It's a strange feeling, one I don't want to sit with for the entire two hours, or I might go insane. So as Ella clears her throat, I take this moment of silence to try and spark some conversation.

"So, Ella, is Leo driving you crazy yet?"

She can only sigh heavily. "He always drives me crazy, but I love him, so I deal with his stupid British ass."

"Don't you mean arse?" Paige asks with a giggle. "All I can think about when I hear him say that is the time you set it as his wake-up alarm."

"Oh my gosh, that was *so* funny! And the fact that he would change it and the next day, it would be the same," Hads says, laughing at the inside joke I am not privy to. Obviously, they aren't doing this on purpose. I'm sure they don't even realize it, but I do.

"I don't know why it took him so long to change his password on his phone if he wanted it to stop. He knew it was me the whole time," Ella says, a proud smile on her face.

"Maybe he thought it was Grant," I say, trying to insert myself into a conversation I wasn't part of in the first place.

"I doubt it," Ella scoffs. "Grant kisses the ground Leo walks on. It's almost comical."

"Really?" I ask, but then I remember what happened at the Halloween party senior year. "Does he do his British accent around Leo, or is he still too scared?"

"It is constant," Hads laughs, some pity in her tone. "Paige and Oliver even did an accent around him and Alissa for Halloween."

"Oliver only did one sentence and then stopped because he felt silly, but Leo and Alissa told me mine is good," Paige says, flipping around in her seat to face Hads and me in the back.

"I remember when we would watch movies with accents, and after, you would be stuck mimicking it for days," I say, reminiscing about a time when I was a part of these stories.

Paige's face falls as soon as I say that. "I still do that."

"Oh," is all I say, and the awkward tension comes back.

"You would know that if you stuck around," Ella says under her breath, but not really. Awkward silence fills the car once again. There are so many things I want to say to them, but I stop myself. I know it's not the right time. It's been all of twenty minutes. I can't just keep spewing stupid shit to distract myself from the giant elephant in the room. Well, car.

"Amelia, do you have some sort of happy playlist in your repertoire that you can turn on for us?" Hads asks me. "I was going to make one for us, but I didn't have time amid all of the Maid of Honor stuff, and I'm sick of the fucking silence in here."

It's like she read my mind.

I grab my phone and swipe through my playlists. "Uh, they're all pretty depressing, but I can make a new one and share it with you guys so you can add whatever you want." I quickly send it to our group chat, all their phones buzzing.

"All depressing songs? Wow, I guess nothing has really changed," Ella says, more silence filling the car as I try to brush off another hurtful but true comment.

"Yeah, that's true," I remind her. Nothing has changed, and yet everything has changed. "A lot more has changed than you guys think, but if one thing is for certain, it's that my music taste is still the same."

"I know, Amelia," Paige says, her voice cracking. "You always did love a good sad song."

I hum my agreement as she pulls it up on Ella's phone, the first song playing off shuffle being one I added to the playlist.

Through the small hums I give, my shoulders feel slightly lighter than they did before I got in the car. I'm going to call this car ride a win so far, since the air has been partially cleared, I guess. I had to start somewhere, and I'll take any win this trip wants to give me, no matter how small it might be.

"OH MY GOODNESS," PAIGE says as she pushes the door to our suite open. Four rooms connect to a main living area with a small kitchen and a table big enough to fit us and then some. I've never been in a hotel this nice, and I'm excited to be able to spend the next two weeks surrounded by the magic I once had with these girls. I know it still exists. It just got a little lost, but with the four of us back together, that magic is bound to come back.

"This is beautiful," I say.

The doors of the room open to a gorgeous living area, with couches that look softer than anything I've sat on. A small kitchen to the right is complete with a table and stools under the counter. There's a sliding door that leads onto the balcony, where a hammock and a few other seats are arranged, looking out at the ocean. It's bright, spacious, and I feel incredibly lucky to even be here to see it.

"Paige gets the room with the biggest bathroom because that's where we'll all get ready. I'll take the room across from her." Ella points to the door to the right by the kitchen. "Hads, since you're the maid of honor, you can have the one next to her." She stops to look at me. "You're next to me, roadrunner."

"Sounds good," Hads says as she grabs Paige and pulls her in for a hug. "Should we rest for a little and then get ready for dinner?"

"Yeah, I figured we could eat at the hotel restaurant, so nothing too fancy. We should all be ready by six so we have a bit to check in with boyfriends and fiancés and squeeze a nap in before then." Ella grabs her bags and wheels them to her room, softly shutting the door behind her. The rest of us do the same, and when I see the bed, I immediately skip unpacking and climb under the sheets.

Today has been exhausting, and not just because of how nervous I've been feeling. I used to beat myself up about how exhausted I would feel, especially when I had slept okay the night before—which didn't happen often. I was always really mean to myself when I would have to lay down or take a nap after doing simple housework or anything that shouldn't require as much energy as I thought I was exerting.

When I realized that was because of my ADHD, I tried to be a little nicer to myself about it. Dr. Elyse has helped me become more conscious of my behaviors and has tried to shift my mindset. I hated myself. I couldn't understand why simple tasks were so draining. I was mad at myself all the time because I felt so messy and disorganized when I wanted to be different.

Now, when I need to rest, I let myself. I've been trying to act kindlier over the past few months, but I still catch myself. It truly has been an everyday battle to try and reframe my mind to stop jumping right to how terrible of a person I am, or to stop blaming myself for the way I am.

I'll be living like this for the rest of my life, unless my symptoms die down as I get older, so this is something I'll have to live with. This is something I have to manage every single day, and some won't be easy, I know that.

I'm trying to be better. Medication has helped. My routine has helped. Having a name for why I'm like this has helped too, but sometimes, I worry the urge to run from every problem will come back, and I'll cave immediately.

Dr. Elyse would say I'm stronger than that feeling now, but I still have fears about that.

Amelia, stop thinking like this before you spiral, I remind myself. I take a deep breath before I grab my phone and set an alarm in case I actually fall asleep.

There's no doubt in my mind that all the girls are talking to their significant others, and since I don't have one of those anymore, the short relationship I had in England fizzling out when I hit rock bottom, I'm all by myself.

I don't know if I'm wired to be loved or in love with someone. I don't know if I should even worry about romantic love, because I'm sure anyone would take one look at the mess I am and run the other direction.

I'm also only worried about repairing what I broke with the girls. Everything else comes second, third, or last in my book. I just have to remind myself I was loveable once. These girls love me somewhere deep down, despite them being pissed at me for what I did.

Platonic love has always felt stronger to me than anything else. It's always been what I'm drawn to in books, movies, and any sort of media, really.

Except him.

I quickly banish those thoughts before I feel myself drift off to sleep. An hour later, my alarm is buzzing me out of a dreamless nap.

Somehow, I get ready, and before I know it, we're all sitting around a dinner table, awkwardly deciding what we all want to eat. I don't know how we got here. The past few hours have been a haze of anxiety, and I wish my memory wasn't so shitty so I could actually remember details.

"We'll take a bottle of champagne," Ella says, looking around at all of us before she orders a few appetizers. "We'll just have those for now. Thank you so much."

The table falls silent as our server leaves, taking the menus with her. Now, none of us have anything to hide behind—physically, at least. I can't pretend to read the same thing a thousand times over, and for some reason, I can't bring myself to speak.

What the hell am I supposed to say? Anything I say will be awkward and pointless, because how do you catch up on this much lost time? Is it even possible? I can't just burst out with all the realizations I've had in the past few months. It would be too much at once, and I don't want to have this serious conversation in the middle of a restaurant.

The champagne comes, and when the server reaches me, I have to decline. Drinking while on a stimulant medication is a recipe for disaster.

"I'm okay with water," I say. "Thank you so much."

The girls are looking at me like I'm insane, and rightfully so. The last time they physically saw me was at Paige's birthday. I drank an entire bottle of prosecco straight from the bottle.

"So, when are the boys getting here?" I ask, deciding on a safe topic to start.

"In a week. Grant planned some sort of greatest hits road-trip for them all," Hads tells me. "My brother is less than thrilled."

"Oh, he'll be fine. He may act like he hates spending time with the boys, but I know he secretly loves it," Paige smiles.

"Oh, that man only wants one thing, Paigey—to marry you. The only reason he's doing all this other stuff is because you wanted to," Ella says to her. "It's cute."

"Oliver has gone soft," I say. "It's going to be weird seeing him like that. The last time I saw him, he was as stone-cold as ever."

"Well, that's because the last time you saw him was eons ago," Ella says as Paige spits her champagne back into her glass.

"You're right, Ells. It has been a long-time," I say before I can stop it. "I've been gone. I've been radio silent, and I have no idea what has been going on in any of your lives. But you also don't know what's been going on in mine." Ella opens her mouth to speak, but I stop her. "And I know that's my fault. I went through a lot over in England, and I'll tell you all about it when I talk to each of you."

All their eyes are latched on to mine. Ella looks pissed off, Hads has more of a neutral expression on her face, and Paige's are full of something I can't place.

"But I want to spend dinner hearing about what I missed. So, give me all the stories that come to your mind, even the comments you don't think you should say out loud. I can handle it, really."

After a long silence, Paige raises her hand. "I have a story."

"Lay it on me," I say to her.

"Okay, so, one day, we all showed up at Hads' apartment for book club, and everything was normal until we saw something peeking out of the corner behind the bookshelf in their living room."

"Oh God, not this," Hads laughs, covering her face with her hands. "I swear, I didn't know he had bought that thing."

"I still wonder how he got a picture of you for that." Ella shakes her head in disbelief.

"There was a sheet over top of it, and when we took it off, it was a cardboard cutout of Hads. Grant got it made and hid it from us for months before we found out about it."

"What?" I say, a small smile coming back to my face. Knowing Grant, that is so on-brand for him. "Why did he have it?"

"Apparently, he gets lonely when Hads stays over at my place or Paige's, so he bought it so he could talk to cardboard Hads instead of simply talking to himself while he was home alone," Ella laughs.

"Oh my," I say with a laugh. "So is that thing on top, or is he?"

Hads lowers her head to the table. "I cannot talk about this again."

"That was my first question too!" Ella says. "And he still hasn't given us an answer."

"Because he doesn't do that with a cardboard cutout of me!" Hads shouts.

"You can't actually confirm that, Hads," Paige giggles. "It's still in the same spot, and we haven't stopped pestering Grant about it."

"I think it's cute, in a way," I say, looking at Hads. "That boy is clearly in love with you if he misses you that much. I'm sure he loves having that around because it can't slap him with a ruler either," I joke, and the three of them laugh.

"My ruler is still kicking. Don't make me use it on you these next two weeks," Hads says.

"I won't," I say under my breath. "Okay, what else?" I ask, and for the rest of our dinner and late into the night, they tell me stories upon stories of all the memories I missed.

For a few hours, I feel included again, and that small pinch of hope I have gets a little bit bigger.

7

Then — July 2025

"Nobody talks about those friends who come into your life when you least expect it. The friends who, from one conversation, make you feel like the most transparent person on the planet from how well they seem to know you." — *Excerpt from Henry Hayes' Notebook*

As I STARE AT the same empty page I've been looking at for two weeks, I sigh heavily.

I don't know what the hell is going on with me. I don't know why I can't seem to put the feelings of this character into words on the page. Usually, when I force myself to write these days, it all comes out sounding flat and uninteresting. The only writing I've been doing lately has been forceful because I need to finish this manuscript.

But my words are dull, vague, and two-dimensional. I'm not sure I can do this anymore.

My phone buzzes, and I don't reach to look at it, already knowing an email is on the other end of it. The same one shows up in my inbox every week like clockwork. It's from my agent, expressing his excitement about how he and my editor can't wait to see what I have in store for my next novel.

I can never seem to reply and tell them I have nothing. At the rate I'm moving, I don't know if I'll ever be able to finish this book.

My first book—the one about a married couple who realize each of them is leading a double life—sold more than I could have ever dreamed of. I couldn't believe the response to it. Then, my second book—the one about a family whose patriarch gets diagnosed with a terminal illness—oversold my first by thousands of copies. I thought I was living in some sort of dream. I couldn't believe it. I was touring with authors I'd long admired and they were asking *me* questions about my process, my characters, and more. These past few years of my career have been beyond my wildest dreams.

Yet, I still can't figure this third book out. The idea I pitched was about a man who survives an attempt on his own life and how he and everyone who loves him come to terms with what almost happened. It's about second chances, seeing life in a new perspective, and how the people who really love you will carry you through the tough times.

I outlined thirty chapters and sent them in, and every week since then, my agent is hounding me for pages to get to my editor. I know they're excited about them, but they aren't even written yet, and I haven't found the right words to tell them I'm struggling.

I know I have to answer eventually, but I'll cross that bridge when I get to it.

When my phone buzzes again, I decide to check it. Rarely does another email come through so quickly, but when I see who's texting me, my heart drops to my stomach.

> **Grant: Is this thing on?**

> **Oliver: Grant, seriously? That's a terrible way to start this conversation.**

> **Grant: I thought it was funny! Sue me, Oliver.**

> **Unknown: I've got a really good lawyer if you need one, Grant.**

> **Oliver: I regret this already.**

> **Grant: Do you think he still has our numbers saved? Henry, it's us, in case you couldn't figure that out yet.**

> **Leo: You've only met me once years ago, but I'm Leo Zimmerman, Ella's boyfriend.**

I can't help the smile that appears on my face as I read all the messages from people I used to call friends—well, and Leo. I'm not sure I can call him anything, because the last time I heard the name Zimmerman, Ella was cursing him out and trying to kill him.

How the hell did they go from that to dating? I would ask, but I'm a little afraid of the answer. I can't help but wonder why they're texting me. The group haven't really stayed in touch since everything fell apart, but I do miss these guys. We got pretty close in college when we were all dating the girls of the book club.

At the mention of that, my breathing quickens, and I have to remind myself to stop thinking about her.

I grab my phone before I can stop myself.

Henry: Hey, guys. Long time no talk.

Grant: Oh my gosh, he answered.

Henry: Why wouldn't I?

Oliver: He thought you hated us.

Henry: Why would I hate you guys?

Leo: There seems to be a lot to unpack here.

Grant: Author Henry Hayes, are you available for a chat perchance?

Oliver: Did you seriously just say that?

Grant: What? He's an author, Ol. I've literally shown you his books in stores.

Oliver: Forget it. Henry, can you hop on a call?

Henry: Sure.

Four seconds later, my phone is ringing, and three faces show up on my screen. Oliver and Grant look how I remember them, but I forgot how terrifyingly suave Leo looks.

"I'm just here for moral support," Leo says in the accent I almost forgot about. Has it really been that long? "Nice to formally meet you again, Henry."

"Yeah, you too," I say, my guard still up. "No offense, but it's been a long time since we've talked. I can't say I'm not a little nervous you're reaching out to me out of the blue."

"And we apologize for that," Grant says. "Not only does life have us all extremely busy, but we regret pulling away from you after everything that happened."

Everything. I don't know how one word can carry such weight, such meaning as it does in that sentence. One word cannot sum up how heartbroken I felt—and still feel—about what she did to me at the airport. I may be a writer, but there will never be any combination of words I could string together that would adequately tell the story of how I felt watching her walk away from me.

"It's okay. I didn't expect you guys to hang around me after..." I trail off, not wanting to say it. "But why are you contacting me now?"

"Well, Oliver here is getting married, and before you ask, yes, you heard that right. Mr. Freeze is the first of us to get married."

I can't help the smile that forms on my face. "Paige is a lucky girl," I tell him. I knew they were both still dating Hads and Paige because I see their posts on social media. Nowadays, it's so easy to stay connected with people because of the internet, and I wasn't going to remove them from anything. Hads, Paige, Grant, Oliver, and Ella didn't do anything to me. I have no reason to hold anything against them.

"I'm the lucky one." Oliver smirks.

"The stone has officially cracked," Leo jokes, and Oliver merely tilts his head as Leo, Grant, and I laugh. I can't help it. The first time I met Oliver, I thought he was going to stab me—especially since he was in the middle of solving a murder case with Paige.

"Why am I friends with you guys again?"

"Because our girlfriends are all best friends. Therefore, we have to be best friends. It's just how it works, Ol," Grant reminds him. "And my girlfriend is your sister, so realistically, you're stuck with me for life, buddy."

"Great," Oliver says in the most monotone voice ever.

"Well, I'm entirely sure the only reason Ella would marry me is to be able to say Alissa is her sister-in-law."

"And because she loves you," I tell him. "She does, right?"

"Most days, yes, although I do piss her off a lot." He smirks at the rest of us. "But that's basically foreplay."

"Is this the reason you called me?" I ask. I don't necessarily have to rush back to writing, but I do want to get some words in before my afternoon walk. I try to keep the same routine every day. That used to help when I was in a funk, but I'm not sure how to dig myself out of this one.

"No," Oliver says as he adjusts his phone. "I wanted to invite you to whatever shenanigans Grant has planned for my bachelor stuff."

"Henry, you're not going to want to miss it. I've truly outdone myself."

"Mate, you say that every time you host, or really anytime you do anything," Leo reminds him.

"And have I been wrong yet?"

Leo searches his head for an answer. "No, I guess not."

"Leo, don't encourage this," Oliver tells him. "He still wants to do a blood oath, and I wouldn't put it past him to lock us all somewhere during these festivities to get it done."

"So, what does this entail exactly? I'm on a pretty rigorous writing schedule." I'm not, but they don't know that.

"Laptops are welcome, Hen. Can I still call you that?" Grant asks me, and I nod. "Okay, good. Basically, we're hitting a few different spots in Virginia for a week before we meet the girls down in Virginia Beach for the actual wedding."

Oh. That isn't at all what I expected. "I don't know, guys."

"Grant, I told you it was too short notice. We would need an answer by September 7th," Oliver tells him. "If you can't make it, it's okay. We would understand."

"And the other reason he's inviting you is because Oliver has no friends and Grant won't stop making fun of him for it." Leo smirks. "Which is valid, because I'm pretty sure Grant and I are his only friends."

"Really? I could end this call right now," Oliver snaps. "Just think about it, okay? Let us know your answer. Festivities—or whatever Grant called them—start two weeks before the wedding."

Well, I guess it can't hurt to think about, right? "Okay. I appreciate the invite, you guys. I don't really leave my little bubble unless I'm going on a book tour or something. It might be good to get out of my apartment for a bit."

"See?" Grant says, raising his eyebrow at the rest of them. "I told you he'd at least be open to it."

"Just let us know, Hen. Take this as confirmation that you're always welcome in our circle—or square, if there's four of us," Oliver tells me.

"And I look forward to learning more about you, mate," Leo tells me, a genuine look on his face.

"Thanks," I say, trying to get the weird feeling in my gut to settle. "I'll give you an answer soon, but I have to get back to writing."

"Sounds good," Oliver says before he exits.

"See you at game night, Grant," Leo says before he also leaves the call.

"You didn't feel bombarded, did you?" Grant asks me.

I shrug my shoulders. "No. A little caught off guard, but I did miss you guys. It's nice hearing from you again."

"Good." Grant smiles. "And seriously, consider our proposal. A lot has changed, and if you do decide to come, I'll update you on all of it to get you back in the loop."

"Thanks, Grant. I would appreciate that," I say with a smile. I can't help all the questions floating around in my brain. What does he mean, things have changed? What could he mean? Am I curious enough to go on this trip to find out? I don't know, and I guess that's what I have to figure out.

"She's going to be there."

She. My stomach plummets at the mention of her. "I have to go."

"Of course," he says with a wink. "Have a great rest of your day, Hen."

"You too, G."

For the rest of the afternoon and all throughout my walk, the only thing I can think about is this very vague proposal that's landed in front of me. By the time I sit back down at my desk, the words still aren't coming, so I close my laptop and decide to wallow in a reread of one of my favorite books.

Now — September 2025

Grant: Have you made a decision yet?

Grant: Not to pressure you or anything, but I made a pretty killer PowerPoint full of all the stuff you missed. It has cool transitions and everything.

Oliver: If you block our numbers and never speak to us again, I wouldn't blame you.

Leo: Maybe just give him a little more time.

"Henry!" My sister shouting at me has me dropping my phone. It slams against my desk, the notepad I'm scratching on breaking most of the fall.

"What the hell, Luce?"

"Did you forget I was here or something? Mom dropped me off twenty minutes ago, and all I've been doing is rummaging around your pantry—which is empty, by the way."

"I didn't even hear you," I say, clearly still distracted by the decision hanging over my head. I wish I was using my brain for productive things like writing, but I can't seem to figure out how to do that anymore. "I'm sorry, sis. I know we were supposed to hang out while Mom goes to the studio."

Our mother is not only one of the best artists in Virginia, but she has a showcase coming up. Since my sister just started school, I told my mom I could watch her while she gets in some time at the studio. Plus, this way, I can spend time with my little sister, who I love more than myself most days. Not only is she more extroverted than I am, but she's grown into someone I admire.

She tells it how it is, and I've never been able to do that. I'm always so worried about what other people think of me. I think it's the artist part of me. Yes, I write books for me and because I love it, but the other part of me secretly craves the validation I get when someone tells me they liked what I wrote. I'm sure my mom can understand that side of being an artist.

At fourteen years old, my sister is all bark *and* bite. I remember when my parents told me I was going to have a little sister. It was the most excited I had ever been, and from the minute she was born, she became my favorite person on the planet. Suddenly, I was someone's big brother, and that alone made me want to shield her from every terrifying thing the world could bring.

Now that we're older, we're still as close as we have been. It's weird seeing her grow up right in front of me, but I'm glad I'm still around so we can have moments like these.

"What gives, Hen? Why have you been so dreary lately?"

I put my pencil down. "Don't you have homework to do?"

"I already did it," she says as she saunters over to my desk. "What are you working on? Is that another book I'm not allowed to read?"

I laugh dryly at that. "You know why you're not allowed to read them yet, and no, it's not. It's a list."

"What kind of list?" Before I can answer, she grabs it from my desk in one swoop and starts reading it out loud. "Pros and cons of going to Oliver's wedding. Who's Oliver? I thought Mitch was your only friend."

I swipe the list back from her. "First of all, ouch. Second, Mitch is my best friend. Thirdly, Oliver is someone I knew back in college."

"Oh," she says as she sits on the small chair in my office. "From Grand Mountain?"

"That is where I went to college," I say to her. I know why she's being so coy about all this. I never talk about college with my family. All they know from back then is that I was dating Amelia one day and she was gone the next. I didn't explain anything to them. I told them to never ask me about it.

I've been struggling for which side to put her on, but since I mostly have pros, I might throw her into the con column just to have a reason to not go.

But going might mean I'll get the closure I've been chasing all these years. Or maybe it'll bring up a whole bunch of other feelings I'd rather keep down. Maybe after we talk a little bit, I can move on and live the rest of my life without that hanging over my head.

"So, why wouldn't you go to his wedding?"

"Lots of reasons, Luce."

"Is it mainly because of her?" she asks me outright. "I know you don't like talking about her, but—"

"I don't, but she will be there," I tell my sister. "Maybe I should go."

Everything happens for a reason, right? That's the motto I live my life by at the ripe age of twenty-five, and since they invited me, there must be some sort of cosmic reason I should take the chance and go. I should bite the bullet that's inevitably headed my way in the form of Amelia Ellis, and maybe there's a slight chance I can come out of this unscathed.

A small, minute chance, but everything she puts her hands on disintegrates immediately, and I wouldn't be surprised if she ruined me even further at this event that's supposed to be about celebrating Paige and Oliver.

"You should," she says, catching me off-guard. "Maybe it'll be good for you to get out of this apartment and actually have a life."

"Hey!" I throw a pen at her. "I have a life! I leave my house all the time."

"Yeah, for like a month when you're on a book tour, but other than that..." She trails off as she turns the pen in her hands. God, I forgot how blunt she can be for a teenager.

"Lucy, I can't just drop work so I can go on vacation. That isn't really how my job works."

"Hen, laptops are portable, you know! You've brought them on planes before, so I think a car ride will be okay."

God, she's right. At this point, I'm just looking for reasons to not go.

So, I crumple up my list and throw it in the garbage, affirming my choice to go to this wedding and confront the person who owes me a hell of a lot of answers. My current manuscript isn't the only unfinished story, and maybe confronting my biggest and toughest one might help the words flow again.

I guess I can only hope she's grown enough in the past two years to want to give me the answers I'm rightfully owed. If not, maybe everything doesn't happen for a reason. Maybe some things are just meant to be left unsaid—unfinished.

In about two weeks, I'll find out if our story is closed, the last words written on our page the ones we barely spoke that day in the airport, or if there are blank pages waiting to be written on with the words we have yet to speak.

Henry: Count me in.

Grant: Hell yes! Oh my God, I'm gonna bring my copies for you to sign!

Oliver: Welcome to the chaos, Hen.

Leo: Welcome back is more like it.

8

Now

Older by Lizzy McAlpine

AFTER I TOSS AND turn for what feels like the fortieth time, I decide to get out of bed because, like always, sleep never seems to come naturally to me. I don't know why I thought it would be easier after dinner, or maybe I thought the weight of seeing my friends and all the anxiety from today would make me crash. It didn't work, and now, I can't sleep.

I get out of bed and head for the small kitchen area. The girls bought a bunch of snacks and drinks, since we'll be in this room for two weeks, and I could not be more thankful. I tiptoe through the suite, and when I reach the cupboards, I pull out a mug and end up finding some hot chocolate mix. Before I head outside, I grab a bag of my favorite kind of chips to keep my hands busy.

I'm sure Ella bought all this for me. Even though our relationship is still strained, that's who she is as a person. Once she knows all your favorite things, she'll always remember them. As much as she probably hates that I'm here, I appreciate the gesture.

I throw my cardigan on and step outside onto the balcony, parking myself in one of the lounge chairs. I've always been a bit too attached to the beach and the ocean. I grew up going to the beach during the summers. Sometimes, I would bring my journal to the beach and have a picnic by myself. Any time I was going through a rough patch, I found myself sitting and listening to the waves that felt as aggressive and loud as my mind did. It was comforting, knowing something as simple as water was able to emulate the emotions in my brain.

Most of the time, it was me and the sand, me and the water. I enjoy the quiet a little too much as someone who lives in a state of constant noise, whether in my head or outside of it. In the state of constant exhaustion I'm always in, the quiet is a nice break. My medication helps to keep my thoughts more uniform, but it's not a total cure.

So, as I sit on this balcony and listen to the sounds of the waves in the distance, I'm jolted back to that time when I used to sit and stare at the water, wondering why I was so different.

When I think about the days I've had since those lonesome ones I spent at the beach, I can't help but smile. I've seen the world. I've seen a lot of the country I live in. I've lived on my own and supported myself. I've hit rock bottom and crawled my way out with the help of my therapist. The moments that often replay in my mind are ones from that little classroom back on campus at Grand Mountain.

Those moments hold the most meaning for me. In that classroom freshman year, for the first time, I was accepted for who I was, no questions asked. Now, I'm back with these girls, *my* girls, and I have so many pieces to patch up before we get back to what we were.

For the last few months, when I came out of the hole I was stuck in, the mistakes I made all hit me in the face at the same time. For a few weeks, I could barely move forward. Every day, my mind was reminding me I was failing—at life, at being a friend, a daughter, a human. I could barely get out of bed. I was not functioning well at all.

Then, I learned to give myself some grace amidst all the change, but it didn't happen overnight. I'm still struggling with it, and my mind is not the nicest place to be sometimes.

It feels as if I'll never stop blaming myself for all of this—the distance, the awkwardness, all of it. Even if we get back to where we used to be, I'll still carry the weight of what I've done. I'm sure of it.

"Can't sleep?"

The voice startles me, and when I look up to see Ella leaning against the sliding door, I set my hot chocolate down.

"No, but now I definitely won't be sleeping, since you scared the crap out of me," I joke.

She doesn't say a word to me as she closes the door, steals my bag of chips that I haven't opened, and sits on the end of my lounge chair. She continues to say nothing as she opens the bag and eats a few.

"Aren't you cold?" I ask her, noting she's only wearing a satin two-piece pajama set and fuzzy socks. Her natural curly hair is up in a messy bun, the loose strands blowing in the breeze.

"I'm alright," is all she says, not looking at me but out at the water. It's a beautiful night, but the wind keeps giving me goosebumps. "I'm actually glad I woke up and saw you out here."

Her words surprise me. "Really?"

She nods. "I wanted to make a few things clear to you before we jump into all these festivities."

I should have known this was coming. Not only is Ella fiercely protective of her friends, but this is Paige's wedding, and I'm sure she wants it to go as smoothly as possible. Paige deserves it. After all she's been through, we deserve to do what we can to make these two weeks perfect for her. I'm a hitch in those plans, and I can understand why she wants to talk to me.

"Go ahead," I tell her.

"We are not ruining this for Paige. Not only did she and Hads work hard to plan all these activities, but this is her wedding, for fuck's sake."

"I know, Ells," I remind her. "It's not my intention to do anything to make this time feel any less special. Paige deserves better."

"Yeah, she does. She deserves a better friend than you've been; hell, we all deserve a better friend than you've been. You disappeared, Amelia, and now you're back, and it's throwing us all for a loop."

I deserved that. "I know—"

"I'm not done," she says, her voice low. "There's no secret there's distance between us and you. That couldn't be more obvious, but we're grown women, and we all need to take accountability for our actions. Part of me is glad you're back, but the other part of me is screaming you're going to disappear again after this. You still feel like a ghost to us, even though you're sitting right in front of me."

I know what she means. I feel it too, and I hate that the distance is there, but again, it's my fault. "I'm not leaving again, Ella."

"I'll believe it when I see it."

"I know me saying this means nothing. After all the empty promises, unread messages, and unanswered calls, my words mean nothing. They shouldn't mean anything to you guys, because not once did they match my actions. I get it, Ella. Any bad thought you've had about me is the same thing I've thought about myself ten times over."

She locks eyes with me, a knowing look passing through her features. She knows I understand what she's saying. I'm not quite sure if she believes me when I say I'm not leaving, but maybe my actions will change that.

"I'm glad you understand it's on you to fix this. You have to have these tough conversations since you were the one who left us, Amelia. It wasn't the other way around."

"I know. I left physically and mentally. I ghosted. I fucked up," I say as a few tears come to my eyes. Normally, I'm not much of a crier, but ever since I left, all I seem to do is cry. I guess suppressing my emotions only worked for twenty-three years. I had a good run, really, I did. "But there's a lot you guys don't know."

"Always so self-aware, aren't you?" she says with a laugh. "If there's a lot we don't know, then tell us. All we've ever wanted was for you to be more open and honest with us. Communication is everything, Amelia. We never needed more than that from you. Just reciprocation in what we give you."

"When the time is right, I will. But we just got here, and I still have to talk to Paige and Hads. I'll get there, I promise, but give me a little grace."

Her eyes pinch at me before they soften, and I can tell she knows something is up, because she goes quiet. For a few minutes, we don't speak.

"Can I ask you something?" She breaks our silence.

"Of course."

"Did you see my messages when I was over in England? Or was I texting a brick wall?"

"I saw them. I even almost responded—twice. I just couldn't. I was afraid to see you after all the time we lost. I knew you would put me in my place—rightfully so—and I wasn't in the right headspace to take that." Not only was I overwhelmed with work, but I was also overwhelmed with trying to figure out where I fit over there—as a person, a partial citizen, and in my life. Her messages were only the beginning of my spiral.

I knew I couldn't handle it, so I didn't even give myself the option. "Why were you in England anyway?"

"Do you actually want to know?"

I grab her hands, my legs crisscrossing underneath me as I sit up fully. "Yes, Ella. I do. I missed out on so much, and any story or detail you want to tell me, I want to hear."

She looks at me, her big brown eyes taking in every word I say before she speaks again. "Leo's father was rushed to the hospital after having a stroke. I came home after having dinner with him to Alissa frantically packing her suitcases, and they asked me to go with them, so I did. We took a flight over there, and I helped them through a really tough time. After he got back is when we finally got together."

"Is his father okay?" I ask. A stroke is a huge deal, and I can't imagine being an entire country away while something as big as that happens. Well, I guess I can, in a way. I was over here when I found out Grant was in a car accident, and even then, I couldn't seem to get myself on a plane. I can't imagine how scared they all were, and I didn't even send a text.

It makes me sick to my stomach just thinking about that.

Ella jumped on a plane to help their family when they needed it, and I stayed put when Grant almost died. That's where she and I differ.

"He is. You would have known that if you met me for a drink back then."

"I know," I say, dropping my head. "I know it means nothing coming from me, but I'm sorry for dropping off the face of the Earth."

"I would say it's okay, but it's been fucking hard. Not only was so much happening in my personal life, but all of us were changing and shifting in so many ways without you. My mom came back, and you weren't here. Hads and Paige got engaged, and you weren't here. Grant was hurt, and you weren't here. No calls—nothing, Amelia. My mother, who abandoned me when I was a kid, came back, and my entire family forgave her, but I couldn't. You coming back sort of feels like that to me, and I don't want to repeat it. I don't want you to waltz back in here with your false promises and break our hearts all over again. I won't do it again. I won't."

I didn't know her mom came back. God, I can't even imagine. Ella never really talked in depth about her childhood or anything to do with her mother, but she was always worrying about her dad and sister. I can't even imagine how hard that was for her.

I wasn't here for her. God, I'm going to throw up by the end of this conversation.

"If it helps, I've pretty much felt like the worst person on the planet. I hit rock bottom, and I knew I wasn't going to be able to get myself out of it, so I had to do a lot of things out of my comfort zone the last few months. In a way, I'm glad I went to England, but I also regret a lot of the decisions I made while I was over there. I live with the regret every day for what I did to you guys, and I'm willing to do anything to prove I'm back for good. I'm not going to leave again, because—" My voice catches in my throat, and the next words I say struggle to get out. "I don't want to leave the only family I've ever really known. Whatever's left of my heart can't handle that again. I can't lose the only people who have fully accepted me, flaws, mistakes, and all. I know you don't believe me, but it's the truth."

The two of us sit with our words, our sentences hanging in the air, and all I can hear are the waves crashing in the background while my brain starts to fill with other things I should blurt out, or other ways I can over explain myself.

It could be one minute, five, or ten before I hear the crinkle of the chip bag.

"Do you want some?" Ella asks me, and I take her gesture as a small lifeline in the middle of my thoughts running wild.

"Sure," I say as I grab a few.

"That doesn't mean I fully forgive you," she says as she gets up, leaving the bag on the chair. "But this conversation was a good start, Ames."

Then, she heads inside, the sliding glass door shutting behind her. When I lean back in my chair and wrap my cardigan around my body, I can't help but realize she called me by my nickname for the first time since I've been back.

A little bit of hope blooms in my chest. I've officially made it through one tough conversation with one girl I care about, and I make a note to update my therapist about all this in the morning.

I guess growth and change aren't so bad after all. Is it terrifying? Yes, but it will be worth it. It has to be.

9

Farsighted by The Band CAMINO

I'M GLAD OUR FIRST day here was a chill one, because last night, I finally got some sleep. Granted, most of it was on the balcony until I slithered inside as the sun started rising, but getting any sleep is good for me. I'm slowly starting to feel more like myself, or this new and improved version of me.

I'm not quite sure who I am anymore, since all I've done is wrestle between two versions of myself—one properly diagnosed, one not. All I know is, I'm trying my best to be someone I can live with every day. I'm not there yet, but hopefully, if I can fix things with the girls, I'll get there.

The group of us are walking to the beach, gearing up for our first full day with the sand in our toes, books in our hands, and the breeze through our hair.

"Is one of you actually going to build a sandcastle with me?" Paige asks, a smile on her face as we walk down the small path.

"Paige, we'll do whatever you want. These are your wedding festivities, after all," Hads tells her. "Plus, it's been a while since I've built one, and I am all for healing my inner child on this trip."

"It's what all of us deserve after the past few years. And well, all of life, I guess," Ella says as she shakes off her sandals and leads us toward a solitary part of the beach. The crowds aren't as bad as they are during the height of summer, but there are still a decent number of people here.

It's been a long time since I've set foot on a beach, and part of me feels nostalgic for the life I used to live. My family and I used to go to the beach all the time, and those are some core memories from my childhood. They're also the only ones I can really remember from way back then. As I got older, they stopped on account of being too busy, but the beach was still my favorite place for solitude and thinking. It was the place I felt most like myself, and now, I wonder what emotions will hit me as the day goes on.

Will I still feel like the mess I'm sorting through, or will I start to remember the girl who used to sit on the beach and journal, wishing for my life to get better?

Nothing hits me as the four of us lay our blankets down and start to set our stuff up. Ella stabs the umbrella into the ground, Paige drops her tote bag, her sand supplies falling out, and Hads puts the cooler on one corner of the blanket so the wind won't take it away.

"I am so excited!" Paige exclaims. "I never went to the beach when I was a kid, and I will not miss this opportunity to build a freaking sandcastle, no matter how stupid you guys think it is."

"We don't think it's stupid," I say before anyone else can. "This entire trip is to celebrate you, and if you want to heal your inner child and take back what you lost, then we'll be right beside you. What part of that is weird? I think it's sweet."

She and the rest of the girls can only stare at me for a few seconds, but I swear, Ella has a slight smirk on her face.

"Thanks," Paige whispers with a grin. "You're right."

I smile shyly as I scold myself for not being able to control my own mouth. Still, that felt good—acknowledging Paige how I did. It slipped out so naturally, just like it did when we used to live together during college. Back then, it was so easy for us all to talk to one another—the complete opposite of how it is now.

Everything really has changed, and I hate it. I'm really trying to get better at running toward the people I'm supposed to when I feel like my thoughts are too loud for me to handle, but it's hard to change something in a few months I've done my entire life.

I just need to remind myself a thousand times over that these conversations are worth having—these relationships are worth saving—no matter how scary it is to crack myself open in front of them.

The four of us read in semi-comfortable silence for about an hour before Paige finishes her book and immediately turns to all of us, ready to tell us why we should read it.

"Guys, he was angry and grumpy for everyone else but her, and he was a retired hitman who killed bad people to protect her. It's the third book of this series, and I definitely recommend it."

"Well, you know I love anything a little morally questionable, so I'll add it to my list," Ella says.

"I'm good," Hads and I say at the same time before looking at one another in surprise.

"You guys know the darker stuff really isn't my vibe," Hads reiterates.

"It has always boggled my mind that Paige loves it," I say, turning my gaze to her. "I remember one time, you burst into my bedroom at like three in the morning to give me the entire rundown of that mafia family you were reading about."

Her mind searches for the time I'm referencing, and her eyes light up when she finally figures it out. "Oh, yeah! That was the second-generation mafia series I was reading at the time. I remember I made you guys listen to me talk about it at book club."

"Those were good times," I say, nostalgia hitting me in the chest over how many times Paige would burst into my room in the early morning hours, knowing I was awake.

Awkward silence covers the group of us before Ella gets up and grabs one of the buckets Paige brought.

"Paige, it would be an honor if we could build a sandcastle together," Ella says.

Paige hops up, shovel in hand, before she raises it to her chest. "The honor is all mine."

I try to focus more on my book as they leave, but I can't because in my mind, Hads is sitting about ten feet away from me. Now would be a perfect time to talk to her.

I should just do it, right?

"Hey, Hads," I say as she looks up from her book. "Can we talk?" *God, I sound like a desperate ex.*

"Uh, sure," she says as she throws a bookmark in her book and scooches closer to me. I'm not quite sure how to go about this. With Ella, it was easy because she surprised me while I was on the balcony. Hads and I are the least emotional members of our little group—well, we were. I'm not quite sure if Grant has softened her out more, but we've never had deep and sensitive conversations like the one we're about to have.

This entire endeavor is a whole new beast for me, but I'm conquering it as best I can.

"Amelia?" Her voice shakes me out of my mind.

"Sorry," I say. "I'm just trying to figure out how to go about this."

"It's easy," she says as I lift my eyebrows at her. "You just have to speak."

I stifle a chuckle before I basically blurt out my apology. "I'm sorry for what I've done, or rather, what I didn't do when I was in England. I screwed up, and I regret falling off the face of the planet. I was a horrible person and friend."

She says nothing, so I continue.

"I'd say I wish I could go back and do everything differently, but I wouldn't. I went through a lot over there that probably wouldn't have happened if not for the decisions I made, but my biggest regret is not leaning on you when I was having a hard time. My biggest regret is how horrible I treated you guys, because I love you all, and you three mean too much to me for me to throw away all we had. You're the only friends I want to have when we're all old and gray, sitting in the same nursing home, reminiscing about the good old days."

She giggles, no doubt at the picture I painted, and right when I think she's going to grab some sand and throw it at me, she speaks.

"I can tell you're trying, Amelia, but it's going to take some time for me to come around to the idea of you being here again. I am happy you're back and trying to fix everything. I may not trust you fully yet, but I'm not blind. You're at least attempting to put the work in, and I think we're all capable of getting back to how we used to be."

"I do too. I'm going to try my hardest to fix everything I broke."

"I was really angry at you—especially after everything that happened with Grant." Her eyes meet mine as she sighs heavily, and I can feel my throat start to clog with emotions. "You weren't here, and Grant almost—" She cuts herself off, no doubt a little overwhelmed thinking about all that happened with the man she's in love with. "Grant almost died. One of your best friends almost died—and you didn't come back.

You didn't even pick the phone up. That hurt, Amelia, realizing you were no longer here and didn't care about us. We knew you saw our social media posts about it, but you still did nothing. That hurt."

One tear falls. I didn't think Hads and I would get this emotional, but I thought wrong. "I wanted to come back. Really, I did, but I was struggling through my own shit. I was a fucking mess. Well, I still am, and that's no excuse, but I've been working on doing better."

"You do seem different."

"I do?" I didn't think it was too noticeable, but I should have known these girls would see that. "That actually means a lot."

"Why did you choose now to come back, though? That question has bugged me ever since Paige told me you answered the invitation."

"That's understandable." I take a deep breath as my hand finds grains of sand, needing to feel something. "I came back because I'm in a place where I'm ready to fix the things I broke. I've been doing a lot of work on myself, and London didn't really feel like home. The invitation showed up at the right time, I guess. If it had shown up at the beginning of the year, I wouldn't be here right now."

"I feel for you, Amelia. I do. All of us have been going through a tough time, but we were still able to talk to one another about it."

"I know. I'll carry the fact that I didn't reach out with me for the rest of my life," my throat breaks, and she hands me a bottle of water. "Thanks."

She nods, taking a second to think about what she wants to say next. "I know this isn't easy, but you hurt me. I can come to forgive you if your actions start matching your words, but everything will always linger in the back of my mind."

"That's totally understandable," I agree. "I don't expect you guys to just forget about that. I just want to show you all I'm trying to do better. I'm learning every single day is different for me and my mind, so I can't tell you I'll be perfect all the time, but I hope you guys can remember I'm trying."

"As long as you stick to your word, we'll be okay." She smiles softly at me.

"I'll try my hardest."

She nods. "I can tell."

"Are you guys okay?" Paige asks as she comes back over, her hands covered in wet sand.

I quickly wipe the tear from my eye before I look at her.

"We're okay," Hads tells her before I can speak.

"Okay..." Paige eyes us skeptically. "Do you want to help Ella and I build a moat?" Her smile lights up this entire beach.

"Yeah," Hads says, grabbing my hand. "We do."

10

"Seeing someone you used to know is always my least favorite interaction. Yes, I remember you. Yes, I no longer know who you are since I last saw you. Yes, I used to know how you took your coffee. Yes, I still remember what you're allergic to. Yes, you meant a lot to me and you still do but somehow we're here—the two of us staring at one another as if we're trying to memorize one another one final time."
— *Our Best Kept Secret*, Henry Hayes

As an audiobook plays softly through my car speakers, I find myself not paying attention to a single word the narrator is saying.

Is this the stupidest thing I've ever done? Am I being a complete idiot for thinking by going down here and surrounding myself with these people again, that somehow, it will magically fix my writing?

It could, but it's not a guarantee.

My mind wanders back to the last time I was in this big of a funk. It was right after the big falling out, and I don't think there was ever a time before then—at least in my adult life—where I had felt so obsolete. Nothing really made much sense to me after Amelia left.

After that, I had a hard time getting out of bed in the morning. I had never felt heartbreak like that before, and going through it once was enough.

But there's a part of me that will always wonder about the what-ifs with her. If she had just talked to me, would we still be together? Would we both be happy? Maybe she is. Maybe she found happiness in England after she destroyed every ounce of mine.

If she's here with a plus-one, I'll have my answer.

But even so, I'm still nervous—not just about seeing her, but about seeing everyone. It's been years since I've seen Grant and Oliver, and I barely met Leo in college. I can't imagine how this dynamic is going to work, but knowing the guys and how they've acted toward me, it will be fine.

The nerves still linger, though. I know they won't go away until I actually see them.

And Oliver is getting *married*. This almost feels like some sort of fever dream. I figured he and Paige would be together for the long haul, but now that it's actually here, part of me feels like I missed out on this wonderful thing I could have been a part of.

These people are like family. It's always been that way, but now more than ever, it rings true. Not only have they all stuck by one another, but they continue to do so.

That's what I've been yearning for these past few years: being able to have that closeness with a group of people. We all fit together in our own weird way back then, and it worked somehow. When Amelia left, I didn't have anything connecting me to them besides some loose threads. When I lost that closeness, it was like running over a speed bump going way too fast.

No amount of success or money could compare to how rich I felt having such wonderful people around me. That's all any human craves, right? We all yearn to build connections and find our people because when it all comes down to it, when death finds us in the end, we'll remember the memories we had with our favorite people. All the other stuff—money, social status, all of it—will mean absolutely nothing.

And that's what I've been missing all this time. So, maybe these next few weeks will give that back to me, only to rip it from me again. Or maybe it will somehow all work out. Maybe the words will flow from my mind again, and I'll be able to continue living out my dream.

So many questions float through my mind, and I have no answers.

If this book can't get written, my publisher will drop me, and maybe I could try being an independent author—I definitely have enough ideas—but sometimes, I worry about what the point of all this is.

If I have nobody by my side cheering me on, if I have nobody to celebrate the milestones with, then why bother at all? Why bother writing stories if my fingers can't seem to type anything? Why not just get a boring, nine-to-five office job with a pension and good health insurance? Why continue to chase my dream if all its showing me is that I'm not cut out for this?

This book officially terrifies me, and I only have a tiny sliver of hope that maybe these next two weeks will help. I'm sure putting myself and my emotions through the ringer will help—it did back when I wrote my first one. Not only did I completely shelve the fantasy novel I was working on, but I channeled all my sad energy into a book about a couple who fell apart and somehow had enough strength to come back together.

I was one hundred percent projecting all of my own feelings into each character, and I know that's not really what you're supposed to do, but in the end, it helped me a lot. I threw all of my shitty feelings onto my characters, let them deal with it, and in the end, it all worked out. One of these days, I'll be able to confidently say it all worked out for me, but that hasn't happened yet.

Mitch would tell me it's because I haven't actually dealt with my feelings, and he's probably right, but that's what this trip is all about. This is basically exposure therapy. I'm confronting something and eventually, I'll forget why I was so nervous in the first place.

Though, I'm downplaying it. This is absolutely going to be more complicated than I want it to be. Nothing ever comes easy where Amelia is concerned, and I'm sure that hasn't changed.

By the time I pull into the hotel, my mind is a mess, and I have to rewind my audiobook. I grab my suitcases from the back of my forerunner before I pull my phone out and message the guys.

Henry: What room number are we again?

Grant: Don't worry, you'll see us.

Leo: Don't ruin the surprise.

Henry: What?

Oliver: Just get in here.

I tilt my head at my phone, confused, but after I gather myself, I head inside.

As soon as I hit the lobby, I not only see a bunch of balloons, but Grant is holding a huge sign, welcoming me into the hotel.

I drop my stuff on the floor before I run my hand through my hair. "You do know Oliver is the one getting married, right? What's the fuss about?"

"Are you serious?" Grant says as he hands the sign to Leo. "The *fuss* is because we haven't seen you in years, and somehow, you're standing in front of us!"

"I wanted to go a more mellow route, but Grant insisted," Oliver says as he comes over to me, his hand out in front of him. "Welcome back, buddy."

I return his handshake, feeling nostalgic. "Thanks, Oliver. Congrats on the wedding."

He can only smile when I say that.

I'm about to introduce myself to the other two, but Grant practically barrels into me, his arms wrapping around me.

"I've missed you," he says into my ear. "How does it feel being a super cool author, and can I tell everyone I know you?"

"Uhh—" is all I can get out.

"Never mind the fact that you already do," Leo says as he saunters over to us, discarding the sign on the floor. "Sorry if this is overwhelming, mate."

"Only a little, but I should have assumed this would happen," I say, my hand massaging my neck. "It is nice to see you guys. I've..." I stop myself from saying I missed this, because that's not something I want to dive into at the current moment.

"Okay, well, we have a lot to discuss," Grant says as he picks my bags up. "Follow me."

"Here we go," Oliver says, a disappointed look on his face. "I'm sorry in advance."

"Wait, why?"

"Because Grant prepared a long fucking presentation to bring you up to speed on all the things you missed, including my relationship," Leo says, and God, he is so much more manly than I remember. That accent is pretty killer too. No wonder all the girls practically drooled over him at that Halloween party senior year.

"Actually, I was curious about that. Last I heard, you two hated one another, and she tried to kill you with a bat." I wasn't actually present for their tiff, but I heard about it a thousand times; Paige would not stop talking about how Ella and Leo were going to get together.

I guess she was right, in the end. She was almost three for three for coupling her friends. I can't help but wish she could have been right about me and Amelia.

"That's foreplay for them now," Grant says as he pushes the conference room door open. "Stop spoiling the presentation. It took me two weeks to put all the information together, and I rented out this conference room in the hotel specifically for this."

"This took you *two* weeks? How fucking long is it?" Oliver asks him. "And where did you find the time?"

"It's a normal length for over two years' worth of life content Henry missed." Grant smirks at us. "Now, gentlemen, if you would be so kind and have a seat. The show is about to begin."

"I can't believe I let you do this." Oliver merely shakes his head as he sits down.

"At least there's alcohol," Leo says, pouring a glass of what looks like bourbon. "Any of you fancy a glass?"

"Nope," Oliver says.

"I'm okay," I tell him.

"The only drunk I am right now is drunk on adrenaline," Grant says as he dims the lights. "Are you guys ready for the best recap of the last two years ever?"

"No," Oliver says.

Leo simply sips his drink. "Lay it on us, Grant."

"I want to say yes, but I'm not sure I'm ready." I will say, I am a lot more nervous than I was before. I know I've missed a lot, but I'm not sure I'm fully prepared to hear *everything*.

"Okay, so starting off with the biggest thing you missed." Grant clicks the slide, and a bunch of photos of everyone together pop up. Most of them have all the girls together—minus Amelia—and Grant and Oliver. Leo is only in the last few, and I assume that's because he's the most recent addition. "All of our themed parties and get-togethers."

"Do we really do that so much?" Oliver asks.

"I think they're quite fun." Leo smiles.

"You know Ella isn't going to find out you aren't the biggest fan of her themed parties. She's miles and miles away. She won't hear you if you actually tell the truth."

"Oliver." Leo rolls his sleeves up. "I love Ella, therefore, I love her parties. Even if I don't see the point of all of them, whatever she wants, she gets."

"Guys, can we focus?" Grant says, annoyed we've already gone off on a tangent.

"These parties look fun," I say, bummed I missed them.

"Obviously, we all struggled to get together sometimes because of our jobs, but when we did find time, we didn't take it for granted." Grant turns to face the screen. "Now, here are all the books the girls and I have bought on every bookstore trip we took."

Grant starts flipping through the slides, and about three seconds later, Oliver grumbles.

"Grant, this is absolutely not necessary. You promised to hit the big stuff only."

"Ugh, fine. You always ruin my fun, Oliver," Grant says as he clicks through what seems like a hundred slides before he gets to the proper one. "Okay, the big moments."

"There were only a few," Leo says as he refills his glass.

"I almost died!" Grant says so cheerfully, I'm sure I misheard him.

"What?" I say, shocked and confused. "You almost died?"

"Well, not really," he tells me. "I was hit by a car, but I only broke my leg and lost a kidney."

"Grant, what the fuck?" I say. "That's terrible."

"And he constantly jokes about it," Oliver says. "Because he's an idiot."

"An idiot you're glad is alive," Grant says.

"Yes, but an idiot, nonetheless."

"Now, gentleman, let's not fight." Leo smirks.

"Well, at least you're okay now."

"Thank you, Hen." Grant smiles at me before continuing. "The only other huge thing besides Amelia dropping off the face of the Earth is that Ella and Leo got together after agreeing to only have sex three times, but they ended up falling in love. The end."

"Wait, go back," I say as I stand. "What did you say about Amelia?"

The three of them are silent for a moment before Oliver speaks up. "I told him not to mention it."

"I'm confused," I say as my head spirals. "I thought she only left me. Was that not the case?"

"Not just you, mate. I'm sorry, by the way." Leo pats me on the shoulder. "I heard about what happened when Ella was ranting to me about how terrible of a person Amelia was—well, is."

What the hell is going on? "But the girls and her were so—"

"Close?" Oliver cuts me off. "Yeah, that's what we thought too. Apparently, Amelia is shitty at being a girlfriend and a friend."

"I thought you guys told me she was spending this week with the girls like I was doing with you all?"

"Well, she is," Leo says. "Ella hated the idea of inviting her, but the fact that she actually showed up and is trying is a good sign. It was Paige's decision."

"She was so excited when she found out Amelia would be coming back," Oliver says, a sad look on his face. "I didn't know how to tell her I don't trust that she won't completely disappear on them again. She was sure these two weeks would change everything, but I'll believe it when I see it."

Wow. I guess I figured I was the only one she cut out of her life when she got on that plane, but I was wrong. She was the most important person in the world to me, but she was also important to the other book club girls, and she left them too. I guess the three of them and I have more in common than I thought.

The four of us are silent as I process all the information they've thrown at me. Not only have I been hurt by Amelia, but the group was too. Maybe I didn't have to be alone all these years. Maybe I could have had these guys around me even though I wasn't dating Amelia anymore. I think, in the back of my mind, I knew they wouldn't mind having me around, but there was something holding me back from reaching out.

Them holding a branch out to me might have been the best thing to happen—especially the timing. It feels like this impromptu trip sort of fell in my lap, and I'm nervous to see if it helps or hurts in the long run.

I guess I'm hoping for the best, but I'm also bracing for the worst. All I know is, I have to face the person who crushed me into pieces, and I'm not so sure my heart is guarded enough to not fall for her trap again.

Her trap being love. She lured me in, made me trust her, and then she crushed me. Us—she crushed *us*.

Wanting to switch the subject off her, I divert the conversation as best I can.

"Wait, you and Ella had a sex pact before you were official?"

"Oh, Henry." Leo finishes his drink. "How long do we have this conference room?"

Grant looks at his watch. "An hour and a half."

"Perfect," Leo says to me as he stands and heads to the front of the room. "So it all started during university..."

11

Used to Be Friends by Searows

I ACTUALLY SLEPT OKAY last night, and I think it has something to do with how much sun we got yesterday at the beach.

I missed the ocean. I missed the sand between my toes, and I absolutely missed feeling like I belonged somewhere. There were many moments yesterday when I felt lighter than I had the past few years, and it's all because I finally understand my mind and why it functions the way that it does.

If I had come back impulsively like I used to, I wouldn't have fixed anything. I would have made it worse, but knowing everything I do and being able to have these conversations with them is a huge step in the right direction.

I've talked with Hads and Ella, and they seem to be open to being able to forgive me if my actions start to match my words, but I still have to have a really tough conversation with the girl I hurt the most. I have no idea how to go about it at all.

I sigh heavily as I drop my blush brush onto the desk. I take a glance at myself in the mirror and remember a time where I could barely look at myself without feeling like I was crumbling.

Now, it's easier. It's easier because I've learned to embrace who I am rather than be ashamed. I still struggle, but I'm better than I used to be. I can get out of bed in the mornings a lot easier now, and my mind is a lot more focused.

But I still hurt the people I love, and that guilt will never go away. Maybe it will lessen with time. For now, it still lingers around every turn. It punches me in the gut knowing I hurt the girls, but with Paige, the ache is stronger. She was the first person who ever wanted to truly listen to what I had to say. Paige was my first true friend, and she once told me being randomly assigned to be my roommate saved her life, but she saved mine too. The girl with clouds over her head, who had too many thoughts to deal with, was saved by the girl who lights up every room despite all she's been through. She gave me a way out of the spiral. Whenever we sat on the floor of our apartment or studied with music playing, my thoughts were quieter than usual.

And I hurt her. I left her like I always said I wouldn't do.

Two soft knocks against my door force me out of my spiral. I already know who it is before I hear her voice against my door. Paige and I always did seem to have a sixth sense with one another. Here I was, just thinking about her, and now she's knocking at my door.

It feels like college all over again.

"Can I come in?" she whispers, her voice timid.

"Yes," is all I can manage to say.

The first thing I see is her smile, brightening up the room like it always does. The second thing I notice are the tears filling her eyes. I guess I didn't have to worry about how to start having this conversation with her. It seems like she's brought it to me.

"I figured this was easier than me waiting for you to come to me." She smiles where she stands. "Can we sit on the floor and talk? Or is this a bad time? Because I can come back—"

"No," I say before she leaves. "Now is a great time. I was just getting ready, but that can wait."

She only nods as she sits on the floor at the end of my bed. I join her immediately. Neither of us speaks for the first few moments, and I feel like I'm teetering on the edge of a cliff, waiting for a small gust of wind to blow me over the edge. I knew this would be hard, but I don't know how I'm supposed to talk without crying.

Sure, I'm close with the other girls, but Paige was... She was everything. My best friend. The other half of me, really, and I hurt her.

"Hads and Ella told me about their conversations with you." She stops to sniffle. "I figured you were struggling, so coming to you felt easiest."

"Thank you," I say. "I was having a hard time figuring out how to approach you. Every time I think I'm ready, the guilt is so heavy and overwhelming."

She takes a big deep breath before she speaks again. "You hurt me, Amelia. You really hurt me. You were my best friend, and you disappeared. For the first few months, I thought I had done something to you. I kept searching my memories, trying to figure out what I could have said or done to make you leave. I still thought you *would* come back." She turns to look at me, tears already falling down both our faces. "Hads, Ella, and even Oliver were pissed at you, and I kept making excuses on your behalf. You weren't even around, and I was still hoping, still believing, that you would reappear one day, but you never did."

I can't even say anything to justify this. I *hate* myself. I hate what I did. I should just leave.

No. No. I'm not running again. God, I hate that leaving is always my first reaction to everything. How fucking long is it going to take to rewire my brain to think differently?

"And then, I got worried something happened to you. I kept telling myself the reason you weren't texting back or answering our calls was because you were hurt somewhere, and do you want to know what made me realize you weren't dead and you were simply ignoring us?"

I'm not sure I want to, but I nod, her stare drilling into me.

"I used to check your music profile," she says with a scoff. "I saw that you were still making your normal monthly playlists. I saw you were active when new albums came out that we used to have listening parties for. You were still listening to the music without me—without us all."

"Paige—"

"Just let me get this out, please," she says through her tears.

"Sorry," I say, wiping some of my own. "Go ahead."

"Did you see me listening to the same music? Did you see me trying to manifest you back into my life by listening to the albums and artists you recommended to me all throughout college? If you did—which I assume you did, hence the guilt—why didn't you reach out? Why didn't you feel the same gut punch I did when I saw your profile picture staring back at me, taunting me because my best friend could somehow keep up with music, but she couldn't bother to reach out and talk to her friends?"

And then, the two of us sit and cry on the floor, not reaching for one another because neither of us knows what to say or do in this situation.

"It hurt, Amelia. God, it really fucking hurt what you did. You should know how much your silence smacked me in the face after everything we had been through, after all the promises you made to never fully leave."

"I'm sorry, Paige." Those three words are all I can seem to get out. If I try to say anything else, I might collapse into guilt. But again, it's my fault I feel this way. All the girls have done is tell the truth about how they felt when I disappeared. It's not like they're lying about any of this. It all actually happened. They're not saying all of this to hurt me; they're simply telling me how my actions affected them, and I know I'm strong enough to hear them, sit with them, and not let it set me back months in growth.

I grab one of my makeup brushes, needing something to stop my hands from shaking.

"I can forgive you, Amelia. Maybe not fully now, but I can find my way to forgiving you if what you say is true," Paige says, her voice low as I go to grab the tissues from the desk, handing her a few. "Thanks."

"You can? Forgive me, I mean," I say as I grab a tissue, my makeup probably running down my face, but I don't care. "If I were you guys, I would have kicked me to the curb the minute I showed back up after all I did.."

"But that's where we differ. We're not you," Paige reminds me. "When things got tough, we ran toward one another, not away."

Again, she's right. I'm a runner. I always have been, but I'm trying to stop. Now, I have a reason why I've done all these things in my life, but it still doesn't change the fact that I fucked up. I have better coping mechanisms now, thankfully, but those aren't some magic eraser to fix all my fuck ups.

"Okay, I'm done, I think," Paige says with a sad smile.

"Saying I'm sorry doesn't really feel like enough," I tell her as a few tears fall. "I fucked up, Paige, and I'll spend the rest of my life trying to prove to you all that I'm not going to leave again. For the first time ever, I'm trying to fix all my faults, because the last year I spent in England was horrible. I was down, and I couldn't pick myself back up. I thought leaving was the best thing for my career, but my career isn't everything, at least not to this version of myself. Moving to England and going through everything I did over there was the wakeup call I needed, and it's a chapter of my life I simultaneously regret and am thankful for. I regret leaving my best—" My throat decides to close at the worst moment, but Paige grabs my hand. I almost pull away at first because of how shocked I am at her sudden touch, but her grip is firm in mine.

"It's okay. Take your time."

I take a moment to collect myself, the tears still falling as I somehow get the words out. "You guys were the best part of my life for four years, and what I did to you guys was horrible."

"Forgive yourself," is all she says. "Us girls are slowly forgiving you if your actions really do match your words, and they have, at least from what I'm starting to see. So, feel how you feel, but at some point, you're going to have to stop focusing on the guilt. You made a mistake, Amelia."

"Well, not just one. I've made about a thousand of them," I laugh at myself.

She giggles across from me, her hand still in mine. "So have I, and so has everyone else on the planet, but there's a big difference between you and some of those other people."

"And what's that?"

"You're doing the work to fix it, Amelia. You came back, owned up to it, and are actually trying to mend what you broke. Most people, when they hurt you, try to make themselves seem like the person who isn't at fault, but you're not doing that. In fact, I can tell you're not because of how guilty you feel."

"You can?"

"It's how I lived a lot of my life. I used to walk around with guilt like it was a cloud always over my head, wondering what I did to make my parents hate me so much because that's how they always made me feel—like I was the problem."

My heart cracks, and I worry it's going to fall out of my body at the reminder.

"You're trying, Amelia, and that means more to me than anything." She smiles at me again, and I wonder what I did to deserve her looking at me like I'm not the most horrible person and friend on the planet. "Give yourself some grace and remind yourself of that when you start to spiral."

"Okay." I nod. "I'm really proud of you, you know."

"For what?"

"You just seem different. You look truly happy, and I'm excited for you and Oliver."

Her eyes widen at me. "Did you just compliment Oliver?"

"Maybe, but don't tell him I said anything nice about him. I wouldn't want the Earth to stop spinning if he ever found out."

We're silent for about three seconds before we both start laughing through our tears, unable to breathe as we lay on the floor, staring at the ceiling like we used to.

Paige gets up first, and before she slips out of my room, I speak again.

"Thank you," is all I say.

"For what?"

"For not giving up on me, even when I felt like giving up on myself."

"It's what friends are for, Ames, and don't ever forget that." She smiles before she closes my door and leaves me to think.

My mind is quiet, a stark difference to what I thought it would sound like after that. I thought I'd be swimming in thoughts of how horrible I am, how much of a mess I continue to be, but I can't hear anything but my own breathing.

These girls are magical, I think to myself. I wish my brain was easier to deal with. I wish I didn't struggle so much with object permanence in my relationships and could have hung onto them when I hit rock bottom. I know they would have grabbed my hand and dragged me out of the hole I was in, because that's just who they are. They are the light when I can't see the way out.

I'm better when I'm beside them, and I hope they'll forgive me fully so I don't have to be without them ever again.

"This game is actually kind of depressing," I say to the girls as Paige spins the wheel for her turn.

"Well, it is the game of life, and life can be pretty depressing, so I'd say it's accurate, if nothing else," Ella jokes.

"Guys! This is supposed to be us getting drunk and having fun before the boys get here tomorrow. I say we spend this round of the game getting as delusional as possible," Hads says, already sounding a bit drunk. Ella poured us all mimosas, and she's having a blast drinking mine. Water has become my best friend, no matter how much I miss prosecco.

After Paige left my room this morning, it took me another half an hour to fix my makeup and get ready for brunch. Ella pulled me aside before we left and thanked me for having these conversations, and I have to say, these past few days have absolutely been a step in the right direction.

I'm proud of myself for not running away from my feelings for once. No matter how much it scared me to do this, in the end, it was worth it. Not only are the girls on their way to believing I'm here for the long haul, but my actions are finally matching my words.

It feels good to have these girls around me again.

We all play a few more turns before each of us lands on the wedding part of the game.

"Okay, who are we all marrying?" Ella asks us.

"Well—" Paige starts to speak but gets cut off.

"We can't say our current partners this time," Hads reminds us before looking over at me. "Sorry."

"It's fine. Harvey and I were a means to an end." I look around at the girls, and they're all staring at me. "What?"

"That's the first time you've talked about him since we got here," Paige tells me.

"I've had other things to talk about, but yeah, I pretty much knew he and I weren't going to last. It doesn't hurt to talk about him."

It only ever hurts to talk about someone else, someone I've tried to purge from my mind, body, and soul. It hasn't worked. No matter how much I try to erase him, I can never outrun the feelings he breathed into me, the memories we created, how his skin felt on mine.

I remember it all—every piece of it, including his face when I ripped his heart out of his chest and stomped on it in front of all our friends.

"But I'm not marrying him," I say, trying to diffuse the tension in the room. "In real life or in this game."

"I am going to pretend the lead singer of my favorite band proposed to me while on-stage," Ella says with a smile.

"I knew that was coming," Paige tells her. "I'm going to marry my favorite morally gray villain from my favorite movie."

"I think I'm going to marry the main male character from my favorite book series," Hads says before she turns to me.

"Oh," I say, thinking. "I guess I'll marry a high up public official so I can blackmail him from the inside."

The girls stare at me before they burst out in laughter, and I join them after a few seconds of confusion.

"And there's the Amelia we know," Hads says.

"I still have no idea how you come up with all those," Ella says as she spins the wheel. "But hey, I won't judge if you were to actually do that. Just don't get caught."

"Well, I'm not Oliver, so I won't," I say as Paige picks up two baby pieces and throws them at me.

"When are you all going to let that go?" she shouts at us all.

"Never," we say at the same time.

We make it almost the entire way through the board, laughing and being delusional as we create fake versions of our lives. Paige has three kids—all girls. Hads ends up with one of each. Ella has two sons and two dogs, and I end up with two kids and a few cats. According to Ella, I have cat mom energy.

"I still can't believe my mom is coming to my wedding. Little me dreamed of her being there, but I never thought we would be close enough for it to actually happen." Paige smiles as she moves her car across the line for retirement.

"I'm really happy she'll be here for you." Hads grabs her hand.

"We're glad she's finally decided to show up for you," Ella tells her. "You deserve the happiest wedding and life possible, Paige."

"Oh, please." Paige waves off all our comments.

"They're right," I say. "This is huge, and I'm excited she's come to her senses and is trying to make up for lost time." All my words come from my own experience, but I know how much Paige's mom hurt her when she was a kid. We used to stay up late and talk about our respective families when we couldn't sleep.

She obviously had it way worse than I did, but she never judged me for saying what I did about my family. She never thought I was being dramatic when I said my family never really knew who I was, how I've spent my entire life running from them and their expectations.

"It's all we really have when it comes down to it—time," I say with a soft smile as I feel tears start to form.

"None of that anymore, please," Hads says, her own voice strained. "We've all done enough crying for the past few days. Let's save our tears for the wedding. I'm sure we're going to need them."

"Everything is going to be perfect," Ella says. "Your wedding is going to be *perfect*, Paige."

"It's already perfect," she sniffles. "Because I've got you all around, my life is nothing short of perfect every single day."

Hearing her say that makes my shoulders drop, my jaw unclench, and my bones settle. These girls are a once-in-a-lifetime group, and I'm somehow lucky enough to be part of it. I'll never take that for granted ever again.

12

Best by Gracie Abrams

"It was Henry."

Three words is all it takes for my head to spiral and for my palms to get sweaty. Ella just got back from getting ice for the drinks. When she threw the snacks she bought on the counter, and came over to me, her eyes said everything she wasn't.

But those three words... I never thought I'd hear his name on this trip, but it seems like these next two weeks are going to be full of surprises.

I touch my necklace, the same one he put around me all those years ago, telling me how beautiful I looked as he latched it on. I can almost feel the brush of his lips against the back of my head, the crook of my neck, my forehead, like he's the ghost haunting me after all these years.

He's here. Henry is *here*, in the same hotel, same place, same vicinity as me, and I can't run from him.

"What?" I can only manage a whisper. "H-Henry is here? Like, h-here, in this hotel?"

"Yes," is all Ella says.

Panic floods my system. I'm either going to throw up, cry, or scream, so I do what feels right.

I lock myself in the bathroom.

I need air. I need space. I need to think, because I never thought I would see him again. I especially didn't think he would be here at Paige's wedding. Did he and the boys stay in touch? Did Paige invite him in case she thought I wasn't going to show up?

I pace around the bathroom for a few seconds before I stop, turn the sink on, and splash cold water on my face. It doesn't help, and I don't know why I thought it would.

When I look up at myself in the giant mirror above the sink, I swear, I can see the girl I was a few years ago. I can see the glow radiating from my skin when Henry was around. I can see a glimpse of real and true happiness I once had before I ruined it.

I know I hurt him. I know I crushed him in that airport, and now, he's back, and I'm going to see the same face I crushed the last time we were together. I'm going to have to acknowledge his pain, the hurt I caused him. I wouldn't blame him if he never wanted to speak to me again.

My breathing starts to become uneven, my mind racing as I stare at the necklace I can't seem to take off, no matter how many times I try. Part of me feels like I kept it around my neck to punish myself—to remind myself of the hurt I caused every time I saw it and felt it against my skin.

The small windmill sits on my neck, reminding me of the happiness I once had that I ruined by doing what I always do.

Running. Bolting. Leaving.

Now he's here, and I can't run this time. I guess this trip really is for me to mend every terrible mistake I made back when I was young and stupid.

Though, it wasn't that long ago. I'm still young. I'm still a mess, but the difference is the work I've done. It's *getting* diagnosed when I thought I was just a rotten person who couldn't handle grown-up life like everyone else can.

"Ames? Are you okay?" Paige asks me through the door.

I can't find the words to answer her as I hear the girls mumbling through the door.

I run my hands through my hair, suddenly feeling like all the walls are closing in on me again. I take a second to gather myself, to remind myself of the techniques Dr. Elyse gave me when I had a panic attack in the middle of one of our sessions.

Let the thoughts exist for a moment. Take a deep breath. Let them go as soon as they take shape.

I feel the cold sink beneath my touch. I hear the girls murmuring outside the door.

Don't run from these, Amelia. Let them come and go like a wave, I remind myself. *It's just the spiral. It's not me. Tolerate these thoughts and move through them rather than shoving them somewhere else.*

I've confronted the hurt I put the girls through. I wasn't expecting to have to confront him and what I did over these two weeks, but life is full of surprises you can't plan for. I need to talk these feelings out, and instead of running away, I'm going to run *towards* the people who understand why this situation is so overwhelming for me.

"Amelia, you never did tell us what actually happened with you two," Paige says through the door.

"Now is as good of a time as any if you have to see him all week," Ella tells me. "We're here for you."

It didn't sound like she said that with an eye roll, but she's right. I never told them anything about me and Henry. I just fucking left.

"Do you want me to get the prosecco?" Paige asks me.

Well, here goes nothing. "We're all going to need a drink," I tell them as I swing the door open. "Well, besides me."

"Why?" Hads asks.

I take a deep breath before I speak again. "Because I'm going to tell you guys everything."

Before I can stop myself, my feet carry me over to Paige's giant bed, and I cover myself in a blanket, making myself as comfortable as I can before I have to tell the most uncomfortable story of all time.

I know it's my fault, which is why it's so hard for me to talk about this. I know the girls have thought I was a horrible person more times than I can think about, but what I did to Henry will solidify my terrible human being status. No diagnosis can undo the fact that I broke the heart of a boy who just wanted to love me.

The girls get comfortable on the bed, Paige even opting to hold my hand as I get my breathing under control.

"Take your time," Paige tells me.

I can only shake my head. "I don't deserve to feel like this. I'm the only one I can blame for all the shit I did."

"Well, yeah," Ella says, affirming my own belief. "But you're still allowed to hurt about the things you fucked up about. That shows me you're a human and not just an unfeeling robot like I thought you were."

"Ells," Paige says, her voice soft as she continues to hold my hand.

"She's right," I agree. "I was a robot, but when it comes to him..." I can barely say his name without wanting to crumble into my guilt. "He was the only person besides you guys who has ever made me feel any semblance of anything."

"What happened on that day in the airport, Ames?" Hads asks.

"I broke him," is all I can get out before the tears start to fall. It feels good to get this all out. I don't think I ever acknowledged how I felt about everything that transpired between us. My journal has heard it all, but I've never spoken the words out loud. It gives it more meaning hearing the words filter through my ears, my own voice sounding far away.

I take another breath before I continue, the girls existing around me as I try to get the words out. "I guess I have to go back a bit."

"Start from wherever you need to," Ella tells me.

"You guys know I had a hard time in England. When we all talked individually, I mentioned it, but what you don't know is how I got out of it. I'm not even sure when it started getting really bad, but I was forced to take time off work. I had a month off, and all I was doing every day was spiraling about every little thing. My head was too loud. I wasn't sleeping. I could barely eat. I felt like I was constantly wrestling with myself, hating how I couldn't seem to get my shit together but desperately wanting to."

"That must have been hard," Paige says. "Dealing with that all on your own."

"She wouldn't have been alone if she had told us about it." Ella crosses her arms. "We would have been there for you."

"I know," I say, wiping a tear from my face. "I started seeing a therapist to help dig myself out of the hole." I take a deep breath. "She diagnosed me with ADHD, and feel free to tell your partners about this, because I can't have this conversation with all of them."

"I don't know if I'm more surprised about you seeing a therapist or you having ADHD," Hads tells me.

A small laugh escapes my mouth. "Looking back on everything, my diagnosis makes a lot of sense. It actually annoyed the shit out of me that it took so long to figure out why I operate the way I do."

"What do you mean by that?" Paige asks me.

"Well, my parents always thought I was a lazy, unmotivated kid. I did okay in school, but I disrupted class a lot. I couldn't seem to slow my brain down. I was always talking over other kids and teachers. My parents didn't know what to do with me. I didn't have a lot of energy, and I got distracted easily when we did things as a family, so they sort of gave up. As I got into my teenage years, I became more forgetful. I'd start to clean my room, then get distracted by something else. I never slept because my mind wouldn't turn off, and I never wanted to talk to them about what I was feeling because they would just tell me to try harder at focusing."

Paige squeezes my hand.

"And when they outlined my life to follow the path they wanted, I just accepted it. Until I got to college and realized I couldn't focus in class and I hated what I was studying because it wasn't something I was interested in. When I switched to journalism, I felt better because I was actually interested in the material, but I still couldn't focus. I forced myself to do my best, and thankfully, I did fine in my classes. It just felt like it took me longer than others to do simple assignments that should have taken all of fifteen minutes. I thought that was just who I was. Now I know that's just the way my brain works, but it was really fucking hard back then."

I look up at all of them, three understanding faces look back at me.

"My entire life I felt disorganized, and I leaned into these stupid quirks because I thought that was just who I was. Amelia the bolter. Amelia the girl who runs away from everything. Amelia the girl who can't ever sleep. Amelia the mess. I was wrestling between two versions of myself at all times—one of them being the ADHD side of me and the other the side of me who wanted so badly to be put together."

"Wow," is all Ella can say. "But why didn't you come to us about all this when it was happening? Why did you cut us off completely?"

"My therapist says it's because I struggle with object permanence, in life and in relationships. If it's not immediately around me or in my circle of everyday life, it's harder for me to remember it exists. I'm not excusing my behavior. It's just how my brain acted before I was medicated. Since I've been on a steady routine and taking my medication every morning, it's been easier to handle things. I'm more focused than I've ever been, and I'm managing things better than before. It was a long fucking road to get here, and I'm still on it, still figuring out how this all works."

"I don't really understand that," Ella says. "But at some point, maybe we can all sit down, and you can tell us how we can help to better understand your brain how it is now."

"We knew what you were like before this, Ames." Paige smiles at me. "We don't know how your brain works now, and I think what Ella said is a wonderful idea."

"Agreed," Hads says.

A few more tears fall from my eyes. "Thank you," I sniffle. "All I really need is your support."

"So, your decision to leave was an impulsive one," Ella says to me. "And your trips you took back in college were the same kind of thing?"

"Yeah," I tell her. "I also went to England to stick it to my parents. They were disappointed in me? Well, look at me, moving to an entire other country because I had a job offer. I didn't follow the path they wanted me to? Well, look at me, landing this job right out of college. Suck it, Mom and Dad. I'm going to be successful without you."

"Why did you decide to come back now? Was it just for the wedding?" Paige asks me.

"After a few months of a solid routine and my medication working, I felt like I was in a good place. I also just missed you guys. You three were the only ones who cared about me, and for the first time ever during college, I felt like I could be myself, and you guys wouldn't judge me for it. You accepted me, flaws and all, and I never had that before. I never had that with my family."

"Well, we definitely made fun of you," Hads reminds me.

"But it was out of love, not disappointment. You guys never tried to change me. You worked around my unmedicated, ADHD brain before I even knew it was that."

The four of us are silent for a few moments before Ella speaks up again.

"So, what happened with you and Henry? Was that an impulsive, split-second decision too?"

"I still struggle with that myself," I tell them. "Impulsive? Yes, but he was someone I never really saw coming."

"Those relationships are the best sometimes," Hads says, no doubt thinking of Grant.

"I told him before we started dating officially that I'm a runner. He knew who I was, though, and he loved me anyway. When I look back on all those conversations, it always felt like I was warning him to not fall in love with me because, subconsciously, I think I knew I was going to do something stupid and hurt him in the process."

No one says anything. They know how I am. They know the decisions I made in the past were stupid and full of nonsense.

"He fell into me anyway, and I fell into him because he made me feel things I had never felt. He understood me—weird quirks and all. I loved him. I really did." Tears start to stream down my face again, and I hate myself for feeling how I do. I was the one who caused all this. I shouldn't be so upset at something I had a direct hand in crushing.

Dr. Elyse told me despite everything I had done, and even though I didn't feel capable of loving myself, I'm still lovable. *It's not something you have to earn*, she told me. *It's something that comes from just being human. Love is given freely, with no expectations or strings, because that's what love is. It exists. Plain and simple.*

That session was a turning point for me.

"Then why, Amelia? Why did you do what you did if you loved him?" Paige asks me.

"It was more about me than him. That sounds cliché, but it was. I had this fierce need to prove my parents wrong. Obviously, I was excited, but the need to stick it to them was stronger. It felt like I had tunnel vision as soon as I got the offer, and of course, I had to take it. Of course, I had to make something of myself, but when I factored in how Henry fit, nothing made sense to me. I loved him, God, I fucking loved him, but I was far too focused on my career to try and balance a relationship from an entire ocean away. I thought it was for the best—for me, for him, and for our collective futures." Which it was, in a way, even if I'm miserable for the rest of my life without him. He's written a few bestsellers. It turned out okay for him. He's achieving his dreams, and even if I'm back to where I started before, I'm glad he's made something of himself.

He deserves every good thing that comes his way.

"I guess it was for the best. Even though I'm a little lost, I had a good run in England. It was nice while it lasted, but I also became a lot more comfortable with who I am, so my stint overseas wasn't a complete failure."

"You're not a failure, Amelia," Paige tells me. "And sometimes, being lost and confused is okay. That just means a new path is about to open for you. At least, that's what I believe."

"Do you still love him?" Hads asks me, my head whipping in her direction.

"Even if I did, I doubt he would care after how badly I broke him." Truth is, it's a question I can't answer. What I did to him haunts me around every turn, and if there's one thing I'll never forgive myself for, it's the decision I made to break his heart in the middle of the airport.

He deserves better than me, and he probably found that after all these years. I won't fuck up his life again, and I'm still working on adjusting to my new livelihood.

"Did you know he chased you through the airport? After you left, he stood there while we all tried to wrap our minds around what we saw, and then he bought a sixty-dollar ticket to nowhere just to chase you down. You never looked back, Amelia. He told us you walked onto that plane without so much of a glance behind you," Ella tells me. I never knew he did that. "I thought he was going to break where he stood after he came back out."

"I didn't know that. I told myself it was the right decision. I told myself the entire flight, the entire first few months I was over there, that I made the right choice. As my life started to spiral, I became more unsure of every decision I made up until that point."

"Would you redo it if you could?" Hads asks me.

Would I? It's a good question, one I've put way too many sleepless hours into wondering about. "If time worked that way, there are a lot of things I would go back and do differently."

"But with him, Amelia." Hads moves closer to me. "What would you do differently with Henry?"

I wouldn't break his heart. "I don't think I'd let him fall for me in the first place."

"Why? Why keep yourself from the good just because you messed something up?" Ella asks me.

"Because I'm not sure it's worth it to feel good for a little while if the only thing I'm left with is the pain over what I did. I would rather feel nothing than feel everything, and I'm sure Henry would say the same."

"What a waste, Amelia," Hads says. "We all saw how you two were in college—enamored doesn't even cover it. Why would you want to erase all that from your memories?"

Because I'd rather be numb than live with the mistakes I've made. That's why part of me was worried to go on medication in the first place. I was afraid I'd be more of an unfeeling robot than before, but that's not true. If anything, I'm more in touch with my emotions than ever.

"So, are you going to talk to him?" Hads asks. "You will have to see him if he's here with the boys."

My head turns to Paige. "I'm not going to ruin the wedding."

"You have to at least talk to him," Paige tells me. "You owe him that much, Ames. After all, you did just up and disappear on him with no explanation."

I know she's right, but I don't know if I'm strong enough for that yet. I'm strong enough to face the girls, but I don't know if I'm even going to be able to look him in the eyes and see the consequences of what I did to him inside his gaze. "I'll think about it, okay?" I shake free from her hand, my palms sweaty before I shake my hands out, needing any part of my body to be moving. "Can we get ready for dinner now?"

The three of them look between the circle we have on Paige's bed before Ella gets up and comes back to top off their drinks.

"Turn on the speaker and get some music going for us, Ames," Ella tells me as she grabs my cup and heads to the kitchen to refill it.

I take a deep breath and take in everything I said to them. I feel lighter than I have in weeks, and now that everything is on the table and I have no more secrets to share, I'd say we're all headed in the right direction.

These girls fully forgiving me is going to take some time, but this entire week has been a step in the right direction. I'm grateful I wasn't stupid enough to keep running from them, because on this next step, I don't know how I'd be able to do it without them.

13

Then — The Summer Before Senior Year

Warm by Ariana Grande

"Paige, I told you, classes are the same as they have been," I say as I adjust my bag on my shoulder. "Boring."

"Then why did you stay on campus?"

"When I switched my major, I fell behind, and if I want to graduate with you at the end of next year, I'll waste my summer here at Grand Mountain." Though, this summer doesn't really feel like a waste. Not only do I not have to deal with my parents at home, the weight of their disappointment on my shoulders twenty-four seven, but I get some time to myself before I'm launched into the real world.

Terrified is an understatement, but it's going to be fine.

"Well, it doesn't seem like a waste, especially since you already had your own personal meet cute at that concert."

I can practically hear her smirk over the phone.

"It wasn't a meet cute, Paige. I'm not even sure if I'm going to text him."

"Amelia! God, you really are the worst, aren't you? Was all the cyber-stalking I did for nothing?"

I can't help my laugh. "I told you not to do it in the first place, but you're crazy!"

"What you call crazy, I call thorough," she reminds me. "But he's adorable, Ames. If you don't text him, I'm going to steal your phone and do it for you."

"Paige Yarrow, you are insane." I say as I open the door to the library, needing a cup of coffee before I lock myself in a study room to get going on this paper due in a week. I knew summer classes were going to be tougher than my normal ones, but the amount of work I have to do has drowned me. I can barely focus on anything besides homework, and even then, I'm still not focusing. This is our first long conversation since classes started, when normally, we debrief a few times a week, especially since she's all the way back in New York.

"And you love me anyway," she reminds me.

"Of course I do."

"So, when are you going to hang out with him again?

"Probably never, P," I reiterate. There's a long pause, and Paige is either too deep into stalking his social media, or she thinks I'm joking. "I'm not kidding."

"I cannot fathom why you wouldn't text him. Not only did you have fun at that concert, but it would make me feel better if you had someone to talk to who wasn't just us girls. Relationships are important, Amelia. You literally need them to survive."

"I have you guys! Why would I need anyone else?"

She scoffs across the line. "In all the time I've known you, I've never heard you so animated unless you were making fun of Oliver. You seem brighter today, more cheerful, even."

"It's the post-concert high, Paigey. I can almost guarantee to you, this switch in my personality isn't because of some boy."

Although, it did feel nice talking to him at the concert. He seemed to understand the music in the same way I did, and it was almost refreshing hearing a guy with as much media literacy as he seemed to have. I enjoyed deconstructing the lyrics to one of my favorite bands with him, but that doesn't mean I want to date him. It was a simple, one-time thing with a person I'm never going to see again.

Those types of interactions are my favorite, and while I've only had the one with Henry, I've come to find I enjoy it. It was easy. There were no strings attached, and at the end of the concert, we parted ways. Easy. Simple. Perfect for someone who can't commit to anything like me.

As Paige would say, I'm allergic to committing to anything besides the book club. It's never been something I've wanted, something I've craved like most other humans seem to. Sure, I've hooked up with guys here and there while at Grand Mountain, but it's never been anything serious, which is the way I like it.

The future to me isn't some white picket fence with kids, a husband who hates me, and neighbors who I talk to on the regular. I'm more career focused, and maybe someday, the white picket fence will come into my mind and not give me hives, but that day isn't today.

I also follow my brain and not my heart. I'm too rational of a person for love, and in the years I've been traipsing around the Earth, not once have I felt an all-consuming, soul-shattering love. I'm not sure I ever will.

"Just don't close yourself off completely, Ames." Paige's voice filters through my ears, but I'm barely listening. When I turn around with my coffee in hand, blue eyes enter my vision.

The same blue eyes I met at the concert a few days ago.

"Amelia?"

"Did someone just say your name? Who is that?" Paige asks me.

"Henry," I say, my voice barely above a whisper. "What are you doing here?"

"I go to school here," he says, a huge smile on his face. "And it seems like you do too."

"Is that him? Oh my God, Amelia, this is fate!"

"Sorry," I say to him as I turn around, my hand gripping my phone. "Paige, I have to go. I'll call you later."

"I want details, Ames! And tell Henry I say—" I hang up on her before he hears her say something insane, and when I turn around, he's leaning against the counter as he pushes his glasses up on his face.

"So, what have you been up to since the concert?"

"Really? That's the question you decide to ask me?" I joke. "Why didn't you tell me you went to Grand Mountain?"

"Why didn't you?"

Well, shit. He's got me there.

"You barely gave me anything but your name, Amelia. When I asked you questions about your life, you changed the subject."

I cock my eyebrows at him. "I just met you. You could have been a serial killer or something."

"Do you often meet serial killers at indie alternative concerts?"

"Well, no, but my best friend Paige always says anybody we walk past could have murdered someone."

"So you didn't want to talk to me in case I was a murderer?"

I nod.

"Then why are we talking now?"

"You're clearly not a murderer, and if you are, you're terrible at it. You've already given up your cover to the first girl you saw."

He smiles as he shakes his head. "I guess I did."

The two of us stand suspended in this moment, and I finally get a good look at him. When I was at the concert, we talked, but I never got to study him. Now that he's in front of me again, I take this moment to really see him.

He's taller than me, which I knew from the concert, but his brown, curly hair is fluffier than it was before. His black, square-framed glasses probably need to be adjusted, because he keeps fiddling with them, and his eyes remind me of the lake I dipped my feet into last summer.

He's beautiful. Anyone with eyes can see that.

He grabs his coffee off the counter. I'm still unsure with what else to say, but he beats me to it.

"Are you headed to study?"

"I am." I adjust my bag. "I have a huge paper to write, and I couldn't focus in my apartment."

"Oh, nice," he says. "What are you studying here?"

"Uh, journalism. And you?"

"Creative writing." He smiles before he laughs to himself. "We're both studying something along the same lines, and I never knew you existed before that concert."

"So?"

"It's just interesting."

"What is?"

"Timing. It's everything. At least, that's how I see it. One day, I didn't know you existed, and the next, I found you at the concert. Now, here we are, on the same college campus, our paths crossing again." He tilts his head. "Don't you think that's a little coincidental?"

"Maybe," I say. "But I'm not a big believer in fate and things like that."

"Well, everything happens for a reason." He steps closer to me. "You haven't used my number yet."

"I haven't," I reiterate. "Maybe I knew the universe would bring us back together."

"But you don't believe in that sort of thing."

God, if he was anyone else, I'd find him annoying, but this entire conversation with him has been strangely endearing.

I think my brain might be broken.

"You got me there."

That only makes him laugh. "You're a very endearing person, Amelia Ellis."

"I don't think that word has ever been used to describe me, Henry Hayes."

"Well, I'm glad I'm the first." He takes a sip of his drink. "Use my number. I'd love to chat more about music and everything in between with you, especially since we're both on the same campus for the summer."

"I'd like that." *Oh, would you, Ames? Would you like that?*

"Me too," he says before he heads for the library doors. "Bye, Mills."

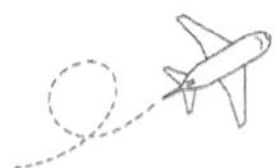

A Few Minutes Later

Amelia: Mills? Really?

Henry: What? Have you never had a nickname before?

Amelia: Of course I have. It just caught me off guard.

Henry: Sorry about that. I won't call you that if you want.

Amelia: No, it's okay.

Henry: Are you sure?

Amelia: Yeah.

Henry: Good luck on your paper.

Amelia: Thank you. Good luck with whatever you're working on.

14

Now

"It was at that moment when I realized I didn't know the person I slept next to every night. And she didn't know me either. The two of us were ghosts, and gone was the person I married all those years ago. My wife was simply a person I no longer knew, and I had to be okay with that because she didn't really know me either." — *Our Best Kept Secret,* **Henry Hayes**

"Did the girls not know I was coming?" I ask the boys as I get back to the room.

"What?" Grant asks, an odd look on his face.

"I ran into Ella in the lobby, and she looked like she had seen a ghost when she realized it was me. Did you tell them I was coming?"

"Paige knows," Oliver tells me. "It's our wedding, so of course she was aware of your invitation. I guess I assumed she would tell the girls."

"If Ella doesn't know, then she must have kept that detail to herself," Leo says.

"Oh, fuck," is all Oliver says before he looks at Grant. "Are you and my wife up to something?"

Grant's hand goes straight to his chest, a gasp coming from his mouth. "How dare you accuse me of something I have nothing to do with." Well, that wasn't suspicious at all. "And she's not your wife yet."

"Semantics," Oliver says as he comes over to me. "It's going to be fine. Paige was okay with this, so I can only assume one of two things."

"And what is that?" I ask him, but Leo is the one who answers.

"Either Paige and Grant are up to something, or Oliver's almost wife thought you two would avoid each other at all costs, so it wouldn't be a problem."

"Bingo," Oliver says with a snap of his fingers. "My money is on Grant and Paige meddling because they are physically incapable of not trying to push two people together."

"Hey!" Grant says as he comes closer to us. "I just want all my friends to be happy and in love like I am. Is that so bad?"

"Well, it can be if you're meddling in people's lives who don't want to be meddled with," Oliver tells him before he looks back at me. "How are you feeling?"

"Nervous, I guess," I say as I run a hand through my hair. "I don't know how I'm going to react when I see her. It's been so fucking long..." I knew she would be here, but nothing can prepare me for actually seeing her.

Amelia has been the longest chapter of my life. Where my brain concerns her, all I can do is write and write. The book of Amelia has never ended, because I never got any sense of closure. I never knew why she chose to rip us apart. She put a period down on a sentence where I thought a comma should have gone.

I haven't been in love since she broke my heart. Part of me secretly wished she would come back, explain why she did it, and maybe we could fix it. I swear, every time my phone buzzed, I secretly hoped it was her, but it never was.

She was the first girl I ever loved. She wasn't simply my *first* love, but my first *love*. I never felt what I did for Amelia for anyone else before, and for some reason, my heart chose the wrong person to give itself over to so completely.

I was also stupid enough to believe every word she whispered to me like it was only meant for me, every secret look we shared that somehow only made sense to us. I truly believed she loved me as much as I loved her.

But she was a con artist, and I was the guy stupid enough to believe her.

"Why don't we watch something before dinner? I can cue up something funny," Grant offers, but I feel my head shake before any words come out.

"I have some work to do, so I'll probably just head to my room."

"Let us know if you need anything, mate," Leo says with a smile.

"I will," I say before I open the door to my suite. "I didn't mean to make this week about Amelia. I'm sorry."

"If anything, I'm glad the spotlight is off me. I just want to marry Paige as soon as I can," Oliver says. "Don't apologize, Hen. This was bound to happen someday, right?"

"I'm not too sure about that." I was fully prepared to never get any answers, but isn't that why I came here? I knew she would be here. I guess I just assumed she would know I was here too.

"What the hell am I doing?" I say as I slump down on the bed.

I glance over at my laptop bag before I decide to decompress inside Mitch's manuscript. I need to live inside someone else's mind for a few hours before I have to face the person who used to know everything about me.

Three hours and multiple chapters later, and my brain is so fried, I hope the anxiety I'll inevitably feel won't show up.

As I exit my room and head down to the lobby to meet the boys, I can already feel my heart rate pick up as I await seeing her again. The last time I physically saw her was when she told me she never loved me.

It really can't get worse than that, can it? Fuck, I hope not.

As I take a deep breath before exiting the elevator, I notice only Paige and Hads are down here conversing with Oliver, Grant, and Leo. Paige notices me first.

She rushes over and throws her arms around me. "It's good to see you again, Henry."

"Uh, thanks," is all I can get out as I nervously adjust my glasses on my face. Hads throws a small wave at me that I return awkwardly, eventually putting my hands in my pocket because I don't really know what to do with myself.

"I'm happy for you and Oliver," I tell Paige.

"Thank you," she says, her eyes gleaming as she looks over at her soon-to-be husband. God, they still look at each other how they did back in college. I can't imagine loving someone so much, it spans years, still looking like it's brand new.

Good for them. I barely scratched the surface of what all these people have been through, but from what I saw our senior year of college, Paige and Oliver deserve this happiness. They've been through enough in this lifetime.

"I forgot how tall you were," Paige tells me with a laugh.

"Our boys are tall, but Henry is the tallest," Hads says.

"Leo could pass him—if his ego counted toward his height," Ella says as she appears from the corner of my eye.

"What was that, darling?" he asks her, a mischievous look in his eye.

"Nothing!" she says to Leo with a smile before turning back to me. "It's nice to see you again."

"Sorry about the awkward elevator ride."

She laughs to herself. "It's alright. I was a little shocked, that's all."

"Henry," Grant says as he slips something into my hand. "I forgot something in the room. Would you mind getting it for me before we head to the restaurant?"

"Sure," I say, a little confused. "What is it?"

"I got Oliver and Paige a present, and I wanted to give it to them when we were all together."

"Is it just a box?"

"With a red bow on it." He smiles at me before grabbing Hads' hand. "Thanks, dude."

As I head back to the elevator, my breathing picks up. Amelia is nowhere to be found. I was fully expecting to see her when I got down there, but I didn't see her.

I've been on the edge of my seat since we got here, and I can't keep hyping myself up for when she finally appears. Although, if she's the same Amelia she's always been, she'll probably run the other direction as soon as we lock eyes.

I wonder if the guilt of what she did keeps her up at night. I have to think it does, especially since she did the same thing to the girls that she did to me. At least she's consistent.

I swipe into the room with Grant's keycard and find the box on the counter. It's smaller than I thought it would be, and I'm curious as to what Grant got them. Gifts could really go either way with Grant.

I really missed these boys, and even if I have to see Amelia and dig up all our shit, I'll still be thankful they invited me. We were close back in college—Oliver, Grant, and me—and I enjoyed being around them. Adding Leo to this mix has only made it more interesting, and it's been fun being around him. He's got the sort of aura that makes you feel more confident just by being near him, and I'm counting on that to help me tonight.

I shut the door, pocketing the key card before I round the corner, ready to press the button for the elevator, but the figure in front of me stops me dead in my tracks.

It's her. I know that frame anywhere, and as if she senses me like she used to be able to all those years ago, her head turns, and her icy blue eyes meet mine.

She looks different. Her hair is the same as it used to be—curly and short—and she still wears those floral dresses that used to overflow in her closet, but something about her looks different. Maybe it's not a physical thing. Maybe I still know her well enough to tell she's a different Amelia.

She doesn't say a word; rather, the two of us continue suspended in this moment, unsure of what to say after all this time has passed. If we said anything, I'm sure it would be fake small talk to avoid saying what we actually want to say. In front of me, she's a stranger. One I know far too much about, but a stranger, nonetheless.

It always amazes me how you can become strangers with someone. Here is this person who used to know every intricate detail of my personality, who used to know all my nuances, all my usual orders, and in between us now is this huge space.

If I think about how many people know such intricacies about me and my life, I might have an anxiety attack, but it's a simple part of life—the fact that people will weave in and out of it. It's natural, like the sun rising in the morning and setting in the evening.

For example, I know Amelia is anxious right now because she still has that same nervous tick—she touches her necklace. To any other person, it wouldn't mean a thing. But to me? To someone who once knew every little thing about her? To me, it tells me she's nervous, scared, even. It brings me the smallest comfort knowing she feels as nervous about this as I do.

The elevator dings, and neither of us says a word as the doors open and we slide inside.

The Elevator by Lizzy McAlpine

It's been eight hundred and sixty seven days since I've last seen him, and my first instinct is to run away.

God, he looks good—different, but good. He's still wearing those same glasses because they always said they made him look more scholarly when I made fun of him our senior year for not being able to see. He told me once he never wanted contacts because of how much he rubs his eyes, and I hate that all these things are trickling back into my thoughts.

My heart lurches as that memory comes back, and my hand goes right to my necklace again. He looked at it before we got in the elevator, and I couldn't tell if he knew it was the same one he got me all those years ago. If he noticed, he hasn't said anything about it.

Neither of us has said much of anything as we stand here, waiting for the elevator to move.

It's a few seconds later I realize neither of us pushed a button to get back to the lobby, so we've just been sitting on the same floor since we awkwardly walked in here.

He must realize it at the same time as me, because we both reach for the button for the lobby, and neither of us actually ends up pressing it. I accidentally graze his hand, and he flinches, pocketing his hand in his jeans.

"Sorry," is the first word I say to him. That single word carries so much weight, and he knows that, even though I'm only talking about the button.

"It's fine."

The two of us are dancing around the actual conversation, but as his voice filters through my ears, I'm hit with a wave of nostalgia. All I can hear is him pleading with me, his voice thick with emotion as I tear his heart to shreds.

"*I love you.*"

"*I don't.*" God, what a liar I was. What a horrible thing I did, breaking this sweet man next to me. Part of me wishes this elevator would crush me after he gets out.

I reach for my necklace again, wanting the smallest bit of comfort it could bring me.

The two of us face the doors, neither of us sparing a glance at one another as Henry pushes the button and it finally starts to move.

I can't think of anything else to say to him. There's no amount of small talk in the world that could fill the awkward tension. We also can't have the beginnings of this conversation in a small elevator before we go to dinner with our friends.

Oh. There's a word I never thought I would say again. Are they our friends again? They're barely even my friends again, so I'm not really sure if I could even say that. How strange to think of us once having a shared group of people who cared about us singularly and as a unit. I ruined that for him. I ruined us, and I ruined his relationship with the guys.

Or maybe I didn't, if they invited him here for the wedding. Maybe they kept in touch. I could ask him, but again, that feels too miniscule. Anything I say besides an apology or an explanation is pretty much pointless.

So, I run away from trying to have any sort of conversation with him, even though I should at least try; it seems like the easiest thing to do right now.

I'm counting down the floor numbers before I hear him scoff and see him shake his head.

"Is something wrong?" I ask, the question slipping out before I can stop it. I don't turn to look at him. I can't. I'm afraid if I spend a second looking into his eyes, I'll see the remnants of how much I destroyed him looking back at me, and I can't handle that.

The elevator dings, and before it opens to the lobby, he speaks.

"You can't spend the entire time pretending I don't exist like you have all these years, Amelia."

"That's not what I was doing."

"Sure it was," he says. "But we'll be seeing a lot of one another, so try to stop running for once, because we have a lot to talk about. I'm not leaving here without any answers like I did the last time you ran from me."

I'm stunned. I've never heard him be so forward before. I thought we would dance around it like we used to dance around serious conversations, but I shouldn't have underestimated him. Of course, he wants answers. If I was him, I would too.

"I'll tell you anything you want to know," I say with a whisper before he turns to look at me, stopping the elevator doors from closing on him.

"Forgive me if I take that sentence with a grain of salt."

And then, he walks away from me, leaving me hoping this elevator crashes. I'm sure it would hurt less than my conversations with him will go. I know he wants answers. I know my words mean nothing to him after what I did.

But it still stings he doesn't think I could change in all the years I've been away. I guess that's what happens when you burn every bridge and make a thousand mistakes you wish you could undo.

He's allowed to be angry at me. He's allowed to because of how I treated him, and I'm going to have to remind myself of that every time I feel like punching myself in the face for what I did to him and the girls.

Deep breaths, Ames. The girls are on their way to forgiving you.

They are, but Henry isn't going to be so easy. With the girls, I said nothing and ghosted them while I was in England. With Henry, every word I said to him in that parking garage is probably burned into his memory. It's easy to take back things I never said or did, but what's difficult is trying to justify my actions. There's no way I can, but I'm sure as hell going to try and make him understand why I did it and what I've been doing since then to work on myself.

Maybe he'll forgive me at some point, but I won't be surprised if he never does. Maybe the two of us were meant to have an unfinished story, or one that ends ambiguously, where the reader and the narrator don't know what will end up happening.

Another hand comes in to stop the elevator from closing in on me, and my thought spiral stops before I fly too far off the handle.

"Is everything okay?" Ella asks as I shake out of my stupor.

"Yup," I say quickly. "Let's go eat. I'm starving."

And when Ella and I see the others, the tension rises, and I'm sure we're in for the most awkward dinner of our lives.

Just don't ruin this for Paige, I remind myself, but that's easier said than done.

15

Then — February 2025, One Month Into Therapy

Growing Sideways by Noah Kahan

"So, how have you been since our last few meetings? I know reaching where we did last time might have been tough for you."

What a loaded question. I guess most of them here are—it is therapy, after all.

"Uhm," I say as I grab my necklace, needing it to ground me as I think about what happened after our last session. "I'm not really sure how to describe what I felt after it."

"Take your time," she says to me. "Last session was a lot at once, and it's perfectly normal to experience whatever you did after you left my office."

Normal. Yeah, because normal is getting diagnosed with Attention-Deficit/Hyperactivity Disorder, leaving your therapist's office, then going home and rearranging your entire apartment. I spent hours moving every single piece of furniture I owned, trying to make sure it was all the way I wanted it. I didn't sleep. I didn't make dinner. I couldn't slow down. I needed the control back. I needed my mind to stop racing.

On the bright side, I built my new bookshelf that had been sitting in the box for months.

"I rearranged my entire apartment."

She scribbles some things down in her notebook before she waits for me to say more.

"A few days after, I felt...foggy. I floated through work, and I could barely sleep at night because I couldn't clear the clouds from my thoughts."

For the first time this session, I look my therapist, Dr. Elyse, in the eye, and I'm met with a neutral expression, a hint of sympathy in her voice so far this session. She's only a few years older than I am, and my decision to come see her has been the most terrifying jump I've ever made in my life.

If my younger self could see me here in England, willingly talking to a therapist after getting a diagnosis we've been waiting our entire lives for, she would probably roll her eyes and make a joke about it.

"Those are all completely normal reactions, Amelia. You were just given a diagnosis, so your brain was searching for a semblance of control. That fogginess you felt has been with you your entire life, at least from what I remember from a few of our earlier sessions."

"I still haven't been able to sleep," I whisper under my breath. "Part of me feels like an idiot for not knowing about this before now. When you told me my diagnosis it felt like the carpet was ripped out from underneath me, but looking back, it all makes sense, I guess."

"Hindsight is tough, especially with mental health. Some people go through a denial phase. Others feel relief to finally have a name for what they've been struggling with. It seems like you were somewhere in the middle."

I scoff. "I guess you could call it that."

"Well, would you think of it as something else?"

"I'd call myself an idiot."

"And why is that?" She scribbles some more things down.

"Because I always assumed these idiosyncrasies I had were personality quirks, but apparently, there's a reason for why I am the way I am."

"Most of the time there is, Amelia."

"Oh, so everyone is just walking around with an undiagnosed mental illness?"

She tilts her head at me as her note-taking stops. "That's a generalization. Not everyone, but more people than we know."

I take a sip from my water bottle, my throat suddenly dry.

"How do you feel now as you sit in front of me? Did you think about what we talked about?"

I take a deep breath as tears filter into my eyes. "Do you want the truth?"

"I never want anything else from you, Amelia."

"I feel like a failure. I feel angry at myself for not seeing the signs sooner. I feel like there's so much regret swimming through my body when I look back at all the decisions I've made."

"Why is that?"

"Because it doesn't feel like me who made those decisions anymore. It feels like my brain and the chemical imbalance inside of it is who has always been calling the shots. I don't know where that ends and I begin. I don't feel in control anymore."

"You are not your diagnosis. I need you to know that this is the first step in creating a healthy routine and managing your symptoms." She crosses her legs in her chair and shuffles around before handing me a tissue box. "With the right treatment, you'll feel more in control. I can't promise our first attempt will be the right one for you, but that's the nice thing about treatment. We can figure out what works best for you and your brain because a diagnosis isn't a one size fits all."

I nod, unable to say much of anything. I know I can't leave this untreated, but it's going to be a long, hard road trying to reframe the mindset I've had for my entire life. I thought admitting I needed help was the hardest thing I've ever done, but that doesn't even come close to the work Dr. Elyse and I are going to do in the future.

"I guess part of me does feel a little relieved," I say as I blow my nose.

"That's wonderful, Amelia." More scribbles in her notebook.

"I really thought I was just a horrible person by making impulsive decisions like I did, not being able to hold relationships for too long."

"I don't think you're a horrible person, Amelia. But don't use this diagnosis to rationalize behavior that isn't healthy. You're going to have to put in the work with me to try and properly treat this. Is that something you're ready for?"

I nod, swallowing to try and help my dry throat.

"Good."

"Can I ask you something?"

"Of course." She closes her notebook and rests her hands on it.

"Why has it always been so difficult for me to do the simplest things? I mean, it's always been difficult for me to answer text messages or emails, and oftentimes, I forget about them until it's been days or weeks and answering would just be rude at that point. But sometimes, even something as simple as doing the dishes felt like... Well, it felt like there was an invisible barrier in front of me that only came down when it wanted to. And why is my memory so terrible? Why can't I remember the simplest of things? Are all these questions I have about myself able to be answered through my diagnosis?"

"Well, some of those things can be explained. Some people with your diagnosis experience situations similar to yours. Others are different. It's not a one size fits all kind of thing. People often underestimate how difficult it is to simply wake up every day and live. With the amount of decisions, interactions, and about a thousand other factors that we go through every single day, it almost feels like a miracle we have time for other things, for other thoughts, for other feelings. When you add a diagnosis on top it, it's astounding how we as humans can be so resilient in the state of brain fog, or the highest highs and lowest lows."

I take in what she's saying as she continues.

"Amelia, your brain spends all day trying to keep up with everything it's taking in. It's a lot for your mind to handle, and after spending all day on high alert at work or school or what have you, when you're out of those situations, you have nothing left to give because you used it all. Your brain works differently, and that's okay. Give yourself the space to really try and understand that, and don't beat yourself up about the past."

I can't help the tears from pouring out. They've barely stopped since I walked out of this office last time, and finally having a reason to why I am the way that I am feels like a breath of fresh air.

I'm not broken.

I'm not a mess who just needs to work harder to get herself together.

I'm not someone who needs to work on her time management skills better.

I'm not lazy and unmotivated like my parents used to think I was as a kid.

And I'm not just forgetful.

I've barely been surviving. I've been giving all that I can, and I'm recognizing it's okay to have been doing that, since it's all I was able to do.

There's something wrong with my brain, and after two decades of assuming I would grow out of it, I finally have a name for it. I finally know why I'm like this. This doesn't erase all the horrible stuff I've done, but it can help me figure out how to fix it going forward. This is the first step in the right direction, and I'm going to take it. I'm going to put in the work to manage this, and then maybe I can work on building back the relationships I lost.

The girls were the first people I wanted to call as soon as I found myself sitting on the floor of my apartment, furniture everywhere, crying my eyes out all by myself.

Then, I had another reason to tack onto my mental list of why I need to put the work in, of why I need to rely on the help from Dr. Elyse and whoever else she might bring in to help me through this.

And she's right. I've come to understand a lot about myself and my life over the past year. I thought being a kid was hard. I could never wait until I was grown up so I could be an adult and people would take me seriously.

But that isn't how it is at all. I've started realizing being an adult is doing your usual routine no matter how you're feeling. If you're happy, sad, depressed, struggling, you still have to wake up every day, go to work, and pretend everything is fine. The worst part is, you realize everyone is doing that all the time. It's not just you; it's everyone. We're all just masks floating through the world trying our best when we ourselves don't feel like we're doing enough.

Being an adult feels like having a never-ending to-do list where you check off something, and four more tasks pop up. It's exhausting, and everyone is going through it, whether they're aware of it or not.

It's so fucking hard, and I've been struggling my entire life. Now, I have an explanation, if I can call it that. It isn't a miracle that's going to fix all my problems and issues, but it is a start to figuring out what works best for me going forward.

Maybe things won't be as bad once I figure it out, but the road to get there isn't going to be easy. I'm going to have to wake up every day and work at this, even when I can't bear to get out of bed.

"Amelia? Are you alright? Our session is almost over."

I'm jolted back to reality as I look at Dr. Elyse. "Sorry. I got a little lost in my thoughts for a second."

"That's okay. What were you thinking about?"

"I was thinking about where we go from here," I say as I grab my necklace. "Can you explain to me what that looks like?"

She smiles at me as she opens her notebook back up. "Of course I can. First things first, we're going to continue our sessions. Routine is important going forward. I really think a set one could help, but we can tweak what works and what doesn't."

"Okay," I say, taking a deep breath.

"And this might be an unpopular opinion in the medical community, but medication really is the best path forward most of the time."

"Why is that unpopular?"

"Well, medication isn't a one size fits all, kind of like a diagnosis, but in your case, I think it could really help."

"You do?" I ask, nerves starting to settle into my body, my foot bounc-ing of its own accord.

"Yes. There's a chemical imbalance in your brain, Amelia, and med-ication can work to fix that."

I nod, unsure how to feel about all this. "So I'll be medicated for the rest of my life?"

"Most likely, yes. Symptoms might lessen as you get older, but it's not a guarantee. How is this making you feel?"

"Terrified. I feel like I've been going through the motions for my entire life, and to fix what's been wrong with me, I have to take medication every day. I guess I'm struggling with the fact that I can't fix myself, and I'll be like this forever."

"It's normal to feel that way. Medication is not a cure, though, Amelia. It helps, sure, but the real work comes from you."

"But what if the person I am when I'm medicated is different from who I really am? What if I don't really know who I am, and I'm going to meet a new version of myself I don't recognize? What if I lose who I thought I was and become someone I don't know when I look in the mirror?"

"Amelia, stop the spiral and come back to the present for me," Dr. Elyse coaxes. "You know who you are. Medication isn't going to change that, but it's going to help your brain balance out. It's going to help the fog clear. It's going to help to keep you focused when your brain normally wants to divert itself. Trust me on this."

"I'm scared," I admit as her timer goes off, tears streaming down my face. Everything is going to change, and I'm terrified I might not be strong enough for it.

"It's okay to be scared," she tells me. "It's going to be a lot of change, and at first, it's going to be weird and tough and terrifying, but that's normal. And you know you can always text or call me in between our weekly sessions. I'm always available for you, especially during this time of change."

She scribbles something down on a piece of paper before she hands it to me.

"I've called in a prescription for you at a local pharmacy. It's fifteen milligrams of Adderall. This is your starting dose that we're going to try out for a little bit. I want you to journal your thoughts every day, and at your next appointment, we're going to talk about how it's helped your symptoms. We'll adjust from there if we need to, okay? Does that seem alright to you?"

I sit with her instructions before I take my journal out and write what she said down—another thing she's suggested I try. I've been keeping a journal on me, writing down notes to keep my brain on track, and so far, it's been working well.

"I can do that."

She grabs my hand as we get up and head for the door. "Yes, you can, Amelia. You *can* do this."

16

Now

From The Dining Table by Harry Styles

DINNER ISN'T ACTUALLY AS bad as I thought it was going to be. We went to one of the restaurants attached to the hotel we're staying at, and it's a nice place. We're on the back patio, away from most other people, and have been conversing since the appetizers were set down.

I've been strategically placed next to Grant and Ella. Grant is to my left; he's the best person in this group for small talk because he can talk about anything for an extended period of time. Ella is to my right, and I'm sure she's trying to keep an eye on me, but I appreciate her keeping me away from Henry after our conversation in the elevator.

He was a lot more forward than he used to be, and I deserved his remarks no matter how much it hurt hearing them. I can't help but steal a few glances at him down the table; he's grown up quite nicely in the past few years. His hair is still that same shade of brown, a little longer than it used to be in college. He never really styled it back then, and I guess he still doesn't, because his wavy hair is all over as the breeze blows through it.

Or it's like that because he won't stop running his hand through it. Back when I knew him, he used to tilt his head when he was nervous. I was never sure if he knew he did that when he was feeling awkward or uncomfortable, but I always noticed it. That's one of the best parts about knowing someone so intimately—you can see things they might not have noticed about themselves.

Now, I can't figure out if him running his hand through his hair so much is a new nervous habit he picked up, or if it's too long and he needs to cut it because it's bothering him.

I'll probably never know him so intimately again, so that thought will remain unanswered.

I'm aching to solve this puzzle just so he and I can both move on and live our lives the way we were meant to—separately. I again ignore how that makes me feel before I grab a chip and dip it in salsa, shoving it into my mouth to try and get rid of the feelings I'm having.

I steal another glance at him, his body like a magnet to mine now that we're back in close proximity, only this time, his eyes connect with mine. Just when I think we're about to share a look or a thought like we used to all those years ago, he breaks contact and turns back to his conversation with Oliver.

I know nothing Oliver says is ever that interesting, so the fact that he chose to talk with him rather than look at me is telling. It hurts more than it should, because every time I had a conversation with Oliver in the past, I either wanted to fall asleep, yell at him to stop being so boring, or some other quip I used to have up my sleeve back then.

But I'm being civil because it is a celebration of his wedding, and I would hate for Paige to have to mediate our quarrels. I have enough shit to deal with on this trip, and adding Oliver to the mix is more of a headache than anything.

Deep down, I am super happy for him, but I'd never tell him that. Not only would it upset the balance, but that's not how our relationship works. The two of us thrive on annoying one another, and I think we both understand that underneath all the shit we've said to one another, it's all out of love.

Actually, love is too strong of a word. I guess I would call it a mutual understanding.

The eight of us order our food, and as the waiter leaves, Grant stands, clinking his glass with his knife.

"As the first official boyfriend, I am honored to welcome the eight of us to the first wedding of the book club."

There's a few cheers around the table, and smiles spread all around as Grant continues.

"To celebrate this momentous occasion, I have a gift for the impatient motherfucker who couldn't wait to marry his girl, even though I proposed first." Grant pauses for the laughter he knows is coming. "I know all of us around the table can agree you two deserve a lifetime of happy memories. So, cheers to a long and beautiful life that the rest of us can't wait to watch unfold beside you."

Glasses are raised, and all of us take sips as Grant slides a box over to Oliver, who already looks a little petrified about what's inside. Honestly, if Grant were my best man, I would be a little scared too, especially with how much he loves giving either weirdly specific gifts or stupidly funny ones.

I've really missed this feeling of inclusion. I remember when it was just us four girls sitting in that small classroom on campus, and now, years later, here we all are, sitting around a table, our group having grown in size.

It almost feels like yesterday Hads was pacing that room complaining about having to tutor Grant.

"You've got to be kidding me," Oliver says, clearly annoyed at whatever Grant gifted him.

Paige looks into the small box, and she bursts out laughing before putting an arm around Oliver, pulling him closer to her.

"Grant, why would you get us these?" Paige asks as she lifts a pair of pink, fuzzy handcuffs out of the box, already laughing.

"It felt fitting!"

"Why? Why did *these* feel fitting as a wedding present?" Oliver groans as he sets them back into the box, probably needing them out of his sight.

"Seriously?" Ella asks. "You don't get the significance?"

"Even I get it," Leo says, and I can no longer hold back my laughter. The fact that this has been the group's longest running joke will never fail to make me laugh. It was always my favorite story to tell anyone who would listen.

"I seriously thought you guys would let it go after a year or two, and for the one thousandth time, I was in a holding cell. I was *not* in jail!"

"Oliver, you were behind bars! That's basically the same thing," Hads tells him.

"I'd have to side with Oliver on this one," Henry says, cocking his head. "He wasn't fully processed and in jail. If Paige hadn't done what she did, he would've landed himself in jail."

We all messily talk over one another before the food comes, and we start reminiscing.

I haven't said much of anything tonight because I've been spending this first full get together trying to wrap my mind around everything that has happened in the past few years—and days, I guess. Not only did I make an effort with the girls, but Henry was a surprise I never saw coming. Him being here is dredging up lots of feelings and emotions I wasn't prepared for—good and bad. Mostly bad, I guess. Whenever I think about what I did to him, I want to curl into a ball and melt into the floor, disappearing physically before the mental assault from my memories.

We all eat until we're full and practically falling asleep where we sit. We're all a little tipsy besides Oliver, Paige, and I, but those two are one hundred percent drunk on happiness.

Eventually, we all disperse. Paige and Oliver head to the beach to walk on the sand. Ella and Leo head upstairs, probably to fuck, according to Grant. All that's left is Hads, Grant, Henry, and me. I would say it's awkward, but that word isn't strong enough for the vibes around this table.

"You guys can leave. It's okay. I'm paying the bill. You don't have to stay," Grant says, trying to disperse the tension. Henry waits all of two seconds before excusing himself.

I take a few deep breaths, Hads locking eyes with me when I open my eyes a few seconds later.

"You okay?" she asks me, her voice muffled by the thoughts in my head.

"Mhm," I hum. "I just need some air."

I don't hear what either of them say as I find myself drifting to the stairwell, not wanting to be stuck in the elevator, forcing other people to bear witness to whatever is going on with me right now. Dots are clouding my vision. My legs turn to jelly as I feel them start to give out. My mind is racing, and I need to make it back to my room before this turns into a full blown panic attack.

I make it up two flights before I collapse, my arm gripping the handrail as if it's the only thing holding me up. I can't tell where my body is, what I'm doing, or what is going on with me.

I somehow move to sit down when I hear footsteps from above me. I can't tell if they're coming toward me or heading away, but I hope for the latter, because even a stranger seeing me like this—barely breathing properly, sweaty, tears streaming down my face—would be enough embarrassment for me today.

I'm not even sure when or why the tears started. I could barely feel them until just now. That has to be good, right? Maybe this feeling is going away. Maybe I'm fine. Maybe if I gaslight myself enough, my body will start to believe it's fine.

"Oh," is all I hear when the footsteps stop.

When I look behind me, blue eyes meeting mine, I curse to myself.

Of course, Henry is who the footsteps belonged to. Who the fuck else would it be on a resort this big?

I can barely manage words, so I just put my head between my legs and wait for him to leave like I assume he's going to.

Except he doesn't, because a few minutes of silence later, I feel him sit down next to me.

"Are you okay?" he asks me in a voice that seems like he really doesn't want to have this conversation with me. I'm sure he doesn't. I'm sure he'd rather leave me here or push me down the stairs or any other horrible thing I can think of, but that's not who Henry is.

He's nice. Thoughtful. Caring. Loving. He's the best person I know. Knew.

"You don't have to do this," I tell him, not sparing a glance at him. I'm not sure I could look at him right now without wanting to crawl into a hole and die. If I was smarter, I would apologize, but I know that isn't what he wants to hear, not after all this time, not after all I've done to him. My words mean nothing if it's not an explanation.

"It was only a question," he says. "And you didn't even answer it."

"I'm fine."

He only sighs. "It always was difficult to pull the truth out of you, Amelia. I guess some things haven't changed."

"Some things haven't changed, but a lot still has," I say as I look over at him for the first time since dinner. Blue eyes look back at me, but instead of seeing them shine at me like they used to, all I see is a blank expression. He's devoid of emotions as he looks at me, tired eyes and dark circles matching the ones on my face, I'm sure.

"Well, that's life, I guess," he says as he runs his hand through his hair. "Can you stand?"

I nod, feeling like my body has returned to itself.

"I'll walk you back."

"Henry, really, it's fine. We don't have to do this," I say as I stand and look down at him.

"Do what?"

"Pretend it doesn't hurt every time we look at one another. Pretend everything is fine, and we're just two people who used to know one another."

The next words out of his mouth crush me more than they should. "I don't know if I ever knew you at all, Amelia."

I don't know if he gets up and leaves, or if I somehow get my legs to move myself up the stairs to my room. I don't know if I fumble around with my room key or if I get it on the first try.

Because of all the things we've said to each other, of all the things I've done, that hurts the most. Henry was the one person who knew every piece of me. He was who I was most myself with, and him saying that just proves how much I took advantage of him and his kindness, of the love he gave to me.

And out of all the things the girls have said to me the past few days, after all the things my brain believes about myself in this moment, those words are the one thing to really cut into me and break me open.

Henry Hayes once knew me to the core, down to my bones. He knew my thoughts with just one glance. So, if he says something about me, then it's true, and there's nothing I can do to change that. No apology from me would fix what I broke.

Sometimes, things that get smashed can't be fixed because the pieces are too small to be put back together, and Henry and I might be living proof.

17

"He wasn't in the room any longer, but his presence still lingered over the rest of us. It's like we were waiting for him to come back and tell us what to do, our family frozen in time and unsure of where to go without his instruction."
— *In A Room With Death*, Henry Hayes

HAUNTED EYES ARE ALL I can see when I wake up, the sun not even risen yet.

I would try to go back to sleep, but there's no point. Once I'm up for the day, I usually can't force myself back to sleep.

After my shower, I sit at my computer, fully prepared for nothing to come out when I set my sprint timer for twenty minutes. But to my surprise, the characters take over, and twenty minutes later, I've written a thousand words.

One thousand words. It's probably been months since I was able to sit down and write that many at once. Before I can even think about it, I pick up my phone.

> **Henry: One thousand words this morning.**

> **Mitch: Holy shit. Should I call your publisher?**

> **Henry: Very funny.**

> **Mitch: Proud of you, buddy. I take it things are going well?**

That's not really the truth, but if it means I'm writing again, I would call that going well. I've got a small part of my groove back, and that is cause for celebrating.

> **Henry: Well enough, I guess. Getting words in is always good.**

> **Mitch: Just take care of yourself first. The manuscript can always wait until after the trip with your ex and all your old friends.**

> **Henry: I'm going to get a coffee. I'll be around later if you want to call.**

> **Mitch: Sounds good.**

I stretch a little bit before I get up, and as I head into the main part of the suite, I run into Leo, who's not only shirtless, but about to make a smoothie of some sort, based on all the fruit he has on the counter.

"Ah, I thought I heard typing somewhere. I figured that was you. Grant types far more like a madman when he's working on his fanfiction."

"Sorry, what?" I hold back my laughter, but in all honesty, Grant writing fanfiction makes the most sense in the world.

Leo merely shrugs. "Probably best for him to tell you. I'm sure he's not mentioned it because he looks up to you."

"That's nice of him, but he really shouldn't. I can barely write these days. I might be a two-hit wonder."

He shakes his head as he cuts up a banana. I move close to the counter, not wanting to wake the other two with our conversation.

"Is that what you think?"

"Yeah," I say as I sit on a bar stool. "I didn't mean to bombard you with my shit, so I'll just—"

"I don't mind, mate. Plus, I barely know you, so maybe it's a little easier with me than the other two. I'm sure Grant would kiss your arse; he's read both of your books multiple times and won't shut up about them. Oliver is okay to go to for advice on occasion, but he doesn't care about anything but his almost wife right now. That leaves me, clearly the smartest, most intelligent one of the group." He slaps me on the shoulder. "You've chosen wisely, Henry. So, what do you need from me? A shoulder to cry on? An ear to listen?"

"Maybe just a listener for now," I say as he throws all his stuff into the blender. "I don't know what's wrong with me, but I can't write. When I wrote my first two books, they sort of...came out of my mind. It wasn't as difficult for the words to come out, but now, it feels like work when it used to feel like the easiest thing in the world. It feels like my job, rather than this thing I love and grew up wanting to do."

Leo simply nods as he turns the blender on, his smoothie mixing as I feel my shoulders relax a little bit. It felt weird to admit that, but it's the truth. All I wanted to do was write and make a living off it, but now that I'm actually doing that, it's harder than I wanted it to be.

It all feels pointless—the words, the characters, the book—when it's just me celebrating and then moving onto the next one. All my accomplishments seem...small. They seem little and pointless, even though some people would kill to be where I'm at. I'm twenty-five, and I've already crossed dreams off my list of where I'd thought I'd be by the time I was forty.

I should be happy. I should be thriving and writing until my fingers hurt, but every time I sit down at my laptop, my brain goes blank, and I have to force myself not to get up and do something else.

"Can I be honest?"

"Of course," I tell him, already weary of his tone.

"I didn't know you back when the girls and the other two did. So, from the outside looking in, I've never seen anyone else with the look in your eyes."

"What look?"

"I can't really describe it. I'd guess I'd call it weighted, if I were to assign a word to it. But you're the writer here, not me."

That makes me laugh. "Some days, I barely feel like one."

"I've had that look you have in your eyes. I've felt it."

"Felt what?"

"Not thinking you're good enough. Not really knowing where you belong. Scared of where you'll end up if all you have are your accomplishments," he says as he scoops his smoothie into a bowl. "If I were you, I would try and figure out what it's going to take to let that go, because it's going to do much more harm than good."

I sit and really think about what he's said. Do I think about all those things? Do I think that, on my own, I'm not good enough? That I don't deserve to have all these good things around me?

Maybe I do. Maybe deep down, that's the root cause of all this.

"What did you do?"

He shrugs. "I talked with my family. I started showing up for people who mattered to me, and I took a look at the people in my life and decided if they were good for me to be around."

"And?"

"And it helped. It helped to have my girl reminding me that life is like the monkey bars. You have to take it one bar at a time, one obstacle, because trying to do it all at the same time is going to make you fall off and have to start all over."

"How did you know where to start?" I ask him, surprised this is the most I've spoken with Leo since I got here. I like this guy. He's good, despite the fact that all I knew about him was that Ella hated his guts.

"The hardest part was figuring out where to start. Everything else seemed to fall into place after that," Leo says as he grabs his water bottle. "I think we all know what the hardest part is for you, but tread carefully. This group is special, really special, and I would hate for people to have to pick sides if you and her can't seem to rewrite your history and be civil for a week."

"You guys don't know the full story, but it was bad," I say to him. "Really bad. So much so that I'm unsure what I want from her now."

"Well then," he says as he heads for the door, "it seems like you've found a place to start."

And then the door shuts, and I'm left alone with the weight of everything we just talked about.

Not wanting to dive into this when the sun is only just coming up, I grab my room key and my wallet before I head to the breakfast bar to grab a coffee. My brain is far too tired, even though I've just woken up, and that needs to change. This week has barely even started.

As soon as I turn the corner and head for the coffee machine, I notice only a few other people down here, but only one short-haired, dress-wearing girl catches my eye.

It's just like it used to be, our eyes always drawn to one another. I've barely moved an inch before she turns around, already sensing I'm behind her.

After a few seconds, she clears her throat and gets back to what she was doing. Four cups sit in front of her as she puts different things in them, presumably one for each of the girls and herself.

She always was an early riser, even when she went to bed in the early hours of the morning.

"I'll be out of your way in a minute," I hear her say as I get closer to the coffee. I grab a cup for myself, standing behind her, suddenly remembering how it used to feel when she would fall asleep on top of me, or when we would walk hand in hand around the grocery store, sharing headphones while we shopped.

I'm about three feet away from Amelia, and I can still feel the ghost of her that used to stand by my side. I can still feel her lean against me in the smallest way, but to me, it was everything.

Amelia doesn't get comfortable with people. She was never one for a lot of physical touch, but every touch, every hand that brushed mine when she slipped me one side of her headphones was like her moving a mountain just for me. It was her building a bridge between us so I could cross and really get to know her. Every piece of music we shared danced between our ears, and sometimes, it felt like she was playing songs just to say all the things she wanted to me that she couldn't form into words.

I was always better at words than she was. Amelia spoke through music, and every melody and lyric shared between us were like her writing love letters to me through songs. Every playlist she sent to me was like getting a peek inside of her head at that time.

Our favorite song we would often send back and forth was from the band we both saw in concert the day we met. I still remember that day as if it were yesterday. It was the day everything changed for me. Here was this girl in front of me, also alone at this concert, and I just happened to run into her and spark up a conversation.

I made a stupid joke, and she rolled her eyes at me, but then she smiled, the softest smile I had ever seen, and I was a goner. Then, we ran into one another on campus because we were both taking summer classes. Eventually, we became friends, and I took everything she wanted to give me because she simply astonished me, this girl in the dress with the yellow flowers on it and a smile that could kill.

Then came the smiles she only gave me, then the moments where we shared a bit too much and she would retreat again. All I did was be there for her. All I did was let her talk because all I wanted to do was listen to her analyze the lyrics and production of different music. Her smile grew when she would talk about the music she loved.

I wonder if she still does that. I wonder if she knows I can't listen to music the same way anymore. I doubt she knows I can't even listen to the band we both saw in concert. It hurts too much. It brought up too many memories of her that I couldn't seem to forget.

How could I? Forget, I mean. How could I forget the first girl who ever loved me back? How could I ever forget the first girl I loved with my whole being?

"Do you often come to depressing concerts in the happiest outfit you can wear, or is this a first for you?"

First was the eye roll. Then, it was a look down at her outfit, paired with the saddest song in the band's discography. *"I guess this is a first. I didn't think I had those in me anymore."*

I never asked her what that meant. My next question was about her favorite song by the band, and we talked through the whole set until that song came on. I videoed it for her so she could go back and listen to it, but while the camera on my phone was pointed at the stage, my eyes never left the mysterious girl beside me. Then, I gave her my number so I could send it to her. She never used it, though, not until I gave her a nickname when I saw her on campus after the concert.

I would say the rest is history, but history has a funny way of repeating itself—or rather, laughing in your face. Because our story doesn't seem to be over, not yet.

"Henry? Henry!" I hear her shout as my hands start to burn. "What are you doing?"

I look down at my overflowing cup, my mind lost in the hazy memory of the stranger to my left. "Being an idiot, it seems."

"Here," she says as she hands me a bunch of napkins before disappearing. Before I think she's not going to come back, she returns with a small ice pack she places on my hand. "For the pain."

I stop myself from laughing at how ironic her saying that to me, of all people, is. Instead, I take a deep breath.

Her hand lingers against my skin for a beat too long, but neither of us mentions it. She doesn't note how she used to brush her hand against mine in a silent plea to hold hands—because she would never outright ask. I don't mention how good it feels to have her touch against my skin again.

"Thanks," is all I say.

She opens her mouth to say something but then stops herself, looking at the four cups she has before speaking again.

"I should get these to the girls."

"Do you want any help?"

She shakes her head. "No, I've got it. Just ice your hand and be more careful next time."

Be more careful with the coffee or with being in your orbit, Amelia? Which one do you mean, because I know I'll never get an answer from you?

"I will."

As I watch her walk away, I realize the place I have to start.

I need an answer. An explanation. I need anything Amelia will give me as to why she did what she did, because I don't think I'll ever move on or figure out anything else without that.

It's going to hurt, I know it will. If the hurt is what I need to move to a new phase of my life away from Amelia, though, I'll do anything, even damage my own mental health, to pry an answer out of her as to why she broke my heart and never looked back.

18

Luna Moth by Maya Hawke

I RUB MY FEET into the sand as I watch my friends run around the beach, and for some reason, all I can think about is my family.

The last time I saw them was right before I left for England, and like my friends, I didn't keep in contact.

The last thing my mother told me was that I'm destined to be alone. Those words have stayed with me over the years. Sure, I wasn't the most forthcoming child, and I didn't really tell my parents much of anything. I kept to myself of my own accord, and I don't regret that. They barely knew my friends, and any interaction we had back then was awkward at best. I could always hear it—the disappointment in their voices when we interacted. I wasn't who they wanted me to be, and they didn't like who I became on my own.

Not only did I disappoint them by not going to medical school or getting a good job like my brother did, but I followed my dreams. I knew they would see my path as a waste of time, which is why I didn't bother telling them when I changed my major. I knew there would be a conversation coming that I didn't want to have. Instead of that, I got a passive-aggressive text, and that was the end of it. We never spoke of it again, even when I graduated.

That's kind of how my relationship with my parents has been my whole life. We don't really talk about anything. Whenever I was struggling, all I was told to do was try harder. Never mind the fact that I already felt like I was trying ten times harder than everyone else to do the simplest of things.

That would always happen when I was younger, too. When my parents were mad at me for whatever reason, none of us would talk about it, and then a few days later, a new notebook would show up on my bed, or something they thought would cheer me up. Life would continue as if nothing had ever happened, and nobody would ever bring anything up.

Therapy has been helping me rewire my brain to actually talk about things, and since being medicated, my thoughts have become less scrambled and all over the place. I block out time specifically on my planner for things I need to do, and they actually get done. Lists with things I can check off is the greatest adjustment I've made for my brain to actually have motivation to do certain tasks. I've done all this work on my own, and part of me wants to mend my relationship with them at some point like I have with the girls.

I want them to be able to understand my brain. I want to be the family I wished we were when I was younger, but we all have to be willing, and I don't know if they'll feel how I do.

I know I'm a disappointment to them, but I still can't help but wonder if they're proud of me. I can't help but wonder what they would say if they saw me now. I'm older. I look a little different. I finally found my own sense of style. I'm basically a grown adult—a real one, not just a kid pretending to be one.

I wonder if I tried to repair my relationship with them, if it would be of any use. Would they actually sit down and listen to what I have to say? Would they be willing to hear me speak, or would they do that thing a lot of adults do and assume I'm naïve because I'm young and the world hasn't jaded me yet?

I don't know how to tell people who think that way that your experiences are what shape you—age doesn't really matter. I've grown so much in the past two years. I want them to be able to see me for who I am now. I want them to be proud of what I've become, despite them not believing in me.

"Amelia!" Grant shouts from across the sand. "Do you want to be on my team for cornhole?"

I come back to reality, digging my hands into the sand to ground myself. "Sure! I'm not the best at cornhole, though. Are you sure you don't want Leo to be your partner?"

"Oliver is about to teach him how to surf. Well, attempt to teach him." Grant smiles. "He's not a great teacher, but Hads is out there too. I don't care if you're good or not; all we have to do is win."

"Who are we playing against?" I ask as I get up.

"Me!" Paige smiles as she comes over to us. "I finished my book, and I need to get my legs moving."

"Let's go," Grant says as he practically pulls me over to the boards in the sand. Paige and Grant say nothing as they head across from me, and I'm about to ask who Paige is playing with, but my question is answered when Henry appears next to me.

"I guess we're board partners," he says, definitely not excited about that.

"Grant, are you sure you want to be on that side? Isn't this side better for your throwing arm?"

He shakes his head. "Nope! I'm okay over here."

Of course he is. I'm going to have a talk with those two later. Anyone with eyes can tell what they're doing, and it's not my intention to hurt Henry more than I already have.

They're trying to get us back together, I'm sure. If by some miracle they're not doing that, then whatever they are doing is cruel. The point of this trip is to celebrate Paige and Oliver, not to make me and Henry talk about what went down at the airport all those years ago.

I don't know if we'll ever discuss it, but Henry has mentioned he wants answers. I just don't know when he wants to actually talk. The only time the two of us have been alone besides the elevator was when he spilled coffee on himself. I know I owe him a conversation, but is now really the best time?

"Can you really not bear to stand next to me for a simple game of cornhole?" Henry whispers under his breath, and I suddenly feel like sinking into the sand.

"No, I just figured you would be more comfortable with Grant over here instead of me."

"Stop assuming things about me, Amelia. You don't know me well enough anymore to be able to do that."

"You're right. I'm sorry," I agree.

"Are you guys ready?" Paige calls out from the other board.

"Yeah!" I say as I swing my arm out. "Bride's team goes first."

Paige throws the first few, and we play a few rounds, the four of us shouting taunts across the sand at one another.

Just being back in Henry's orbit has made me feel off my axis, and I'm sure it's noticeable. After a few more tosses, we're down to the wire.

Grant needs to make it into the hole and another on the board. Paige has to do the same. So far, neither of us has points this round because Paige and Grant have tied what they've gotten.

"You've got this." Paige is hyping herself up for her final shot. When she misses the board entirely, Grant smiles at me. He throws and makes it on the board. Now, it's up to me to close out this game.

"Alright, Amelia, bring it home for us, okay?" Grant smiles at me before I hear Henry scoff beside me.

I look over at him, and I can tell that was a reaction he didn't mean to say out loud.

"Something to say?" I ask, my voice low so only he can hear it.

"No. Sorry," he says as he shifts the beanbag from hand to hand.

Suddenly, the sand feels coarse beneath my feet, and I can hear my blood pumping through my veins. I somehow throw my shots, but Henry and Paige end up winning. As they celebrate, Grant comes over to me.

"Do you need some water?"

I nod, unable to form words to speak.

"Here," Grant says as he pulls up one of the beach chairs for me, and I sit down. "Are you good?"

"Yup," I say as I choke the words out. "Swell."

"You always were a terrible liar." He smiles at me before looking at the sand. "You know you can talk to me, right?"

"Why would you want to talk to me, Grant?" I snap at him, regretting it immediately. "I didn't mean to sound so—"

"Cruel?"

I laugh, and my mind starts to settle. "Yeah."

"And as for why I want to talk to you, it's because I've missed my friend, Amelia, and you look... Well, if I'm being honest, you look like shit right now, and I want to help however I can."

"Even after I left and never looked back? Even after you almost died and I didn't even call to ask if you were okay? I'm a terrible person, Grant. I don't deserve any kindness from you."

"You've made mistakes, Amelia, and you're aware of them. I'm not going to give you more reasons to hate you than you're already giving yourself."

I take a deep breath as I take a few more sips of water, the coldness bringing me down from whatever weird spell I just had.

"I'm sorry I wasn't here, Grant, and I'm sorry I didn't call. I should have, but—"

"Hads told me everything. She told me about your diagnosis and the conversation all you girls had in the hotel room." Grant grabs one of my hands and smacks it. "That's for leaving." He gives one of my hands a squeeze. "And that's me being proud of you for finally talking to someone."

"It helped more than I thought it would."

"It always does." He hands me another bottle of water. "How are you feeling about all of this? I know you've made your peace with the girls, but how is it being around Henry? Is that what's causing this spiral of yours?"

I've always loved Grant's ability to get the point. He's also one of the most hopeful people I've ever met. In the back of his mind, I'm sure he's hoping Henry and I will work out our shit so we can eventually be together again. I don't know how to tell him all his hope is for nothing. I'm sure Henry wants closure so he can move on without me.

Hell, I don't even know if I'm in a place emotionally and physically where I can handle a relationship. For now, I'm focusing on myself like I've been doing for the past nine months.

"It's weird. Uncomfortable is the only word that comes to mind. Did you know he was going to be here? You are the best man, after all."

He nods. "Well, Oliver invited him, so I was aware he was going to be here. I think most of us were unsure if you were actually going to show, so we figured it would be fine. Obviously, you're here, and we're happy you are, but we never anticipated what would happen if you were both in the same vicinity again. You two seem to be okay, despite the tension."

"Tension?"

"In my eyes, it's obvious."

Of course it is. "There's nothing between Henry and I."

"But there used to be," he raises his eyebrows at me. "With the way you guys left things, there's got to be some unresolved feelings."

"What would you do if you were Henry in this situation?"

He takes a moment to think about it before he opens his mouth. "I would want to know why you left. I would have a thousand questions about the relationship, and I'd want answers as soon as I could get them. Hell, even as myself, I have a lot of questions for you, but I'm not trying to overwhelm you. You two loved one another, and then you smashed his heart to pieces. If I were him, I'd want to know why you played with my feelings like that, just to end it the way you did."

I guess I should have known that. I have some questions I'd like to ask Henry myself, but I'm too scared. I don't want to know the answer to some of them, but I know at some point, we'll be talking about all of it, and I can't do anything to prepare myself.

There were a lot of reasons why I did what I did. Fear. Impulsivity due to an undiagnosed condition. Wanting to spite my parents and prove I could be successful and have a career despite not following the path they wanted for me. More than anything, I wanted to prove to myself I could have a life outside of the place I grew up in, surrounded by loneliness and people who didn't really know me until I got to college with the girls.

Well, I succeeded in spiting my parents, but I also lost the only true people I ever had around me, and by some miracle, I got them back because I'm putting the work in.

"I don't want to ruin the wedding our shit. If anything, I was going to talk to him after it was all over."

"Don't waste this precious time, Amelia. If my accident taught me one thing, it was that. You can't spend your entire life waiting for the right moment for things to happen. Sometimes, you have to make it happen for yourself."

"Thank you."

He hits my arm softly before he pulls me in for a quick hug. "Listen, I know Ella already knocked some sense into you, but we really did miss you, and I hope you don't run away again. I'd hate for this to become a recurring theme, and I really don't like having a ghost for a friend."

"Don't worry," I say as I pull back. "The only other time I'll be ghosting you guys is if I die and haunt you from the grave."

"That's fair, but go to Oliver's house first and scare the shit out of him before you come and chill at ours."

I laugh as I imagine that. "I wouldn't dream of anything else."

19

"Where did my wife go? Where did I go? Did we grow apart from one another or ourselves? Is who we were when we first met still an accurate portrayal of who we are now?" — *Our Best Kept Secret*, Henry Hayes

SINCE WE GOT BACK to the hotel room a few hours ago, all I've done is stare at my computer and wish this book could write itself. I thought all the sun I got earlier today would have helped kickstart my brain, but apparently, all it did was make it worse.

This book is going to be a gigantic failure. I can feel it in my bones—something isn't right, and it's showing through the struggles I keep having when I try to write it.

I'm practically pulling my hair out every time I open this document, knowing everything I'm going to end up writing will probably be deleted or reworded by me or my editor at some point.

It would be nice if I could just finish this draft and actually turn it in, but even that feels so far out of reach from where I'm at now.

When I outlined this book, I was excited about it. I called Mitch after I was done and practically vomited the entire story out to him. He could barely keep up with me because of how excited I was.

Somewhere along the way, all these thoughts started to creep in, and eventually, they swallowed me whole. That's the thing about having my books do well. Don't get me wrong, I'm grateful to even be having these experiences, but the fear and worry this book is going to be unsuccessful and not live up to the others eats away at me every single day.

Even if it somehow manages to get written and do better than my second novel, I'm not going to have anyone to celebrate with. It's going to be exactly how it always has been—me alone in my apartment, getting a call from my parents about how proud they are of me.

That's great and all, but I wish I had a partner in all this. I wish I had someone to share my success with. I wish I had someone to walk around the bookstore with and obnoxiously point out my books.

But when I picture the future in my mind, it all feels fuzzy and out of reach. I'm halfway through my twenties, and while I have success in my career, I can't help but crave success and fulfillment in other parts of my life.

My timer goes off, and I realize I just spent the entire twenty minutes spiraling and thinking about how my personal life is going nowhere.

No wonder this book isn't getting finished.

I reset it, but before I press the button, Oliver pokes his head into my room.

"I thought you were having dinner with your parents?" I didn't think Oliver was still up in the room. Tonight is free rein for all of us, since we spent the day together. Oliver's family arrived earlier today, so he and his sister, along with Paige and Grant, are going to dinner. Leo told me he and Ella are also doing a candlelit dinner somewhere fancy.

It seems everyone has dinner plans besides me.

"I am. I'm waiting on Grant, but I wanted to check-in with you before I left."

"That's nice of you."

"Well, you've been holed up here since we got back. You should go out and explore the resort. This *is* supposed to be a vacation, and all you've done when we're not hanging out is work."

I shrug my shoulders. "Well, that's pushing it, Oliver."

"I'm just saying, Henry. It wouldn't kill you to put the voices away for one night and let loose in whatever way you see fit."

I can see where he's coming from, I guess. I mull it over before I eventually close my laptop and turn my timer off.

"You ready, Ol?" Grant says as he comes in, his face lighting up when he sees the two of us. "What are you two talking about?"

"Oliver was telling me to get out of the room tonight and enjoy myself."

Grant starts to laugh before he notices neither of us are, although I've only heard Oliver laugh a handful of times. Most of the time, he scoffs or simply grunts in the direction of the joke.

"You're being serious?"

"Yes," I say. "I'm actually going to take his advice and leave my manuscript for the night."

"Oh my gosh, you're working on your next book while you're here? I will sell you one of my kidneys to be able to read it early."

"Grant, you only have one kidney left, remember?"

"Oh, right," he says as he thinks. "What do you want, Hen? An arm? A finger?"

"You are free to keep all your body parts, especially since I can't seem to write this book without wanting to erase everything." Both look at me as if they want me to dive deeper into that, but I don't. "Don't you guys have dinner to get to?"

"Shit," Oliver says as he checks his watch. "Come on, pretty boy."

As I hear the door shut, my phone pings with a notification—Grant sent me fifteen dollars. I'm about to text him and ask why, but a text comes through.

> **Grant: Buy yourself a celebratory drink on me.**

> Henry: With fifteen dollars, I could buy a few.

> Henry: And what am I celebrating?

> **Grant: Well, you're writing a whole ass book, aren't you?**

> Henry: I guess I am. Thanks, man. I appreciate it.

> **Grant: I've been your silent cheerleader from afar, but now that you're back, consider me a loud and proud supporter.**

> Henry liked a message.

AFTER A SHOWER AND a quick call with my family, I've officially made it out of the room and onto the elevator. The hotel we're staying at has a really nice bar we've passed a few times, and even though I'm not a huge fan of alcohol, maybe I need to loosen up a bit.

Hell, I'll try anything if it will make writing my book a tiny bit easier.

The bar overlooks the ocean, and as soon as I step out and feel the warm breeze on my face, my bones start to settle. I've always loved Virginia. Growing up here, I knew I never wanted to leave. I feel content here, settled, even, and not once have I wanted to run from this place and never look back.

Well, that's not technically true. There was one point when I thought about getting on a plane and leaving this all behind, but in the end, I'm grateful I didn't—especially since the reason I didn't go was because I wasn't actually wanted by the other person.

By some stroke of something, that person happens to be sitting at the other end of the bar.

I take my seat and flag down the bartender. "I'll have a beer please."

I see her head turn to look at me, and I also see about eight shades of panic cross her face before she downs her drink in one go and starts gathering her things.

Just as the bartender sets my drink in front of me, Amelia gets up, but she has to come this way if she wants to leave.

I'm tired of this. I'm tired of her running from me.

"Sit down and have a drink with me, Amelia," I say as she passes me, freezing in her spot when I speak. "Get her another of whatever she was having."

"Henry, we don't have to—"

"We're just two people having a drink. Or can you not handle being in the same vicinity as me for more than a few hours?"

"I don't want to make things uncomfortable."

There she goes with her assumptions again. "Who says you make me feel that way?"

"Shirley Temple, please," she says to my surprise. She sits next to me, the bartender placing the drink in front of her. "Thank you."

I can practically feel the anxiety rolling off her, or maybe that's just the leftover emotions from me thinking about my manuscript earlier.

The two of us sit quietly. I take small sips of my drink, and she doesn't touch hers. I'm not sure how to break this silence. I don't know what to ask her, but I was the one who invited her to sit down for some reason.

"I should go," she says, fidgeting where she sits.

"For fuck's sake, Amelia, can we just talk?" I say as I grab her hand, trying to calm her down.

"T-Talk? You mean about—"

"I think we both owe it to ourselves to clear the air before the wedding."

She looks down at our conjoined hands, and I shake out of her grip. "I wanted to keep our shit away from the wedding. I was going to find you after it so we could talk."

Is that so? I don't believe it. "I figured you were off on a plane to England after the wedding."

Her face pinches, but she masks it immediately. "Do you want to take a walk on the beach?"

I'm surprised at her offer. "Of course." I motion for her to lead the way, and the two of us take our drinks and start off. I have to admit, this isn't how I thought tonight was going to go, but I can't say I'm disappointed.

After all, finally being able to get some answers from the girl walking next to me is all I've wanted since she left. I don't really know where to start, but luckily, as our feet hit the sand, she speaks first.

"If I were you, I'd hate me so much, I wouldn't even want to talk to me."

"I wish I hated you, Amelia. Really, I do. It would make this all so much fucking easier."

She looks over at me, eyes wide and mouth slightly open. "What do you feel for me then?"

"That's a complicated question," I say as I take a deep breath. "I know you're right next to me, but you've never felt as far away as you do, even though you've been in an entirely different country."

"What do you mean?"

"When we were in college and I first met you, there was a tower with eighty floors built around you, and eventually, I cracked through, and you were right in front of me. I could read your mind. I could tell what you were thinking before you even thought it, and everyone else noticed it too. You felt like mine, Amelia, and I was wholly and completely yours. But as we walk, I can't help but feel like you're still a thousand miles away from me."

"I'm not trying to be. I..." She trails off, and I can tell she's nervous. She keeps touching her neck. She used to do that all the time, but the only difference is, the necklace I once bought her was underneath that touch. She used to tell me it calmed her down, but now, it looks like it's still a nervous tick.

"Do you even regret what you did?" I whisper, letting the words flow into the breeze like a special correspondence. "Because to you, it might have been one minuscule conversation before the rest of your actual life started, but my world ended when you told me you never loved me."

She stops walking and looks up at me, her eyes glassy. "Of course I regret it. What kind of person do you take me for?"

"The kind of person who would rip my heart out in the middle of the airport and never look back. That's the only memory I've had of you since it happened. It plays on repeat because I couldn't fathom how someone I loved with every fiber of my being could do that to me. I couldn't fathom the girl I thought I was going to marry would break my heart and leave."

"I had to do it, Henry. I wouldn't have dragged you to England because you would have been miserable, but you would have been equally miserable doing long-distance. We both had careers to focus on. It would have been too much. I thought it was the right decision for us, but every time I look back on it and see your face, I second-guess myself."

I shake my head at her, invading her personal space. "You didn't have to do that, Amelia! There were so many other options, and we could have made it work. I would have made anything work for you, and I don't know how you didn't know that."

"We would have both been unhappy." She shrugs her shoulders.

"You couldn't have known that. You made the decision for the both of us, and you didn't even bother asking me how I felt. You just did what you always do and assume you're not worth the effort, but I would have stood by you. The fact that you didn't understand that makes me question how real our relationship was. Did you even love me back then, or were all those whispers in the silence of the night as you slept against my shoulder a lie?"

A single tear falls from her eye as she looks at me. "You are the only person I've ever loved, and what I did doesn't negate that, no matter how much you might want it to. But I did what I had to do, Henry, and it was what was best for the both of us."

"For you, Amelia," I remind her. "It was what was best for you. For some reason, you think it's all a choice—love or success. You can have both. It's not going to kill you if you have both of those things."

And then, I see it. I see the necklace I bought her still resting around her neck, tucked underneath her floral midi dress flowing with the breeze.

She still wears it. Why does she still wear it?

"I'm not sure I deserve either of those things anymore."

"Don't say that."

"Why? I'm a horrible person. I let people get close to me, only to leave them when I see fit. I play with people's feelings and use their fears against them. I disappear, only to come back whenever I want. I never let anyone truly in to see who I am because I'm sure they'll see the same thing I do—that I'm a horrendous, mean, jaded person."

She's saying these things, but for some reason, it doesn't feel like she actually believes them. I sigh heavily as I finish my drink and set my glass in the sand. "You were all of those things, Amelia." I run a hand through my hair. "But you're also secretly soft. And once upon a time, we used to share headphones. You would speak to me through music, and for those few minutes, I felt like I knew you. You just have to stop running, for once in your life, Amelia."

"I'm trying," she whispers. I take a step back. I feel like I just got grounded after being up in the air for the few minutes we were talking.

"Why do you still wear my necklace?"

Her lips part; I'm sure she wasn't expecting me to ask her that. "Because it's my favorite, and it calms me down when I feel…"

"When you feel what, Amelia?"

She locks eyes with me. "When I feel anxious. It helps me, Henry, because you bought it for me, and it's the nicest gift I've ever received from someone."

Why the hell does she still wear it after all this time? A thought enters my mind and lingers, but there's no way it can be true. Amelia is not still in love with me. You don't treat the people you love how she has, but then why keep the necklace I bought her?

Suddenly, I'm jolted back to when I first put it around her neck, her eyes shining at me in the mirror as I latched it on. Amelia isn't one for many emotions, but her eyes always told me all I needed to know. I thought buying her jewelry at first was a bad idea because of how specific she is. She wears the same rings every single day, and she doesn't have her ears pierced, so earrings were out. She also hates the way bracelets feel on her wrists, so I decided on a necklace with some special meaning—a windmill because of my nickname for her. Mills.

The first time I called her that, it sort of slipped out, and it stuck. Then, I got her the necklace, and she never took it off, a constant reminder of the two of us hanging around her neck.

"A necklace? Is this to show everyone I'm yours?"

"No, Mills. This is just between us, like a secret that hangs around your neck. Nobody else needs to know what it means except us."

"I love it, Hen. And I love you."

God, it felt so easy back then—loving her.

Before I can stop myself, I kiss her. Because in the moonlight, here on this beach, she's wearing my necklace, and we're finally talking about all our shit. As soon as our lips touch, it's a shock, but eventually, we both give in, and I'm catapulted back to when I could kiss her simply because she was mine.

It feels just how it used to—her soft skin beneath my touch, goosebumps all over her neck as I cup my hand around her neck and pull her closer. I need to be closer. I need to be able to reach into her mind and somehow figure out why she killed us back then.

Because her lips were always meant to be on mine, and this is proof of it. But she's not mine, not anymore, and the two of us should not be doing this.

I pull back just as she starts to melt into me, and the breeze flows between us as I take a few steps back.

Why the fuck did I just do that? It's going to make everything so much more complicated. I didn't even get the answers I was hoping for tonight. We talked, but we didn't really discuss everything. The two of us aren't going to fix our shit in one night.

Why did I do that? Why did I fucking kiss the girl who destroyed me?

"I-I'm sorry. I shouldn't have done that."

She says nothing as she simply looks at me, shock and confusion written across her features.

"Shit, I'm sorry," I say as I walk away.

I don't bother looking back.

HENRY JUST KISSED ME.

Henry Hayes—the boy I used to know and love—just kissed me on the beach as we talked about our past.

I'm not sure where we go from here. I'm not sure what he wants from me. Hell, I'm not sure what I want from him. All I want to do is clear the air and apologize, but there's some part of me that feels uneasy, knowing after we talk about all this, we'll both go our separate ways.

I didn't lie when I told him he was the only person I ever loved. That's still the truth. He was the only guy I let in enough to love me, to see who I really was beneath my harsh exterior. I used to be really good at keeping people out, but now, after all I've done and been through, it's harder to build my walls back up. I don't want to. I want people to see me. I'm tired of hiding.

When I used to let Henry see the real me, he never judged me. He got my weird, dry sense of humor, and not once did he try to change who I was.

He was the first person to truly understand me besides the girls. Sometimes, I didn't even let them all the way in. Henry truly smashed my reinforcements to pieces as I tried to keep us strictly in the friend zone.

But one night, it all changed. When the break-in happened back in college and I realized he was the only person I needed beside me, something shifted between us.

Tonight, I felt that same shift when he touched his lips to mine.

My hand moves up to my lips, still feeling the ghost of him there, wishing I took more time to savor the feeling, because it might be the last time I feel that with someone—with him.

By some miracle, could Henry and I actually work things out and be together? Could we get back to where we once were? Is that something I want? Is that something *he* wants?

I have more questions than answers, and I know for sure I'm going to have to think about what all of this means. For now, I'm going to sit down, listen to the waves, and think about what it would feel like to love someone again.

Is that delusional of me? Probably. But if I can imagine loving someone again, maybe that means I'm not totally unlovable. Maybe I'm not going to end up alone forever like my parents thought. Maybe that means I deserve to be happy, even if I'm still working through my own shit.

20

Then — College

How Sweet It Is (To Be Loved By You) by James Taylor

As I THROW MY noise-cancelling headphones on and shuffle through my overflowing music library, I decide on my sixties playlist with some of my favorite bands. I was going to go with a classic—my movie scores playlist—since I'm trying to make some headway on studying for this test, but my vibe tonight is more nostalgic.

I love Grand Mountain so much, and I love receiving a well-rounded education since I chose a liberal arts college, but sometimes, I wish I didn't have to learn about stuff that doesn't interest me. I'm all for learning about history, but this test being one hundred questions about the Mongols is making me tired, and I haven't even started yet.

Paige left the apartment a few minutes ago to go study at the library with Hads, Oliver, and Grant. Part of me wishes I went with them, but I need to get something done tonight. I love my friends, but sometimes, it is so hard to concentrate when we're all together.

It takes me a half an hour to really get into my groove, and for the first time tonight, I actually think I can pass this test.

My playlist is about to switch to another song when I hear the door fly open. My headphones are great for cancelling out noise most of the time, but I assume Paige forgot something and is trying to mimic how I've entered the apartment a few times.

I turn around to face her, taking my headphones off my head, but when I spin around, my heart drops through my stomach. It's not Paige. It's not one of my friends. It's a man, I think, wearing an all-black outfit and a ski mask.

I'm frozen where I stand, my heart beating out of my chest. My first instinct is to scream, but when I try to, no words come out.

Who the fuck just walked into my apartment? Is this some sort of sick joke or something?

"Oliver, if this is your idea of a prank, it's not a very good one," I say, my voice starting to shake as the very tall person stands in front of me. It almost looks like they're sizing me up or something.

Is this a robbery? Am I being burglarized or something? Now, I wish Paige were here, because she would probably tell me how those are two different things and then go on an entire spiel about what was actually happening in this moment.

Something shifts in the person's hand, and when it shines towards me, my stomach drops.

It's a knife—or worse, a gun.

I think they're going to kill me.

I barely think before I reach for my phone where it lays on the couch, but as I move to do that, so do they. The person rushes towards me as I try to get my bearings. I'm grabbed from behind and thrown to my floor, my phone still in my hands. Through the haze of pain, I try to send a text, but they grab my phone out of my hands and toss it somewhere.

"Get off me!" I scream, trying to get them to leave but knowing it's no use.

They're standing over me now, and I'm probably going to die. I'm going to die in the middle of my college apartment with nothing to show for my life. I didn't even get to start it yet, and it's already going to be over.

Even worse, Paige is going to find my body when she gets back here. Then twice this semester, she'll have walked in on someone dead, but this time, it will be me, and I don't think I can handle watching her go through that after I'm gone.

"Please don't," I say, unsure if they can even understand me, but at least I can say I fought back, right?

I'm not finished here yet. I don't want to be gone.

There's going to be nothing to write on my tombstone because I haven't even achieved anything. My life has barely begun. All I've done is do what everyone else has told me to. I've gone to school. I'm in college. My life has been fully at the hands of what I'm supposed to do. Nothing I've done yet has been what I've wanted to do with no rules, no schedules to adhere to.

How long does it take to die? Minutes? Hours? Days? Seconds? I'll never know.

As they stand over me, weapon raised in the air, I suddenly can't think as something hits my head, and I'm out cold.

I WAKE UP WITH a sting on my face, my eyes scanning the room, terrified I'm in Hell until I see I'm surrounded by my friends. Well, Oliver is here too.

They're all talking, but I can barely register what's going on. My body feels like it's moving a thousand miles a minute. Somehow, I can tell my mouth is moving and words are coming out, but I can't tell if anything I'm saying is making any sense.

Paige excuses the rest of them, and my head still really fucking hurts, but as I'm describing to her what I saw, it all clicks into place. Her room was ransacked. The person in here almost looked surprised to see me, didn't really know what to do with me.

This has something to do with Paige and Oliver's investigation. I'm sure of it. Those two psychos are the only people I know who would see a dead body on campus and decide to try and solve it. I feel like it's a prerequisite to being a criminal justice student to be the slightest bit insane when a case literally drops into your lap.

Why else would this person have come into our apartment? We're two college students living on campus. There's no way this was some random person deciding to steal a bunch of shit from us.

Tears flood my eyes as I think about what I thought were my last moments on the planet before Paige's voice comes through my mind.

"What can I do to help? Do you need anything? Just tell me what I can do, and I'll do it."

"Henry. I need Henry." The words come out before I can stop them.

"Okay. I can call him. Where's your phone?" I point her towards the couch where I think they threw it, and Paige excuses herself before Ella grabs me a glass of water. Hads throws a blanket over top of me, and even though I'm still shivering, the gesture is nice.

Oliver eventually stitches my head up, and I'm still floating through these conversations, feeling like I want to lay down forever. I know they're probably not going to let me sleep in case I have a concussion, though.

I need Henry to get here. I need a tether or something to carry me through this. That's the one thing I knew I needed when Paige asked me. Sure, I'm grateful for the people already around me, but Henry has always been the one person who brings me back to Earth. His presence has always felt different to me. I knew it when I first met him at that concert, and I knew it when I ran into him on campus after the fact.

He's always been around, in our own weird way, and even though we're not dating, I need him. At this moment, I'm choosing to run toward him instead of keeping him at an arm's length. Suddenly, I regret not having been with him this entire time. I could have died tonight, and it's hitting me that my biggest regret would have been not being loved by someone.

I would have died alone, physically and mentally, because I never allowed anyone to get close enough to see who I am underneath all the jokes and dry humor. I would have died tonight, never having been loved, never having felt it from another person.

I can't keep doing this. I can't keep running away from these emotions that terrify me just because I've always assumed I was better off alone. Nobody is better off alone, and of course, I can be loved despite all my flaws. Those are what make me who I am.

Maybe I deserve love. Maybe I am the type of person who people drop anything for when I need them.

I can't believe it's taken me so long to realize this. I can't believe almost dying is what it took for me to finally believe I am a person capable of feeling true, unconditional, stupid, dumb love.

"Paige, where is she?" I hear the voice of the person I need most, and as soon as he locks eyes with me, he takes a few steps, stops, and takes me in. I've never seen him look so disheveled before, so panicked and worried. He's always been so calm, always so go-with-the-flow, but seeing him panicked like this at the thought of me being hurt? God, that's unraveling me too.

It seems he needs me just as much as I seem to need him.

My legs weaken, and I stretch them out in front of me. That somehow shakes him out of whatever haze he was in before he comes over to me and runs his hands all over my body. When he opens his mouth, he can barely speak.

He takes one look at the stitches on my head before his eyes finally latch on to mine. "Who the fuck did this to you, Amelia?"

"I-I don't know, Hen," I say, the shaking in my body calming down now that he's here. "Thank you for getting here."

His gaze flies all over my shriveled up form, as if he's scared I'm going to disappear under his touch. "I brought my headphones, and I have some snacks in my pocket, tissues too. I didn't know what happened, so I just grabbed what I could hold."

"Henry—"

"I figured music would help, but when Paige called me, I was so fucking scared, Ames. She didn't tell me what happened, but her voice was so defeated, and my mind jumped to the worst of the worst. I should have come over tonight. I should have been here studying with you, and—"

"Henry—" He stares into my eyes, searching for an answer, but I know he can't find one. "Will you just hold me?"

His eyes soften, a smile overtaking his face as he settles in next to me. I lean my head on his shoulder as his arms wrap around me. All our friends are gone, most likely outside giving us a minute, and I appreciate that.

"You don't have to tell me what happened yet, but whenever you decide to, just know I'll be here for you, Mills."

I know, Hen. "Can you play that song you showed me the other day?"

I'm not good at talking, and Henry knows that. Music has always been my favorite way of explaining my emotions. For some reason, I've never been able to articulate things how my favorite lyrics can. In this moment, I need to remember something good. In this moment, I want to live in a good memory instead of the one from earlier tonight.

The other day, I went to Henry's place, and when I opened the door, he was standing right in front of me, smiling from ear to ear. I have to admit, I was a little nervous, but when he sat me down, gave me a headphone, and pressed play, I knew why he was so happy.

For months, all I've done is show him new songs and artists he had never heard of, but this time, it was the opposite. He found a song I had never heard, and he was so excited to play it for me.

He hit the nail on the head. It was everything I loved about music. The production was dreamy, the lyrics were beautiful yet haunting, and all night, we sat there with our headphones in and did a deep dive into the artist's discography.

It was one of the best nights of my life, and I know if I hear the song again, it will take me right back to one of my happiest memories. I fell asleep on his couch and woke up covered in a blanket, wrapped in his arms.

He squeezes me a little harder before grabbing one headphone and softly placing it in my ear, and I do the same for him as the music filters through our ears at the same time.

In the dark of my messed up apartment after the worst night of my life, I feel safe. Here in his arms, it's impossible not to feel that way. As the music floats between us, I cry. I cry so hard, I can barely think straight. I let out all the fear, all the sadness, all the terrifying emotions I felt in the past hour into his chest.

"What else do you need from me, Mills? Do you want me to stay over tonight?" He wipes my tears with a tissue.

"Just don't let me go," I say into his arms.

And he doesn't.

My phone alarm jolts me awake, and when I look around and see Oliver missing, clearly not watching for whoever broke in earlier, I panic.

My feet are moving before I can even stop them, and as I swing open Amelia's door, scared she's not going to be on the other side of it, I'm met with something being thrown at me.

One of her favorite pens sits at my feet as I see her body relax when she realizes it's me.

"I didn't mean to scare you."

"Entering my room like that after the day I had was certainly a choice, Hen."

Guilt races down my body. "I'm sorry. I wasn't thinking. I—"

She shuffles over to the side of her bed, her long legs swinging over. "Let me guess: you saw Oliver was gone and got nervous that whoever broke in earlier somehow got past you while you were sleeping and came for us all?"

"W-Well, yes, actually."

She smirks to herself, but I can tell she's still shaken up. Obviously, she is. It happened only hours ago.

"Paige was having a nightmare a few hours ago. I wanted to handle it like I always do, but Oliver," she rolls her eyes at his name, "beat me to it."

"And he's still in Paige's room?" I had the weirdest conversation of my entire life with him earlier. Not only did I get the feeling he hates small talk, but we also said a lot of things without really saying anything. He told me I was a good friend for speeding over here for Amelia. I said he would do the same thing if it were Paige, and then we fought over the air mattress until the girls came out and we pretended we didn't know one another.

Today has been one of the most bizarre days of my entire life, one of the scariest too. The fear I felt racing over here rivaled the emotions I felt when I found out my dad had been hit by a drunk driver. Terror, pure terror is all I have felt in both times, and I hate it. I'm not built for these kinds of situations, and I hate that it's happened to two people I couldn't live without.

I've never been so out of control. Paige didn't even tell me what happened, but in my gut, I knew it was bad. When she said something happened to Amelia, I could barely think. I grabbed my keys and threw my shoes on, driving way too fast to get to her.

"Yes, I would assume so," Amelia says as she picks up her favorite book from her bed, returning to what she was doing before I got here.

I pick her pen up off the floor and hand it to her. "Here."

"Thanks, Hen." She tucks a loose strand of hair behind her ear.

"I'll be in the living room if you—"

"Would you stay with me?" Her sentence surprises me. "I know most of the time, I prefer being alone, but I don't want to be alone tonight. At least, not now that you're awake."

"Of course, I'll stay with you, Mills," I say as I try to hide my smile, knowing I'm failing miserably. Honestly, I'm happy she asked me to stay. I feel much better actually being able to see her and know she's alright.

Well, as alright as she can be after what happened.

"Thanks," she says as she shifts on her bed, making just enough room for me to slide in next to her.

"You know I'd do anything for you, don't you?"

"I always thought you were joking when you said that before," she whispers, closing her favorite book. "But now, I know you're being serious."

"Why did you think I was joking?"

She simply shrugs, and before I change the subject onto something else, Amelia surprises me by elaborating.

"I've never felt like a person someone would drop everything for. I'm pretty solidified in who I am, so I guess I always thought you were kidding." She fiddles with one of her pens as she locks eyes with me. "Tonight made me think differently about that."

I shift closer to her, needing to be more in her orbit. I know she hates physical touch, and we are just friends, but I can't help this pull I feel.

I don't break eye contact as I speak. "Why do you think you're not enough as you are, Amelia? Why do you assume nobody would break about a hundred traffic laws to get to you? Because I sure as hell did tonight."

"I've always felt...different, I guess. I didn't make friends easily when I was younger, and when I did, I wasn't ever anyone's favorite friend. I was never anybody's first choice in any of the relationships I had growing up. I should have seen that coming, I guess. I was never my parents' first choice."

I sigh heavily as I reach for her hand, surprise coursing through my body when she takes it, squeezing. "Did you tell your parents what happened?"

She shakes her head.

"Amelia, baby." I stop myself, because that term of endearment just slipped out without me thinking. "Why didn't you call them?"

"Because I'm fine," she says, as if that's enough. "They wouldn't care anyway."

"Don't say that."

"It's the truth, Hen." She swipes a tear from her face as soon as it falls. "Steven has always been the favorite. He was born first, and my parents were actually trying to have kids when he was conceived. I was an accident, the surprise they didn't want or see coming, and that stayed with me my entire life. Steven was a multi-sport athlete growing up. He was the popular one with a bunch of friends my parents knew by first name. He was the academic standout—the one getting all the awards—and I existed in the shadow of his greatness. Steven was the one my parents bragged about, and I was the daughter who couldn't keep friends. I was the daughter who couldn't wear certain clothes because I didn't like the feeling of them. I was the problem child. I was the second choice to everyone and everything in my life."

"Mills—"

She cuts me off, clearly emotional, and I wish I could take all these notions she has about herself away. "I don't know why I'm getting so worked up about this."

"Because it hurts. Believe it or not, you are still a human being, no matter how hard you try to hide behind those walls." I grip her hand a little tighter. "And do you want to know a secret?"

She nods.

"You're always going to be my first choice."

The look on her face as those words settle into her mind might be enough to kill me. She's never heard those words before, but I mean them with every fiber of my soul. I'd do anything for her, and she knew that, but I think this is the first time she's really hearing it. I think this is the first time she believes she's someone's first choice.

"Really?" she says as disbelief flashes across her face. "Because you know me, Hen. I'm a handful, and sometimes, my brain is so loud, I can't figure a way out. I can be a lot—"

"Amelia Ellis," I say as I grab her free hand. "You're my favorite person on the planet, so yes, even when your brain is loud, even when you think you're not enough, you'll always be my first choice. No matter what."

"Thank you," she whispers as I wipe her tears.

"I mean every word," I remind her. "If you ever doubt that again, just come to me, and I'll remind you how much I like being in your presence, no matter the clouds in the way."

She takes a deep breath, trying to balance herself back out after the emotional whiplash of the last few hours.

"Do you want to know something?" she asks me, her voice lower.

"Always."

"You're my first choice too."

"Is that so?" I say, my tone playful so she doesn't feel as awkward.

Another nod, her curly hair moving around the bandage on her head. "When Paige asked me if I needed anything earlier, I didn't even hesitate to ask for you."

Her candor surprises me. Tonight has opened my eyes more and more to what Amelia and I are to one another. Well, I always knew what she was to me—everything—but I'm starting to understand I might be the same for her.

"I'm glad you did," I say as I hold my arms out for her. She turns, her body sliding right into my arms as I close them around her. "Now, try and get some sleep. I'll be here, so you'll be safe."

Another nod. "I know, Hen. I think I'll always feel safe with you."

I reach for her lamp and turn it to the dimmest setting as she adjusts how she's sleeping against me, getting more comfortable in my arms, as if she's always belonged here.

If it were up to me, she would always be.

Because to me, Amelia Ellis is the brightest star in the galaxy. To me, she's a book I never want to put down. To me, she'll always be the girl who stole my attention that day at the concert, and since then, I haven't wanted to look at anything else but her.

And if she'll let me, she'll never know what it feels like to be anybody's second choice ever again.

21

Now

"Mistakes are human. They're as natural as death itself. To live a life is to live with mistakes." — *In A Room With Death*, Henry Hayes

"WHY ARE WE HERE again?" I ask as we get out of the car at the golf course.

"I don't even like golf," Oliver says under his breath.

"Yeah, well, it's been a weird week, and I figured we all need to whack balls with clubs. It's a nice stress reliever."

"Unless you're bad at it," Leo says, and I nod. I'm not the most athletic person on the planet. In high school, instead of being out on the field, I was in a classroom at the creative writing club.

My dad was always a huge football fan, but when I tried to play when I was a kid, I was far too lanky. The gear was always too big, and eventually, my mom was worried another kid was going to tackle me too hard and I'd be broken in half, so they pulled me out after one season.

It's safe to say, I have low expectations for this round of golf. Not only is Grant a former hockey player who plays golf regularly, but I'm sure Leo is good at it too. He just gives off an energy that he's good at everything. Maybe it's his ego, or he's just built like an athlete.

Grant goes to get us all checked in, and the rest of us hang out by the first hole. He comes back a few moments later with two keys and a huge smile on his face.

"Are you guys ready for the best round of golf ever?"

Leo and Grant are in one cart, and Oliver is with me. I'm driving ours because Oliver won't stop shaking. The last time I remember him doing that was when I brought him to the hospital after Paige got whacked back in college.

I wonder if he ever got over that fear, or if it's just now manifesting in a different way.

"Are you okay over there? Any more shaking, and I'll think you're trying to tip this cart over," I say as I slow down. Our balls aren't too far apart because neither of us hit them very far. It's only the first hole, and we're off to a rocky start.

"I just want to be married already."

"Don't rush this, Oliver. Enjoy this time with your friends," Grant says from his cart.

"I am, but this week is taking forever, and I'm tired of waiting. No offense to you guys, but if Paige and I could get married today, I'd drive this golf cart back to the hotel and do it now."

"Is this the beginning of some sort of wedding freak out for you?" Leo asks him, and Oliver shakes his head. "It's fairly common, I've heard."

"No, it's not. I'm just impatient and worried about everything coming together perfectly for Paige."

"It'll be fine, Ol. Don't you trust me and Hads to make this perfect for you two?" Grant asks as Oliver steps up to his ball, taking a swing. It lands just shy of the green. "Damn, that was pretty good."

"I trust you guys, I swear. It's all the things I can't control that I worry about," he says as he slides the club back into his bag. "I want this to be perfect for her. After all she's been through, a smooth wedding and a lifetime of happiness are the least I could give her."

"Don't put so much pressure on yourself," I say as I step up to my ball. The three of them go silent, and I swing, feeling decent about that shot, only to have it land in the sand to the left of the green.

"Henry is right," Leo agrees. "You're only feeling so anxious because of the standards you're projecting. Just let it be, and it will all work out."

"Yeah, I guess," Oliver says as we get back onto the cart. We head off for the green, and my head jumps back to the other night, when I kissed Amelia.

I wasn't thinking. Clearly, the drink I had was clouding my thoughts, but I haven't been able to stop thinking about it since it happened. That's the bad thing about being in Amelia's orbit again. I'm sucked back in just how I was in college, and I can't seem to let her go. Here she is, back in my vicinity, clouding all my thoughts, just how she used to.

I sigh heavily, trying to force the girl out of my head but knowing it's not going to work.

"Dude, are you good?" Oliver asks. I feel the breeze stop as the cart slows down.

"Not really. I did something stupid the other night, and I can't stop thinking about what a dumbass I am." I park the cart and grab my wedge—I think that's what Grant called it—before trotting over to my ball resting in the sand. I have no idea how to go about this, so I'll probably just smack it and hope for the best.

"What did you do?" Oliver asks me, and after a few hits trying to get my ball out of the sand, it pops up onto the green.

"I kissed Amelia."

"What?" Grant practically shouts as Leo is about to swing, though he stops immediately.

"Well, that's...insane," Leo says. "And also not what I meant when I told you to figure out where to start. You skipped like a hundred steps, mate."

"You kissed Amelia? And you didn't immediately melt? I don't know how you do it, Hen. Really, I don't." Oliver pats me on the back.

"You guys seriously kissed again?" Grant is smiling so wide right now, I feel like the Earth suddenly has two suns. "I need to know everything."

"It was a mistake, a one-time thing, and I can't have it happen again."

"Why not?" Grant asks me.

"Because we still haven't talked about what happened. We started to, and then I saw the necklace she was wearing, and I just..." I trail off, losing my entire train of thought. "Being around her has brought all these confusing feelings back, but they're pointless to have. Amelia and I will never be anything again."

"Do we need to lock you two in a room so you can sort your shit out or something?" Oliver asks, and Grant punches him in the arm. "What the fuck?"

"We're not doing that," Grant looks at me. "Unless you think that will help?"

I shake my head. "I doubt it. Amelia has always been good at avoiding her real feelings. I'm sure anything she tells me, there are about a thousand other things she's not. And why would she want me back after what she did to us?"

"I think this could just be a proximity thing. You guys are around one another again, and all those feelings are coming back," Leo says. "Ella and I had the same kind of thing. We were just...always around one another, and it brought up a lot of confusing feelings on my end."

"All I really want from her is answers. I want to know why she left, why she broke us up." I run a hand through my hair, annoyed I let myself get so worked up over this situation. Amelia always seems to seep into every crack and crevice in my body, and I don't know how to stop her. I don't know how to get her out.

It's been years since she broke my heart, and not once have I forgotten about her. I thought I knew where we were headed back then. I thought I knew where our story was going, but then she took over, left, and I never bothered to finish it.

Not just because I couldn't, but maybe somewhere along the way, I knew our paths would cross again, on purpose or on accident.

"Good luck getting anything out of her," Oliver says.

"She was pretty honest with me the other day," Grant says. "I talked to her on the beach, and I've never seen her so open before. Hads said the same thing too. When Amelia talked to all the girls, they weren't just short, stupid talks. They were long, honest, and open about all the things that hurt while she was away. I'm pretty sure Ames and Paige talked for over an hour. You can say a lot about Amelia now, but you can't say she's not trying."

The three of us take a minute to sit with that, and he is right. She is trying more than I've ever seen her. She told me she was going to wait until after the wedding to talk so as to not ruin Paige's moment.

She was also the one to suggest a walk on the beach after I asked to speak. For once, she wasn't the one who ran away—I was. After I kissed her out of the blue, I left her on the beach with no explanation as to why I had kissed her.

"God, this sucks," I say as I plop back into the golf cart.

"Yeah, it does, but nobody ever said love was easy," Grant states as they join me.

"It definitely wasn't with me and Ella. We were practically biting each other's heads off all the time." Leo smirks.

"Hads let me in and then chased me away multiple times, but look at us now. We're both thriving and loving life alongside one another."

"Paige and I obviously had some bumps, but shit, I'm grateful we're both still alive to see our wedding day."

"So?" I ask, wondering what the point of all this is.

"So, you have to figure out who you want by your side for the highs, lows, and everything in between. It's not going to just come to you. Sure, it could be Amelia, but it could also be someone you haven't met yet," Grant tells me. "But if you want to work things out with Amelia, we'll be here to talk it through with you if you're confused."

"Thanks, guys." I smile, feeling grateful I returned their messages to come to the wedding. "I hope that, even if I'm not a part of the boyfriends of book club anymore, we can all still find time to get together."

"Of course we can, mate." Leo pats me on the shoulder. "Now, can we finish this round and go have a pint to celebrate?"

And for the rest of the afternoon, I laugh and smile with these guys alongside me, even as I play the worst round of golf I've ever played. Even though I did terribly, I still had fun. Because when I'm around these people, I suddenly remember what it's like to be a part of something. I desperately want to hang on to these moments, because it could be the last time we're all around one another like this before we all start truly living our lives with our families.

I hope I'm lucky enough to have these guys be part of mine someday, but I'm not sure if Amelia and I are meant to be. Maybe she was meant to be my first love in this universe and that's it.

Maybe in another life, we somehow made it work, but I'm just not sure we can in this one.

22

That's What I Get by Wallows

MY BRAIN HAS BEEN a mess for the last twenty-four hours, but as I listen to the girls talk about the most random things, I realize I have three wonderful humans in front of me who are on their way to forgiving me.

My brain is so scrambled from that kiss, I can't even begin to sort through everything my mind, body, and heart are feeling.

"Ella, you promised me you didn't do anything too over the top." Paige smirks, knowing over the top and Ella are words that often go together. "I said I didn't need anything too crazy."

"And it's not!" Ella says, but I can tell she's lying. She told us to expect the unexpected tonight, and there's not a doubt in my mind that she has something up her sleeve.

"Ells, I love you, but you said the same thing about your birthday this year, and Alissa dragged us all to a strip club," Hads reminds us, but I wasn't present for that. Some of these conversations they have from when I wasn't around make the ache in my chest stronger, but I always remind myself I'm here now. One day, we'll tell stories about these moments while sitting around with our families, catching up.

I can't wait to get to those moments, but I also want time to slow down so I can savor this with them.

"Ames? Are you okay?" Paige asks me. "You've been more quiet than usual tonight."

"I think I'm just a little tired," I lie, and I can tell the three of them can see right through me. I don't want this week to be all about me. That's not why I came back.

"Don't start lying to us again, Ames," Ella says. "If you're struggling with something, tell us about it."

"Isn't that what you promised the three of us when we all sat down to talk?" Hads reminds me, and I nod.

"Yes, but it's Paige's wedding, and I don't—"

"Stop with the bullshit excuses," Paige tells me, and we all turn to look at her. The three of us are shocked at not only her tone, but her candor. "What? Just because it's my wedding doesn't mean we can't talk about anything else."

The three of them turn and wait for me to start speaking. Not knowing where to start, I just open my mouth and let whatever comes out come out.

"Henry kissed me the other day."

"What?" Paige all but leaps out of her spot on the couch.

"Henry Hayes? Kissed you?" Ella asks, shock lacing her tone.

"On purpose?" Hads asks, and then I launch into what happened on the beach.

By the time I'm done, I've paced around the entire living area, and I'm worried the chain on this necklace is going to break with the number of times I've moved the charm back and forth on it.

"I don't know what to do going forward. Do we talk about the kiss, or do we pretend it never happened?"

"Well, how did it make you feel?" Paige asks me, and I freeze.

"I don't really know the answer to that," I say as I start to think. How *did* it make me feel?

"Just tell us the first words that pop into your mind when you think about the kiss," Hads says.

"Familiar. Confusing. Terrifying," are the first three words that come out. "Wow."

"That sounds about right, given your history with him," Ella says. "And how you left things."

"I know I fucked up. I thought it was best for us in the long run, but I went about it in the worst way possible. My therapist told me it's because of my fucking brain. My stupid, impulsive, annoying, chemically unbalanced brain." Sometimes, I feel okay about getting a diagnosis and knowing why I operate the way I do. Other times, I get frustrated I won't ever be different from this. This is one of the frustrating times when my brain feels so disorganized, I can't think straight.

"Maybe you should call her and update her about what's been going on?" Hads offers.

"It's not the worst idea," Ella says. "But I'm glad you decided to talk to us about this, Amelia. We're your friends, and we can understand how difficult it must be for you and Henry to be in the same place again."

"Open communication is good. It's what we need from all of us from now on," Hads says.

"I'm working on it," I remind them. "I can't promise it won't feel like pulling teeth sometimes, but I'm trying to get better. I *want* to get better at letting you guys in on everything."

Paige sits next to me, her hand on my arm. "That's all we ask, Ames."

"I'll call her at some point. We have things to celebrate, and I don't want my stupid feelings to intrude on them."

"Good, because we only have a few minutes until my surprise." Ella smirks before grabbing the champagne. "And not for nothing, an apology would go a long way, Amelia."

"I tried to apologize on the beach, but it was all too much at once. The words could barely come out." We both acted on emotions and not rational thought on the beach the other night. Plus, that was the first time we really talked about everything. It was bound to be how it was, but I wish I was better at talking. It used to feel so easy with him, and now, we're strangers trying to talk about how we once loved one another.

It's a difficult situation to navigate, and it's difficult because I made it so.

"That's understandable, but apologies go a long way, especially now that you're actually backing your words with actions. We can all see that. Since you apologized to us, you've been more present, more open. So, just show him the same, and you'll be golden," Hads tells me as a few knocks hit the door.

"Thank God. We need some better vibes in here," Ella says as she goes to answer it. "Who is it?"

There's no answer, but as I look around the room, I feel nothing but warmth. Paige is smiling from ear to ear about whatever is going to happen tonight. Hads is sipping wine and relaxing for once, and Ella has just let in a giant cake, or so it appears.

"Oh my God," I say, knowing exactly what tonight entails.

And then a stripper jumps out of the cake, and the four of us scream as the party begins.

I KNOCK TWICE ON the door to the hotel room all the boys inhabit, and I unfortunately don't have time to second guess my decision to come here at two in the morning, because the door opens immediately.

Honestly, if I didn't do this tonight, I would give myself a thousand reasons not to do it in the next few days. I know myself well enough, and I would do anything to avoid this conversation. But the girls were right. I need to apologize and back up my actions, because when I look back, I want to be able to tell myself I did the right thing in trying to mend my mistakes. I want my future self to know I tried my hardest. I won't be able to live with myself if I didn't.

"What are you doing here? I thought Grant already saged the demon out of our room?"

"Funny, Oliver. Always so funny," I say as I stand in front of him. I would have loved for literally anyone else to have answered the door—even Leo, who I don't know as well, would have been a better option.

"I'm surprised you were even here when I opened the door and weren't playing ding-dong ditch."

I cock my head at him, already annoyed. This is not how I wanted to start this out, especially since I'm already feeling self-conscious. "Are you done?"

"No, but what do you want, Amelia?"

That's a fair question. "Can I come in? I need to talk to Henry."

"How do you know he's awake?"

"I don't," I tell him.

"So, you just showed up here wanting to talk to him in the early hours of the morning?"

"Yes. Now, are you going to let me in or not?"

He says nothing as he moves out of the way, and I take that as a silent invitation in, noticing their room is exactly the same as ours, just mirrored. I look around, not knowing which door he's behind as I feel Oliver staring at the back of my head.

"Lucky for you, he's still awake. I've heard him typing for the last hour. He's almost as bad as Paige and Grant."

"Which door?"

He points to the one in the corner, and I don't bother thanking Oliver as I knock on the door, mentally preparing myself for whatever lies ahead.

I hear the typing Oliver mentioned stop, and when he opens the door wearing no shirt and just sweatpants, I freeze. Every word I had memorized to tell him is suddenly gone.

"What are you doing here?" he asks, running a hand through his hair.

"Can we talk?"

He looks at me for a moment and, under his gaze, I start to wrap my cardigan around myself. "Uh, sure."

I head into his room, and he closes the door, the air thick with tension as I turn around and face him, doing my best to keep my head up and not fall into myself and my thoughts like I often do.

But I have to do this. He deserves to hear this from me. After all I've put him through, he deserves for me to not be a coward, to not run for once.

"I'm sorry," is all I can manage to get out.

"What?"

"I'm sorry, Henry. For all of it. For breaking your heart, for saying what I did at the airport, for running from you when—" My voice breaks, and I remind myself to breathe. I'm talking way too fast.

I'm sorry for running when all you wanted to do was love me.

"Amelia?"

"Just please, let me get this all out," I say as my mind spirals. I take a deep breath as I get my breathing back under control. The weight of all I've done crushes me, but I muster through. "I'm sorry, Henry, and I know saying this doesn't erase what I did. It doesn't take away the pain I caused you, and it doesn't make me feel any less shitty, but I need you to know I think about that conversation we had at the airport a lot."

"You do?" Surprise covers his face.

"Of course I do. I was horrible to you. I said all this shit I didn't mean, and I broke your heart because I thought it was for the best. I regret every single thing that came out of my mouth that day."

"So you regret what you said but not what you did? You regret the words but not your actions?" No. No, I regret all of it. Fuck, how did I ruin a fucking apology? He sits on his bed, his head in his hands. "Amelia, this is so typical of you."

"What?"

"Did you know I chased you through the airport? I bought a ticket and got through security, feeling like a madman as I ran through the airport trying to catch you at your gate so I could try to convince you that you were wrong." He shakes his head as he runs his hands down his face, discarding his glasses next to him. "I screamed for you through the airport as one last ditch effort to get you to talk, and you didn't even turn around."

"Nobody can blame me more than I blame myself, Henry. I regret everything I did, but I thought leaving was what was best for me and my career. I can't apologize for doing what I thought was best for myself at that time." I truly thought getting on that plane was what I had to do. If I could go back and do it all differently, I would, but in another way, I wouldn't, because it led me here to the person I am now.

Living abroad changed me. It changed how I view every single thing about my life. By leaving the place I had known all my life, I learned new things. I had new experiences. I grew as a person. I lost who I was too.

If I had stayed here, I don't know if I would have had the same epiphanies. England taught me a lot about myself, but it also smacked me in the face with a lot of different things.

"So what exactly are you apologizing for? For the words you said to me that day? You can't take them back, Amelia. Unlike you, I understand the words I say have meaning, and I would *never* have said to you what you said to me."

"I'm apologizing for all of it, Henry. I needed you to know I regret how I went about everything, and—"

"I understand why you feel like you had to leave, but I'll never get why you destroyed us before you left. You could have broken my heart in a thousand different ways, but choosing to do it at the airport on the day you left was cruel. Amelia, you're a cruel person, and I know you know that, but if you had just talked to me…" He trails off, his voice thick with emotion as I stand in front of him, suddenly wanting to collapse. "I was blindsided at that airport."

"I know, and I'm—"

"Stop with the half-assed apologies. Why did you leave how you did?" He stands and comes over to me, fresh tears washing down his face as he looks at me, eyes pleading for me to tell him the full truth. "The night before you left, you whispered that you loved me before we went to sleep. We shared headphones, we connected, we *loved* each other. I kissed your neck where your necklace sat before we fell asleep, and I heard you say it back to me, only to turn around the next day and tell me you weren't capable of loving me."

"Henry, I'm—"

"No, Amelia. I don't think you're capable of being sorry for what you did. I think you feel guilty and are trying to erase that to make yourself feel better." He walks toward me, and I step back, trying to get the truth away from me but knowing he's right. My back hits the dresser, and he cages me in with both arms so I can't run. "Why did you leave like that? I know there's a reason, and I've racked my brain for years trying to figure out what would make you run from me like that."

I can't tell him. I can't tell him about how scared I was of how serious we were getting. I can't tell him what I found that day in his apartment.

"Because I had to, Henry. We had careers to start, and we couldn't have done that tied together how we were." I'm afraid of forever. Forever feels like a death sentence if I think about it too hard. It's the walls closing in on me, and at twenty-two, forever felt impossible. I wasn't looking to attain it back then, and maybe not even now.

My brain can barely handle a few minutes ahead, let alone years. I made the decision impulsively, not thinking about the ripple effect it would cause. That's not how my brain works.

I meet his gaze, our breathing matching as what I said hangs in the air between us. And then, he pulls away, standing as far from me as he can as he motions for me to leave, his hand outstretched for the exit. I don't wait for him to say anything before I head for the door.

"Did you even love me?"

I stop in my tracks, my hand resting on the doorknob. "I love you with every molecule of myself I'm capable of."

As I look back at him, I find his entire body stopped dead in his tracks. He knows what I said. He knows I didn't say it in the past tense, but I leave before he asks me about it, feeling too overwhelmed.

I get back to my room, the tears still flowing, because everything he said about me is right. I'm a coward. I'm cruel. I was an idiot to think that, in the future, Henry and I could be some sort of civil, even friends. Because after what I did, how could we get back to even a semblance of how we were before? I ruined any shred of that when I stood in front of him and lied right to his face.

23

Then — Spring Semester in College

All I Know by asiris

"Here," I say to Henry as I hand him one of my Bluetooth head-phones.

Every week, Henry and I go grocery shopping together. We don't live together, but we both grab food for our places since we're over at one another's apartments more than we're apart.

It's been a weird adjustment, Henry being my boyfriend. I never thought someone would willingly be around me this much. Besides my friends, I figured a relationship like this was never going to find me just because of how I am.

Brash. Cold. Unnerving to most people. I run from my feelings more than I run toward anything, but Henry was the biggest surprise. I'm still not sure I deserve him, or if I ever will, but for now, I'm going to enjoy his company before he realizes I'm not the one for him.

Because I do. I enjoy being in his orbit. What used to be shopping alone every week with my headphones in so nobody would talk to me has turned into Henry and I sharing headphones and shopping together.

Each week, we trade who plays music. This week, it's my turn, and I have a perfectly tailored playlist for tonight. I spent all day yesterday combing through my catalog to find the perfect mix.

Now, on this cold, rainy Sunday night, Henry and I are going to shop and listen to the same songs together. We always come late on the weekends, when it's less crowded and calmer than having to maneuver around carts and annoyed people yelling at workers.

"Are you ready?"

I roll my eyes as I laugh. "Why are you making this sound like some sort of race?"

"You know what I mean, Mills. Are you going to press play?" He gets out of my car and shuffles around to my side, umbrella in hand as he opens my door for me.

A year ago, I would have gagged and thought love was gross.

Now, I love sharing an umbrella with someone, him holding it for me as I carry our tote bags and make sure the playlist plays in the correct order. As I grab a cart and he shakes out the umbrella, he meets my eyes and smiles at me.

I feel like the luckiest girl in the world, having that pointed at me and not someone else.

"Let's go, Hen," I say as he sets the umbrella in the cart and takes over steering it. I have the list on my phone for both of us, and most of our trips go the same way.

He steers the cart and practically follows me around the store. I grab everything off our list and place it in the cart, and neither of us says a word.

It's perfect. It's my idea of quality time. Just being able to exist in his presence is enough. Still, I do love it when he opens his mouth to talk about something he loves or to tell me about his day.

It's weird. In a way, I'm still in the adjustment period. For once, I don't want to run. My entire life, I've run from every emotion, every attachment formed with family or people who wanted to be my friend, only to give up when they realized how strange I am, how cold I am.

But with him, it's different. College has been so different than I imagined it ever would be. Not only has Grand Mountain brought me the girls, but it's brought me to him. Henry Hayes, lover of words and nerd stuff, who tilts his head when he gets nervous.

For once in my life, I have a lot to lose, and it's terrifying to think about that. I know now more than ever that I don't want to lose what I have around me. I can't. If I do, I don't know who I'll become, and as soft, slow music flows through my ear, I feel it for the first time.

Love. I'm in love with Henry. I *love* him.

My first instinct is to shove the feeling down, but I block it out. I let it settle in my mind, my heart, my bones. Right in the middle of the fucking fruit section, I feel content. I feel this is the exact place I'm supposed to be at this point in my life, and no matter what shit comes my way, I couldn't care less about it.

Because I have him, and for some reason, in every way that matters, I want to run to him instead of away.

Henry Hayes, this sweet, kind man in front of me, who doesn't mind my dry humor. He doesn't care about my resting bitch face and how unapproachable I always look. He shares music with me, and umbrellas, and he lets me read what he's written sometimes, and I love him, but he doesn't know that yet.

I simply say nothing as he taps my leg with the cart, probably wondering why I've been staring at the pomegranates for so long, but he doesn't break our no talking rule.

I look over at him leaning over the cart, smiling at me with confusion written all over his face. I smile back at him, grabbing two pomegranates and setting them in the cart.

The rest of our shopping goes on without a hitch, and he puts the bags in the car as I hold the umbrella for him, walking him to and from the cart return so he doesn't get wet. The two of us get into my car, and I start it, wanting to get warm for a few seconds before I start to drive us back to campus. As I do, I feel Henry's hand on my forearm.

"Mills?"

"What?" I don't like the look on his face. Is he about to say something stupid? Leave it to me to find out I love this man, only for him to break up with me. "Is something wrong?"

He smiles, shaking his head as he reaches for my hand on the wheel, interlocking it with his. "No. I wanted to do our debrief about the playlist now, if that's okay?"

Seeing him look at me, his eyes cast down behind his glasses, a soft smile on his face as I hear the rain tapping against the windows, the low light of the parking lot casting shadows across his features, I'm ruined.

His love is the only romantic feeling I've ever felt, and all I know now is, I don't want to experience this from anyone else. His love is all I want to know for however long I have it. I'd hope for forever, but I can't think too far ahead, or I'll panic. So just for now, for however long I'm able, I'm going to love this man in front of me.

"That's okay, Hen," I say as I squeeze his hand, placing our interlocked hands in my lap as I turn to face him from the driver's seat. "Was my playlist that good?"

"It always is, Ames." He smiles to himself again, and the weirdest feeling floats through my body as he keeps talking. "But this one felt different."

"It did?"

He nods.

"Why is that?" I reach for my necklace, suddenly feeling nervous. I never touch it, though, because he grabs my other hand and stops my nervous tick.

"Well, I don't know if you know this, but you speak through music. I think it's something you've always done, and I wanted you to know it's been an honor trying to decipher you through the songs we've shared. In fact, us meeting at a concert just confirms my theory."

"And what theory is that?"

"Now, don't throw up on me, but I think you and I were fated to meet, Mills. I think something out there knew our paths had to cross, and I am thankful for whatever cosmic force sent us together."

My breath catches in my throat. "You are?"

"I am." He squeezes both of my hands. "Because it's been an honor being able to share music with you. It's been an honor to peek inside your thoughts through each song you choose to share with me. You've changed the way I view music. You're one of a kind, Amelia Ellis, and I'm grateful I broke down most of those walls while we were still just friends."

That earns an eye roll, but he simply laughs, as if he knew that was coming.

"I know you hate emotions and stuff like this, but... Shit, I don't know how to even fucking say this."

"You might just be the only writer on the planet who can't find words to say something, Hen." I lean closer to him, and all he does is tap his forehead to mine.

"I'm a big believer that everything happens for a reason, Mills. I think meeting you was proof of that for me."

"What does that mean?" I ask him, and suddenly, all I can focus on is the rain, his eyes, and the turning in my stomach.

"I love you."

My breath catches in my throat as I digest three words I haven't heard in a long time from anyone other than my friends. I don't think my parents haven't said them to me since I was small, and if they did, I don't remember it.

"I know this could make you retreat from me, but I can't spend another second of you not knowing. I couldn't spend another second pretending like I'm not hopelessly in love with the way you view music, the way you touch the necklace I bought you because it brings you comfort. I can't keep pretending silently grocery shopping with you isn't my favorite part of the week because even though we're not saying a word, we're still saying so fucking much." He presses a small kiss to my forehead. "And I can't keep almost saying those words before you leave but getting worried it's not the right time. I love you, and I don't want to spend another second without you knowing that."

Paige always tells us Henry and I have telepathic conversations when we're in a room full of people, and I never knew what she meant. Yeah, I can tell what he means just from a look sometimes, but I think tonight might actually be the first real evidence of us communicating telepathically.

"If you end up running from me, just know I'll be chasing you, Amelia, because I love you. I hope that's something you realize you can't outrun."

I feel tears spring to my eyes as I look up at him, his eyes also gleaming in the middle of this parking lot in the rain.

"All I know is that I love you too, Hen, and believe me, I never want to outrun you, no matter how terrified my own feelings make me feel."

He jumps back, as if he wasn't expecting me to say that. "You love me?"

I nod.

"Say it again, Amelia."

"I love you, Henry Hayes, and I realized it in the middle of the fruit section of the grocery store," I say as a laugh bubbles out of me.

And then he starts laughing, and the two of us are lovesick idiots in the middle of a parked car, admitting we love one another after floating around for months and months.

"In the fruit section?" he giggles. "Why?"

"Who the hell knows?" I say as I laugh, leaning into his shoulder as his arms come around me. I still feel like my stomach is going to fall through my feet, but as his arms swallow me into his body, I realize this is what love feels like.

It's warm, inviting, and a little terrifying.

"Don't ever let me go," I whisper to him.

"I won't."

Then he kisses me, and it feels different from all the ones we've shared. It feels new. This man sitting in my passenger seat loves me, and I love him. We're just two idiots in love.

I've read hundreds of romance books, swearing on my life that the feelings described in them weren't real. But here in this car, I'm surrounded by the love Henry has for me, and there aren't enough words in any language to describe what it feels like to love him.

No longer are there thoughts in my head of being unlovable, because Henry has proven all of those to be wrong. In fact, my head is quiet for the first time in a while, the only thoughts floating around of him. As I put the car in drive, his hand in mine, both of us smiling like idiots, the playlist I made playing softly in the background, I want to freeze this moment forever.

Henry loves me, and I love him back.

I'm not running from that for once.

24

Now

Speyside by Bon Iver

THE LAST PLACE I want to be the night after a breakdown is an escape room, but here I am. The eight of us are signing all the paperwork in order to actually do it. I had no idea these places were so detailed, but I get it. These things are supposed to be a little scary, right?

It makes sense why Grant chose this as a group activity.

"So, which of you are doing the *Saw* inspired one, and which of you are doing the asylum?" the guy at the counter asks us before Grant speaks up.

"I've got teams covered," he says with a smile. "I put all of our names in a random generator, and this is what popped out."

"Oh, this ought to be good," Oliver says as he hands his form in.

When the girls took one look at me coming out of my room this morning, I barely lasted two seconds before I burst into tears and told them how my talk with Henry went. They were sympathetic, of course, but I know Henry was right. I just can't think about it anymore, and thankfully, they've done a good job of keeping the two of us separate for today.

"Okay, so, Leo, Hads, and Paige are with me in the asylum, and the rest of you are doing the other one." Grant smiles, but I feel like my heart just fell to my feet. Henry and I are going to be trapped together in a small room with Ella and Oliver, and we're all going to have to work together to get out.

Fuck my life.

"Did everyone hand in their forms?" Ella asks as she brings hers to the front.

The guy at the counter counts them all, and once he confirms we're good, he puts on a video for us to watch about the rules, and after that's done, we're all good to go.

Except Grant failed to mention the theatrics of this before we got here—their group is getting fake handcuffed as they head to the room they have to escape from.

"Oh my gosh, Oliver, is this what you felt like when you got handcuffed?" Hads asks him with a fake smile as he flips her off.

"If anyone comes within five feet of me with those things, I will be screaming," Ella says. "But I'm sure you're used to this." She smacks Oliver on the arm, and he sighs heavily.

"Can we just get this over with?" he asks, already annoyed.

"Alright, if you guys could just put these over your heads before we go in, that would be great." He hands us all burlap sacks. "And two of you have to go ahead of the others."

"Are you serious?" I ask, knowing Oliver and Ella were about to say something much harsher to this poor dude.

"Yup," is all he says. "And you two," he points between me and Henry, "you both can follow me while the other two figure out the sacks."

Ella and Oliver groan, and I'm literally going to throw up as I toss the sack over my head and wordlessly follow this guy down a few different dark hallways. Henry has barely said a word, but I can feel the awkward energy coming off him. I would rather die and end up a prop in one of these rooms than talk with him. As we turn into the first room of our adventure, the guy instructs us to get into a small cage in the corner of the room.

"The other two have to figure out how to get you out. It's the first part of the puzzle."

"Is this a joke?" I ask, and he shakes his head.

"Let's just get in, Amelia. The faster we get in, the faster we get out," Henry says as he heads to the cage.

"He's right, you know." The worker smirks at me as I roll my eyes and watch him lock us both in the cage.

As he leaves and shuts the door, I rip the sack off my head and fix my hair, Henry doing the same.

"Where do you think we should start?" I ask, breaking the silence.

"I think we should wait for Ella and Oliver, since they're not trapped in here and can actually figure out the puzzle."

Well, there goes working together.

As soon as they get inside, they both start laughing.

"I could make so many jokes about this, but I'll refrain," Ella says.

Oliver comes up to the edge of the cage. "How does it feel, Amelia?"

"I'm sure you would know, Oliver. I don't think you need me to describe it for you, not with all the experience you have being behind bars."

"You know what, Amelia—"

"What, Oliver? You are the living embodiment of the color beige. What could you possibly—"

Ella cuts our bickering off. "Look, we all know why Grant put the teams like this, so if you three could shut the hell up and be civil for five minutes, maybe we'll win this thing and beat Leo's team."

I love how competitive Ella is, but an escape room in the middle of nowhere in Virginia is not where I want to sort my shit out with Oliver, and especially not Henry.

"I can be civil if they can," Henry says as he opens and shuts the small locker in the corner of the room.

"I'll be nice," I say, looking at Oliver to see what sort of remark he has for me.

"Let's just get the fuck out of here, okay?"

"Glad we're all on the same page," Ella says as she picks up a small piece of paper. "Now, let's figure out how to get you two out of there."

"Thank God," Henry says under his breath, and I roll my eyes as I start to look for clues.

This is going to be the longest hour of my life.

"LOOK AT HOW CUTE this picture is, you guys!" Paige waves the photo around as if we all weren't in it just a few minutes ago. Paige's team won, and the worst part is, they only beat us by a few minutes. We had around ten minutes left to escape when we finally got out, and we only used one clue. Turns out, Oliver forgot to grab one of the vials we needed from the second room. I thought his literal job would have made him great at these, but I guess not.

And yes, the *second* room. This is probably my last time doing an escape room. I thought I was going to get murdered.

"I'm gonna frame this!" she says as we head back to the car.

"You tried your best, darling, but we were just better than you guys this time," Leo gloats to Ella, and she glares daggers at him.

"Grant, you are never allowed to assign teams ever again." She looks over at me. "No offense. We did get out of there before the time was up, so it wasn't a total loss."

"None taken, Ella. I actually agree with you," I say as I joke with Grant. "I know what you're up to."

He feigns surprise while putting his hand on his chest. "It was a randomized generator, you guys! Blame the generator. I'm simply the messenger."

Ella and I look at one another, shake our heads, and get into the car. The girls and the guys drove separately, but we're all headed back to the hotel to recuperate before we have dinner together tonight.

Hads starts back for the hotel, and just when I think this is going to be another awkward car ride, Ella speaks up.

"Paige, here's your twenty bucks."

"Thank you! I told you they wouldn't claw each other's eyes out." She smiles at me from the front seat. "Sorry, Ames."

It all clicks in my head. "Did you guys bet on Henry and I trying to kill each other or something?"

"Ella thought you guys were going to ruin your chances of actually getting out of the room, since you two were on the same team," she says quietly. "But I knew you would be fine."

I can't help the laughter that comes out, and as it really hits me, I can't stop it. So, I sit in the back seat of the car and laugh my ass off, the rest of the girls eventually joining me. Now, the entire car is filled with laughter as the music plays softly through the speakers.

It feels like the four of us are back in college, making bets on if Oliver will say more than three sentences. Right here in this car, years after we graduated from that small classroom where we held book club, I've found a small sliver of home I once felt.

"I've really missed you guys," I say as I wipe the tears of laughter from my face. "Truly. I've missed feeling like this."

"Like what?" Hads asks me.

"Whole again. So, thanks for not turning me away when you saw me again. You guys could have been as cruel as I was and left me standing outside with my bags in hand, but you didn't. I'll never forget that. I know I didn't deserve a second chance, but you guys gave me one anyway." They gave me a chance, let me back in, and I hope I'm almost on the way to proving I'm not going to leave again.

I'm so many things, but I'm not stupid enough to leave these girls behind again. Never again will I leave this safe, comfortable home I've found with these three girls.

It feels right to be known and loved by them. I feel more like myself when I'm with them. I should have never tried to hide from them how I hide from myself most days. But I'm trying to fix that. I'm trying to change to be a person they deserve as a friend, because the old version of myself was not one who deserved these girls, yet they loved me anyway.

Paige reaches for my hand from her seat in the front and looks me in the eyes, fresh tears brimming. "We're glad you're back. Book club just isn't the same without you, and you've made us a whole group again."

"There's no book club without you," Ella agrees. "And even though I was skeptical at first, you've continued to prove me wrong. I'm glad you're here for this big moment, but I hope that even for all the little ones, you'll still show up for us."

My voice is thick with emotion, but I somehow manage to get the words out. "You bet your ass I'll be here for all of them."

"Okay, I love you guys, but I am tired of crying so much on this trip, so I'm going to turn this song up, and we're all going to sing it, okay?" Hads says as she turns the volume dial.

The entire car ride back to the hotel is filled with off-key singing, upbeat songs, and laughter. I know no matter what ends up happening with Henry, I'll still have these girls.

Because even if I can't find romantic love at any point in my life, I'll have these girls to remind me I am capable of being loved. I do deserve it, even though I've made some mistakes.

At the end of the day, we're just four girls who went to college in a small town called Grand Mountain, and no matter where we end up, that will always be true. That was where we started, and I hope our ending will be just as magical as the beginning.

25

"I don't know who you are anymore. I can't stand up for you knowing all I know. After all I've seen, after all you've done, I can't keep making excuses for you." — *Untitled Henry Hayes Manuscript*

THE PAST FEW DAYS have been a whirlwind of emotions, and since we don't have group plans for today, I'm headed out to a small coffee shop to try and get some words in.

I'll be honest, all this emotional shit that has dredged up inside me where Amelia is concerned has helped the words flow a bit easier. I knew it would. There's a reason my first book did so well—I wrote it only a few months after Amelia and I had our falling out.

If I can even call it that. She and I never fell in the same direction. It was more like she pushed me off a cliff and didn't stick around to see if I hit the rocks or the water.

Mitch and my family have been constantly checking in on me, my sister especially. It feels good to have some people care enough to call and want to talk to me. According to Mitch, he's made decent progress on his manuscript while I'm over here ignoring the emails from my editor asking for an update. I sent one back about a week ago, just so they didn't think I was dead or something, but I was vague on purpose.

I don't want to jinx myself, and if I tell them everything is going well, it might jump me back into the block I had before I came face to face with my own form of emotional torture. At least I'm actually writing again, though. That has to be a good sign or something.

It does feel good to pretend I could still be a writer, even after wanting to trash this manuscript about a thousand times since I started it.

Two sharp knocks on my door as I gather my laptop and notes into my bag make me pause, and I already know who stands on the other side of the door. When Oliver's face greets me with a weird smirk, I get worried.

"Is everything okay?"

Now he looks confused. "Yeah, why?"

"Your face looks weird."

He sighs heavily. "I was trying not to look so menacing."

"Honestly, I get more worried when you don't look how you normally do." I wave my hand out, and he comes in, sitting on the edge of my bed as I lean against the small desk I have in my room. "Did you want to talk about something, or is this some sort of wedding freak out Grant thinks you're going to have?"

He only rolls his eyes. "I'm not going to freak out, so if you could all stop assuming I'm going to, that would be wonderful." He rubs his hand down his chin as I wait for him to hopefully explain himself.

Or he could just not say anything. That used to happen a lot when I first met him at Grand Mountain. He would talk, and I would always assume he had more to say, but he would remain quiet. As I got to know him better, I realized he's not a small talk kind of guy, and I got used to his one and done sentences.

"So, what's up?" I ask again, a bit worried about whatever he came in here to say.

"I just wanted to check in with you about things."

I pinch my eyebrows, still confused. "Uh, why? And what things?"

"Why do you sound so confused?"

"Because you came in here willingly to ask me how I am."

He throws his hands up. "Why is that so weird?"

"Have you met yourself?" I say, a laugh slipping out on accident. "Oliver, you and I have never made small talk about our feelings ever, so color me confused."

"That's not true!" he says as he stands. I've never seen him so animated before, and all of us should really thank Paige. She's softened him immensely if he's really in here to talk with me about how I'm feeling. "When you picked me up from the police station, we talked about stuff."

"Yes, but you also yelled at me for not driving fast enough when I was already at fifteen over," I joke. "And that was a few years ago, so don't blame me for reacting like this when we've barely seen one another."

Out of everyone, Oliver and I stayed in contact the most. Grant was here and there, but Oliver and I probably checked in about once a month. After Grant was hospitalized last year, Oliver called me to talk it out. I was worried, but Grant sent me a bunch of memes when he was feeling better.

"Whatever," he says as he sits back down. "I just wanted to ask you how you're doing being back in close proximity to the devil."

I scoff as I sit in the desk chair, knowing he's talking about Amelia. I thought for sure when I saw them both again, they would get along, but I guess some things never change.

"It's weird, honestly. We've had a few conversations with one another about everything that happened, but they always leave me feeling more confused."

"Well, that tracks. Amelia is the most confusing and terrifying person I've ever met."

My knee jerk reaction is to stand up for her, to tell Oliver he's wrong. She's just complex, complicated, and has made more than a few mistakes, but I bite my tongue. I no longer know who Amelia is. I'm not hers and she's not mine, and I'm not going to defend her actions. Even I don't understand why she does what she does.

I'm also tired of making excuses for her when I talk about our situation. I've defended her in my mind so many times, I often forget how badly she hurt me. I'm done pretending like there's an excuse for what she did, because there isn't.

If I was in her situation, I never would have done what she did. In fact, I doubt running and never looking back would have ever crossed my mind.

"Do you still love her?"

His question surprises me. "You of all people asking me that feels a little crazy. In another timeline, it's Grant asking me that."

"I'm just curious, Henry. Have you seen the way you two still look at one another? If I didn't know your history, I would think something was up."

"What do you mean?" The two of us haven't interacted much since we've been here, at least not as much as everyone else. Most of the time, we're separated in group settings.

"I can't really explain it, but it's something in your eyes when you look at Amelia. They almost sparkle in a way, as if you've just discovered a new galaxy or something. She looks at you the exact same way, but her eyes are more downturned, full of sadness."

"I didn't know you paid such close attention to anyone besides Paige," I joke.

"Consider it a one-time thing then," he says, looking at his feet.

The two of us are quiet for a few moments before the words come tumbling out. "Of course, I still love her. With the way things ended, I felt suspended in time, with nowhere to put my feelings for her, so they sort of festered. I have lots of confusing emotions about Amelia. I hate her, but I wish she would talk to me. I love her, but I wish she didn't end things how she did. I'll never be able to forget her, but sometimes, I wish I could wipe my brain of knowing her. It's the weirdest thing."

"Do you think you could want what you two used to have, whatever it was?"

"I don't know," I say truthfully. Besides an actual answer as to why she did what she did, I'm not sure where the two of us go after we sort our shit out—if we even can. "I thought I knew how our story was going to unfold. I thought we were on the same page when it came to our collective future, but we weren't."

"Then maybe just take it one step at a time. Maybe just get some answers while she's here and go from there." Oliver stands and comes over to me. "But be careful. I'm still not fully sure Amelia is here for the long haul. Just...protect yourself and that heart of yours. I don't want a repeat of what happened last time when Amelia ran out on everyone."

I nod. "Yeah, me neither."

"Good. Now go write that damn book of yours and enjoy today by yourself."

He's about to leave my room before I speak up. "Thanks, Oliver."

"For what?"

"The invitation," I tell him. "And for everything, really."

"You're a good guy, Henry. Try not to forget that." He shuts my door before I continue to pack my bag, hoping a change of scenery will help me chip away at my manuscript.

I can't help that my mind floats back to Amelia. All of us around her are in the same boat. There are a few options in terms of what could happen after all of this is over, but the one thing I know for sure is, I'm not going to have any expectations.

26

I Met You Too Soon by asiris

WHILE EVERYONE ELSE IS out doing date night, I've decided to grab my journal and take a walk on the beach. This week has been a mixed bag emotionally for me, and most nights, I've been far too exhausted to get my journal out. Which is good, actually. I'm sleeping well again, so that's a good step in the right direction.

Though this trip has thrown my routine out of whack, I've been handling it pretty well. I think it's because my brain has been so distracted by a thousand other things, so my body just goes with whatever is happening.

I take a sip of my favorite tea before I set my beach towel down, throw my shoes to the side, and sit. The light from the hotel and the moon are all I need to see what I'm writing. Most of the time, my entries don't make much sense, at least to someone who picks up my journal randomly. To me, the chaotic scribblings are a direct reflection of what my brain feels like.

I don't know how long I'm out here journaling, but the moment I feel another presence coming up behind me, I'm barely thinking before I turn around and throw my pen at them.

It knocks against Henry's chest, falling to the sand with a small thump.

"I think we've been here before," is all he says as he grabs my pen. "Here."

"Thank you," I say before I shake the grains off of it, tucking it into my journal as I shut it. My heart starts to race as I realize he's not leaving. "Do you want to sit?"

He adjusts his bag on his shoulder, and I can't tell if it's because he's uncomfortable or if it's something else. "Uhm, sure," he says, running a hand through his hair.

"I mean, you don't have to," I say, stumbling to get the words out.

He stops as he's almost sitting down. "D-do you not want me to sit?"

"No, you can sit if you want to. I just—" I cut myself off. "I can't figure out what I'm trying to say." I laugh myself off as I fiddle with the rings on my fingers.

"I didn't mean to throw you all out of whack," he says as he makes himself comfortable on the beach towel. "I didn't even know it was you, actually. I came out here to get some fresh air after a small writing session."

"Oh," is all I can say. "How was writing?"

He looks surprised at my question. "It was okay, actually. More pro-ductive than most of mine lately."

I want so badly to ask him what that means, but I remain silent as we sit beside one another, listening to the breeze and the waves crashing out in the ocean. I should say something, anything to break this tension between us, but I feel like anything I try to say is going to be the wrong thing.

"Do you ever wonder?"

I look over at him, his eyes still trained on the ocean in front of us, as I think about the question he asked me. I know what he's asking. He doesn't need to elaborate.

"All the time," I whisper back to him.

He turns to meet my gaze. "Do you even know what I'm referencing?"

"Of course I do."

He sighs heavily. "Will I always wonder what happened between us, or do you think someday, we'll get a second chance?"

I had no idea he was even thinking about another chance with me. Maybe what I said to him in his room the other night made him think about it, but I don't think he's actually serious. I assume he's just wondering what it would look like. I don't think he'll ever let it happen. Not after everything I said to him. Not after all I did.

If I was him, I wouldn't give me another chance.

"I don't think those words belong in the same sentence with my name, especially not after what I said to you."

He turns to the ocean again. "I'm not sure that's true." He must sense my confusion, because he continues. "If the world didn't have or give second chances, all of us would be a lot lonelier. Everyone deserves a second chance, even after fucking up."

"I mean, unless you killed someone, I'd agree."

He laughs. "Well, yeah, Amelia. That, we can agree on."

"Wow, I never thought I'd see the day you agreed with me on something again."

Another laugh, and then we're back to silence. This time, it doesn't feel awkward or tense, just familiar. It reminds me of when we used to have study dates, the only sounds between us were either the music I played or our typing on our laptops.

"What do you wonder most about?"

A stray tear falls from my eyes as I think about what we could have been. "I wonder what would have happened if I made a different choice."

"And what have you found out?"

"A lot of different things, I guess. Mostly, I've found out things about myself I don't think I ever would have had I not been in England."

I can tell he thinks this conversation has gone too far, because he adjusts his glasses and how he's sitting. "We don't have to talk about any of this if it's too much."

"No, it's okay, Henry." I reach out, my hand brushing his arm, goosebumps traveling all over my skin. I take a deep breath, needing all the air I can get. "I was in a really bad place over there. So bad, I decided to talk to someone about it."

"Good for you, Amelia."

"A month into our sessions, I was diagnosed with ADHD."

He studies my face, and I'm not sure why I'm so fucking nervous but I am.

"That's not me excusing my behavior or what I did to you at the airport, but it felt good knowing there was a reason behind how I've felt my whole life. I sort of spun out over there, but with more sessions and medication, I couldn't believe how much better I felt."

"Wow," is all he says.

"Mhm," is all I can muster.

It could be minutes or hours before one of us speaks again. "I'm really proud of you."

He says it so quietly, I almost think I misheard him. "What?"

"I'm proud of you. The Amelia I knew in college would have run the opposite direction from a therapist's office. I know that was a big step for you. I can't imagine what it must have felt like getting the diagnosis."

"Part of me was relieved to have a name for it. I had been wrestling my own mind for my entire life. The last year has been a good step in the right direction."

He smiles at me, one I've never seen before. It seems I've unlocked a new version of Henry. I try to take a mental picture of this moment, knowing I'm probably not going to get many more of them.

"That's good, Amelia. Really good."

"Thanks," I say, taking another sip of my tea. "You know what I think about a lot?"

"What?"

"That maybe we were just too young back then. Maybe we met a bit too soon."

He tilts his head at me. "Is that so?"

"Well, young and confused is still the story of my life, but when I think about the girl I used to be, I wish I could tell her so many things I know now."

He clears his throat. "That's the good thing about growing up." He smiles to himself. "You're always learning and growing through your experiences. You never have to know who you are so completely that you can't change. You have a lifetime to figure out who you want to be and the life you want to live."

I sit with his words for a moment. "Wow, that was beautiful."

"Thank you."

"You should be a writer or something."

He laughs again, the sound music to my ears. "You always did believe I'd make something of myself."

"Of course I did." I still do. I still think he's on his way to fame. The way he writes, the way he explains emotions, God, all of it—he's talented. Anyone who reads a single page of what he wrote knows that.

"It just sucks that you could have been beside me for all of it like we planned."

My eyes fill with tears at the picture coming together in my mind. Henry and I at an apartment that's ours. Pages of his manuscript all over the bed as he watches me read it. Happiness. Pure happiness floats through my mind at what could have been.

"Henry, I—"

I hear him sniffle as he grabs his bag. "I have to go." He doesn't even bother dusting the sand off himself before he walks away, getting smaller and smaller as he heads for the hotel.

27

I Told You Things by Gracie Abrams

Us girls get ready in Paige's giant bathroom, music playing over her speaker as we all get ready for a night on the town. It feels like just yesterday the four of us were getting ready for some party or night out at the Hidden Bear back in college, when Ella used to drag us out of our dorms to socialize.

God, nostalgia has been punching me in the face all throughout this trip, and I can't believe Paige is getting married at the end of the week.

"Is another glass a good idea, Ames? We are going to a club, and I know drinks are expensive, but I've never seen you pregame so much," Hads says as she notices my full glass again.

"Drinking when you're stressed about..." Paige pauses to think of the right words. "When you're stressed about certain things is not the best idea."

"Take it from me," Ella says. "The first time I fucked Leo, I was tipsy, and I swear, he put some sort of horny spell on me. It was not my finest hour."

The three of us look at her like she's crazy, because we all know she loves the guy.

"Back then, it was," she reiterates. "I almost missed my weekly coffee chat with Hads because I was too busy sleeping on his stupid chest."

"I *knew* it was Leo you had that regrettable hookup with, and now I wish I asked you more about it. I would have loved to know all the details back then. It would have been a great distraction from what was happening with Grant." Hads swipes some blush onto her face, and the three of us look at her confused.

"It's sparkling juice," I tell them. "Ella grabbed some for me after I told you guys I was on medication."

"Can we just focus on the fact that we're all here with the people we love instead of harping on the past?" Paige smiles at us, and we nod collectively. "And I never hated Oliver, so that is where I differ from you two."

"Yes, but you were scared to have feelings for him," I remind her. "And I don't know how Hads didn't see that. You two were glaringly obvious. I mean, the first time you guys messed around, Hads was at Oliver's door minutes prior, and you were trying not to giggle behind the door." I laugh.

"What?" Hads shrieks, and I forgot Paige only told me about that. "Are you serious?"

Paige only blushes, and Hads throws a makeup brush towards her, but she dodges it.

"My bad," I say to the room, still giggling into my glass.

I don't know how tonight is going to go, especially after Henry and my impromptu chat on the beach yesterday. It was weird, the two of us having a civil conversation. Not only did we talk about the past, but Henry knows about my diagnosis now—not that it's going to change anything. Both of our walls seem to be down, the two of us suspended in the air because neither of us knows what we want from one another. Sure, we still have some things to talk about, but maybe we'll be civil enough to chat about us after the wedding. Maybe we can make the next few days not as horrible as it started out.

Though it is getting late, and I'm worried about what could happen tonight when my medication wears off. I told my therapist there's a noticeable difference when it wears off before I fall asleep, and I'm worried my brain might turn on me at the blink of an eye. I guess we'll find out as the night progresses.

Nothing in my head is ever really silent when my medication wears off, but I'm having fun while I dance with my friends. Still, I can't help but steal glances at the guy I used to know.

Once upon a time, he loved me, and I loved him, but now, we're strangers again. That cuts me open, and I can practically feel my blood spilling out all over the place. I wonder why he came up to me at the beach the other night. I wonder what happened after he left. I wanted to chase after him, but I figured he needed some space after the conversation we had. It was heavy and full of questions neither of us could answer because we can't repeat the past.

I step off the dance floor to grab some water, dehydrated and sweaty.

All the boys are sitting at a table, talking amongst themselves while us girls are dancing and enjoying ourselves. I have to say, we all look super hot, and being able to get out of the hotel room has done wonders.

Well, it's done what it can. I don't think there's any way to outrun Henry and our collective past, but I feel like the two of us are in a decent place, despite not having said a word to each other all night.

By the time I get back to the dance floor, Paige grabs my arm and pulls me into her.

"I've been looking for you for a few minutes. Where did you go?" she shouts over the music.

"I needed some water," I shout to her. "I went back to the table for a second."

"By yourself?"

"Yeah," I say, confused as to why that would matter. "I'm not drinking, I promise."

"That's not why I asked." She flicks her eyes to Henry and then looks back at me. "Are you two okay?"

"As okay as we can be," I tell her as a new song comes on, and Ella grabs both of us to dance. She must have requested this one, because it's one of our favorites. On every playlist we ever made, this one was always on it. It's basically the soundtrack to our friendship, and I could cry in the middle of this dance floor thinking about the four of us.

It feels good to dance it out with them around me. It feels like the old days, when everything was okay and we were all just four girls who bonded over books. Now, we have so much more life under our belts, yet somehow, we're still here.

I'm thankful I was brave enough to get on the plane and come back here, because I truly can't imagine not being around them.

Oliver interrupts our moment when he whispers in Paige's ear, and her face lights up as she jumps up and down on the dance floor.

"What's going on?" Hads asks.

"She was excited to finally hear Oliver speak!" I joke, and he shoots me a glare.

"Sadie is here! Her flight just landed! I thought she was supposed to get in tomorrow, but apparently, she caught an earlier flight," Paige tells us.

"Are you going to pick her up?" Ella asks.

"Yes! I'm not letting her take a car to the hotel when we can just get her. I'm sorry I'm leaving earlier than intended, but—"

"Paige, don't apologize." Ella smooths her hair down. "It's late, and we've been out for hours. It's okay."

"Grant and I are probably heading out too, so can we catch a ride with you guys?" Hads says as she looks up from her phone. I assume Grant texted her something from over at the table, because I've never seen her look at her phone how she is now.

"Where are you two going?" Oliver asks his sister.

"Back to the hotel." She smiles, and Oliver practically gags as he realizes what she means.

"Good for you, babe," Ella says. "Make sure Grant puts the other set of keys in my purse before you leave."

"I will," Hads says as she hugs us all. "I'll see you all tomorrow."

"I love you guys! I'm so excited for everyone to get here!" Paige shouts. "This is the best week ever!"

Oliver only smiles as he whisks Paige away, the rest of us following them back to the table to say goodbye before they leave. After they're gone, it's just me, Ella, Leo, and Henry. It's not the oddest pairing you could have in our group, but I can't say it's not going to be awkward.

I practically stumble out of the chair I sat down in, and Ella catches me before I fall, all but dragging me outside before I make a complete fool of myself.

"Ames, what is going on with you tonight?" she asks as I take a deep breath, feeling the warm Virginia air down my throat.

"Nothing," I tell her. "I'm just a little dehydrated, I think. I've been a bit dizzy tonight, and I don't know why."

"Is that a side effect of your medication?"

My head tilts. "It might be. Can we get some water?"

She then jumps into normal Ella mode, ready to take care of me as soon as I ask.

"Not for nothing, but I'm glad you found Leo."

"Why?"

"Because he takes care of you how you always take care of others, and there's nobody more deserving of that than you."

"Thanks," she says as she sits me down at the table, Leo and Henry barely stopping their conversation as Ella goes to grab me some water.

My head is spinning in more ways than one. Since my medication wore off hours ago, I can feel my brain being pulled in a thousand different directions. Part of me wants to insert myself into Leo and Henry's conversation. The other part wants to dance, but I'm too dizzy for that, so I can't. I could go outside and get some air, but standing feels impossible.

I'm also just exhausted. Maybe I should go find somewhere to lie down.

As I'm getting up, Ella reaches me. "Where are you going?"

Shit. Where was I about to go?

"Uhm," is all I can say before she hands me some cold water.

"Drink this."

"Thanks, Ells." I take a long sip as the sounds of the bar float in and out of my ears, everything so overstimulating between the noise, the lights, and the way my dress feels against my skin. It feels like too much.

Then, a single word from Henry's lips sits on my eardrums and won't leave.

"Here," Ella says as she hands me another glass, and I take a few sips, my throat suddenly feeling dry. "Drink the whole thing before we leave."

"You're telling me you'll probably never get married? We're at a wedding, mate," Leo tells him. "I assume everyone is always thinking about their own wedding while at another one."

"Not me," Henry says, rubbing the condensation off his glass. "I've never been one hundred percent sure it's something I wanted."

I can't help the scoff that comes out of my mouth before all of them look over at me, confusion on all their faces.

"Is something funny?" Henry asks, a bite to his tone as he looks at me.

"Yeah, actually," I say as I lean forward. "You saying that is the funniest thing I've ever heard."

"Amelia…" Ella warns me, her eyes widening as she tries to get me to stop talking before this conversation gets heated.

I should probably listen to her, but I can't find it in me to care too much right now. Not after what I found. Not after what he was going to do.

"And why is that funny?"

"You know what? Maybe we should go outside," Leo says. "I need a cigarette. Henry, care to join me?"

"Sure," he says before they walk outside, but I've already locked on to the memories flooding my brain of what I found that day in his apartment.

"Amelia, whatever it is you're thinking about doing, don't," she warns. "The impulsive part of your brain is overriding everything else. Do not make this worse for yourself." My mind is already made up as I head for the door, my feet moving of their own accord toward him in the parking lot.

"You're a liar," I say as I point my finger in his face. "Look, I'm aware I fucked up, but at least I don't go around lying to people."

"Well, that's debatable," is all Ella says from behind me.

"What the hell are you doing?" Henry asks me.

"Darling, let's go inside," Leo says as he throws his cigarette out, barely having smoked it.

"I'm talking! I'm giving you answers. Do you want to know why I left?"

"Of course I do!" he says back to me.

"Then why are you telling Leo you never wanted to get married when I found a ring on your bookshelf back in college?"

28

Then — Finals Week of Spring Semester

So Real by Jeff Buckley

I LET MYSELF INTO Henry's apartment because I know he's not back yet. His mom bought a new washer and dryer over the weekend, and Henry offered to help install them, since he didn't want his dad to do all the heavy lifting.

I'm over here earlier than I planned, but I wanted to get his place ready for the small surprise I got him. Honestly, it's not a big deal, but I went book shopping with the girls over the weekend, and while I was there, I bought Henry this series he's been eyeing for a few weeks. He keeps mentioning it, but he never bought them because of how busy school has been keeping him.

Senior year has not been easy, and with finals week in full swing, I wanted to do something nice for him. I have the books, his favorite snacks, and even a new writing notebook tucked into this small basket. He told me his last one was almost full, so I figured he needed a new one.

It's been hard for us to see one another with how much studying and shit we've had going on, so dinner and a movie on this slow Sunday is my idea of a perfect night.

Sure, we sleep in the same bed most nights, but I miss having actual conversion with him, even when we barely speak. Some nights, we study together, but lately, we've only seen one another before we sleep, and I hate it.

I never thought I would crave someone's presence as much as I do his, but I do. Henry and his quiet love are all I need when life feels too overwhelming, and with graduation looming, everything has felt too open-ended for my liking.

For once, I have no plan. My job applications have come back with nothing so far, and I worry about the future if I can't find something. My internship supervisor, Kacey, apparently put some feelers out for me after I compiled my portfolio, but she hasn't updated me in a few days. I'm starting to get worried about what my life will look like if I can't even get a job right out of college. All the success I crave will be gone. I'll be a failure before I've even had a chance to start, and my parents will have been right.

Wanting to banish those thoughts, I place some confetti around the basket on the counter, and eventually, I wander over to the bookshelves in his living room.

My fingers trace the spines of the books he has on display; I know this is just a small collection of his books he brought with him. I'm sure he'll bring a few back from his house like he always does when he visits.

I grab a copy of his favorite book, noting the scribbles in the margins. I love that I've found someone who doesn't mind writing in books. Some people are very particular about that, but I've always loved to doodle my favorite lines and paragraphs. Plus, I bought them, so I can doodle to my heart's desire.

I'm not sure what time he told me he'd be back, so I put the book back, opting for another one I might start to read just to pass the time. As I do, something falls out of the spine.

That's weird, I think to myself. Henry isn't a trinket kind of guy, at least not on the shelves out here. The ones in his room are a different story. Those are filled with figures of his favorite movie characters, including the ones I've bought him over the past few months.

I can't find what dropped until a small, shiny glint catches my eye under his couch. As I reach for it and grasp it, I'm sure this isn't what it seems.

When I pull it out and open my hand, an engagement ring staring back at me from the palm of my hand, I freeze.

A small diamond sits in the center of a beautifully crafted vintage setting.

Is Henry going to propose after graduation? No. No, he can't be doing that, can he? We've only known one another for a year. That's way too soon to get engaged, let alone *married*.

We're so young. We're so young, and we have so much time. Is he really serious enough to want to lock me down this early into our relationship? I love Henry. Of course I love him, but I am in no way ready for this kind of commitment.

I thought we had talked about this? I thought he knew we were taking it slow and at our own pace? Not once has he brought up marriage or kids or the rest of our lives. He knows how I feel about thinking about that stuff.

I can't do this. I'm not ready for this, and I won't be the one to turn him down when he ultimately gets down on one knee. I can't say yes to him, not right now. Maybe ten years in the future, but now? No way. I can't break his heart when I say nothing to his proposal.

It's not that I don't want to marry him. It's that I didn't know he was so serious. I'm not ready for this level of commitment. I have an entire life to kick-start after graduation, and as selfish as it may be, I want to be secure in that before I decide to get married. I want to have a career and be successful and show my parents they were wrong.

I have all these things to do before I get married, and I won't put them on hold.

What the fuck am I going to do?

This is too much. The ring stares back at me in the palm of my hand, but all I see when I look at it is a prison sentence. So, I do what I know best—run. As I grab my phone from my purse on the counter, I notice a text from him, and I freeze, as if he can sense my thoughts spiraling all the way from his house.

Henry: I'll be back soon. What should I pick up for dinner on my way back?

I can't do this tonight. I can't look him in the eye after what I found. God, I feel like I'm going to be sick or something.

Amelia: I'm actually not feeling too well. Rain check?

His reply is almost immediate.

> **Henry: Are you okay? Do you want me to drop something off at your place?**

> **Amelia: No, it's fine. Paige is taking care of me.**

> **Henry: Oh, okay.**

> **Henry: I'll see you tomorrow? We can study together in the library after class.**

I don't bother answering him, because I'm already halfway out his door, trying to calm myself down and failing miserably.

I'm officially losing my mind, and as I speed back to my place, I turn my phone off, not wanting to deal with anybody or anything but my racing thoughts about the future and what it holds for the two of us.

29

Now

"Everything happens for a reason, but I don't know the reason behind all of this." — *Excerpt from Henry Hayes' Text Messages*

"I'm talking! I'm giving you answers, Henry. Do you want to know why I left?"

"Of course I do!" I shout back at her.

"Then why are you telling Leo you never wanted to get married when I found a ring on your bookshelf back in college?"

Oh, fuck.

Amelia found that? The pieces fall into place as soon as the words fall out of her mouth. I remember that night so clearly. I came back to school to a small basket on my counter, no Amelia in my apartment after she said she wasn't feeling well. I always assumed she had set it up at random, but now, the picture becomes clearer.

She went to my place before I got there. She set the basket up, perused my bookshelves like she always does, and found the ring I hid—not very well, in hindsight.

The ring scared her off, and throughout the rest of finals week, she almost avoided me on account of our schedules being the exact opposite, but normally, when she'd make time for us, she didn't. I chalked it up to being busy—I knew how Amelia felt about me—but looking back, it was obvious.

That was when Amelia started retreating from me. That was also probably when she decided she was going to leave and never look back. Pre-finals week, she had no job opportunities, so I'm not sure when she got the call about leaving, but as soon as she did, the plan was in motion. Everything moved so fast back then, and I obviously wasn't going to talk her out of her dream, so I went along with it.

"You found it?" I whisper, suddenly feeling like the biggest idiot in the world.

"Yes." She stares back at me, her lips trembling. I can't tell if it's because she's cold or nervous about having this conversation. "Why did you have it, Henry?"

"My mother gave it to me over Thanksgiving break that year," I say to her, not wanting to do this in a parking lot. Still, if we're finally talking about all this, I'm not going to stop on account of us being in public. "It was my grandmother's ring, and she gave it to me because she knew how I felt about you, Amelia. I was serious about you, about us, so she gave it to me to save for when the time was right."

"And the right time was graduation?" she spits at me, her eyes wide and angry.

"No," I say, getting into her personal space. "I wasn't going to propose to you after graduation."

"You weren't?"

"No. And the fact that you assumed I would is ridiculous. Amelia, all of this could have been solved if you had just talked to me! I would have been honest with you."

She shakes her head as I feel a few raindrops fall onto my skin. "But you wanted to give it to me. You were going to."

"When the time was right! When we finally had our lives sorted out, I was going to get down on one knee and promise to love you for the rest of my life, but we had barely cracked the surface of life in college."

"I don't believe you."

"Believe whatever you want, but I'm serious. I wasn't going to do anything we both weren't ready for. I knew I was going to have to wait a few years, but you were the first and only person I ever thought of giving it to. When I looked at my future after college, you were still in it—until you broke my heart at the airport and wrecked all our plans." I shake my head, my hair suddenly wet as it starts to rain harder, Amelia and I both shouting now. "Why did you break us? Was it your commitment issues again, or does running make you feel better than I ever did?"

"I was scared!" she shouts as she looks up at me. Her hair and outfit are soaked as well, but neither of us moves to get under cover. "I was terrified of what I felt for you, so I ran! It was impulsive, I know that, but it's all I've ever done. I'm still trying to fix the part of myself that runs instead of talking about things."

"You ran toward me before, Ames! What made you believe you couldn't come to me about the ring?" I take my glasses off; I can barely see out of them with all the water on the lenses.

"I don't know! I was scared back then!"

"Scared of the idea of marrying me, or scared of committing yourself to someone who just wanted to love you? Or both, Amelia? What was so scary about loving me? Because last I checked, you loved me, and then you turned around and left, taking my heart with you on that plane!" She's crying, I think, and I might be too, but I can barely see between the rain and tears. "I was bleeding out right in front of you that day, and I wanted you to fight for us. I wanted you to risk the idea of being hurt, of us not working out—which wouldn't have happened, by the way. I would have gone anywhere in the world with you! I would've...I would have done anything to be with you forever, Amelia.."

She just shakes her head at me again, her face pinched as she takes in what I said. "You didn't want to marry me, Henry. If I look at myself back then and where I am now, I wouldn't have married me. We made the right choice. It was for the best."

I can't decide if she's trying to convince me or herself of that. I don't think she believes it, not after all we've talked about. "No, Amelia," I say as I cup her face with my hand. "*You* made the choice. You're the one who gave up, but I would have fought for us. I would have risked everything to be loved by you, and that's where we differ. I chose you a thousand times over, and not once did you choose me."

"We wouldn't have worked!" she yells, her lips inches from mine.

I push away from her, needing some space as I rub the back of my neck, my entire body tense and tight. "Do you remember the day I told you I loved you for the first time?'

Her eyes droop as she nods. "What does that have to do with any-thing?"

"Today reminds me a lot of that night. It was raining then too."

That only earns me a shrug.

"I didn't tell you I loved you that day to hear you say it back to me."

"But I did," she says as she comes closer to me. "And I meant it."

"I know you did," I say, emotions bubbling up my chest. "But I told you I loved you because I wanted to make sure you knew you were capable of being loved. I wanted you to know I was hopelessly, completely, insanely in love with you, just as you were. I never wanted to change you, to make you someone else, or anything stupid like that. I wanted you as you were, and I loved you like that too."

The two of us let the words hang in the air, the weight of them crushing me as I think about how much we could have solved just by having a conversation. Amelia Ellis is the worst communicator I've ever met, and all her feelings could have been solved if she had talked to me instead of running to another country.

"So, there you go," she says. "It's all on the table now."

"Yeah, I guess it is," I agree. "It's just hard to believe what one person can do to either fuck up your life or make existing feel better. Sometimes, I think about what would have happened if I never met you."

"Do you wish you never did?" she asks.

"Sometimes," I tell her. "But I would never regret loving someone how I loved you. I grieve what we could have been if we had just talked. One conversation was all it would have taken, Amelia, but for some reason, you didn't want to have one with me."

She's crying harder now, and I can feel the weight crushing the both of us after all we've talked about. "I know, and I will live every single day regretting what I did, Henry. We're grown up now, and everything has changed. I can't get any of the good times back because I ruined it all. Everything is different, and maybe it's too late for us."

That last sentence punctures my chest. "One day, you'll realize, no matter how much you run from something, you'll never be able to beat it. Another day, you'll realize that, despite all you've done, you still deserve to be happy with or without someone. Time will always pass, and we can't get it back, so yeah, sometimes, I wish I never met you in the first place. But I'll never regret giving you the parts of myself I did, because what we had was real, and I would never erase that. I can look back and say I was loved, happy, and it changed me. But I can't save you from your guilt, Amelia. Only you can."

I walk over to her and grab her hand, the two of us crying in the rain, thinking about the life we could have had that is no longer within our grasp.

Then, she lets go of my hand, reaches up to her neck, and unclasps the necklace I bought her before she tucks it into my palm, her eyes meeting mine. She doesn't let go of me, she doesn't say a single word—just a look, the necklace between our palms as the rain soaks us.

It could be a few minutes or hours we stand like this, just existing in one another's presence one last time. As Ella and Leo come out to the parking lot, our hands fall, and it feels like we're both letting each other go.

Amelia and I are no longer tied together how we used to be. We knew one another, we loved one another, but now, we're past that. Someday, I'll look back on this moment and realize this was what was best. We would never work. Amelia has a lot of personal shit to sort through, and I'm finally going to be able to move on from all my unanswered questions.

I'm letting go of what could have been. Amelia is right. In a way, maybe we wouldn't have worked. Maybe we would have crashed and burned, and she just sped up the process by pouring lighter fluid over our relationship.

"Are you guys okay?" Ella asks as she comes over to us.

The two of us nod, not saying a word. As we all pack into the car and head back to the hotel, I find myself wondering what the rest of the week holds. After the wedding, Amelia will be back in England, I'll be back at my apartment, and I'll probably never see these guys again.

But how lucky am I to say I once loved, had a friend group that felt like home, and experienced life alongside these people? Pretty damn lucky, if

I say so myself. Grand Mountain changed my life forever, and one day in thirty years, when I think back on this week, I'll look back with joy in my heart that I had one last chance.

30

As It Was by Harry Styles

Since Paige and Hads are down greeting their guests who arrived this morning, I've taken this morning as an opportunity to apply to some jobs and even read a little bit. It's been an absolutely overwhelming few days, but I'm still grateful I can find these moments to unwind.

Not only have Claire and Jacks finally arrived—Grant has been talking about them nonstop—but so have Nick and Noah, Oliver's only two other friends on the planet. I didn't know they all still talked and kept up with one another, but if I couldn't even keep up with my best friends' lives, then I definitely wasn't going to check up on Oliver's.

Paige and Oliver have kept this wedding small, the only people coming to it being those who truly matter to them, and I'm still honored to fit that bill. Still, I can't help but feel like an outsider. I know I apologized and everything, but the disconnect is still present, and I doubt it will be going away anytime soon.

Sometimes, I think about what would have happened if I never met you.

That one sentence infiltrates my thoughts again and again, because everything he said was right. Sometimes, I wish I didn't know me. I wish I could undo every mistake, bad move, and dumb thing I've ever done, but life doesn't work that way.

I cannot believe I yelled at Henry in the parking lot. I can't believe I got in his face and made a fucking fool of myself in public. It was impulsive and stupid and I was clearly off my medication. If I wasn't, I would have at least thought about the repercussions.

I have to apologize. It was the wrong way to go about all of this, and I regret not only that Henry saw me like that, but that Ella and Leo had to witness it as well.

The entire conversation has been replaying in my mind on a loop. I remember every single thing about the way he looked at me, the number of droplets on his glasses, the feel of his hand when I gave him the necklace back.

And since the end of our conversation felt how it did, I can only assume it was the end. No longer are Henry and I intertwined as we were. When he dropped my hand in that lot, it's like he severed the tie we had with one another, and no matter how shitty that makes me feel, I have to accept it. I know he can't look at me without seeing the girl he loved in college, and I can't look at him without seeing the boy whose heart I ripped to shreds.

The only love I've ever felt was from him, and I don't know if it feels this horrible when other people fall in love, but Henry and I almost felt cosmic, as if some greater power was at work when we first met.

I reach for my necklace, suddenly feeling anxious, only to remember I gave it back to him. I couldn't have kept it anymore, and maybe it was never really mine to begin with.

A Few Hours Later

"WHAT COLOR ARE YOU going to get?" Hads asks me as I flip through the color selection. All of us girls—the book club, Claire, and Sadie—are getting our nails done before the rehearsal dinner tonight. Paige thought we all deserved some girl time while the guys got settled, and I'm excited to have my nails done again.

I usually just do my own, but when I was over in England, I really dropped the ball on self-care. Not only was I falling apart on the inside, but I feel like people could tell on the outside too.

"I'm thinking of a soft blue," I say as I bring the book closer to her. "I can't decide between these two."

"I like the one on the left." Ella pokes her head over, already having chosen a red that looks stunning. Paige is getting French tips, but with lavender instead of white so she matches her bouquet.

"Sold," I say as the technicians all lead us to our spots. Hads, Paige, and Sadie are behind where Ella, Claire and I sit, and I try to fully relax myself as I hold my hands in front of me.

"So, Claire," Hads says from behind us. "How has photographing the Appalachian Avalanche been?"

"It's the best job ever, honestly." She smiles next to me. "Thankfully, I'm only ever doing home games, so I don't have to travel as much, but it is insanely fun."

"That's really cool, Claire," Paige smiles at her. "Has Hads shown you some of the pictures she took for our engagement pictures? The first time I saw them, I cried."

"I saw them on social media." Claire smirks. "I keep telling Hads to start a side business, but she won't listen to me or Grant."

"Maybe if we all bug her, she'll do it," Ella says.

"So, Sadie, what do you do?" I ask, trying to get us all involved in the conversation.

"I work for a hospital." I can feel her smile from behind me.

"That's putting it lightly," Paige says. "She's a registered nurse for the biggest hospital back home."

"Oh, wow," I say, forgetting she was on the path I once was in college. "Good for you."

"Thanks, Amelia. And I hear you live in England, right?"

My throat dries up as soon as she says that. "Mhm."

"That's really cool. And you work for National Geographic?"

"Yup."

"Do you, by chance, know of any good travel spots on the west coast? I'm looking to go somewhere this summer, and I want it to be warm, but I don't really know where to start."

I don't know why I assumed she was going to yell at me on behalf of Paige or something, but her question reminds me not everyone is going to be against me. "I can put a packet together for you after the wedding, if that works?"

"That sounds perfect."

"I told her to go to that one haunted museum in Vegas, but she wasn't interested," Paige says.

"Babe, not everyone is ecstatic about terrifying things like you are," Ella jokes, and the rest of us laugh. "You are the only person I know who willingly watches horror shit by herself just to feel something."

"She's been that way since she was a teenager," Sadie says. "And I am *not* a horror girl, but she always begged me to watch them with her. The only times I ever agreed were on Halloween. Do you remember that one time we watched that freaky movie and were convinced the thing from the movie was hiding in my closet?"

Paige immediately starts laughing, the memory crawling back into her head.

"That was hilarious," she says through her grin. "I've rewatched that one a few times since, and it's actually pretty good."

"You are insane," Hads says. "I'm with you, Sadie. I am not a horror girl at all."

"Well, that's why I love you guys," Paige says. "You may not like those movies, but you've all watched them with me. True friendship is being scared together, and you all put yourselves in front of the screen with me."

"And we're all glad we get to be here to celebrate love this weekend," Ella says. "This is going to be the best wedding ever."

"It will be," Paige says, but I can tell by her tone, something is off.

"Your mom will show up," Hads says to her. "Maybe her phone is just on airplane mode."

"You're right," she says. "It'll be fine."

For the rest of the appointment, the six of us girls trade stories and laugh before the rehearsal dinner. Since I'm not in the wedding party, I have another few hours to myself.

I'm either going to go crazy or I'll actually pick my book up. I hope for the latter as I dive into bed, needing to rest my brain before I see Henry again and decide if it's worth it to apologize to him or to just leave us where we belong—in the past.

31

"Humans are made for connection. We crave that feeling of being in a crowded room and having someone light up when they see our face. It gives you that single split second of a reminder that someone out there is happy you exist."
— *Our Best Kept Secret*, Henry Hayes

After writing almost six thousand words today while everyone was getting ready for the rehearsal dinner, I feel lighter than I have all week. Paige, Oliver and the rest of the wedding party did a walk through for what tomorrow will look like, but all I've done today is write.

The words have been pouring out of me, and after months of pulling my own hair out over this manuscript, things are finally moving in the right direction.

I should feel excited about it, but it's left me feeling a bit empty. After everything that has happened over the past two weeks, I thought I would be elated to write again. That is why I came here, isn't it? I wanted to subject myself to the emotional torture that is being around Amelia because I knew it would work, and it has, but I don't feel how I thought I would.

"Hey, buddy," Grant says as he hands me a drink. As the best man, I assumed he would be hanging around Oliver all night, but he and Paige are mingling. "Figured you would need this."

"Thanks," I say as I take a sip of the mixed drink.

"It's weird," Grant says, taking a sip of his own drink. "Seeing everyone here is an odd feeling I can't quite place."

"Well, this is the first wedding to come out of your group. There's bound to be some big emotions and nostalgia."

"Sometimes, I want to go back," he tells me, smiling from ear to ear as he settles his gaze on Hads across the room. She's talking with Claire, who's leaning against Jacks, but her eyes find him in an instant and she winks. He's blushing when I look back over at him.

"Back to where it all started? Didn't you two hate one another back then?"

"She disliked me, but I was a goner from the moment I saw her." He looks at me. "Do you ever wish to go back when everything felt easier?"

"All the time," I tell him. "There's this ache of remembering I have every once in a while, and somehow, I don't think it will ever go away."

"Well," he taps my arm with a small box, "it's nothing, really, but I wanted to get something for you."

"Why?"

"Because you're my friend, Henry, and I know this week has been tough for you."

I open the small box to find a t-shirt that says 'Team Henry.' I thought Grant made these before Amelia and I got together in college, but maybe I'm misremembering. He must sense my confusion, because he speaks again.

"I'll always be in your corner, man. No matter if you're around or not, I'll always be cheering you on from afar. If you have no fans, it means I'm dead."

I laugh before he brings me in for a hug. "Thank you, Grant."

"Anything for my favorite author." He clinks his glass with mine before we're interrupted.

"I don't mean to break up whatever interaction this is," Amelia says as she steps up to us. "But can I steal Henry from you?"

"Of course." Grant tips his glass to Amelia. "If you need me, I'll be stealing my girl from everyone else."

I try to swallow, but my throat feels thick as her presence overwhelms me.

"I wanted to apologize again. For everything that happened in the parking lot, for leaving, for all of it. And this isn't some guilty, bullshit apology. I'm just...I'm sorry for everything."

I set the shirt on a small table before I turn back to her. "I'm sorry too. For yelling, for doing it in public. I didn't want it to happen like this."

"I know," she says, her face falling as she looks around the room. "I just can't help but think about what would have changed if I just asked you about the ring."

"We can't really know that, Ames."

She shrugs her shoulders before taking another sip of what I assume is a mocktail. She hasn't been drinking this week, and I assume it's because of whatever medication she's taking. "I know, but maybe we would have been celebrating Oliver and Paige together instead of...this."

I shake my head at her before I slam the rest of my drink and set my glass down. "Look, Amelia, I appreciate the apology, really, I do. I just don't know what else you want from me." I'm glad we've cleared the air, but I can't keep doing this. I can't keep throwing myself back into her orbit because I know how this all ends. She has to focus on herself for the time being, and I don't know if we'll find our way back to one another again, but I can't see that happening.

She gave me her necklace back. That to me is the biggest signal in the world that we're done, no longer intertwined how we've been since college.

"We're over, Amelia." The words somehow escape through the thickness in my throat. "What happened between us happened, and we have to accept that we lost one another. I won't give myself over to you again. I won't do it."

She nods. "I've broken your heart, Hen. I know I did, but truth be told, I'm not sure what I want. I'm still adjusting to this new part of my life."

"Well, maybe you should figure that out before you run back to England. I won't let you play with my feelings again, Amelia, especially not when I still have love in my heart for you somehow."

"What?"

I look over at her, confusion and shock on her features, as if she didn't know, as if she couldn't see. "When you left, it didn't just disappear. It lingered, it changed, but it's still there. The other day, I told you I wish I hated you because that is so much easier. I wasn't lying when I said you were the first and only girl I was ever serious about. That kind of love, the one that consumes you fully, doesn't just leave. I love you, and I'm sorry, but I won't let you do this to me again."

"Henry—"

Hads clinks her glass, and everyone gathers around the table. I leave Amelia standing where she is as I head to my seat. I've been placed between Leo and Jacks, and I couldn't be happier to be as far away from Amelia as possible.

"Thank you," Hads says as everyone settles in. "Before we all eat and celebrate my brother and one of my best friends, I wanted to say something."

Hads turns to her brother and Paige, and I swear, I can already hear sniffles. I think that's what is so special about this group. They all love each other endlessly. They've been through so much, so many highs and lows, so many scary moments, yet they all still surround one another with love and warmth.

"Growing up with someone like Oliver as my brother was the biggest honor I could have. Being able to call myself your sister is the greatest thing in the world to me. I can't imagine having someone better to look up to, to make fun of, to talk to when I have no idea what to do in certain situations. He was always a great listener, even when I came to him with my boy troubles."

Everyone laughs.

"Hey, I was right about Grant, thank you very much," he says to the room.

"Appreciate it, bro." Grant nudges Oliver, and Oliver leans away, trying to escape.

"But when I found out Paige over here was in love with him, I freaked out. I almost couldn't wrap my mind around it," she says, pausing to take a breath. "But the first time I saw Oliver smile at her, I knew. I knew these two were meant to be, and I wasn't going to stand in the way of that. Not only did my brother deserve a love that would soften his life, but Paige deserved someone who would move mountains for her. Both of them have found that in the other."

Paige slumps her head on Oliver's shoulder, and he wipes her tears from her face like I've seen him do so many times.

"So, to you two, my brother and my almost-sister, I am so happy to be here to celebrate the beginning of your forever. There are no two people more deserving of this happiness than you, especially after almost dying for one another—literally."

More laughter floats around the table, and I can't believe it was only a few years ago those two were dodging bullets and intruders together. Their kids are going to hear some wild stories in the future, and I can't even imagine them trying to explain how they get together. That's going to be the funniest conversation in the world.

"To Oliver and Paige," Hads says, and we all raise our glasses, toasting to them.

For the rest of the evening, stories are traded over good food and even better dessert.

Maybe this isn't the end for me. Maybe one day, I'll be around a table in a similar manner, trading stories with new friends I haven't met yet.

It's a shame this one didn't work out, but that's the thing about life, right? You have so many chances for a do-over, and even when you feel sad about something ending, there's an entirely new door somewhere, just waiting for you to open it.

Amelia by Mimi Webb

"Tomorrow is the day." Hads sniffles as we all get comfortable on Paige's bed. There was only one thing on the schedule for after the rehearsal dinner, one final slumber party between the four of us.

Since we got back up here, we've all been a mess of emotions. Not only did Hads get us matching lavender silk pajamas for tonight, but we're piled into Paige's bed for one last girls' night before tomorrow.

It's terrifying to think about how time is passing us by so quickly. I wish it would stop. I wish we could go back to that small classroom at Grand Mountain and relive all the wonderful moments. All the laughter we shared. All the books we argued over. All the charts Hads made for us until, eventually, our group got larger. I want to live in these memories and never come out.

I'm nothing if not a person who longs to return to the moments I took for granted when I was in them. I often find myself wishing to go back, to have a redo, but I can't. All we can do now is reminisce, the memories floating in and out of our heads as we talk about them.

"Do you guys think we're friends in every universe?" Paige asks as we all settle in.

"Where did that come from, P?" Ella asks, grabbing her water bottle.

"Well, we read all these books about romance and platonic love, and in them, there's always that feeling of knowing those characters will always find one another. I guess I just wondered if you guys ever think about who we would all be if we weren't in this timeline right now."

"I don't think there's a universe where we all don't find one another," Hads says, leaning into her almost-sister.

"It would upset the balance," I say as the girls laugh. "I'm glad you guys welcomed me back. I'm sure there's a universe where I don't get a second chance."

"It wouldn't be the same without you, Ames." Paige grabs my hand. "We're glad you're back."

I look at Hads and Ella, and they nod in agreement.

"No more apologizing," Ella says. "Let's just be in one another's company, okay?"

"Got it." I smile. "Are you guys hungry?"

"I could always go for some snacks." Paige answers.

"What do you say we head for the kitchen and sit on the floor while we eat?" I ask. "For old time's sake?"

After the words come out of my mouth, I realize how sad they are. Here I am, sitting with my three favorite people in the world, telling them we should sit on the floor because those are some of my favorite memories. So many nights, I met Paige in the kitchen and sat with her after she had a nightmare, or she couldn't sleep, and we ate snacks until the sun came up.

As the four of us grab blankets, water bottles, and ourselves, we head for the kitchen area and plop down in our spots, grabbing snacks and passing them around, huge smiles on all our faces as we settle in.

"Do you guys remember when we got drunk on Ella's birthday and ended up on her kitchen floor until the sun came up?" Hads asks us, and we all laugh. "That was one of my favorite moments of sophomore year."

"What I remember is you talking about how dreamy Grant's eyes were that night," Ella jokes, and Hads throws a chip at her.

"It was Amelia's fault! She was the one talking about lakes, and it made me think of his eyes!"

"I haven't been that drunk since then," Paige laughs. "But my favorite part of that night was the next morning, when we made breakfast and listened to music. It was another one of those moments where I healed my inner child. There were so many mornings I either skipped breakfast or made it myself because my mom was too busy."

A few tears fall from Paige's eyes; I know she's still worried about not having heard from her mom. She's supposed to be here tomorrow, but the radio silence has us all worried she won't show.

"You guys healed every bit of my inner child that you never broke in the first place. I really love you guys so much. I can't imagine my life without you all in it."

"Paige, oh my gosh, I cannot keep crying," Ella says as she grabs the tissue box from the counter.

"To be fair, this is the most I've seen Amelia cry ever," Hads jokes as she hands me a tissue. "It's still freaky seeing you have emotions, but I like it. It suits you."

"Thanks...I think," I chuckle as I wipe my tears with my pajama sleeve. "To be honest, it's still weird to me. I think my therapist broke me."

"More like healed you, Ames," Ella tells me, grabbing my hand. "And we're thankful for her doing God's work."

I shove her arm as we all laugh until we cry.

I wish I could send a message to the version of myself back in England who was terrified, lonely, and worried she was broken. I would tell her we made some mistakes, but we survived them. I would tell her we lost our friends, but we were smart enough to fight to get them back. I would tell her life doesn't end when you graduate college—it actually begins, and you'll fail a thousand times at a thousand different things, but you'll come back from them every single time.

I would tell her she started completely over once, and she can do it again.

No matter how many times life tried to knock me down, throw me off track, I eventually figured it out, despite feeling every time like it was over.

I would tell her the friends she left would forgive her, and eventually, we would sit on the floor with them again and laugh until our ribs hurt, until we cried, because we're all grateful to be next to one another.

"Do you guys want to know what I thought a lot about tonight?"

"Sure," Hads says as she passes a snack to Paige.

"The Halloween party our senior year. The one where Ella and Leo matched." I smile as I remember that night. "That night feels like a fever dream looking back. I mean, now Ella and Leo are dating. Oliver and Paige are getting married. Hads and Grant are still going strong, and even though I ruined everything with Henry, that night makes me remember all the good things about college with you guys, like a mirror to the one we just had, except this time, I didn't fall asleep early."

"That was a weird night," Hads says. "I don't know how I was so oblivious about Paige and Oliver. Looking back on it, I was an idiot."

"Maybe a little bit," I say as she throws a chip at me. "I'm kidding!"

"That was an interesting night," Ella says, a blush creeping up her cheeks. "Even now, I would still swing that bat at him. He still pisses me off, but I can't imagine not loving him as much as I do now. God, how everything has changed. It's making my heart want to explode."

"Mine too," I say as I grab another tissue. "It's weird thinking about how things have changed but also kind of stayed the same."

"That's what growing up feels like." Paige smiles sadly to herself. "I used to wish I was an adult when I was a kid, but now that we're here, I wish it would calm down a little. I know we're all still in our twenties, but for some reason, it feels like our lives are almost over."

"They're not, though," Hads reminds us. "We have so much time to change, to grow, to experience all the beautiful and terrifying things life has to offer. And the best part is, we get to experience it all together. That's the best gift this life has brought us, at least in my opinion."

"Agreed," I say as I raise my water bottle, the rest of them following suit. "One final toast between the four of us. To the tiny classroom where this all started, and to the lives we made together."

We clink our water bottles together, and for the rest of the night, we're just four girls who happened to find one another at a small campus in Virginia.

Everything is going to be fine, I remind myself. As long as I have these girls, how could it not? As we all fall asleep on the floor of this hotel suite, I'm blasted with a wave of not wanting to miss out on these moments right now.

I can't keep living in the past, wishing I did things differently. I have to live here and now, because one day, this will all be a distant memory. I don't want to waste these moments thinking about what could have been. I want to *live* them with my best friends.

As my eyes flutter shut, I make a promise to myself to only look forward, because past me got me to where I am now, and I should be thanking her for finding her way back home to these girls. Through the struggle, through it all, I've come out stronger than I ever knew I was capable of.

Thank you. I forgive you, I say in my mind as I finally drift off to sleep, dreaming of sand between my feet and ocean waves in the background.

33

Feels Like by Gracie Abrams

"It's my wedding day!" Paige shouts as she sprints around the room, Hads and Ella next to me as she jostles me awake from the floor. "Wake up, Ames!"

"I'm up. I'm up," I say, smiling as soon as I see the three of them. "Holy shit. It's tomorrow."

"I'm going to make pancakes," Ella says as she stretches before giving Paige a big hug. "Happy wedding day, Paigey."

"What the fuck?" Hads says as she grabs her phone. "Ugh, I'll be right back."

"What's going on?" I ask her, confused.

"My brother is having some sort of freak out over the color of his tie, according to Grant." She sighs heavily as she whips the door open. "I knew this was coming."

Ella and I start laughing as she leaves, wondering what a freak out from Oliver would look like. I'm sure even his freak outs are bland.

"Paige, why don't you start the music and get the bathroom set up with all your makeup? I can grab your dress and hang it on the door."

Just then, Claire and Sadie join us, Claire's camera in her hand. I'm already emotional thinking about seeing these pictures after the fact.

"Sounds good!" Paige says, her smile bursting. "Sadie, did you bring the thing?"

"I did." She smiles, handing Paige a small velvet bag. "Your something blue."

Paige throws her arm around her best friend before she drags Claire and Sadie into her room, leaving me and Ella in the kitchen. I don't even bother asking Ella if she wants me to help—I jump right in, grabbing some plates and utensils for us all.

"Are we going to ever talk about what happened in the parking lot that night?"

Her question doesn't surprise me. In fact, I thought she would have asked me about it before. "In college, I found an engagement ring in Henry's apartment hidden in a book."

The spatula falls from her hand as she looks over at me setting the table. "What?"

"I found the ring and ran from him, Ella. It was the weakest moment of my life, same as what I did at the airport. I was weak, and I left because of how terrified forever felt to me at the time."

She flips a few pancakes on the griddle. "You came back, Amelia. I think you keep forgetting that. Yeah, sure, you had a weak moment, but you had enough strength to come back and fight for your friendships. Don't you think you could do the same with him?"

"I don't want to hurt him again, Ells." I loved him and then I broke him. I don't think I have the strength to love him again if I know, deep down, I might panic and leave like I did last time. I'm trying to do better, but the what-ifs don't ever stop.

And then she says two words that stop me in my tracks. "Then don't."

Sometimes, it really is as simple as that, but with me and Henry, I don't think it ever could be. We're messy. Complicated. We're too intertwined, and we can't just forget the past. I really wish it were that simple. If it was, I'd run right back to him at this very moment.

I have no time to form any words before Hads comes back into the room, her face a sliver away from laughing her ass off. "My brother is insane. It's official."

"Well, jail will do that to a person," I joke, and Ella throws a chocolate chip at me.

"Did Oliver figure out a tie?" Ella asks, and Hads nods.

"And he calls me the dramatic one." She shakes her head. "He settled on the one he originally picked because Leo told him to go with his gut. That's all it took, and the freak out was for nothing."

Sadie pokes her head outside of Paige's room as Ella finishes the pancakes. "Are there mimosas, by any chance?"

"I knew I liked you," Ella says as she grabs the orange juice and champagne, already one step ahead of her.

AFTER THE MOST NOSTALGIC morning of my life and having to hold back my tears, I'm now standing on the beach, away from the hustle and bustle a few yards from me.

Weddings are notorious for thinking about love, life, and everything that comes with celebrating two people starting their forever together. All I can seem to think about is Henry.

At the rehearsal dinner, he told me he still had love for me. That almost knocked me over, him saying that. It brought me right back to the moment he said it for the first time in that grocery store parking lot. I've replayed that moment a lot when I've felt unlovable, and I wish he knew how much that one conversation affected me.

Henry Hayes is the only proof I have of being loved, and I destroyed him.

Could I still love him? The answer is obvious. Of course I could, but *should* I? Should I subject him to this version of myself, who has no clue what the hell she's doing? I can't. I can't throw myself back into his orbit if I don't even love or understand who I am yet.

Maybe we could slowly get back to being friends, but I can't force my way back into his life just because I regret the mistakes I made.

Ella is right, though. I know I don't want to hurt him, and I don't have to. I could just fade from his life as if I didn't exist, and we'll forever be a could have been. I'm not sure how this ends, Henry and I, and he'll always be the biggest what-if of my life.

Neither of us can erase the memories of what we once were. If only there were some way to do that, but even then, I wouldn't ever erase him from my head. I showed him every part of myself I hated, that I was unsure about. I gave him every piece of me, even if not vocally all the time. Henry understood the songs I would play for him, understood those were me telling him the things I struggled to say.

I take a deep breath as I stare out at the ocean, feeling the water hitting my feet, my shoes hanging from my hand on my side. Maybe that's what we are. We're not stars dying beside one another in the sky. We're not an unfinished story he has yet to write. We're a wave coming from the ocean, heading to shore, only to return to wherever it came from. This part of our story is simply the wave hitting the sand, some of the water dissipating beneath someone's feet.

I'm not totally sure of anything in my life, but I am sure Henry and I are meant to be intertwined. I thought there was nothing left between us, but him saying what he did at the rehearsal dinner has given me hope, and even if it might be false, I still have to try.

My phone buzzes, and as I grab it from my small purse and see who the message is from, I have to grip my phone tighter so it doesn't fall into the water.

> **Kacey: We can absolutely set up a meeting. Just send me some times you're available and I'll make it work for you, Amelia.**

> **Kacey: I'm glad you're back over here. You've been missed.**

I don't have any time to process the message before I feel a hand on my arm.

"Paige needs us," is all she says before I follow her lead. By the time we get to Paige, my heart drops to my chest.

"Ames is here," Ella says softly. "What's going on, babe? Are you having second thoughts?"

She shakes her head into Hads' shoulder before she grabs her phone from the pocket of her wedding dress, opening it to a text conversation. I know all of us are feeling the exact same thing as we read it.

Feeling guilty about missing half of her child's life is the lamest excuse for not showing up for her wedding—especially after they've been working to mend their relationship.

"She's not coming," Paige sniffles as a single tear drops from her face. "My own mother is going to miss my wedding."

Hads blots her tears from her face before she gets right into Maid of Honor mode. "It's going to be okay, Paigey. Do you want me to ask Grant to walk you down the aisle? I'm sure he would do it."

"Or I can grab my mom?" Sadie offers. "We always joked she was like a second mother to you when we were kids."

"Or I could do it?" Hads says. "You are marrying my brother, so it would work, right?"

We all nod in agreement, but Paige shakes hers. Her sadness is still written all over her face, but a small smile comes through.

"No." She walks around a little bit, pacing while her dress trails behind her. "I'm going to walk myself down the aisle. As long as I've got my girls, everything is going to be okay."

We all hug before I go back to my seat behind the front row next to Jacks. Claire is off to the side, her camera at the ready.

The music begins, and I know nobody here is going to make it through the ceremony with dry eyes. The love that blankets our corner of this beach is tangible, and I'm grateful I get to be here to witness it.

34

"Everyone always told me the true foundation of a good marriage was love. I'm not sure that's true. I think it's friendship. My wife and I have had some rocky moments, but at the end of the day, we're still the same two people who fell for one another way back when. Deep down, those versions of us still exist. Sometimes, they're just buried." — *Our Best Kept Secret*, **Henry Hayes**

As I watch Oliver, Grant, and Leo take their places, soft music sifting through the speakers, I can't help but steal glances over at Amelia. I had to stop myself from going over to her when she was sticking her feet in the water, and when I finally decided to pull the plug and go talk to her, Ella pulled her away.

I should take that as a sign we're done, but for some reason, I still can't shake Amelia's hold on my heart or my head. I thought our conversations would purge her from my system, but it didn't. I wish it did. I wish I could unknow her. I wish I could leave her in my memories, but the stupid part of me thinks we might be able to work this out. She just needs to prove she can fight for me and stick around. Which already, I know, isn't going to work because she's going back to England after this is over.

I still have the ring my mom gave me. It sits in my drawer next to some pens, random scribbles on notes, and junk. I put it away because I couldn't bear to look at it. It reminds me of her. It reminds me she ran from me. It's a constant reminder of Amelia because she's still the only person I ever thought of giving it to. Even though we've changed so much these past few years, that has stayed the same. That ring was always meant to be hers, and she was the only girl I wanted to give it to.

I come back to reality as I see the girls start to walk down the aisle: Sadie first, then Ella, then Hads. Everyone stands as the music changes to Paige's favorite song, but this version is more instrumental. When Paige emerges by herself, her bouquet in her hands, tears already in her eyes, I know I want to feel that one day.

I want to love someone with my entire body. With every atom, I want that. And as Noah hands me a tissue, I realize I'm getting emotional at the thought of simply loving someone so much, their mere presence moves me to tears.

The thing that sends me over the edge is when I look at Oliver, Mr. Unemotional, with tears streaming down his face.

Their love is absolutely beautiful, and no two people deserve this happiness more than them. The things they've been through would have crumbled me, but these two are strong, and their love for one another makes them even stronger.

Paige eventually reaches the altar, handing her bouquet off to Hads as she blots Paige's face, Hads handing Grant some tissues. He's officiating the wedding, but he needs to be able to speak to do so. The rest of us sit down in our chairs as the wedding begins.

"You look beautiful," Oliver says as he grabs Paige's hands, pressing a small kiss to her knuckles.

"I love your tie," she jokes. "It's as perfect as you are."

Grant clears his throat before speaking into the microphone. "We are gathered here today to witness the love Paige and Oliver share. I know all of us can attest to them being perfect for one another, and as I look around at this group of people, I feel incredibly lucky to be a part of this moment."

My head shifts to Amelia out of habit, and she turns at the same time I do, throwing me a small smile as she reaches for her neck, the necklace she used to wear no longer there.

"I'll keep this short and sweet, because I know this one wants to marry this girl as soon as he can." Grant pauses as we all laugh. Then, he goes through the usual things, and as we get to the vows section, the microphone goes to Oliver.

"Paige Yarrow, I once stood on a beach just like this one and told you you were my sunrise. I still stand by that statement, but you are *everything* to me. Every smile you throw in my direction, every time your face lights up, all of it. I feel like the luckiest fucker on the planet that those are somehow pointed at me." Tissues are passed around, and I take a few. Being able to witness them from where they started until now is making me emotional.

"You are the strongest person I know. You are the light of my life, and I promise I will never try to dim you. I promise to fill our house with tote bags, physical copies of movies we love, and so much happiness, we don't know where to put it. I promise to brighten your life, to hold you when you cry over dog videos on the internet, and to love you until the moon and the sun finally meet in the sky."

She smiles at him, her face full of tears as the microphone turns to her.

"Oh, shit," is all she says, the crowd laughing through our own tears. "I always thought I was destined to be alone, to give more love than I would ever receive. But as soon as I met Oliver, I realized the future had different plans for me. I went from being a lonely kid to someone who had everything to lose, and now, as I stand here today, I feel like the luckiest person in the entire world. Because not only do I feel loved every single day when I open my eyes, but I never have to go to bed crying anymore. And even if I am crying over dog videos, or whatever it is, I know I have two strong arms to wrap myself in that will hold me and tell me everything's okay."

She takes a deep breath before she continues.

"Oliver Baker, I promise to love you with everything I've got. I promise to stop trying to solve cold cases in the middle of the night. I promise to *never* try to solve a murder case ever again, because, well, we all know how that ended last time."

Everyone laughs, but Oliver simply tilts his head at his almost-wife.

"And most of all, I promise to show you every single day that you deserve to feel as loved as you make me feel, because even in the silence, you are loved. You never have to question it. I will go anywhere in the world as long as I'm with you, Ol."

The rest of the ceremony goes off with even more tears, Oliver's parents smiling ear to ear. As they're pronounced husband and wife and they walk toward their collective future together, I'm grateful to have witnessed such a small part of their story with my own two eyes.

Maybe someday, I can have this. Maybe one day, I'll be able to look back and say the journey was worth it. Maybe instead of writing happy endings for my characters, I can finally have one for myself.

Everything happens for a reason, right?

35

Ghostin by Ariana Grande

I'M GOING TO BE hungover from this trip for weeks, socially and physically.

I've missed my friends, and I made the right decision coming back here for good. I can't wait to keep making more memories alongside them.

Everyone scattered last night. Well, everyone let Paige and Oliver have the boys' suite to themselves for their wedding night. All the boys roomed with their girls, though Henry left during the reception, according to Grant.

Part of me still thinks we could work it out. If given the chance, I'd love him right this time. I'd love him louder than I did. I'd show him off every moment I could because he's an incredible person. He *deserves* to be loved out loud, with no hiding or secrets.

I need to talk to him again, but I'm going to give him some space before I do. I can't just jump into this with no plan. I need to prove to myself I can keep showing up for people. I have to work on my own shit before I can love Henry how he deserves. Plus, seeing me in such close proximity for two weeks was bound to fuck his mind up, so he needs some room to digest his feelings.

I zip up my last suitcase before heading out to the rest of my friends, all of them gathered by the table in the kitchen, looking at something. As soon as Grant locks eyes with me, he clears his throat, looking guilty.

"Uh, hi?" I say as I drag my stuff over with the rest of their luggage. "What's going on?"

"Nothing!" Paige says, her adorable white sweat-set making her pop even more than she usually does. "I'm actually afraid to ask, but when will we see you again? I'm assuming your flight to England is today or tomorrow."

Ella locks eyes with me, and I forgot I only mentioned to her that very first night that I was staying.

"I'm not leaving."

"What?" Hads questions.

"Like at all?" Grant smirks towards me.

"I swear, if you say the words for now, I'm going to punch you," Paige threatens with the biggest smile on her face.

"God, we really can't get rid of you, can we?" Oliver rolls his eyes before Paige and Leo smack him. "Ow!"

"How is it that you just got married, and you're still an arsehole?" Leo jokes.

"When it comes to me, Oliver will always be annoyed," I say, and he nods as he agrees with me. "But I'm not leaving. I'll be here for the long haul, if you'll all still have me."

Paige shrieks, and Grant envelops me in a hug.

"This is the best day ever!" Paige squeezes me the hardest, and even after everyone else pulls away, she's still holding me. I can't help the smile that comes from my face.

"Oof, that's not what you want to hear the day after your wedding, is it, buddy?" Grant elbows Oliver in the side.

"I'm going to go pack up the car," Oliver says.

"I'll join you, mate," Leo says as he grabs some suitcases. I'm driving home with Ella and Leo while the Baker family and Grant drive in the other car. Grant and Hads are dropping Paige and Oliver off at the airport for their honeymoon in Vermont.

"So, you're actually staying?" Hads questions again, probably not believing me.

"Yeah. I quit my job and sold my place in England. My routine is all out of whack, but that's a decently easy adjustment. A fresh start, if I can even call it that."

"You absolutely can," Grant says. "And if I say so myself, you're already doing a great job."

"Thanks. I mean, I don't have a job or health insurance or any of those important adult things, but I do have a place to live. And I have you all again, so I'm doing alright." I smile as I look around the room at my favorite people.

"You'll figure it out, Ames," Ella tells me. "We'll help in any way we can."

"We can have book club in person again!" Paige's excitement is making all the difficult stuff I've been through worth it. I didn't think anyone would care that I was back for real, but of course, I underestimated the people around me again.

I really need to call my therapist when I get back.

"I'm excited for this new chapter," I say as I spot a small box on the table. "It's going to be good."

"When I get back from Vermont, we're going to have a huge debrief, okay?" Paige looks at me for confirmation, and I nod my head. "Good! Ah, it will be just like old times!"

"I can't wait," Ella says as she gathers our remaining bags. "Now, let's go help the boys load all this up."

"Paigey, you're not lifting a thing!" Grant says as she goes for her suitcase. "Neither are you, Hades."

"You're going to get all of this stuff downstairs by yourself?" Hads questions him. "No way."

She grabs a suitcase in each hand as he drags a hand down his face.

"Just go with them, G," I say as I head for the door, but he stops me with his arm across my body. "What?"

"I have something for you," he says as he grabs a small box from the table and hands it to me. "I don't know what it is, but he gave it to me before he left and told me to give it to you."

I stare down at this small box, wondering what Henry could have given Grant for me before he left. Part of me is sure I should never open this box, just leave us in the past. But the selfish part of my brain feels like there is hope behind this gift, whatever it is.

"Do you want to open it now? I can leave—"

"Stay. Please. If I'm alone, I'll go insane or something," I say as I carefully open the box, a small note falling out. As Grant reaches for the note, I'm shocked by what I see staring back at me.

The necklace Henry once bought me—the one I gave back to him—shines back at me, and my heart is going to explode. He gave it back. Why did he give it back?

"Here," Grant says as he hands me the small paper. "I only read some of it, and it's not my fault. It's not folded."

I chuckle as I take the necklace out of the box, already fastening it around my neck. As soon as it's around me, I feel calmer. I don't know what's in this necklace, or maybe it's a psychological thing, but it has always been helpful in calming my racing mind.

This was never meant to be mine. It will always belong to you. Take care of it and yourself, Mills.
I hope you find what you're looking for, and someday, maybe I can hear all about it.
Never forget you were loved by someone, even if it was only for a moment. This necklace is proof of that.
– H

A tear slips from my eyes before I can stop it. Grant says nothing as he wraps me in his arms, comforting me when it's the furthest thing I deserve right now.

Henry Hayes is proof I can be loved, and I had it, even if it was momentary. It still existed, and that's enough.

I CAN'T STOP STARING at the note he left me. None of us have said anything during the drive back besides Ella getting mad at the traffic and Leo trying to calm her down. Neither of them asked me about the tears in my eyes when Grant and I got down to the car, and my brain is spiraling in about forty different ways.

Henry and the love we shared was...God, it was legendary. It was everything.

But does what I did negate it all? I don't think it can, but maybe in his mind, it does. All I can see when I close my eyes are his somber, broken, and disheartened eyes. Until he's out of my system, my memories, my everything, I think that's all I'll see.

"Amelia?" Ella's eyes meet mine in the rearview mirror. "Did you hear what I said?"

"No." I grab my headphones out of my ears. They're not even on. That's how I know I'm struggling—I didn't even bother turning on my music to cloud out the rest of my thoughts.

"Told you, darling." Leo smirks. "Did Grant try to clone you or something? Did he make you do a blood oath while you two were up there?"

"No, but weirdly enough, both of those things have almost happened," I laugh. "I'm just thinking about Henry. He gave me back my necklace before he left."

"I noticed you wearing it when you came back down. I was going to ask about it, but I didn't want to press," Ella says. "You know he's not going anywhere, right? And neither are you, might I add."

"What do you mean?" I ask her.

"Just because your mind thinks this is the end doesn't mean it has to be. Henry is in Virginia. You're in Virginia. It's never really over until you both decide it is. Did you guys talk about that in any of your arguments—I mean, conversations?"

That earns an eye roll, but I know she's coming from a place of love. "We never explicitly stated it was completely over, I guess. But that feels like a technicality, Ells. I don't know if Henry can ever get past what I did to him."

"The girls and I did," she reminds me. "Granted, what you did to him was a lot worse—"

"True that," Leo jumps in. "Sorry."

"It's fine," I tell him. "I know you all got past me ghosting, but—"

"Stop," is all she says. "If you're truly serious about trying to win Henry back, then prove it. If you do what you did with us, then you two could be really happy. When you two just met, I almost didn't recognize you. You were softer. You smiled and joked around more. You were in love, Amelia, and if you really love Henry like we all think you do, then work it out."

"But don't just run back to him because he's familiar. You have to truly love him, or it won't work," Leo adds, and even Ella is surprised, looking over at him in the passenger seat.

"Leo's right," she says with an eye roll. "You have to really want to make it work. Do you think you can do that with Henry?"

"I don't want to hurt him again."

"Then don't, Ames. Fight like hell to break your own pattern of running, and prove to the people you love that you're here for the long haul. Don't let a few mistakes keep you from the life you deserve. But if you're going to fight for him, you better fight like hell, because he deserves that and more."

I touch the necklace again, dragging the pendant on the chain.

Of course I still love him, and not just because he was my first and only love. Henry truly feels like the missing piece I've been looking for my entire life. When I was with him, I felt whole again. I felt like I mattered, like I was good enough.

He filled up my cup that he never spilled in the first place. I didn't have to beg him to love me, he just did, as if it was as easy for him as breathing.

"Don't you guys love the groveling trope?" Leo says.

Ella and I can't help but laugh. He's right.

"Yes," I say with a smile. "I'll be living in mine for as long as it takes, it seems."

I'm going to love him right this time. I'm going to prove to him he's worth it, because he always has been.

36

Two Weeks Later

Miles to Go by Gregory Alan Isakov

"I'M SO HAPPY TO see you!" Paige squeals as she throws her arms around me.

"Thanks," I smile. "But can we actually get inside your apartment? I'm freezing."

"Oh, yeah." She lets go as she ushers me inside, everyone else staring back at me.

"What?"

"I assumed you were a figment of my imagination," Oliver jokes as he goes to the kitchen for a bottle of water.

"I'll take this to-go in case you poisoned it." I pat him on the arm, and he moves away from me.

"I wouldn't waste poison on you, Ames."

"Aw," I say, my hand on my heart.

"Guys," Hads threatens. "Don't make me get my ruler out."

Oliver and I look at one another before we move to sit down, Paige clearing a spot on the couch for me. Oliver takes the floor in front of his wife.

"So, lovebirds," I joke, "how was the honeymoon?"

"Ugh." Paige's head falls back. "It was amazing. It was the New England trip of my dreams. Thanks to Grant and his mom, we had the most adorable cabin on the water, and hearing the birds chirp when we woke up in the mornings was so peaceful. It was the detox we both needed." She puts her hands on Oliver's shoulders. "Right, Ol?"

He nods. "It was wonderful, but my favorite part is getting to call you my wife now." He presses a kiss to one of her hands, and we all groan.

"We get it, you're married." I roll my eyes.

"Do you have pictures?" Ella asks.

"I made a PowerPoint!" Paige says as she hops up to get her computer, I assume.

"I've heard the scenery is phenomenal up there," Leo says as he sips his drink. "Darling, we should plan a trip at some point."

"As soon as you're not so busy at work, that sounds like a plan." Ella tilts her head at him. "You're a worse workaholic than I was."

"Am," Leo and Grant say at the same time.

"Oh, come on," Ella groans. "I own my own business, which means I can work from anywhere! Vacations are easy for me."

"No offense, Ells, but when was the last time you actually took a break?" I ask her, and she goes quiet. "Exactly."

"Oh, don't even." She points her drink at me. "You dropped off the face of the Earth."

"She's got a point," Oliver agrees.

"You know what?" I scoff. "I deserved that one, but let's not make that a longer running joke than Oliver almost ending up in jail."

"Ha!" Oliver says as he stands up. "You said almost!"

I don't think I've ever heard him speak this loud in my entire life.

"You know what I meant."

"No! You can't joke about it anymore because you said I *almost* ended up in jail, not that I was in jail!" Oliver looks around for support, but nothing happens.

"You were behind bars," Grant says.

"And you lied to me for months," Hads says.

"You told me you were over that! Don't tell me you're still mad at me?" he asks his sister, and she simply shrugs.

"It was a stressful day, Oliver."

"Paige almost got killed," Ella reminds us. "And you were behind bars."

"Sometimes, I think I'm happy not having known you all well prior to last year, but other times, I feel like I missed all the crazy shit." Leo shakes his head. "Probably for the best. I would have made it worse, knowing my track record."

"Okay, everyone sit down," Paige shouts as she plugs her laptop into the television. "What were you guys just talking about?"

All of us are quiet for a few seconds before Oliver sits down and Ella speaks up.

"We're just excited to see pictures."

Paige smiles before she launches into a very thorough slideshow of her honeymoon. I have to admit, some of the pictures of the food they had make me jealous. I desperately need a vacation, but in a way, I was on an extended one for two years.

It feels good to be around these people again. Over these past two weeks, all I've done is talk to my therapist, figure out a plan for a new routine over here, and apply to jobs in case the one with Kacey ends up being a dead end. It's been a big adjustment, but the girls have been here for me through all of it. They even helped me shop for furniture a few days ago.

An hour later, Paige finishes, and we all clap, not only for the artistry, but because the last photo was a picture of Oliver falling off a paddleboard.

"So, what's going on with everyone else?" Paige asks as she closes her laptop.

"Same old shit, really," Ella says. "It was only two weeks, P. All of us mostly went to work and did our usual routines."

Everyone nods before they all turn to me, as if they're waiting for me to say something.

"Uh, can I help you?"

"Has anything…" Grant pauses, "interesting happened to you lately?"

"With you and perhaps another person…" Paige smirks as she sits back down, her eyes bright and wide, as if she's waiting for me to give her the right answer.

These two could not be more obvious.

"Wow, way to be nonchalant, you guys," Leo jokes.

"Oh, come on!" Paige scooches closer to me. "What is going on between you and Henry? Are you going to get him back or what?"

"Paige—" Ella starts, but I cut her off.

"It's okay," I say with a small smile. "I want to try, but I have no idea what to do or where to start."

"You really want him back?" Hads questions, and I nod.

"I'm terrified, and I really don't trust myself yet, but I will," I tell them. "Of course I still love him. After all we went through, after all I did, it was hard to just let him go. I don't think I'll ever be unlatched from him, and I don't want to be."

Another thing I've done over the last two weeks is think about the guy I'm still in love with. I can't get him out of my head.

"Just don't fuck it up again," Oliver says. "He doesn't deserve that. Not again, Amelia."

"Can it, inmate. I'm trying to be better, to do better. Have some faith in me," I tell him, and he holds his hands up in defeat.

"So, what are you going to do?" Leo asks me. "Have you figured that out yet?"

"No," I say as I grab my necklace. "I figured you guys could help me." I look around at the girls, and before I know it, Paige has grabbed her whiteboard. She and Hads are setting it up, drawing some sort of list.

"Okay," Hads says as she waves her ruler around as if it's a pointer. "We need some suggestions, people. Let's hear them."

"This feels all too familiar," Oliver says. "Why do we do this so often?"

"What? Use the whiteboard?" Hads asks him.

"Yeah. We can't just talk things out?"

"No, Ol," Paige smirks. "We're visual people."

"Can we focus?" I ask before my mind starts to spiral.

"Sorry," Hads says. "Okay, you could send him flowers once a week or something?"

I shake my head. "That's not enough."

"You could make some sort of public grand gesture to show him you're not scared of loving him," Paige suggests, a glint in her eye as she speaks. "Grand gestures are important, right?"

Ella shakes her head. "Not in their case."

"What do you mean, Ella?" I ask her.

"All Henry has wanted from you, or at least what I think he wants from you, is for you to prove you're going to stop running."

"Yeah, that tracks," Grant says as Hads scribbles it down.

"As long as you show up for him like you have for us, I think he'll realize you're serious about making it work," Ella tells me. "I mean, over the last two weeks, I've seen you more than when we were in college. You're putting the work in with us, Ames. You essentially have to do the same thing with him. It's not going to be easy, but as long as you keep showing up, that's all he'll need to trust you again."

"Do you think that's all it will take? If I were him, I wouldn't trust her one bit," Hads says before she apologizes. "Sorry."

"I was thinking the same thing," I tell her.

"Prove to him you're planting roots and making a home here." Paige smiles. "Henry will come around like we all did. You have to love him loudly, Ames. You have to run toward him when you're scared, not away, and I think he understands it will take some more time for you to do that. But I'm also betting he's willing to give you another chance, especially with how he looked at you during the wedding."

"You think?" I ask, and everyone nods.

"The guy was heartbroken, but those eyes?" Leo shakes his head. "The eyes never lie, and he is still madly in love with you, even if you did break his heart."

"He doesn't even know I'm still in Virginia," I tell them. "I never told him I was leaving England." Everyone starts shouting, and I get immediately overwhelmed. "What?"

"Why didn't you tell him?" Hads asks, shouting at me.

"It never came up. We had more pressing things to discuss!"

"You have to go show him you're back for good!" Grant says as he scribbles something down on a piece of paper. "Someone get Amelia's purse for her."

"What? Why?"

"You have to tell him, Ames." Grant hands me the paper while Ella grabs my purse. "Here's his address. Go."

"Right now? I thought we were going to have—"

"Movie night can wait! This is more important," Paige shouts, her voice filled with excitement. "Go, Ames!"

And they practically shove me out the door. As soon as I get outside, my heart starts to race as I sprint to my car, needing to show Henry I'm capable of planting roots and building a home somewhere.

Not anywhere, though. Here. Here in Virginia, with the family I never knew I needed but somehow was lucky enough to find.

My mind went into tunnel vision mode as soon as Grant gave me Henry's address. I left right from Paige's place, not wanting to waste another second. I've wasted enough time in my life, and I won't spend more of it letting Henry slip away from me.

I want our life to start as soon as it can. I know it's going to be a long time until he fully trusts me again, but I'm going to put in the work. He is worth it.

I don't want to erase our past together—there's no way we could—but I want to use it to remind myself what not to do, to remind myself what happened when I left him the first time. I'm going to learn from every mistake I've made, and I'm going to try my fucking hardest to not make them again.

I'm still a human, so I know I'm still going to mess up, but hopefully, this time, I won't be consciously aware of my fuckups.

I turn into the lot of his building, no music playing through my speakers as I practically jump out of my car. I find his door immediately, and before I think about turning around, I knock.

The small light outside flicks on, and it only takes a few seconds for the door to open. When he sees it's me on the other end, his mouth drops open ever so slightly, and I can't tell if it's because he's surprised to see me here, or if he wants me to leave.

"Hi," is all I can say, kicking myself for somehow being the most awkward person on the planet.

"Hey," he says as he puts his hands in his pockets, the door swaying between the two of us. "Do you want to come in?"

"No," I say as I grab my necklace, needing a bit more strength. "This won't take long." That earns me a head tilt. "I need to know if you could ever forgive me."

"What?"

"Please," I beg. "I need to know if some day, by some miracle, you could forgive me for breaking us. I might not be sure of anything in my life at this moment, but the one thing I am sure about is you. I was giving you space after the wedding, but I can't do that anymore. When I realized I still loved you, after all this time, I came right over."

"So this is a recent revelation, then, isn't it?"

I shake my head.

"Don't play with my feelings again, Amelia," he says as his head drops. "You know what I said to you at the rehearsal dinner, and if this is some—"

I cut him off. "It's not. I just need to know if you can ever forgive me. I need to know if we have a shot at being happy again, because if we do, I'm going to fight like hell for us."

His eyes get heavy as he takes a moment to think, and I can tell all our best and worst moments are filtering through his head. Part of me is terrified to hear his answer. If he wants me to leave and never come back, I will. I have to respect what he says, but if there's even a small sliver of hope he can forgive me, I'm putting my fucking game face on.

"I don't exactly trust what you're saying to me, but..." He trails off, and my stomach flips as I await his next words. "I loved you once, Mills. With how easy it felt for me, I could absolutely do it again."

"You could?"

He steps closer, getting into my personal space. "Yes, but I've also watched you leave before. I watched you fade from my life. How do I know this isn't just you showing up at my door, wearing your best apology, telling me what I've dreamed about you saying for two years?"

"Because I'm not the same person. In some ways, I might be, and I'm still terrified about so many things, but I'm trying to be better. That's the difference. I actually want to be the person you and the girls thought I was back in college. I'm going to be better, and I'm going to prove to you I can love you louder than the voices in the back of your head telling you it's all bullshit."

He looks down at me, his eyes hooded as the smallest smirk appears, then vanishes in a split second. "No." He grabs the necklace on my neck and rubs the pendant between his fingers. "You're not the same person you were all those years ago."

I want to ask him how he can tell, but his breath on my face and his eyes staring into mine have suddenly made me forget every word.

"But we can't just pick up where we left off," he whispers, his face coming closer as he lets my necklace drop and traces his thumb over my lips. "If you want me back, Amelia, you'll have to earn me."

"I will," I whisper back to him. "I'll do whatever it takes to rewrite our story, Henry. I'm not giving up on us again."

"Good. I am a writer, after all. I know how powerful words can be, but it's the actions backing up those words that mean the most to me," he says as he steps back from me. "Did you fly all the way here from England to tell me this?"

"No. I drove over here from Paige's place," I say as I try to hide my flushed cheeks.

"How long are you staying with her?"

"I'm not." He tilts his head at me again, still confused.

"Then how long are you back?"

I turn around, heading back to my car, knowing I have to prepare myself.

"Amelia?"

"I'm back for good!" I say as I spin around, his smile overtaking his face. "Like I said, Hen, I'm not messing this up again."

"Then I'll leave the light on for you," he says as he shuts his door, and I smile like an idiot all the way home, my music blasting, my windows down, and the wind in my hair.

It feels good to be home.

37

"I didn't think she could surprise me anymore, but I guess that's the thing about surprises—they come when you least expect." — *Untitled Henry Hayes Manuscript*

I'VE BARELY HAD TIME to think or breathe the last few weeks between trying to polish off my manuscript, seeing my family again, and the signing event my publisher threw on me at the last minute.

Amelia has kept popping into my mind since she showed up at my apartment. If I'm honest with myself, she never really left to begin with, but the big declaration she made on my doorstep has left me smiling a bit too much.

Obviously, it feels good to know she's going to fight for us, but I'm not totally giving in yet. She needs to prove she can show up and stop running, but I'm not going to make it easy for her. I don't know if she expected me to take her back the other day, but I'd like to think she's smarter than that.

Either way, she has been answering me more, and she has even called me a few times to chat.

I shake my head of all thoughts of Amelia as I finish signing some copies. This event isn't going to be a huge thing because of how last minute it was. Not even my family is coming because they all had plans, which is fine. They've been to enough of my tour stops in Virginia to last a lifetime, but they were upset they were missing this one. It's the two-year anniversary of my debut novel that went number one on multiple charts, and to celebrate, my publisher printed an exclusive edition that will only be on sale for a limited time.

And there's even a bonus chapter at the end, as well as a few book club questions in the back for people to discuss if they choose to do so.

This event doesn't come with a question-and-answer portion, just the signing, but as I step out onto the floor and notice a long line of people swinging around the store, I smile. I can't believe this is my job, that people actually read what I write. Today is one of the days I feel lucky for all the hard times writing has given me recently; no matter what happens in my personal life, writing will always be a place I can go to create something, even if it's just for myself.

That small ache still filters through my body at having nobody here to celebrate with me, but if everything works out, maybe Amelia can be by my side for these in the future.

"Thank you all for coming," I say as I try to project my voice. Heads turn as they see me, eyes lighting up. It's still weird having that effect on people, but I know I would look the exact same if I saw one of my favorite authors.

I start signing the book that started it all for me as people filter through the line, multiple people telling me they're excited to see what I do next, which makes me equally excited and terrified. I just turned in the first draft last week after struggling with it forever. The trip to Oliver's wedding helped more than I thought. I came home from it feeling recharged and full of complex emotions. The words eventually poured out of me as I sat at my desk each morning, and I couldn't believe I wrote as fast as I did.

Even Mitch was surprised. I ducked some of his calls a few times because I was too enthralled in my manuscript to stop. He also got an earful of what happened at the wedding when I eventually answered him. He was proud of me for sticking up for myself and my feelings, and even though he doesn't trust Amelia, he trusts I'm doing what I know is right.

In my mind, Amelia has always been right for me. She's always been *the* one, but this time, she has to prove it. I don't know how it happened, but we've switched places. Back in college, I was the one chasing her. Now, it's the opposite. I hate that it feels good to be wanted again, and I'm trying my hardest to keep my walls up when it comes to her, but it's been difficult keeping her at an arm's length.

As if she can sense I'm thinking about her, she suddenly appears in front of me, a small smile on her face as she gets up to my table.

"Hi," is all she says. "Can you make them out to Mills, please?"

I smile, aware of what she's doing, but as I open the book and try to get to the title page, my eyes catch on the small scribbles in the margins of my debut—the original cover. Actually, as I sift through the pile she brought, I realize she has every single edition, foreign and domestic, of my books, all of them with scribbles in the margins.

I look back up to her, my mouth slack. Even while we were apart, Amelia still read my books. Amelia Ellis has read both of my books, and she even has multiple copies of them.

Surprise doesn't even begin to cover what I'm feeling.

"The second one was my favorite, but I was also a huge fan of the way you showed the relationship throughout the first one. It was...complicated, messy, and all too familiar."

"Is that your review?" I ask, a small smile overtaking my face.

"No," she says as I sign her books. "But I always knew you would make it as a writer, Henry. I'm still mad you wouldn't let me read your fantasy project when we were in college."

"Well, that's not entirely true," I remind her.

"The first ten chapters of a first draft fantasy novel don't count. It was all world building."

I laugh as I sign the nickname I gave her way back when, and I can't help as my heart starts to beat faster in my chest. Some strange hit of déjà vu overwhelms me, even though Amelia and I have never been in this situation before. "These books seem well loved."

Her hand drags over the tattered cover of my debut novel, and I can tell by the way the spine is cracked that she's read it more than once. She still uses different colored pens when she rereads. Whenever Amelia rereads a book, she uses a different colored pen than the time before, so she can tell how her opinions or feelings have changed.

There's a rainbow of colors throughout my books, and I wish I had more time to ask her about them. I want to know every single thought she had; talking with her about music and novels used to be my favorite thing to do. Her eyes always lit up when she got in the zone, and I want to see that happen when she's talking about the words I wrote.

As I sign her last book, she smiles at me as she looks at the inscription.

For Mills, my first reader, my favorite chapter, and the best plot twist.

She was always the person who wanted to listen to me talk about my ideas, no matter how fleshed out they were. We would take turns, in a way. One night, she would talk to me about an album or lyrics, and other times, she would let me rattle on about my ideas.

She was the first person I felt comfortable enough to share my ideas with, and I'll never forget that. She was with me before I ever became somebody.

"I'll always be your biggest fan, Hen," she whispers to me. "Now, I won't hold up the line." She grabs her books from the table, and my hand grazes hers as she does.

"Thank you for coming," I say, grasping her hand. "It means a lot."

She smiles at me, her cheeks growing pink as she looks around. "I'm going to browse a little bit. I'm going to wait until you're done, if that's okay with you?"

"That's perfectly fine with me," I say as I press my glasses up onto my nose, the next person coming up to the table and holding her books out to me. As Amelia moves to my peripheral, I let my smile take over my face, unable to hold it back any longer.

THE SIGNING ONLY TOOK a few hours, but with how late it is, I'm surprised to still see Amelia roaming the aisles of the bookstore, a few more books in her hands.

When she realizes I'm near, her head turns to me, and she looks down at her basket of books, a tote bag I assumed she borrowed from Paige hanging from her shoulder.

"I swear, I only meant to browse," she laughs. "But you know how it is."

"Browsing always turns into buying, Mills. As a fellow book lover, you should know that."

"Guilty," she says as she holds the basket up, the two of us browsing before we come up on the shelf that holds mine. "I know him," she says as she points at my books.

"Amelia..." I can feel my face get bright red as she says that.

"Come on," she says, grabbing one off the shelf and handing it to me. "Hold it up for me. I want to take a picture of you with your debut novel that got you on all those lists you used to dream about being on."

I can feel my smile sparkle. "You remembered?"

"Of course I did." She smiles behind the camera. "I'm really proud of you, Henry. You were meant to be an author."

"Thank you, Amelia. That means a lot," I say as I stare at the book on my desk next to my laptop. I've written plenty of manuscripts, but this one will always be special to me. Not only was it the one that landed me the deal with my publisher, but it was the book I threw part of my soul into. As I skim the pages, I'm hit with a wave of emotions.

My third book is slated to come out next year. I have lines of people excited to meet me. My life is what I always wanted it to be, and here's Amelia, pointing out my books on the shelf of this bookstore, forcing me to take a picture with it.

"Are you all done meeting readers?" she asks, breaking me out of my haze.

"Yeah, I'm all set," I say as we head for the checkout counter. "What do you have in that basket of yours?"

"Just a few recommendations from the girls and Grant. I missed a few books while I was gone, and they gave me a few of the top ones they still rave about. I figured I'd catch up. I have a lot of time on my hands since I'm unemployed."

"Oh, that's nice," I say, my voice fading a bit as she checks out. I feel a bit out of place, unsure of what to do with my hands. Does she want to talk? Or is something else on her mind?

"Thank you," she says as we head for the door. As soon as we step outside, the cold Virginia air hits us both at the same time. "I don't mean for this to sound so forward, but did you maybe want to come back to my place for some hot chocolate?"

My eyebrows shoot up, and before I can stop myself, I nod.

"Trust me, I would have offered to go out to some sort of coffee shop or something, but I assume they're all closed."

"It's okay, Ames," I say as I look around. The parking lot is fairly empty, but as she starts for her car, I grab the bag from her hands and escort her. "I'll follow you?" I say as I grab the top of her car door, handing her the tote bag.

"Sounds good." She smiles at me. "I'll try not to drive too fast."

"Mhm, I bet," I say as I shut her door, a memory of Ames driving back in college popping into my head.

As I get back into my car, I let myself remember all of it. We had left the grocery store one night, and she had her windows rolled down, music blasting how it always was, and then we heard sirens behind us.

Ames got pulled over. The cop gave her a ticket for driving fifteen over the speed limit in a school zone. I never let her forget it, and even Paige and Oliver brought it up the entire semester.

Lately, I've been letting myself remember all the things I tried to push out, and while the ache still exists, Amelia has really surprised me.

Fifteen minutes later, I'm pulling into what I assume is her complex. We haven't really talked much, besides updating one another on our days. Hers are mostly filled with applying to jobs. Mine are usually filled with writing or admin tasks. Even so, it's nice having her take an interest and be consistent with reaching out to me.

I've been leaving that up to her. I wasn't lying when I said I wanted to stop chasing her, and every time we've talked, it's been because she has wanted to, her always reaching out first.

But I'm still cautious. Sure, she can do this for a few weeks, but I need to see the longevity in her showing up and proving she's not going to run again. Until I'm sure of that, we're going to keep doing whatever it is we're doing now.

I follow her to her place, watching her turn the key in her lock before she opens the door to a place that screams Amelia. Photo frames with her favorite lyrics line the walls of her living room, all her furniture a different shade of blue that reminds me of the ocean. Most of her bookshelves seem to be out here, and I even see some National Geographic magazines on an entire shelf. I wonder if those are just her favorite issues, or if those are the ones she worked on in England. I'm about to ask her about it, but she beats me to the punch.

"Make yourself comfortable," she says as I stroll around her place. "The couch is brand new, along with half the other furniture."

"It's all new?" I swing my head around to her in the kitchen, where she's prepping the hot chocolate.

"When I sold my place in England, I sold it with all my furniture. I got more money for it being furnished, but I had to get out of there." She scoffs. "It seems I have a track record."

"Had," I tell her. "You *had* one."

"Right." She grabs her necklace as she pours hot chocolate into mugs for us. "Thank you for giving it back to me."

I don't ask for context; I know what she's referring to.

"It was the right thing to do," I say as I head over to her small counter, leaning on my forearms as I look at her. "It will never belong to anyone else but you."

She stirs my mug before handing it to me, leading me over to her couch. I take a sip, thankful to have something to hold while we talk.

"So, why did you really invite me over, Mills?" I ask, wondering if another shoe is going to drop kick me any second.

"Well, I wanted you to see how serious I am about staying here. Not only do I have a job interview next week, but I have a new place. This is my fresh start, Henry, and I'm not going to fuck this one up."

"The hot chocolate was just a ruse, then?" I say as I shake my head, setting my mug down as if I'm annoyed. "God, I'm an idiot."

"You poor man," she jokes. "Held hostage by hot chocolate."

I take a sweep around her place, noting how much it feels like I just walked into her brain, and I take a deep breath. I can almost believe her, but there will always be a part of me waiting for her to leave. Maybe in time, that will go away, but for now, I have to protect myself.

"It's a beautiful place, Ames," I tell her.

"Thanks." She smiles. "I'm thinking of having the girls over for a housewarming party next weekend."

"It sounds like they've forgiven you," I say as I sip my hot chocolate.

"As much as they can, I guess," she says, gripping her mug with both hands. "But like I'm doing with you, I'm still proving to them I can show up and stick around. It may not look like it, but I'm trying my fucking hardest to have my actions match my words."

"Everyone can tell how hard you're trying, Amelia. Sure, we might be a little worried about the future once this sudden urge to fix things ends, but we can all tell you're trying."

"I worry it's not going to be enough," she says, her eyes falling.

"Why? Why do you always think you're not enough?"

"I've been trying to be enough my whole life, Hen. People either couldn't understand me or didn't want to stick around enough to deal with me and my not-so-glowing personality. Now, I realize it's my ADHD that has made me think and behave how I have my entire life, but the fear is still there. It still lingers until I'm asking the people who love me if they still like me, or if I'm too annoying."

"Then they're not the right people for you," I remind her. "Only you can decide what's good enough. Don't let other's skewed projections of you cloud who you know you are."

"Trust me," she wipes a tear from her face, "my therapist and I are working on it."

"That's good, Ames," I say as I grab her hand. "I'm proud of you."

"You are?" Her face is more shocked than I thought it would be. "I've barely done anything, Hen."

"Stop selling yourself short," I remind her. "You're trying. The hardest I've seen you try at anything, really."

"Henry, I didn't bring you over here for this. You should not be making me feel better. I should—"

"You need to hear it, Ames. Because if you keep assuming you're not good enough for the people around you, you'll run again. You are enough for the girls, and you are enough for me, even if I'm still terrified you're going to wake up one day and leave."

She lets the words sit for a second. "Then I've got more work to do to prove your mind otherwise," she says as she takes my mug from me. I follow her to the kitchen, grabbing my jacket off her coat rack.

"Thanks for the hot chocolate," I tell her as she heads to the front door with me.

"I'll call you at some point."

I press a small kiss to her cheek, unable to help myself but knowing I can't fully kiss her. If I do, I'm not sure I'd stop, and right now, I can't afford to give in. I need a little more from her. It's only been a few weeks since she declared on my doorstep that she was back for good. Two weeks is nothing compared to the scale I've known Amelia on.

She tripped and fell into my life over three years ago, and since that moment, I've never been the same.

Lately, I've been thinking about my life as two different periods: before Amelia and after Amelia. Now, I'm starting to think there is no after

Amelia, at least not for me. I'm starting to think there is no *without* Amelia.

Maybe in my head, after Amelia simply means we're an us again. Maybe this is the point in our story where we make it to the ending neither of us thought we would write.

"I know you will, baby."

38

Ordinary People by John Legend

My foot taps nervously as I sit in the passenger seat of Henry's car, and, as if he can read my thoughts, he turns the music down before he parks in his driveway.

"They don't hate you, Mills. They're not going to be mean or turn you away." He grabs my hand. "It's just dinner."

Just dinner? "Henry, after what I did—"

"I never even told them what happened." His admittance surprises me. "I told them we broke up, but I didn't talk to them about what happened. It was too hard."

That kills me even more.

"Everything is going to be okay," he says as he presses a small kiss to my knuckles. "We can leave whenever you want, okay?"

"Should we have some sort of signal or something?"

He shakes his head. "We don't need signals, Amelia. I can read your mind, remember?"

I laugh—of course he can. "Okay," I say as I pull my shoulders back. "Let's do this."

Even though I've only met his parents a few times, that hasn't stopped the spiral. I spiraled so bad last night after my medication wore off that I called the girls, and they helped to soothe my thoughts. It was actually really helpful, having them be here for me when my mind got too loud. Then, I cried to them on the phone for not giving up on me. Let's just say last night was an emotional one, but I actually slept through the whole night.

He opens my door for me, and as we walk up the beautifully gardened path to the front door, I can hear my heartbeat in my ears. I want so badly to cower behind Henry, but as soon as the door opens and their familiar faces hit my mine, they smile.

And they both bring me in for a hug.

"Amelia!" his mother says into my ear. "We're so happy you could make it tonight."

I have to stop myself from questioning that; my own parents would never be this happy to see me, so it confuses me as to why his are, especially after I broke their son's heart and left the fucking country.

"Hey, Dad," Henry says as he hugs his father. "How's the recent puzzle coming?"

"Well, if you head to the dining room table, you'll find out."

I step into the house, Henry's hand on the small of my back as the scent of garlic bread hits my nose. This house is more home-like than the one I grew up in. Colors look brighter here. It's an exact contrast to my childhood house that's devoid of the things that make a house feel like a home.

"Hen, he refused to move it off the table," his mother says as he takes my coat. "I knew he took his puzzles seriously, but he's making us squish around the table in the kitchen because he didn't want me to move it."

"It's the puzzle of both of Henry's book covers, Sheila," his father says. "I couldn't move it when I'm almost done!"

"You have a puzzle with his covers on it?" I ask, wanting to see it for myself.

"Come on," Henry says as he leads the way. I find myself remembering the layout of the house since I came here for Thanksgiving our senior year, then a few times after that for dinner. It's weird how certain memories don't fade.

As soon as I see the red cover of his debut, I smile.

"Wow," I say as I run my hand over the completed sections. "This is so cool. Where did he get this?"

"Henry made it for me on some create your own puzzle website," his dad says as he hands us both a glass of water. "It was a wonderful birthday present a few weeks ago."

"Where's Lucy?" Henry asks.

"She's out with some friends at the beach," his mother says from the other room. "She's not coming, unfortunately. You know how teenagers are."

"I know how excited you were to see her," his father says. "And she was excited to see you as well."

It takes me a moment to realize he's talking to me. "Really? Me?"

"Amelia, you were her favorite person to talk to way back when. She would not stop mentioning her new friend Amelia to all her classmates."

My throat practically closes. I guess I didn't just break Henry when I left. I loved his little sister, and even though most children annoy the ever-loving crap out of me, she never fit into the category. Matter of fact,

I remember telling Henry multiple times that I thought his sister was marginally cooler than him. He agreed, of course.

I swallow the knot in my throat—the memories overwhelming me—and I have to remind myself to stay in the present. Henry is on his way to forgiving me. I'm showing up for him. I'm here and trying not to run from the things that terrify me.

Henry meets my eyes, and I can tell he's asking me if I'm okay.

I nod, and then he shows me that beautiful Henry smile.

"Feel free to help me out a bit," his father offers. "I'm going to help your mother with dinner. Okay?"

"Sounds good, Dad," Henry says before he pulls one of the dining room chairs out for me, the two of us sitting down to work on a puzzle before dinner.

And for the next few minutes, Henry and I fill in parts of the puzzle, the two of us working silently as my shoulders loosen and I feel my breathing get easier.

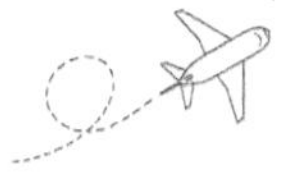

Henry

AMELIA HAS BEEN STRANGELY quiet since she got here. I'm unsure if this is overwhelming her, but when I asked her if she was okay, she said she was.

It must be something else, but I'm not sure what. I know she doesn't have the best relationship with her family, so maybe seeing me with mine is too much.

Back in college, anytime she talked to her family, Ames curled in on herself. It was hard seeing her like that, but her parents always made her feel small, unimportant, as if her dreams were useless. I can only imagine how she feels thinking about them now. I know her main reasons for leaving were to prove she could be something despite them not believing in her, but I wonder how she's going to navigate that relationship since she's back on U.S. soil. Especially after all she went through alone in England, I wonder if she thinks about mentioning any of that to them.

Back then, I never pressed on the things that made Amelia curl in on herself. I didn't like seeing her in that state, and she didn't deserve to be living in it. I wanted to make her happy, so we avoided talking about it.

Looking back, I wish we laid it all on the table then. Maybe the past two years would look a little different, but I'm glad we're here now. I'm glad she came back and we're on our way to repairing what she broke.

"So, Amelia, you worked all the way in London for National Geographic, is that right?" my mother asks as she sets the bread down. "That's very impressive."

"Oh, please." Amelia waves her off. "It's not as fancy as it sounds."

"You traveled all over Europe and wrote articles about different parts of the world, Amelia," I remind her. "That's impressive."

"Yes, well, you wrote and published two books, Hen," she tells me. "That's far more incredible than anything I've done."

"Now, honey." My mom reaches for her hand, and I feel Amelia's entire body tense. "Do not downplay your accomplishments."

"I keep telling her that, but she doesn't listen," I say as she jostles me with her elbow.

"I remember when you sat at that table and talked about your major." My dad pauses to take a drink. "Journalism, right?"

"It was, yes," Amelia affirms.

"Your eyes lit up like Henry's did when he talked about being an author." He smiles to himself. "You should be proud of yourself, Amelia. You had a dream, and you made it a reality."

"Not many people can say they did that," my mom reminds her. "You two have already achieved so much."

"Mom, please don't start crying during dinner," I tell her, knowing how emotional she gets when she thinks about Lucy and me.

When I look over at Amelia, she has a look on her face I've never seen before. It almost looks like surprise mixed with longing. Her eyes are glassy as she looks between my parents, her chest rising steadily as she fiddles with her fork.

"I won't, Hen," she says as she looks at Amelia. "Is everything alright? Is the food okay?"

"It's perfect," Amelia says before I can answer for her. "Everything is perfect."

I can hear the wispiness in her voice, and just before I think she's going to excuse herself, she launches into questions for my parents. For the rest of the night, we chat around the dinner table, and Amelia surprises me in a thousand different ways.

She's leading the conversation most of the time, and she laughs like she hasn't a care in the world. I can't help the smile on my face the entire night; it feels like old times, before everything got complicated.

It feels like the clouds are starting to clear, and even though the sun isn't fully through yet, I can feel it coming on the horizon.

39

"Relationships are never equal. Some days, you can only give ten percent. Other days, your partner can only give the same. It's constant, but it's also the most rewarding thing—being able to grow alongside someone like I have with her." — *Our Best Kept Secret*, Henry Hayes

IT'S BEEN A MONTH of Amelia proving she can show up for me, and at this point, I don't think anything can slow her down.

We've had lots of long talks about our feelings. We've been chatting almost every day, and she's constantly updating me on her job search, which hasn't been going well, but she hasn't given up yet. I keep joking she could work as my assistant, but I know she would hate it.

Amelia was always destined for bigger things, and I know the right opportunity will find her soon enough.

After dinner with my parents, we took the long way home and parked at a lookout point over the beach. She told me that was the most she had ever talked while sitting at a dinner table. Most of the time when she was younger, she would be talked over, or she would fade into the background and say nothing as her family talked around her.

She told me she had to hold back tears when my parents told her they were proud of her because her parents had never said that to her. Her entire life, not once did they tell her that, and my heart sank as soon as the words left her lips.

I know family looks different for everyone, but anyone can see Amelia misses hers. It's blatantly obvious to me, and I hope one day, her parents will come around. I know she didn't follow the plan they had for her, but they're still her parents. As long as Amelia is happy—which I think she finally is—shouldn't that be the only thing that matters?

My phone rings, and I already know who it is.

"Hi, Ames," I say as I pick up.

"Hi, Hen." I can hear her smile through the phone. "Any chance you can be ready in fifteen minutes?"

"Ready for what?"

"A surprise date night?" I can hear her holding her breath. "Only if you want to, of course. If you're busy, I can call Hads or something."

"I'm never too busy for you, Mills."

"Great. I'll be at your place in ten minutes."

I hang up, feeling my stupid smile spread over my face, unable to stop it.

That has been happening a lot lately when I talk to Amelia, and I always feel catapulted back to when we were two idiots in college, and I was pining after her for months. After I met her for the first time, I couldn't stop thinking about her, and I didn't expect to see her so soon.

I was confused as to how she had gone to Grand Mountain for the same amount of time as I had, and I only met her the summer before our senior year. Amelia was a puzzle I desperately wanted to solve, and I spent months in her orbit, falling in love with her while she tried to keep me at arm's length.

Now, here we are, years later, and the same thing is happening. *I'm* trying to keep her at an arm's length because I don't fully trust her, and here she is, pining after me, trying to prove she can love me how I deserve.

I can't deny what I'm feeling now. I can't deny that every time I see her, my breath catches in my throat. I can't deny the way my heart speeds up when I know she's near, or the way we can somehow still communicate with a simple look.

Amelia Ellis makes me whole again. I might be the biggest idiot for giving her another chance, but I knew if I let her go, I would have regretted it.

We're not out of the woods quite yet, but in time, I know everything will be okay.

Amelia: I'm here.

Henry: I would offer you to come up, but it seems like we're in a rush?

Amelia: A little bit, but maybe after?

Henry: Sounds good.

I grab my wallet, keys and shove my phone into the pocket of my button-up before I head down to the lot, spotting her car almost immediately on account of the music blaring at a normal Amelia level.

As soon as she spots me, she fiddles around in her seat and opens her door, a bouquet of flowers in her hand as she waits for me to come toward her.

What the hell is going on?

"Uh, hi?" I say with a chuckle.

"Hi." She grabs her necklace with her free hand. "These are for you."

"For me? Why?"

That earns me a shrug. "Why not?"

I guess I can't argue with that. "Thank you, Mills. These are beautiful."

"They correspond with your book covers." She smiles. "I figured they could sit in your office."

"That's the perfect spot for them," I reassure her before I press a kiss to her forehead. "Shall we?" I say as I open her door for her, Ames sliding into the seat. I have no idea where we're headed, but the butterflies in my stomach make me feel like an idiot in love again.

"AMES, WHY CAN'T YOU just tell me where we're going?"

"Because that's the thing about surprises, Henry." She looks over at me while we're at a stoplight. "You don't know what we're doing until we get there."

"Fine," I concede. "You look beautiful, by the way."

"You've said that already," she reminds me, moving her free hand back and forth on her sweater dress.

"There is no limit on telling you how beautiful you are, Amelia." I run my hand through my hair before I grab hers on her lap.

"You look amazing as well, Hen," she says. "Especially since I only gave you fifteen minutes to get ready."

"Thanks," I say, shifting in my seat as Ames turns into a lot and parks.

By the time we get in, the surprise is over, but I'm very excited. I should have known this was some sort of art thing when she mentioned taking Hads if I couldn't go—it's an immersive experience for Van Gogh. I've seen these on the internet sometimes, but I didn't know it was coming to Virginia any time soon.

We head into the exhibit, the first area with a bunch of smaller paintings and quote projections, Ames and I stopping to read each of them. Neither of us speaks, just enjoying one another's company.

It is a full immersive experience, and as I reach for her hand while she's reading a quote, fully invested in what it says, she doesn't pull away. Her hand slides firmly into mine, and I see her lips turn up as it does. I can tell she's trying not to make a big deal out of it.

Amelia isn't the biggest fan of physical touch, so her grabbing my hand feels like a decent step in the right direction.

I don't try to guide her anywhere; instead, the two of us float through each room, as if we're on the same path through this exhibit. We don't need words. Just one look is all it takes for us to read what the other one is thinking.

When we get to the last room, it's a large open space, a few people walking all around as the paintings move on the walls, the floor, the ceilings. His art is *everywhere*, and as a creative myself, it's easy for me to appreciate every single brush stroke, every color used, all of it.

Stunning doesn't even begin to describe the work he put out, and one day, I hope to inspire someone with my writing how I'm sure he's inspired millions of artists. That's the dream of most creatives, right? To inspire someone with the work they put out like other work has inspired us?

"Do you ever look at something and ask yourself if other people see it the same way you do?"

Her question throws me off as I lead her over to a small bench off to the side. "What do you mean?"

"I don't know," she says as her gaze flows throughout the room. "I look at these pieces, and I'm filled with a longing I've never felt before. It almost feels like I can float through the room like the brush strokes do."

"When I look around, all I feel is respect," I tell her. "His work is so influential to have carried him throughout the ever-changing time periods. I guess I hope my work could have even just a fraction of that."

"It will," she says immediately. "I know I'm biased having read them so many times, but your books are special, Henry, and I'm excited to see what you're going to tackle next."

"Thank you," I say as I press a kiss to our joined hands. "It means a lot knowing you've read them."

"It was purely selfish," she says. "I was lonely in England, and I saw them in a bookstore. I grabbed them because you were familiar to me. Even though I was terrible to you, I was selfish because I was clinging to any semblance of the past I could get."

"That is a little selfish," I joke with her, and she shoves me. "But it's okay to be selfish sometimes when it's not hurting anybody else."

"Well..." She trails off, her head hanging low, before I grab her chin with my hand.

"We should make a rule," I tell her as she stares into my eyes. "Let's not talk about the past unless it's about how we're learning from our mistakes."

She nods her head in my hand.

"I want to hear you say it, Amelia. I want to hear you say you're not who you were before."

"I'm not who I was before," she whispers to me.

"Good," I say as I release her face. "Because our story isn't over, Ames. Not on my watch."

"And are you the one writing it?" she smirks.

"Why would that matter?"

"Well, I want it to be written well, and if you're the one writing it, all will be fine."

I scoff, my cheeks heating up at her compliment. "We're writing it together, Ames. And it will be messy, chaotic, and beautiful."

"Do you promise?" She smiles at me, her eyes gleaming under the lights of the paintings.

"I promise."

40

All I Need to Hear by The 1975

"Did you want to come up?" Henry asks me as I park.

"Oh, I don't have to," I tell him, not wanting to make anything weird. I know we had a wonderful date, but I'm not expecting anything else from him tonight. I'm still working to make him trust me, and I wasn't lying when I told him I'm willing to work as long as it takes.

It's only been a month and a half, and I'm sure he needs more time.

"Amelia." He tilts his head at me. "Stop being weird and help me put these things in water." He notes the flowers currently sitting in my back seat.

"Okay," I concede, and the two of us head into his place. There's a card burning a hole in the pocket of my purse that I didn't include with the flowers; I was worried it was too much.

But maybe I should just go for it and take a risk? Most of the time, the risks I would take didn't actually make me feel nervous—it usually involved me running from my feelings.

This is an entirely different scenario. My throat is dry, this sweater dress I'm wearing suddenly feels itchy, and my palms are starting to get sweaty.

As soon as I step into his space, I feel immersed in another world. Somehow, he has more books than he did in college, and the earth tones mixed with splashes of lighter colors make it seem not too big or too small.

This apartment feels like the most familiar place I've ever been. Henry always was a creature of habit, and this apartment reminds me of the one he had back in college—mostly because there are books everywhere. It sort of feels like I walked into a library.

"Hot chocolate?" he asks as he fills his vase with water.

"That sounds perfect." I smile as I trace his bookshelves with my fingers, eventually seeing the shield he has for every single copy of his favorite book of all time. There's a few translations of it, some sprayed edges, and his original copy he was nice enough to lend to me back in college.

"You want to read my favorite book?" he asks me, a confused expression on his face.

"Of course I do," I tell him. "It's the closest I can get to understanding you on a different level. Unless you want me to poke around in your brain. I'm sure I can arrange something of the sort."

Then he laughs at me, wrapping me in his arms in the middle of the study room, and I don't tell him to pull away.

He brought it to me the next morning before he stole my favorite book from my nightstand.

"Here," Henry says as he hands me a mug, breaking me out of the memory I was in before the two of us take a seat on his couch.

"Do you have a CD player by any chance?" I ask before I can stop it.

"Uh, yeah," he says as he sets his mug down on the table, heading to another room. I hear him fumbling around for a few minutes before he returns with a pair of headphones as well. "What is this for?"

"Another surprise," I say as I grab my purse and pull out the envelope, handing it to him. "For you."

"Wow. First flowers, now a card," he smiles at me. "What did I do to deserve all this?"

"Everything," I say, tears already filling my eyes. "This is merely a fraction of what you deserve, Henry."

He reads the card before he takes the disc and inserts it into the player, my heart beating out of my chest. He goes to press play, but I grab his hand before he presses the button.

"Headphones," I remind him, plugging them in before handing him the one for his right ear as I put the other into my left. "I know we used to do this and we wouldn't say a word, but this time, I have some explaining to do."

"Then I will sit back and let the master work," he jokes, and I laugh as the first song plays. It's the song playing at the concert when we first met.

I let the lyrics play for a few seconds before I open my mouth.

"This song reminds me of the first time I saw you," I say, my voice already shaking. "Obviously, it was playing when you came up to me, but the first thing I noticed about you was how familiar you felt when I had never met you before."

"Really?"

"There was just something about you," I tell him. "I still can't put my finger on it."

When the song finishes, another comes on by a completely different artist. This one is more upbeat, but underneath it are dreamy lyrics and beautiful metaphors about life.

"This one reminds me of your smile," I giggle to myself. "Honestly, I have no reason, but every time I listen to it, all I can see in my head is you smiling at me, but in that specific Henry way."

"What does that mean?" He laughs with me.

"Well, you smile differently. If you're with your friends, you show your teeth a bit more. When you're focused on something you just wrote and you like it, you only turn your lips up, as if that smile is for you and your characters." I start to trip over my words. "But when you smile at me, it's unique and beautiful, and I've only ever seen it pointed at me."

He tilts his head with the exact face I just described, and I don't even think he knows he's doing it.

The song finishes and another starts, and I'm thankful I burned this disc properly. Well, properly, with help from the girls and Oliver.

"This song reminds me of our first kiss." I smile as the memories play in my mind.

"This was the exact song playing as we walked around campus, a shared headphone between us."

I nod, happy he seems to remember it too. "It was a perfect night."

"It was," he agrees with me.

"You told me you loved me to this song," I say as we let the music flow. "I was in that parking lot, terrified you were going to say something else, but then you said you loved me. For the first time ever, I believed it. I *knew* I was capable of it because I felt the exact same way you did, but hearing it..." I trail off, unsure what to say. "It changed a lot for me. *You* changed me, Henry, and I'll never be able to properly thank you for that."

He shakes his head. "You don't have to thank me for loving you, Amelia. It's the most natural thing in the world. Hell, even when I was supposed to hate you, I couldn't—not fully, at least."

Henry grabs my hands, and I meet his eyes.

"Loving you made me realize what most writers talk about in their novels. I never understood it—the feeling, at least. Obviously, I love my family and my friends, but romantically? I never understood it until you came into my life, and that changed. You made the words on the pages I read have meaning, and any time I thought of love, or read about love, or wrote about love, all I could see was you."

"Henry—"

"Amelia, I love you. I have always loved you, and I always will. All the days we have left together, I'll spend every single one of them loving you."

I feel it again. I feel like I deserve this man in front of me. Somehow, he's forgiven me for what I did, and out of the billions of people on the planet, he's chosen me to love.

And I'm choosing him.

"You're the only man I've ever loved, Henry." I smile as a few tears come through. "I'm so excited I get to keep it that way."

He grabs my face in his hands. "You love me?"

"Fuck, of course, I love you, Hen."

"No more past tense?"

"We're in the present now." I smile as he captures my lips in his, the two of us connected in more than one way—our lips, our bodies, our shared music playing between us, our souls. Henry has and always will be part of every atom in my body. I can recognize him simply by his presence, the way his body takes up space in rooms, and I never want to be apart from him. Not now. Not ever again.

He leans me back on the couch, deepening the kiss as the two of us get tangled between the strings of the headphones.

"Henry," I say as he presses kisses to my neck.

"Just let me enjoy my beautiful girlfriend properly," he tells me. "God, you're ethereal, Ames."

"Girlfriend?"

His eyes meet mine. "Is that okay?"

"Say it again."

"Amelia, my beautiful girlfriend," he says. He presses a kiss to my shoulder before he slides his arms underneath my body and lifts me up. He pulls the headphones out from between us as he carries me to his room.

I can't help the laugh that comes out, happiness radiating throughout my body as I squeeze my arms around his neck.

"Is this too fast?" I ask him as he sets me carefully onto his bed, the two of us knowing where this is headed.

"Amelia, it's been years," he tells me as he starts to unbutton his shirt. "I want to worship you properly tonight, if that's okay?"

"That's perfectly okay," I say as I slip my dress over my head.

A moan slips out of his mouth as he runs his hands all over my body, kissing every single inch of skin he can.

"My God, Amelia," he says. "You're perfect."

"How do you want me?" I ask, my body buzzing.

"Take off all your clothes," he says as he slides his pants off. "Keep the necklace on, baby."

I comply, and within seconds, Henry is on top of me, his soft skin brushing mine as he cups my face, kissing me deeply, his tongue threading with mine.

"Just the necklace? Really?" I joke, knowing he loves seeing me wear it because he bought it for me.

"It's not because I want to own you, Amelia," he says as his head settles between my legs. "I'm just gonna love seeing it around your neck while I make you mine again."

And then, his tongue is on me. I can barely think, react, anything because I've never had so many feelings in such a short time before. But that's what Henry does to me. He makes me feel things, and sometimes, those are magnified more than they should be.

It's overwhelming in the best way. I'll never forget this moment with him, this start of us again. Eventually, all of the old, bad memories will be replaced by the new ones we create.

"Are you ready for me, Ames?"

"Please," I say as I grab him by his hair and drag him up toward me. "I need to feel you, Henry."

"Your wish is my command," he says as he grabs a condom from his side table, rolls it on, and presses a kiss to my forehead as he slides into me in one thrust. His head falls to mine, the two of us overwhelmed by emotions. I slide his glasses off and set them on his side table. "God, you feel—"

"I need you to move, Henry," I tell him as I squirm. We had sex when we were in college before everything went to shit, but this time feels different. I don't know if it's because it's been so long or because we're different people now, but I can barely think or breathe unless it's about the beautiful man in front of me.

He starts slow at first, and I'm memorizing every ridge of his body, every face he makes as he slides in and out of my body. My hand goes to his back, and I feel the same birthmark there, nostalgia hitting me in the face from the last time we did this.

He picks up his pace, and I can't help my moans as he starts to fuck me harder, deeper, hitting spots I haven't hit in years.

"Henry—"

"That's it, baby," he says with a smirk. "You're taking me so well."

"Fuck," I say as he speeds up, my orgasm building as he coaxes me into it.

"Look at you, my beautiful girl," he says, his hand coming behind my neck as he forces me to look at him. "I need you to come for me, Ames. Can you do that?"

I nod, and when he lifts my hips, it pushes me over the edge, his name the only thing on my lips.

"Amelia, fuck," he says as I feel his dick twitch as he comes with me, the two of us a mess as we ride it out at the same time. I've never felt so close to anyone else before, and as I catch my breath, Henry discards the condom.

I feel like I'm lying here for hours until something comes up to my mouth.

"Drink, Mills," he says as I take a few sips of water.

He sets the bottle on his table, immediately engulfing me in his arms as he gets us both comfortable underneath his sheets. He plays with my necklace with one hand while the other runs through my hair, and I could stay like this forever.

"Do you want me to leave?"

"What kind of question is that, Ames?" He presses a kiss to my shoulder. "You can stay here with me forever."

"I'd like that," I say as a tear slips from one of my eyes. "I'd like that a lot, Hen."

"To our new beginning, Ames," he says as my head turns to meet his.

"Our new beginning. I love you so much, Henry Hayes."

"I love you, Amelia Ellis."

Then he kisses me, and I fall asleep tangled in his arms, feeling more like myself every moment I'm with him. This is where I'm meant to be. After years of running and searching for a place to call mine, for a place to be comfortable in, I've found it wrapped in the arms of Henry Hayes.

41

"I always love the slow mornings with her. I love seeing her in my clothes, and smelling her on my sheets the day after she stayed over. She was everywhere, and I finally have her back." — *Excerpt from Henry Hayes' Journal*

I WAKE WITH HAIR against my face, but I don't make to move—the hair belongs to my favorite girl on the planet.

I can't believe this is real, waking up and still seeing her sleeping against my chest.

This is how I wanted to start our new beginning—the two of us tangled between the sheets of my fucking bed, her pressed against me as I run my hand through her curls.

As I look at her peaceful face and watch the rise and fall of her chest, I can't help but feel like the luckiest fucking guy on the planet. Not only did we find our way back to one another, but she was able to prove to me she was serious about us.

I can't help my smirk as my phone starts to ring, and I answer it so Ames doesn't wake up.

"Hello?" I didn't bother looking at who it was before I picked it up.

"Um, hi?" Mitch says across the line. "I thought we were going to write this morning?"

Oh, fuck. "I'm sorry, dude," I whisper to him. "I totally forgot."

"Henry?"

"Yeah?"

"Why are you whispering?"

I don't bother lying, but by his tone, he already knows what I'm about to say. "Amelia is sleeping, and I don't want to wake her up."

"So I take it you guys talked it out and then some last night?"

"We did," I tell him, my smile still stuck on my face. "I'm happy, Mitch. I'm *so* fucking happy."

"Good," he says as I hear him typing. "That's all that matters, buddy. When can I meet her?"

"I can have you over for dinner whenever you're in town again," I tell him. "Maybe we can talk to our publishers and set up something for my next book tour?"

"That sounds perfect, Henry. Since you're not available, I'm going to go write by myself."

"Sorry, dude. We can figure out a schedule for our sprint sessions this weekend."

"It's fine, Hen. You sound different already," he tells me. "Happier."

"I am."

"It's noticeable, even just over the phone."

All I can do is smile as he tells me that. I know he was skeptical when I told him I was giving Amelia a second chance, but I'm glad I have him. He's a wonderful friend.

"Thanks, Mitch."

"Have a good morning, buddy," he says as he hangs up. I turn my attention back to Amelia, who's staring at me.

"Good morning, sunshine."

"I'm mad at you," she tells me with a tired smirk.

"Already? Wow, that has to be a record."

"I was going to wake up before you and make you breakfast in bed with whatever I could find in your kitchen, but my plan was thwarted."

"I'm sorry, Mills," I say as I press a kiss to her head. "Why don't we make something together?"

"Fine," she grumbles. "But this isn't how I wanted to start our new chapter."

"How did you sleep?"

"The best I have in years," she whispers to me. "And it's all because of you."

I throw the covers off us and grab my shirt, walking around to where she sits in bed, putting it around her and buttoning it up. She stares back at me, her beautiful eyes shining in the low light of my bedroom.

"You know, I thought our new chapter started pretty well," I joke as she whacks me with a pillow.

"Shut up," she says with a laugh, the sound filtering through my ears and flooding my body.

"Come on, beautiful," I say as I grab her hand and lead her into my kitchen. "Let's get you some coffee."

"You always know the way to my heart, Hen." She smiles as she sits on my counter.

"Always have and always will." Once we're caffeinated, I start to make some pancakes while Ames turns the playlist on from last night and connects it to my speaker, the music quietly playing in the background.

I was always worried my story would end with me being unhappy for the rest of my life. I know there's a phrase that says the good guys get to be happy, but I always had a hard time believing that. I thought I was doomed to some existence where the happiness I was meant to find was simply through my books. I always worried I'd be too busy making fictional characters happy, and I'd never achieve it.

But as I watch Amelia float around my kitchen wearing my shirt, a huge smile on both of our faces, I realize happiness isn't a stranger to me anymore.

In fact, it's my companion as I enter this new phase of my life with her by my side.

"I'll set the table," she says as she grabs plates and silverware.

"Thank you."

I plate the pancakes and grab some fruit, throwing it into a bowl before I meet her at the table. Sitting down next to her, I'm unable to stop myself from grabbing her hand and kissing her.

"I wanted to talk to you about something," she says as I grab her a pancake. "It's not bad, don't worry. I just didn't get to say it last night."

"Well, we were busy doing other things, so that's okay."

Her cheeks turn red at the memory of last night. "I know communication is the most important thing going forward, at least for me it is. My mind works a lot differently than most, and it's been less than a year of me having a diagnosis. I'm still figuring out what works best for me, so there might be some trial and error until I solidify a routine."

"I know, Ames," I agree. "I want to know everything about how your brain works. It might take me some time to adjust, but I'll do anything to help make things easier for you and that beautiful brain of yours."

"Thank you," she tells me. "Support is the biggest thing I've needed lately. It's been easier to manage with a routine. I drink tea now. I cut out alcohol. I feel more like myself, but some days are still a fight in my head."

I grab her hands. "Mills, no matter what, I'm here for you. As long as we communicate about things, we're going to be okay. I trust you to come to me when you feel scared or nervous or anything. You should trust yourself—I'm not worried about you leaving me again."

"Because you would chase me down?"

I nod. "Always, Amelia. I'm not letting your fears get in the way of us again."

"And I won't either."

"Good," I say as I pop some fruit into my mouth. "Now, hurry up and eat so you can call Paige and debrief with her."

The rest of our morning is filled with laughs, gossip, and Amelia's presence all around me in my apartment. It's the best morning I've had in a long time, and there are a thousand more like this to come.

MY PHONE RINGS A few times, and I swear, I could bite my fingernails off as I await to tell them all about what happened last night.

Paige answers first, and eventually, Hads and Ella filter into the call.

"Good morning!" Paige smiles, and I hear Oliver groan in the background.

"God, I really haven't missed this," he says as he gets out of bed.

"Just go have your coffee, you big grump," Hads jokes with her brother.

"Amelia, care to explain where the hell you are?" Ella asks me. "That's not your apartment."

"What?" Grant shrieks as he comes into frame. "Oh my fucking God."

"Are you..." Paige trails off before she too screams. "Holy shit!"

"Am I missing something?" Leo asks as he hears us all freak out.

"I'm turning the volume down because I know Paige and Grant are about to scream or something," I say as I laugh. "And yes, I'm at Henry's apartment."

"Did you spend the night?" Ella asks, probably noticing this isn't my shirt. I sent all the girls a picture of my outfit for my surprise date night with Henry, and they agreed the sweater dress was better than the floral one I had originally.

"Ahh!" Paige squeaks.

"Love, please breathe. I don't want you passing out from excitement again," Oliver tells her as he returns. "Do you want some water?"

"Stop asking dumb questions, Oliver!" Grant says, his chin on Hads' shoulder. "Amelia, tell us everything."

While Henry is in the shower, I spill every single thing that happened last night—minus some explicit details. I do not want any of the boys to hear details about my sex life. Well, except Grant, I guess. He's one of the girls, and I have missed being able to gossip and talk shit with him.

"It was...the best night of my entire life," I say as I let my smile take over my face. Back in college, I would have tried to hide all these mushy and gushy feelings, but now, all I want to do is tell my friends every single thing.

It feels good being open with them, and since they have already seen us as a couple, it's almost better. Their excitement has made me even more ecstatic about this fresh start, and I know this is where I'm meant to be.

At this phase in my life, I thought I would have had everything figured out. But it's so easy, isn't it? It's easy to look to the future and assume you'll know where you want to be in a few years. You think you'll get there because not only do you believe in yourself, but it's *so* far ahead. How couldn't you be where you want to by then?

My life looks so different than I imagined it. Getting to where you want to be isn't just from one point to the other. It's a thousand small steps, a few big ones, maybe some setbacks along the way, and eventually, you might be where you thought you would be. Or maybe your mindset changes, and you end up somewhere you never even thought existed.

I'm on a path with so much uncertainty still ahead, but deciding to come back was the best decision I never thought I would make. It was one I never saw coming, and it led me to a new beginning.

When I got on the plane to London all those years ago, I thought that would be the last time I would have to start all over, but here I am, back in the same place I once was.

Life, I've come to understand, doesn't have beginnings and endings, at least not finite ones. Our friends, our family, the people we love, they live on through the stories we tell, through the memories we have of them. Sure, relationships can end and new ones can begin, but nothing is ever truly over. Every experience brings a new opportunity to learn, whether it's a new start or something ending. I don't want this version of my story to end.

With these people around me, I can't imagine our love ever ending. In fact, if I think about how close we are, I'm sure our love will never end. It can't—not when it's this real.

"So, when can we get together and have a proper date night with all of us? And when can Henry bring me a new copy of his latest project?

I'm ready to saw my arm off and give it to him if it will help him write faster."

"No need to remove any of your limbs, Grant," Henry says as he comes out of the shower, a towel hanging low on his waist.

"Oh, hello." Ella winks at me through the camera as Leo rolls his eyes.

"Shit," he says as he slides out of frame. "I didn't know it was a video call."

"It's okay, babe."

"Oh my God, she called him babe!" Paige shouts. "This is the best news I could have woken up to. I am so happy for you two."

"Thanks." I smile as Henry locks eyes with me where I sit on his bed. "We're happy too."

"You two deserve it," Hads tells me. "When is everyone able to get together? We need a group debrief."

"Can everyone put their work schedules into the shared calendar? Then we'll be able to see what weekend is best for everyone," Ella says as she taps on her phone.

"I'll send it to Henry," I let them know.

"Thanks, Mills." He comes over to me, now fully dressed, and presses a quick kiss to my lips before he heads for his computer. "I'd love to stay and chat, but I have a book to write."

"Hell yeah, you do!" Grant shouts. "Thanks, Hen."

"Well, I don't want you to lose any more limbs," he jokes. "Stay as long as you want, baby. I don't mind the company."

"Okay." I smile at him, knowing I'm going to make myself comfortable with one of the hundreds of books he has on his shelves. "I'll talk to you guys soon?"

"Thanks for the update, Ames." Paige smiles. "I missed our morning chats. It feels like we're in college again."

"I've missed them too."

"Bye, Amelia," Ella and Leo say at the same time before they hang up.

"Mr. Grouch? Anything to say?" I note how quiet Oliver has been throughout this whole thing.

"Seeing you this happy is weird as fuck. Go back to being cold and annoying, or the planet is going to spin off its axis."

I throw a smile his way. "Yeah, well, now you know how it felt watching you fall in love with Paige. You've gone soft, dumbass."

Paige just sighs heavily as she looks between Oliver and the phone.

"Sorry, P," I say.

"Sorry, my love," Oliver says as he kisses her on the cheek. "Bye, psycho."

"See you later, loser," I joke. As I grab a book from Henry's bedroom shelves, I hear him laugh to himself in the other room, probably from eavesdropping on our conversation. "I love you."

"I love you too, Mills."

42

Martingale by Searows

"SHE OFFERED ME THE job on the spot," I tell Henry as I walk out of the building. "Kacey was excited to know I'm back in Virginia for good."

"I told you, Ames." I can hear his smile over the phone. To say I was terrified for this interview today was an understatement. Knowing I was going to be interviewing at the place where I did my internship helped to ease my anxiety a little. Kacey, my old supervisor, helped me get the job over in England, but I was still worried. For some reason, even though I did great work, I thought I was going to look stupid coming back to the place I once worked at. I thought she would ask me about the forced leave I took at the beginning of the year, but that never came up. Sure, my work faltered a little bit, but it went right back up to where it was as soon as I had better coping mechanisms and understood my brain a little better.

But, like everything else, it had changed. Kacey was elated to have me back. She was going to try and poach me anyway—at least, that's what she told me. Apparently, the position I had at National Geographic in England is a direct mirror to the job I'm going to have starting Monday.

"I'm excited," I tell my boyfriend. "I really feel like this is where I'm meant to be."

"I'm glad," he says as I hear him typing something. "You deserve this, Mills."

"Thanks, Hen." I smile as I get into my car. "I'll see you tonight?"

"Sounds good to me."

"I love you."

He giggles a little. "I love you too."

And as I hang up the phone, a stupid smile on my face, I take a deep breath before I start my car. My therapist told me to try and start taking in the big moments a few months ago, and instead of focusing on the future and the next thing, I've been trying to live in my emotions when they show up.

Part of me still feels like something is missing, though, and I know exactly what that is. That's the good and bad part of being so self-aware. It's good because at least I know what's bugging me, but it's bad because I'm not sure how to face the things that make me ache.

I turn my car on and drive, already knowing where I'm headed, the familiar streets of my hometown burned into my memories.

Looking back on when I would wander these streets searching for something I thought I would never find, I wish I could have coffee with my younger self. I'd tell her it's all going to be relatively okay. I think she would ask about our travels, and I'd be able to show her photos of all the places we've gone on our own. She would ask me if we found people who could handle her sense of humor and odd personality, and I'd tell her we did, and even though we lost them for a little bit, we found our way back. She would ask if our brain ever started to make sense, and I'd tell her about our diagnosis and how grateful we are to finally understand.

I'd tell her we're still scared of talking to our parents because we didn't follow the path they wanted for us, and she'll hold my hand and tell me she understands.

As I park in the driveway of my childhood home, spotting the window I used to climb out of, I take a deep breath. I've changed throughout the years, but I'm still terrified to talk to my parents and finally have an open conversation—if they'll even have one with me. I probably should have done this sooner, but I was too busy trying to get my life back on track. I was securing my future first before I tried to figure out my past. My new routine has been okay so far, and now that I officially have a job, it will be even better.

The last thing my mother said to me before I left for England was that I was destined to be alone, and I thought she was right. I've barely talked to my father in the last two years. I have no idea who they are. They feel more like strangers to me than my parents.

But my mother wasn't right, and I'm tired of running from the past and the people who created me. I want to think she didn't say that to be mean—maybe it was simply an observation—but she was right for a period of time. I was the loneliest I've ever been.

I get out of my car, trying to even out my breathing as I head for the door and knock. It takes a few seconds longer than I thought it would for them to answer the door, but as soon as my mother sees me, she wraps me in her arms.

"Amelia, it's been too long since we've seen you," she says into my hair, and I'm frozen, my arms glued to my sides as I take in her words.

The only other time my mom hugged me was...never. At least from what I remember growing up in this house.

"Uh, hi?" I say as she pulls back, her arms still on my shoulders as she takes a long look at me.

"George! Come here! It's Amelia," she smiles as she ushers me into the house, and I'm still confused at this reaction. My dad comes into the foyer then, and his eyes light up as he sees it's actually me. His arms are around me too, and I'm practically robotic as I hug him back.

"Okay, this is not what I was expecting when I drove over here," I say as I take my shoes off. "Did you guys get abducted by aliens or something? Blink twice if you need help."

They just sit and stare at me, huge smiles on their faces. "Do you want some coffee? Or hot chocolate? Or water? Please, Amelia, let's sit down and catch up." My mother grabs my hand and leads me into the kitchen, the familiar environment making nostalgia float into me.

"Uh, coffee is fine," I say as I shed my jacket. "I'll be honest, I was expecting you guys to turn me away."

"Why would we do that, honey?" my father asks as he sits next to me.

"Because of how I left," I say as I grab my necklace. "And because we're not a family who talks about feelings and stuff. At least when I was growing up, we weren't."

"Amelia, getting emotions and feelings out of you as a kid was worse than pulling teeth," my mother says as she pours me a coffee. "We didn't want to pry because you would only retreat further."

"You always did like to sort through your feelings on your own, so we let you," my father says as he sips his own coffee. "We've realized over the years that wasn't the best way to go about it, and we're sorry if you ever felt like you couldn't come to us with what you were feeling, especially if you were struggling."

This is the exact opposite of how I thought this conversation was going to go. If anything, this house feels warmer and more inviting than it did when I was a child. I thought the rose-colored glasses of childhood were supposed to go away as you got older, but that isn't the case here.

"Okay, pardon my confusion," I say as I adjust how I'm sitting on the chair. "But when I changed my major in college, I was terrified to tell you guys about it because I wasn't following in Steven's footsteps like you wanted me to. Every conversation I had with you back in college, all I could hear was disappointment in your voices."

"Well, we were disappointed at first, but then we kept seeing pictures from your travels all over social media—"

"Which Steven had to teach us how to use," my mom says with a laugh. "You looked so different from the daughter we knew, almost carefree in those photos."

"That's how traveling made me feel. It's how I *still* feel, but I've realized over the years that Virginia is where I'm meant to be."

"George, go get them," my mother says.

My father jumps up from the table, already knowing what she's referring to.

"Wait," I say before he rounds the staircase. "Can I tell you both something before you grab whatever you're grabbing?"

"Sure, honey," he says before he comes back over, still standing. They wait for me to continue, but for some reason, telling them about my diagnosis is terrifying.

"I know you guys thought I was a lazy kid who was unmotivated and moody, but when I was in England, things got dark. I was depressed, unhappy, and I couldn't figure out why my brain was being as mean to me as it was. So, I went to see someone about it, and she diagnosed me with ADHD."

They let what I say settle into the air, and before I know it, my father has his arms around me.

"I'm sorry for not getting you the proper help you needed as a kid," he whispers to me.

"We always thought it was just your personality," my mom says. "I wish we tried a little harder and noticed the signs sooner, Amelia. That must have been hard for you discovering that all by yourself."

I can only nod. "It was, but I got through it. I'm handling it a lot better. I'm on medication for it, and I don't feel as messy as I did before."

My dad squeezes me a little tighter before he pulls back, rounding the stairs before looking back at me. "Please don't leave until I come back, okay?"

"I'll be here, Dad."

"Good." He smiles before he's out of sight, and it's just me and my mother at the table.

"It might take him a few minutes, but I really am glad to see you, Amelia."

"Can I ask you something?"

"Anything," my mother says as she grabs one of my hands.

"What did you mean when you told me I was destined to be alone before I went to England? Because I've tried saying it a thousand different ways, and none of them end up being taken well."

Her head falls a little as she finds my eyes again. "I shouldn't have said that."

"But why did you?"

"The therapist we've been seeing the past few years tells me it's because I was projecting my feelings onto you," she tells me, and my eyebrows shoot up in surprise. "I always felt so far away from you, and I blamed myself for not being able to tell when my own daughter was struggling. I apologize, Amelia. I'm sorry I said that to you as your mother and as a person."

A tear falls from my eye, and I swipe it away. "Wow. It's kind of funny that we're both seeing someone," I tell her. "Dr. Elyse has helped me get a better handle on how my brain operates. She's also helped me to stop running away from things and instead run toward them. Which, I guess, is why I'm here right now."

"Your father and I are so glad you're back." My mom squeezes my hand. "We can't wait to hear all about England, if that's something you want to talk to us about. And we'd love to hear about that brain of yours and what we can do to help."

"I'd like that," I tell her.

"I found them," my father announces, and as soon as he gets to the table, he pours a bunch of issues from National Geographic onto the table. "These are all the issues you worked on, Amelia. We bought all of them."

"You're a wonderful writer and journalist, honey," my mother says, and I'm about to burst into tears.

"You guys read all of them?" I say as I filter through the magazines, remembering each piece I did.

"Of course we did," my father says as he wraps his arms around my shoulders. "We're really proud of you for all the wonderful work you've created."

"You're proud of me?" I say, tears filling my eyes. "Really?"

"Of course we are," my father says. "We're sorry it took us so long to see this was the path you were meant to be on."

"And we're proud you were brave enough to change it, despite us not trusting you knew what was best for you," my mom tells me. "Steven even has them all on his shelf in his office at the hospital. We bought two of each so he could read them too."

"I don't know what to say." I smile through my tears. Growing up, I always saw my parents one way, but now, I'm seeing them through an entirely different lens. They are right—I do like to sort through my own feelings, but I'm also trying to get better at being more open with the people I love. I can't keep picking myself back up all the time. I need to rely on the people who love me to take some of the weight and vice versa.

Maybe the same goes with my parents. It is their first time living on this planet too, and we're all just trying to be the best we can be with the short time we have. We're all growing up. Every day, each person on the planet gets older, and we're all just trying to be good people.

Existing is difficult sometimes, and the fact that my parents and I are both seeing someone and trying to do better is proof we can always evolve, we can always grow, and it's never too late to rewire your brain.

"Maybe you can come to dinner next weekend? We can even call your brother and see if he's available?"

"A family dinner?" I ask my father, wondering if I heard him right. "Like we used to back when I was a child?"

"If that's okay?" my mother asks, and I can tell she's worried about my answer.

"It's perfect," I say. "Can I bring Henry?"

"Henry? The boy from college?" my father asks.

I nod. "There's a lot to catch you guys up on."

"We want to hear it all, honey." My mother refills my coffee for me. "If you want to share it, that is."

"I do," I tell them, and for the rest of the afternoon, I sit around the kitchen table and talk with my parents about the life I've been living the past few years. Tears are shed, laughs are traded, and for the first time in my life, I feel like I have a family who understands me. It's the opposite of my childhood, where I used to sit around the table quietly and wish for a time when someone would understand me.

I thought I would only experience a close knit family unit in another life, but this timeline is the only one I want to be present in, because I'm somehow lucky enough to have two close family units.

43

A Few Weeks Later

Ribs by Lorde

"Guys, did anyone write on the banner I bought?" I ask my apartment full of my friends. Nobody says a word. "I'm going to assume that's a no."

"Come to think of it, I was wondering why we were going to hang up a blank sign," Grant says, and Hads smacks his hand as he tries to blow up a balloon.

"I can write on it, babes," Ella says as she grabs the roll of light blue paper from me. "What did you want it to say again?"

Ella has the best handwriting of us all, and I sigh with relief that they all came over to help me. It was a little last minute, but thankfully, everyone was able to make it over to my place.

Tonight, I'm throwing an impromptu party to celebrate Henry turning in his book. I know how much he struggled with this story, and finishing it is a huge deal, so I wanted to throw him a little something to celebrate.

I am so fucking proud of him.

"Something about him finishing his third book?" I state.

"Well, we know who the author is here," Oliver jokes as I shoot him a dirty look.

"Don't make me call the cops on you," I threaten.

"Don't make me—"

Hads cuts off our bickering. "I'm going to get my fucking ruler if you two don't stop arguing all the damn time."

"I don't understand the animosity between you two," Leo says as everyone murmurs in agreement. "It doesn't make any bloody sense."

"Can we just finish decorating before he gets here?"

"Where is he coming from again?" Paige asks as she hangs streamers from all the doorframes in my apartment.

"He's having dinner with his sister," I tell them. "He invited me to go, but Lucy is actually doing me a favor by distracting him until we're done."

"Oh, right." Paige smiles as she steps off the small stool I gave her. I have to say, this impromptu party has come together quite nicely, even though I planned it in only a few days. I sort of feel like Ella right now. That girl can whip up a themed party like nobody's business.

The theme for tonight is writers across the centuries. I basically forced everyone to dress up as one of their favorite authors to celebrate *my* favorite author.

I'm dressed exactly like Henry—with fake glasses I got at the store, along with blue jeans and a button up top. I even have a notebook attached to my hip for when he gets here, because whenever he starts a new story, he always buys a new notebook.

"Okay, and do you guys think we have enough food and drinks? Because I can go to the—"

"Girl." Paige grabs my shoulders. "Everything is perfect. There's enough food for a small restaurant and drinks to last us a year. Everything is perfect," she reassures me and I take a breath.

"Okay." I shake out my shoulders. "I don't know why I'm so stressed about this."

"Welcome to being the host," Ella jokes with me. "It may be my favorite thing to do, but when this one over here," she gestures to Leo, "first hosted a party for all of us, you should have seen how freaked he was."

"I was not that bad," he tells us.

Ella only shakes her head as she disagrees, and Leo shoots her a look of disgust.

"Fine, then how about we each host a party and leave it up to our lovely guests to judge who is better?" Leo asks her, and Ella's eyes pinch in thought.

"Done," she says, holding out her hand. He shakes it, pulling her into his body.

"You two are the most competitive people I've ever met," Oliver says as he turns the speakers on.

"It's foreplay," Paige tells him, and he shakes his head. "What? It is for them!"

I can't help but laugh at this chaotically wonderful group of people, but it's short-lived when I feel my phone buzz in my pocket.

"Okay, he's almost here," I say, and everyone scrambles into gear. Ella and Leo hang the sign on my living room wall. Oliver and Grant blow up some more balloons, randomly throwing them all over the place. Paige rips streamers off the roll and throws them around too, while Hads turns the playlist I made on.

I wouldn't call this a surprise party, since we're not jumping out and surprising him, but I think he will be shocked to see everyone.

I can't wait to see the look on his face. Even though it's a small celebration, he deserves it. Writing a book is no easy feat, and knowing how much he struggled with this one, this is the least I could do to show how proud I am of him.

"Why is my heart beating so fast? Am I going to have a heart attack?" I turn to Ella, and she simply shakes her head.

"Reel it in, girl. It's just a get-together, and he's going to love it."

"Ames, do you think he'll be mad at me for not dressing as him?" Grant says as he adjusts his outfit.

"Babe, I think he'll be okay." Hads motions to his custom-made shirt with Henry's name and face on it. "Given the circumstances, I'm sure he'll be more confused than anything.

"He's going to be so mad at you," Oliver jokes—as much as he can for one day—and Grant's face falls before he turns to Hads.

"Grant, it's fine," she reassures him. "Plus, I'm glad you dressed as who you did because, without that book, we would not be here right now."

"Thank God for my man Fitzy."

"And his wife," Hads reminds him.

"Guys, get the streamers ready," I say as I hear footsteps outside. "Hads, hit the music."

She does, and as soon as it starts playing, the door opens. His face pinches in surprise as he sees me and all our friends greeting him.

"Woah," he says as Paige sets off a few hand-popping streamers. "What's all this?"

"Well, we had to celebrate," Grant says. "Someone over here finished their third book!"

Everyone sets off their streamers as Henry comes closer, a smile I've never seen from him before showing up on his face.

"Congrats!" we all say as he wraps me in his arms.

"I'm proud of you, Hen," I whisper into his ear as he buries his face in my shoulder.

"Thank you so much, Mills." He presses a quick kiss to my lips. "What the hell are you all wearing?"

Laughs echo around the room as he stares at all of us, and I can tell when recognition hits.

"Are you guys all dressed as authors?"

"Our favorite ones!" Paige says while she pops another streamer. Hads reaches over and takes the bag from her.

"And since everyone has to be dressed according to the theme," I say as I open the door to my bedroom, "I left you a very important outfit in there. So, go get changed, and when you come out, we can fully start the celebration."

"I love you," he says as he presses a kiss to my forehead. "Although, it feels weird saying that to you while you're dressed as...me, I assume?"

"You're my favorite author, Hen," I remind him. "And I can understand that."

As soon as he gets dressed, he comes back out and greets the boys, the four of them trading hugs as us girls watch Ella mix our drinks for us. My drink of choice tonight is a Shirley Temple, and I've been in the biggest hyper fixation of my life for the past few weeks.

"Proud of you, buddy," Oliver says quietly.

"Good job, mate," Leo says. "I'm not much of a reader, but I can't imagine actually writing a story, let alone three."

"Thank you, Leo." Then his eyes land on Grant, and I swear, he's about to cry.

"I'm just super proud of you, dude," Grant tells him, his voice sincere as they hug. "I remember rooting you on from the book club classroom all those years ago, and now, you're published three times over."

"Fuck, that feels like forever ago," Henry says. "I think you called me your favorite almost-author or something?"

"This whole getting old thing is driving me nuts," Oliver says, and for once, I agree with him.

"Me too," I say to the room, and I swear, you could hear a pin drop if the music wasn't playing. "What?"

"You just agreed with Oliver," Paige says, her eyes shining. "I never thought I would see the day it happened in front of him."

"What do you mean in front of me?" Oliver asks as I shake my head.

"She means nothing," I tell him as I sip my drink. "Now, can we get to celebrating?"

"Of course we can!" Ella shouts as she pops the champagne while also pouring me a glass of water. Everyone cheers as glasses are poured, conversations are had, and snacks are eaten. Eventually, the karaoke machine is brought out, and just like old times, Grant and Ella sing a duet, Paige and I sing at the top of our lungs, and Oliver pretends to hate it, but I can see him smiling to himself as he watches his wife.

"I am so glad Paige and I practically trapped you two at her wedding," Grant says, his lips loose from the alcohol. "Oh, shit."

"Grant!" Paige says into the microphone as her solo song ends. "Out of the two of us, I thought I was going to be the one to blab!"

"Shit," is all he says as we all stare at the two of them.

"Are you guys serious?" I ask them. "You pulled a parent trap on us?"

"A what?" Leo asks.

"It's a movie," Oliver tells him. "I knew those two had meddled in your relationship."

"Well, it worked, didn't it?" Grant reminds us, and Henry starts to laugh as he pulls me onto his lap.

"We should have seen that coming," he tells me.

"Oh, absolutely," I agree as I laugh into his chest. "But I guess we owe you two a thank you."

"I'll take my form of payment in you naming any future pets or children after me," Grant jokes. "Or a simple thank you during a wedding speech would be nice."

"I don't need anything," Paige says. "Except for you two to last forever. Deal?"

"I think we can manage that," Henry says.

"God, I thought Paige was bad back in college when she tried to ship us all together," Hads says. "But you two were right, so I guess we all owe you a thank you."

"No need," Paige says. "The biggest gift of all is seeing us together in this room, drinking and laughing and having fun. It's what we all deserve, and I am so grateful we're all here."

"Now, for this last song," Ella says as she takes a deep breath, grabbing the mic from Paige, "I want to invite my favorite book club girls up to the stage with me."

"All of us?" Hads questions as I take her hand and drag her up to where Ella and Paige stand.

"Yes," Ella says into the mic. "This is a special one."

As she hits play, Paige and I share one microphone while Hads and Ella share the other, our favorite song comes on. The last time we all heard it was when we danced to it at Paige's wedding, the four of us in a circle as we screamed the lyrics. Before that, the last time was when Ella made us all go on a drive the night before Hads and Grant graduated. The three of them might have played it without me while I was gone, but I'm choosing to remember the moments we were together, singing until our lungs gave out.

I remember the first time I showed the girls this song. It was basically my way of showing them how I felt because back then, I never outwardly shared my feelings.

As the chorus starts and the four of us are up here singing our hearts out, I can't help but feel the words tumble out of my mouth.

"I fucking love you guys."

"Come on, boys," Ella shouts into the mic. "Get the hell up and dance with us," she says as the beat speeds up. Then, the eight of us are dancing around my living room, balloons and streamers everywhere.

None of us cares about the mess. All we care about are the feelings we're having right now, echoes of who we once were in that small classroom at Grand Mountain.

I always wondered if I'd ever have a place to call home, since growing up, I never felt like I belonged. Well now, my biological family and I are on great terms. Henry and I had dinner with my parents and brother the other day, and it was wonderful being able to sit around the table, guiding the conversation and being a part of it. It ended with my parents hugging me before we left, leftovers of our dinner in a small box for us as they hugged me goodbye and told me they were proud of me.

I cried in front of them again when they said that, and it was one of the best nights of my life.

After that, I started my new job, and the moment I walked back into my old internship office, I felt like I belonged. I couldn't explain it—at least not with words. All I wanted to do was run feet first into anything I could get my hands on because of how excited I was to be back.

When I went to Henry's apartment after my first day, I talked the entire time about all the exciting things I was going to be doing, and he let me. He watched me in awe as I barely touched my food because of my excitement.

And then I ended the night in his arms, which was the best present of all, because loving him is the easiest thing I've ever done. No matter what happens in the future, I'll always be running back to his arms, knowing there's a safe place for me there.

As he wraps around me again, I shove the microphone into his face as he looks at me, the both of us singing, surrounded by the love we share with our friends. I feel my heart settle in my chest as I take in the scene surrounding us.

Over the past few months, I've come to realize the home I've been searching for isn't me running away. It also isn't one specific place. It's not just my childhood home. It's not just in Virginia.

Home is laughing with my friends as we sing a little too loudly. Home is hearing Hads smack Grant or any of the boys with a ruler. Home is Ella asking us if we need water after a long night out. Home is Paige calling me every Saturday morning to debrief our week. Home is sitting on the floor with the girls late at night and eating chips right out of the bag. Home is that tiny classroom at Grand Mountain College, where these three girls first came into my life.

Home is wherever these people around me are, and even when they're not near, I still have tiny pieces of them I can use to ground me when I feel stressed or when the world gets too loud.

We may have doubled in size since we met, but I am forever grateful I get to go through life with the same people I met when I was terrified of never finding anyone who could understand me. These girls were dropped into my life at just the right time, and I'm the lucky one who is able to say, years later, we're still surrounding each other. I can still hear their laughter. I can still see them smile, cry, scream, and joke around with me.

And I still have Henry, who I was lucky enough to fall in love with twice. At least, that's how I'm choosing to see it. In one lifetime, I was lucky enough to find him, know him, and love him two different times.

I once sat on a plane after making the most life-altering decision of my life and wondered how it was possible to leave a place you were so familiar with.

Well, it turns out, I figured out the answer after all this time.

How *do* you leave a place you're so familiar with?

You stay.

Epilogue

Henry

A Few Years Into the Future

"For Amelia Ellis—My wife, my partner, my forever. This book was always going to be dedicated to you. Thank you for giving me our beautiful family and the life we live together." — *Dedication from Henry Hayes' Eighth Novel*

"Spread your legs for me, Mills," I say, and my beautiful wife listens to me so well. "That's it. Let me see all of you, baby."

"Henry, please," she begs beneath me.

"God, I love it when you look at me like that," I tell her as I lower my head to her center.

"Like what?"

"Like you want me. Like I'm the only guy in the world who can give you what you need."

"Because you are, Henry," she reminds me as I finally get a taste of her. "Now, please, get up here," she says as she pulls me up to her mouth.

"Someone's needy for me." I smile against her lips, and in one, swift thrust, I'm inside her, the two of us moaning against each other's lips.

Amelia and I are at a resort in Turks and Caicos for our vacation this year, and this place is beautiful. Our days have been filled with trips to the beach, delicious meals at local restaurants, and so much sun, we aren't even thinking about going back to the cold that waits for us in Virginia.

Most of our nights are filled with us getting lost in one another's bodies. After a few years of Amelia being my wife, I can't imagine not being as infatuated with her as I am now and forever will be.

Her legs wrap around my back, pulling me deeper inside her as her back arches, my dick hitting her favorite fucking spot.

God, I love seeing her like this. I love making my beautiful, enchanting wife moan and groan until I give her what she needs from me.

"Amelia Hayes, you look like a fucking dream when your eyes roll to the back of your head."

"Faster, please," she groans as I hoist her legs onto my shoulders, pumping in and out of her. I know she loves it when I make that necklace bounce between her breasts. She's so close, I can feel her clenching around me, but I don't give in just yet. I want to drive her as crazy as she makes me feel.

"On second thought, I want to take my time," I say as I lower her legs, pulling out as I kiss her on the lips, then the jaw, then her cheek, then slowly down her body. I take one of her nipples into my mouth, biting on it ever so slightly so her back arches again, the light touches to her skin driving her insane.

She's been on a different level lately, and I don't think the two of us have ever had sex as much as we have in the past few months. My wife has been insatiable, and I'm loving every second of it.

"Henry..." she whispers to me.

"Let me savor you, Mills," I whisper against her soft skin. I kiss her chest, her belly button, her hip bone, down her legs, and eventually, when I'm worshipping her at her feet, I flip her over, wanting to cover every inch of her beautiful body with my lips.

"I swear if you don't—"

"What was that?" I say as I wet my dick with her pussy and slide back home. God, she feels so fucking good every single time. "Were you saying something, baby?"

"Please keep going, Hen."

I give her what she needs, and as she unravels around my cock, I can't help but spill inside her at the same time, chanting one another's names until we come down, the only sound the waves crashing outside of our room and our panting breaths.

"I love you, Mills."

She flips around and slips her tongue in my mouth. "I love you too, Hen."

I bundle her in my arms before I feel and hear her stomach grumble.

"Do you want me to grab us some food while you shower?"

"I think I just fell more in love with you," she says as the two of us laugh, taking as many seconds as we can wrapped in one another's arms before we untangle.

As shock filters through my system, I do the only thing I can and pick up my phone, dialing the only people I want to talk to.

"Why are you calling us on vacation?" Ella asks me. "Damn, your tan looks wonderful, though."

"I'm freaking out."

"Amelia, I thought we were done with the whole running thing when you came back here all those years ago?" Hads asks me, but my mind can only focus on the thing in my hand. Where the fuck is Paige? I need *all* my girls here with me. Just as her phone clicks in, I see Oliver on the other side of it, and I groan.

"Seriously? I thought I was going to get a week off from you and your incessant calls. Isn't that the point of a vacation?"

"Shut it, Nosferatu," I snark as I pace around the bathroom. "Where is your wife?"

"In front of the toilet." He sighs heavily. "Her morning sickness has been horrible lately, you guys know that."

"That means the little bean is growing properly!" Grant pops his head into the screen, and I'm still freaking the fuck out.

"I need Paige," I tell him. "Like right now."

"Amelia..." Grant trails off. "What's going on?"

"I need my girls," I say as I sit on the floor of the resort bathroom, my head in my hands. "Please, Oliver. I need Paige."

I think he realizes how dire of a situation this is, because I've never been so nice to him. He shuffles over to his pregnant wife, and when I see Paige sitting on the floor of her bathroom, crackers and ginger ale in hand, she shrieks.

"Did I almost miss a debrief? Ugh!" she says as she throws her hands up. "I miss you, Ames! What's going on?"

"She's having a tsunami-level meltdown," Ella says. "At least, that's what I think is happening."

"Is everything okay? Where's Henry?" Hads asks me.

"He went to get us some food," I say. "I stayed in the room."

"And that became a full-blown meltdown?" Paige wonders.

"Well, yes."

"How?" Hads asks, and before I say anything else, I flip the camera to show them the reason I'm going insane.

"Is that what I think it is?" Ella asks, and I shake the camera to match my nodding behind it.

"You're pregnant?" Paige practically screams over the line.

"Oh God, there's going to be another Amelia? Prayers to us," Oliver jokes, and I wish Hads could smack him with something.

"What?" I hear from across the other side of the door, and when I hear Henry's voice, I unlock it, his eyes already filled with tears. "Did I hear that right?"

"Mhm," I confirm. "And I'm terrified, Hen, because this wasn't part of our plan—"

He picks me up, and my phone falls to the floor as he spins me around the bathroom. "Fuck the plan, Mills. This is—fuck." He sets me down and cradles my face in his hands. "This is the best thing that has ever happened to me."

"Really?"

"Yes, really," he says as a few tears fall from his eyes. "My God, Amelia, *you* are the best thing that happened to me."

He leans his forehead against mine, and tears fall from my eyes as I think about the life we've created. "I'm scared."

"I'm scared too," he tells me, a huge smile still on his face. "But this is just another chapter of our story together."

"We're having a baby," I tell him with a smile as I look at this astonishing man in front of me.

"Hell yeah, we are," he says as the voices of our friends filter in. Everyone is crying, save for Oliver, and as I look at Paige, I find tears pouring from her face.

"We're pregnant at the same time," she tells me.

"Which means our kids are totally going to be best friends."

"At this rate, all of our kids are going to be as close as you girls are," Grant reminds us. "And what a beautiful family we're all creating together."

"Our master plan is complete," Ella jokes as Leo comes into frame.

"Why are you all crying?"

"Amelia's pregnant," Ella tells her husband, because Henry and I are too speechless to say anything.

"That's wonderful news. Congratulations, you two," he says to us. "Now we're going to have two babies to spoil at the end of the year."

"Thanks, Leo," Henry says. "But I'm going to spend some time with my beautiful pregnant wife, so we'll see you all when we get home."

And with a parade of well wishes, he hangs up the call and captures my lips, whispering sweet nothings as we start this new, terrifying, exciting life together.

Extended Epilogue

Years Later

When We Are Together by The 1975

"Mommy, why are we doing this again?" my daughter, Kaia, asks me.

"We're surprising your daddy with a mix of songs that describe his latest book," I tell her as I move the files onto a disc. Henry is already at the venue for his last book tour stop, and since this tour is coming to an end and he's finally back in Virginia, I wanted to do something special.

Not only does he not know we're coming, but he also doesn't know the apartment is decorated for when we all get back. Our kids, Kaia and Rowan, helped make the decorations, and I know he's going to love it. I can't wait to see the look on his face when he sees us in the crowd.

We've been married for years, and it still feels like I'm finding more reasons to love him. When I got pregnant with our twins, I was terrified. I was worried about being a mother. This wasn't in the plan we had for our lives—at least not at that point.

But these past years with our kids have been some of the best of my life, and I can't imagine not having these little bugs around to ask me a thousand different questions.

"I can't wait to tell Dad about my playdate with Riley," Rowan says as he paints with his fingers on a sheet of paper.

"He's going to be excited to be home," I tell them as I finalize the songs for the disc. "I sent him pictures of you guys all playing while we were at Aunt Paige's house."

"Oh yeah," he chirps, and as I look at the time, I realize we have to get a move on. Getting two kids dressed, into the car, and fed is a pain in the butt, and I don't want to be late to this.

Henry has been away for about a week, and we've missed him so much. I cannot wait to see him.

We moved into this small house near the beach before I gave birth to the twins, and while I love our house, it is a bit farther from things than I would like. Granted, we're still pretty close to all our friends, but this small bookstore we're headed to is far, and I really need to pick up my pace.

"Okay, my loves," I say as I close my laptop. "Can you go wash your hands and get dressed for Mommy so we can go see Daddy?"

As squeals and screams fill the house, I smile to myself.

I love this life I've created with Henry, and I'm grateful I get to be living it. I was smart enough to come back and build the life I knew I wanted—the one I *deserve*. Because every time I look into the eyes of my kids and see the echoes of Henry in them both, I have to stop myself from crying.

No longer does it feel like I'm breathing when I'm running from things. Now, the only time I feel like everything will be okay is when my two kids and my wonderful husband are around me.

And to think, I almost gave all this up by not coming back all those years ago.

"Alright, are you guys ready?" I ask as the two of them come out, showing off their outfits. As I grab their hands in mine, their little fingers wiggling in my closed hand, tears start to form in my eyes, but I push those down before I get too overwhelmed.

Henry

EVEN THOUGH I'VE DONE multiple book tours and this isn't my first rodeo, I still get nervous as I walk onto the small stage, a microphone in my hand as I wave to the crowd.

"Thank you all for coming. Oh my goodness," I say as I settle into my chair, Mitch sitting across from me. "This is wild. I can't wait to meet all of you after this."

Murmurs of laughter echo around the shop as I hear Mitch start to ask some of the prepared questions.

"Henry, I think the most asked question most people want to know is where you get your ideas from?" Mitch adjusts how he sits. "Because obviously, you write about all sorts of things, complicated family dynamics, relationships, and most recently, a friend group with multiple points of view. I figured we would start off with a bang."

"Oh gosh, yeah," I chuckle. "Most of my ideas come from wanting to explore certain types of relationships. I think that's what I love writing most about, because we as humans are such connective people. As I look around at the world and see all these types of dynamics, I've always wanted to explore it through my writing. It feels natural to me—exploring dynamics and molding a story around those."

"And you guys should see this guy outlining a novel." Mitch points to me. "I've never seen such chaos turn into what his drafts look like. It's honestly impressive from both a writer and a reader standpoint, Henry."

"Thank you," I laugh. "It works for my brain—the organized chaos."

More questions are asked, and as soon as I really take a look into the crowd and see my beautiful wife and two kids, I almost start crying. I even fumble over some of my words when I recognize them in the audience. I didn't know they were coming. I knew Amelia had planned to pick me up when it was over, since these things can go all night, but I'm shocked.

I love traveling and chatting about my novels, but I fucking miss my family. Before Ames and I had kids, she would travel with me to these events, and we'd spend time together in different cities.

But now that we have Kaia and Rowan, it's harder. The fact that they came to watch my last stop and support me from the audience makes my heart soar. I used to dream of times like this—being able to see the people I love looking back at me from the audience—and now, I've made it.

I don't have just Amelia to celebrate with anymore. Now, we have two pieces of us to remind us of our love. We loved each other so much, we created two tiny humans to love us no matter what happens.

When I started my career, I was celebrating my wins all by myself. Now, I'm not alone. Now, I'll never be alone again.

The question-and-answer section ends, and it takes about three hours for me to get through the line of people. The real prize of tonight is seeing my kids run into my arms, their beautiful voices filtering through my ears.

"I missed you guys so much," I say as I squeeze them.

"Too tight, Dad!" Kaia says as she pulls away from me.

"Did you bring us anything?" Rowan asks me. I started a new tradition of bringing them each back something from my trips.

"Is that all you want me for? The gifts?" I joke as I fluff my son's hair. "Of course I got you guys presents, but they're in my suitcase, so we can open them at home."

I stand from the floor and press a kiss to my wife's lips, melting into her embrace as she throws her arms around me.

"I'm glad you're home," she whispers. "Were you surprised?"

"I was." My smile slips onto my face. "I missed you guys."

"Do you want to go home?" she asks me, and I nod before the sentence is even over. Mitch and I had dinner as soon as we got to the airport, and as much as I'd like to see more of him, I've also missed my family. It's time for some much needed rest and relaxation with my favorite people.

Ames and I get the kids into the car, and as soon as my hand grabs hers as she drives, I feel a sense of peace wash over me.

This is the life I've been chasing since I was in my twenties, and I swear, I blinked and it arrived. Time needs to slow down. I swear, Kaia and Rowan were kids just learning how to walk.

"Daddy, we made you something special!" Kaia says to me, and I see her excited face in the rearview. "Mom, can you play it?"

"Of course I can, baby," Ames says as she fumbles with the console, and as soon as the music starts, I want to cry.

The song Amelia and I danced to at our wedding plays first. Then comes the songs playing in the hospital when our kids were born. Every song holds a sentimental value from the life Amelia and I have shared.

Tears fall from my eyes as I squeeze Amelia's hand.

"What is this one called?"

"Our life together," Amelia tells me. Just like every playlist we both make has a name, every disc burned also gets one. This one being just for me, made by my family, is...too much, almost.

"It's been the best one I could have ever imagined," I tell her. "And I owe it all to you."

"Us, Henry. It's not just you and me anymore, remember?" She tilts her head to the back seat.

"God, I love you so much, Ames," I tell her. "I love this life we have together."

"Me too." She smiles as a tear falls. "It's everything I could have imagined."

I used to believe everything happens for a reason, but now, I know things happen because we make them happen. Amelia and I made this happen—together.

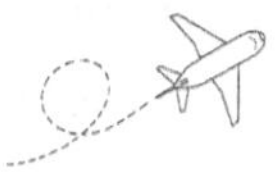

True Blue by boygenius

As I CARRY ONE of our dogs out to the living room of our home, I see my beautiful wife scrambling around, trying to get everything ready for the family Christmas party we're hosting. My parents flew in the other day, and Ella's dad and sister are on the way as well. Part of me feels nostalgic seeing Ella run around like this, remembering how she bossed me around the first time I freaked out about hosting our friends.

It's funny how things never seem to change much.

"Ella, darling," I say as she looks over at me, "do you want some help?"

"You've got Rosie girl in your arms," she tells me as she hangs our decorations on the tree. "Do you think she'll let you put her down to help me?"

I shrug. "I can at least get the food out."

"That actually would be helpful," she tells me as I walk by, grabbing her in my free arm and spinning her around, needing to feel her lips on mine. "What was that for?"

"Why do you question me every time I want to kiss my beautiful wife?"

"Because you always seem to want something after." She smirks, knowing I'll never be able to get enough of her, in this lifetime and the next. She's all I've ever wanted, and the life we've created together is just as I imagined.

We have two codependent dogs, no children, and beautiful properties around the States and back in London. We vacation a lot, despite how hard it is to pull my wife away from her business—which continues to thrive as the years pass.

I've officially taken over Loft Media since Imogen moved on to bigger and better things. The transition was rough, but I'm grateful to be able to run the company I started at all those years ago. Not only did I work my ass off to get where I am, but I was able to do it with Ella by my side.

"Am I too early?" my sister says as she waltzes through the door.

"I regret giving you a key now," I say as I hug her. "But I am glad to see you."

"Alissa, thank fuck," Ella sighs. "Can you help me set up everything before our parents arrive?"

"Is Lizzie coming too?"

"Yes, and her husband." Ella smiles. I let the two of them settle in and finish up everything while I get the food ready.

I'm grateful my parents made the trip over here. Obviously, we stay in touch, but I've missed actually seeing them. Ella and I got to London over the summer, but it's still been too damn long.

Soon, this house will be filled with two families, lots of laughter, and probably too much cursing, but I love it. I was so afraid of missing out on things being in the States, but now that I'm older, more secure, Ella and I are able to travel and see them whenever we can.

No longer am I worried I'm not doing enough for my family—Ella wakes up every morning and tells me I'm enough for her. Those words are all I need, and I can't believe she still deals with my annoying arse.

I thought she would tire of me. I thought she would get sick of me one of these days, but every morning, I get to wake up to her beautiful face, those curls sticking to my face as our dogs lay between us. I thank my lucky stars she opened the damn door for me all those years ago.

I've reached the other side of the monkey bars, all thanks to Ella, and I can't wait to see where this next phase of our life takes us.

"Leo?"

"Yes, darling?"

"Can you get the door? I think everyone is here."

As soon as I'm back in reality, I hear knocks, and as I open the door and both our families filter inside, I send a thank you into the universe for being so good to me.

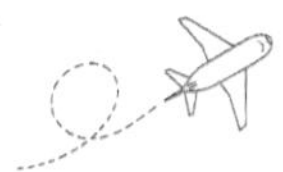

AFTER THE BEST DINNER I've ever prepared, our families are all gathered in the living room to open presents. I can't believe we're all here together; I never take this time for granted—sometime in the future, this won't be possible.

But I can't think about that right now.

"Okay, so before we open presents," my sister says as she gets up, "there's something I want to tell you all."

"Lizzie, please don't tell me you got another piercing," my dad groans. "Just don't tell me where it is this time, okay? I do not need the details."

Matthew, our other dog, crawls into my lap while I wait to hear what my sister has to say.

"Dad, calm down," she says. "It's not a big deal." Lizzie reaches into her bag and pulls out two small boxes, one for my dad and one for me. She hands them to us and looks over at her husband, her eyes shining as bright as the lights on the tree.

"Can we open them?" I ask, petting my very needy dog. "Lizzie, you're kind of scaring me."

"Don't be scared. Just open them," she tells us, and as I pull out a shirt that says Aunt Ella on it, tears burst from my eyes.

"Are you serious?"

"Yes!" she tells me. "You're going to be the best aunt ever, Ells."

I practically scream as I hug my sister.

"We're going to spoil that child rotten," Leo says as he hugs her. "And you can't say a word about it."

"I would never tell you two what to do with your money," Lizzie says as I wrap her in another hug.

"I'm so happy for you, sis." I squeeze her. "You're going to be the best mother."

"I was worried at first." She locks eyes with me. "I was scared I didn't have it in me because of—"

I shake my head. "No. No, you're nothing like her," I remind her. "Your child is going to be so full of love, they won't know what to do with it all. And I will be here by your side through it all, Lizzie."

"Thank you, Ells." A few tears fall as we hug again. "Thank you for taking care of me all those years. I'm pretty sure I wouldn't be here now if not for you."

"I love you," I tell her. "And I am so proud of you, Lizzie."

Tissues are passed around the room. As we settle in for the remaining presents, I really stop and take it all in.

I'm surrounded by my family, the one I was born with and the one I inherited when I chose Leo. The love in the room is astounding, and it covers me like a warm blanket.

When I was a child, I grew up so fast, I never thought I would have a chance to really live my life to the fullest. I thought I was always destined to take care of others and put their lives above my own.

But sitting here now, I realize I not only have a partner in my life who reminds me to slow down, but one who takes care of me. He loves me for who I am, and he's never tried to change me. He only lifts me up when I'm not strong enough to do it for myself.

I still have my friends to remind me of all those things too—when they're not too busy with their own families and children. I've taken my life back from all the years I spent working myself to the bone, trying to remind myself I was good enough.

Well, now, I have nothing to prove. The only life I want to live is one beside Leo, hearing him cheer me on so loud, I never remember what it was like to be on my own.

In the years to come, I hope we can fill this house with more parties, more laughs, more friendship, and more love.

Because not only do we deserve it, but we earned it.

Walking in the Wind by One Direction

"What do I do with this, Dad?" my daughter Riley asks me as she holds up the pasta dough. "It feels weird."

"Put it through the roller a few more times until it's nice and long," I tell her. Not only is my daughter my favorite assistant in the kitchen, but being able to teach her one of my favorite things has been the best part of being a father.

Well, among the other million things I love about it.

Aspen is with Paige in the other room, the two of them playing with her toys before Hads and Grant get here with their kids. Never did I imagine my sister having four kids, but that's the reality.

"Am I doing okay?" my daughter asks, and I move from what I'm stirring to help her handle the dough.

"You're doing great, sunshine," I tell her. "Now, lay it out on the counter, and I'll cut it while you set the table, okay?"

"Okay." She hops off the small stool I keep for her in the kitchen before she grabs the plates to set the table.

"Winnie, no," I say to our dog, who sits patiently, waiting for small scraps of food to fall off the table. "It's not dinner time for you yet."

A heavy sigh and a flop to the floor is all I get from her.

"Hey, Dad?"

"What's up?"

"Do you think one day, I can have a book club just like Mom does?"

Her big green eyes shine back at me, and as I set the spoon down to let the broth rest, I sweep her up in my arms. Most of our kids are readers, thanks to the girls and all their meddling, and even the young ones who can't form words yet will probably follow in their footsteps.

"Is that something you want?"

She nods.

"Then one day, you'll find your people." I tap her on the nose. "Just how your mom did, you'll find the people who will love you as you are, not as who you pretend to be."

"Do you think so?"

"I know so," I tell her as she nuzzles her head into my shoulder. "Just don't force friendships, okay? When you find your people, you'll know."

"Like how you knew you loved Mom when you first met her?"

"Yeah, baby, kind of like that."

I hear Paige laughing from the other room, our daughter's laughter echoing into the kitchen as well, and I try to wrap my mind around the past few years. I never thought I'd find a home like the one Paige and I have created. I always thought my future would be full of loneliness because I refused to let anyone in.

Then, along came Paige, and everything changed for the better. That girl saved my goddamn life—more than once. I'll never be able to thank her for giving me our two beautiful daughters and the life we live now.

It's perfect. It's everything, and Paige gave that to me.

"Now, go wash up with your sister before your cousins get here," I tell her as I set her down, heading to see my wife before all hell breaks loose.

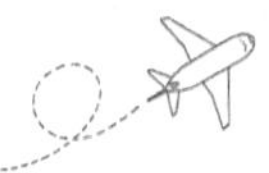

Paige

I FEEL OLIVER'S PRESENCE before he makes himself known.

"Hi, my love," I say as I swing around, grabbing some toys and putting them back in their bin in the toy room. Aspen barrels out of the room, following her sister to the bathroom. Oliver and I laugh as he pretends she knocked him off his feet. "How is dinner coming?"

"It's almost done. Are Hads and Grant on their way?"

"They are," I confirm as I get up and throw my arms around his neck. "What are you thinking about?"

"You," he says as he presses a kiss to my forehead. "Our life."

"Oh, so nothing too heavy," I joke. "What about it?"

"I'm just lucky, P," he says as he spins me around. "I'm so fucking lucky to have found you."

"Likewise," I tell him as I press a kiss to his lips.

Lately, I've found myself thinking a lot about the past—mine specifically. Growing up, I never could have imagined my life would look so...happy. All I knew when I was a kid was sadness, loneliness, and every other horrible emotion in between. I was scared, so often terrified I wouldn't be around to grow up and escape the house I was raised in.

I broke that cycle. *I* did that, and I am so fucking proud of myself for creating a life with the man I love.

I have children I love more than myself most days, and I cannot imagine my life without them in it. I can't imagine not being here for every big, small, and in between moment.

I'm not alone anymore—in fact, I'm so far from it, I can barely remember what that emotion feels like anymore. I have a family, one I chose and one who chose me right back.

Gone is the girl afraid of her own shadow, and in her place is someone strong, confident, and brave.

"Can we watch the sunrise with the kids tomorrow morning?" Oliver asks me, and I smile into his lips.

"Of course we can," I tell him.

As we take a moment just with us, Oliver's hands around my waist as we silently sway to no music, I take a mental picture of this moment.

The childhood my kids will have will only be one full of laughter, light, and happiness—the exact opposite of what I grew up in. The home Oliver I have created despite all we've been through is something worth celebrating.

"Can you believe we made it here, love? I can't thank you enough for giving me our beautiful children and this life of ours."

"We made it because we deserve it, Ol," I remind him. "And you as a father is quite literally the hottest thing I've ever seen."

He presses a kiss to my lips, deepening it before a knock on the door breaks us apart, our kids rushing down the hall to open it to their cousins, Uncle Grant, and Aunt Hads.

"Are you ready for the chaos, my love?" I ask him, a huge smile on my face.

"I wouldn't want it any other way, Mrs. Baker."

The Manuscript by Taylor Swift

"Claire, how does this look?" I say as I hoist Caleb, my youngest son, over my shoulder. "Do you think this would look good on the Christmas card?"

"Well," she laughs as she clicks some photos, "per Hads' instructions, no, but I can always give you copies for your latest scrapbook."

"Were matching sweaters really necessary?" Oliver asks as he walks over with Aspen in his arms. "And outside in this weather? If one of my kids gets sick, it's on you, Carter."

"Ol," Paige says as she grabs Aspen from him. "What did I tell you before we left the house this morning?"

"No arguing with Grant." He rolls his eyes. "I know we've done the whole matching thing before, but it feels cheesy."

"Cheesy, yes, but adorable and family-like was the main goal here," my beautiful wife says as she holds our newborn, both of them wrapped in coats. "We're a big family, Oliver."

"Well, I wonder why that is." He smirks.

"What did I do?" I feign innocence.

"You procreated a bit too much with my little sister," he jokes. I know he's joking, because he cried every time he held one of our kids in the hospital. Uncle Oliver is a big softie, but he's too afraid to admit it.

"Hads and I wanted a big family," I reiterate.

"Claire and I stopped at two," Jacks says as he carries more equipment over for his wife. "And remind me to send Ella and Leo a gift for watching them while we're here. Cece and Ezra were a bit fussy this morning."

"Ezra Grant Moore was being fussy?" I say, my hand on my chest. "Well, it looks like he takes after his namesake."

"Oh, then we can blame you for him not wanting to sleep all last night?" Jacks jokes.

"I've never had any problem getting him down when I watch him."

"Because you have the secret touch," Claire tells me, and I fist bump her.

"Ella and Leo are the best babysitters," Paige insists. "But can we get this show on the road?"

"We have book club tonight," Hads reminds us, as if we could all forget it was Wednesday. Little does she know, I have a surprise for her, and I'm practically itching to tell her about it.

The boys and I have been planning this for weeks, and I don't think any of the girls suspect a thing.

"We'll be home in time for that," I say as I press a kiss to Hads' forehead. "Don't worry, baby."

"How do you want us, Claire?" Paige asks, and Claire goes full-on photographer mode as she sets us all up. The Carter family is on the left, the Baker family on the right, and with six kids between our two families, I can't help but smile.

I always wanted a big family—growing up an only child made me yearn for this, and now I have it. Hads and I are outnumbered by two, but somehow, we still make a great team. That girl is my rock, my support. My wife. My soul. My future. My light. I finally reached her all those years ago, and now, as we stand here with our families, I find myself wanting to slow time down.

It's going too fast. It's speeding through the years, and I'm desperate to savor more of these moments with her. No amount of time in the world will ever be enough with Hads, and I hope in the next life we're able to find one another again.

"Jacks?"

"Yes, gorgeous?"

"Can you move my light a few inches to the left?"

"Of course." He does, and the rest of us hold our positions as we await further instructions from Claire. She is the professional, after all.

"Hads," I whisper to her, not moving my head. "Remember when I told you that you were like the spring?"

"Yes..." she says, a confused expression on her face.

"Well, I was wrong."

"You were? The most beautiful thing you said to me when we first got together, you were wrong about?"

I nod.

"And what does that mean?"

"You're not just the spring, at least not anymore." I shove her with my shoulder. "You're all the seasons, every single one of them. You are my forever, Hadleigh Carter. Not just one season, but somehow, all four wrapped into one."

"I love you, pretty boy."

"I love you too, Hades."

"Are you guys ready?" Claire asks us all. "Everyone smile for the camera!"

The camera flashes, photos are taken, but one thing will always remain the same—our family. We're messy and dysfunctional, but we're ours. I'll always be grateful to the four girls who sat in a classroom to read a book. Somehow, by some stroke of luck, I'm able to be a part of this journey we're all on together.

Hadleigh

"Did I really need to be blindfolded for this?" I ask my husband as he leads me up the stairs. "I'm having déjà vu."

"Yes, baby," he tells me. "A few more steps, and we're almost there."

I sigh heavily as I let him lead me to our destination. The boys texted in the group chat earlier, letting us girls know we were in for a surprise tonight, so I assume the rest of the girls are also being blindfolded and led to the same place. I can't lie, I'm nervous for some reason.

Jacks and Claire are watching all of our kids, and bless their hearts for agreeing to take *all* of them on such short notice.

"It took you long enough," I hear my brother say. "What took you two so long?"

"Traffic," Grant tells him.

"Can we take off these blindfolds now?" I hear Amelia say, annoyance in her tone. "I only agreed to wearing this for a short amount of time."

"We're almost ready, Mills," Henry says to her.

"I bet this is foreplay for you two," Grant snarks, probably aiming it at Ella and Leo.

"Not this time," Leo affirms.

"I will claw your eyes out if you ever try to get me to wear one of these again, Zimmerman," Ella threatens her husband.

"We have the same surname, darling," Leo reminds her. "You don't quite scare me anymore."

"Keep one eye open tonight while you're sleeping," she tells him.

"Now that we're all here, can we take these off?" I ask Grant as he moves around me.

"One moment, girls," he says, and I hear a lock click, a door slowly opening before he grabs my hand, leading me inside. "Okay, now you can take them off."

I undo mine, and tears spring to my eyes almost immediately as I recognize where we are.

Grand Mountain College—the same classroom where we started book club in all those years ago.

"What are we doing here?" I ask as I turn to meet Grant. "Are we even allowed in here?"

"Celebrating," Leo says as he grabs a bottle of champagne from next to a bunch of snacks and our book club choice for this month.

"Celebrating what?" Paige asks, her eyes also full of tears.

"You guys," Oliver tells us. "Because without your book club, none of our lives would be where they are today."

"And that's the truth," Henry reminds us. "You four are responsible for the lives we're all living."

"What's that?" Ella asks as she points to a small plaque on the wall. The four of us walk over to it, reading the small inscription.

For The Grand Mountain Book Club: Hads, Paige, Ella, and Amelia. Four started as strangers, four ended as family.

Plaque donated by Grant, Oliver, Leo, and Henry.

"You guys did this for us?" Amelia asks, tears falling down her cheeks.

"It was the least we could do," Grant tells us.

"You four are special," Leo states. "And though we let you know every day how thankful we are for you, this plaque is there to remind you."

"Books brought you together, but the impression you made on one another will last lifetimes," Henry reminds us. "Lifetimes in the form of our kids."

"You guys..." Paige sniffles.

"I can't believe this," I say through my own tears. I used to hate crying. Now, I find myself doing it constantly at the littlest things. Rosalie, my daughter, latched onto my finger the other day, and I started bawling.

"Do you guys remember the first time we all sat in here?" Amelia asks us.

"Of course we do," I answer. "It was the day everything changed."

"Can you believe where we are now?" Amelia asks, and we all stand silently, really taking in the moment.

"And it's all thanks to books." Paige smiles before she wraps us all in a group hug. "I love you guys so much."

"Books are magical," Ella says, squeezing us all a little tighter.

"You four are the real magic," Grant reminds us.

And as the eight of us reminisce on the good old days, I find myself thanking the college version of myself for walking into this room on campus. I never would have guessed this is where it would have led me—sitting here years later with the same girls I started this journey with.

"Can you guys believe I once paced this room at the thought of tutoring Grant?" I smile, my cheeks flushing at the memory.

"And four children later, we're as happy as can be," he reminds me.

"My fondest memory was when Oliver practically shoved me to the classroom next door to secretly talk about our investigation." Paige smiles as my brother hugs her from behind. I can't believe I was ever so blind to those two and their feelings for one another. Paige was the best thing to happen to my brother.

"You wouldn't stop staring at my arms, love," Oliver reminds her before I roll my eyes.

"I remember all the times I cursed out Leo while sitting in this exact chair," Ella says, giving Leo a dirty look.

"Was that before or after our first slip-up, darling?" he asks his wife, a challenge in his voice as she flips him off.

"I have nightmares about that first conversation when you all met Henry," Amelia says. "I have never been more terrified in my entire life."

"I remember that night fondly," Henry tells her. "We had the best dinner after, and you kept denying your feelings for me."

The room erupts with laughter, and stories are traded well into the night. I take a deep breath before we leave, the four of us girls looking back at this classroom that holds our most special college memories.

When I first walked into this room all those years ago, I never would have guessed what was to come. I got to watch Paige fall in love with my brother and find a family in all of us that she didn't have as a kid. I was lucky enough to see Ella finally let someone take care of her after all the years she's spent taking care of her sister and the three of us since we became friends. And I got to watch Amelia come back and fight for her friendships after struggling to stay in one place. Now, we're all here, still choosing one another every single day. We've created one giant family, the four of us, and all of them got to watch me fall in love with Grant, finally learning to trust again after all I had been through.

I can almost see the younger versions of ourselves looking back at us. I hope they're proud of who we've become. Actually, I know they are; those versions live inside us no matter how old we get, and the girl I was back then always reminds me of how lucky we are to have gone to that book club meeting in the first place.

I never would have imagined books could have brought me this life I'm living, but damn, I got super fucking lucky.

The End.

Authors Note

And with that, the Grand Mountain series is officially complete.

I'll be honest, I never thought I would be typing that sentence. There were so many times I wanted to shelve this book and delete every single word of it. This story felt like pulling teeth at times, and there were so many moments I sat at my desk, my fingers resting on the keyboard of my laptop thinking to myself I wasn't cut out for this. I truly lost my passion for telling stories when I first wrote this book. Every word I wrote was stale and horrible. I wanted to delete it all and end my debut series with the third book.

But when I thought about doing that, I got even more upset. I knew if I didn't figure this story out, I'd regret it.

And boy, was I right. Eventually, the words and the characters fell into place. After an entire rewrite, a long session with my therapist about why I was struggling so much, and *many* tears, the words started to flow. The characters finally felt like *mine* again, and I couldn't be happier with what this novel has turned out to be.

I have spent over two years with these characters. The first book, Re-playing the Game, came out originally in February of 2023, the original idea for this series was born in November of 2022. Now, it's July of 2025. So much has changed since four girls sat in that original document, outlining what would become the Grand Mountain series. Now, there's three of us. Unlike this series, the characters we loosely based on how we met, got their happy ending, but in real life, it didn't really work out that way. I still wonder sometimes, but I'm happy to know that in another life, these girls got a happy ending, even if I didn't. But that's life, right? As you grow, friendships change. People change. You will change so many times throughout the course of your life. Just in the years I've spent with this series, I've changed so much. I almost don't recognize the version of myself that started writing my debut novel. It sort of feels like a lifetime ago.

This series has followed me from being in college not really knowing what I wanted to do with my life, to graduating and still being as lost as ever, to working at the same part-time job I had all throughout college, to being unemployed, and now, here I am, typing these words with a full-time job, still creating stories during the lulls at my day job. These characters have grown with me, and now, they belong to you. Through whatever phase of life you're in at the moment, I hope you find some comfort in this series and the family these characters have created. It's an honor you've chosen to pick up my story and spend some time in the universe I created way back when stories felt like all I had.

This series was my way of highlighting platonic love, something I have long lived as a companion with. Romantic love is obviously just as important, but friendships like the one the book club girls have are just as important. I hope that's something you all take away from this series, whether you've only read this one or the entire thing. If you've been with me since the beginning or just recently, thank you. I couldn't do any of this without the readers. You don't know how much you mean to small indie authors like me.

This series now belongs to all of you, and I hope it brings some light when things get dark. I hope it reminds you that you are worth more than what your grades are. I hope it reminds you that family isn't always just the people you're related to by blood. I hope it reminds you that leaning on others when things get tough is okay. And I hope it reminds you that to make mistakes is to be a human being, and sometimes, all we need is another chance to make things right again.

GM4L.

— Emily

Acknowledgements

Being an author would not be possible without the amazing people I'm lucky enough to have around me.

Hannah & Lexi—Holy crap. The series we manically thought of one day as a joke is now complete. I know we all didn't think this would really come, but now that it's here, I'm really going to fucking miss it. From having you guys watch me write Hads and Grant to watching me write the extended epilogue, all of us in tears as I typed, I will never forget that this is where we started, but it's also not where we're going to end. Lexi, I couldn't do any of this author thing without you. I know you know that, but it's important to me that I tell you that anytime I can. Thank you times a million for *everything*. Though sometimes, thank you does not feel like enough. From calling in a manic state to try and figure out where this story went wrong, to finally typing the end, this entire series would not have become what it is without you. And Hannah, these beautiful covers and interiors would not exist without your beautiful brain. I will always smile until my cheeks hurt when I get to tell people one of my best friends designs the covers that wrap around my words. It's an honor. And I hope we can all look back on this series with fondness because I will always be proud of what we've all created together. Thank you. I love you both. Here's to more books together in the future.

My Beta readers—Amy, Shannon, Soph, and Baleigh. Thank goodness for you guys. Seriously. This story would not be anything without you guys. You truly helped me wrap up this story and give these characters the story they deserved. I will always be thankful for that. Thank you times a million.

Josh—For everything you do. Sometimes, I don't know how you deal with me between the manic writing episodes, to the not drinking water or eating sometimes because I'm too in the zone. Thank you for feeding me, loving me, and reminding me why I write stories in the first place. Whenever I felt down on myself, crying because I didn't think I could do this anymore, you were always there to remind me that I was doing okay. Thank you. I love you so damn much.

Sarah A. Bailey—For letting me pick your brain about ADHD and for helping me through the spiral. You understand more than most how hard it is to push through the hard manuscripts, and I am so grateful for you and every time you helped me talk the problems out when they felt too big for my brain. I feel so lucky to be on this journey with you. Thank you for everything.

My sensitivity readers—Kait, Noe, Hails, & Catarina. Thank you to each of you for answering all the questions I had about ADHD. Amelia would not be the character she is without all of your help. I am so grateful to have readers like you all, who were willing to share tiny bits of your stories with me. I will forever cherish that. Thank you *so* much.

My therapist—who may or may not read this. I know you've only started to understand how this all works through our sessions together, but this book would not have been remotely possible without all the advice you gave me when I spent an entire session working through the struggles I was having with this manuscript. And thank you for all of the wonderful insight you gave me on ADHD. I feel so lucky to have someone like you in my corner when things get too loud.

Alyssa—My girl forever. I cannot believe I have known you for over twenty years, and you're still my favorite person to laugh with. I can't imagine not knowing you, not being in your orbit, and not perusing the bookstore with you, pointing out all the books we love and have read before. You are one of the reasons I understand what platonic love is, even if we don't hug because we're so awkward. Thank you for *everything*. I hope one day we're sitting on our porches, drinking a glass a wine, and still talking about the same twenty things we just *love* to keep rehashing.

My editor—Alexa, at The Fiction Fix. You always make my stories shine, and I so appreciate every *that* and *just* you remove from my manuscript. I adore you, and it is an honor to be included amongst your client list. Thank you for everything you do to make my stories the best they can be.

Shannon—Again, because you truly helped me through every step of this book. From outlining, to writing, to spiraling, to the final product. I could not have done this without you reminding me every other day that even if I didn't feel like it was good enough, that it was. You've believed in me since the beginning, and for that, I am grateful for. I will always be thankful for the job we worked at together for bringing us together. At least they did one thing right.

Mom—For the creative genes. Growing up and seeing you paint and create art for the plays when I was younger totally had a direct effect for my love of telling stories. I'm sure of it. Thank you for reading my books with the dog and coming to all my local events. It means the world that you continue to show up for me.

Shauna—My favorite local bookstore owner. For believing in indie authors, and for being the absolute coolest and wanting to host a launch party for this book. Being able to have a store like yours local to me is one of the best things to ever happen to me. It's an honor to know you and

I will always shout out the beautiful atmosphere you've created at Burn Bright.

Loretta—For helping me not spiral when I was writing this book at work. I probably should not have written any of this novel in public, but alas, a girl has to do what a girl has to do. Thank you for always listening when I would turn to you and say, "Can I ask you a question?" and then launch into a spiel about whatever it was that night. Thank you for not only being the coolest ever with immaculate music taste, but for reading all of my books one after another when you found out I was an author. It made me feel so much cooler than I am.

To everyone at work who has read my books or talked about them—On the days I felt my passion for telling stories dwindling, you were all there to remind me how cool it is that I write books. I'll never forget that. So, thank you to all of you, and thanks for listening to my aggressive and incessant typing. I know it's loud, and I am very sorry you have to deal with it when I'm on a deadline.

And finally, to me. This book was the most difficult time I've ever had creating something, and I am really bad at being proud of myself for doing just about anything, but right now, I don't really care. I am *so* proud of the girl who thought of this idea with her friends. I am so proud of the girl who took a year off from this series because it just wasn't working. I am so proud of the girl who jumped back into this universe and made it mine again. And I am so proud of this story and what it turned out to be. To the girl who was worried this book would never feel like hers, I hope you feel how proud each and every version of us is of you. Thank you for not giving up on us.

Also by Emily Tudor

<u>The Grand Mountain Series</u>
Replaying the Game
Redefining the Rules
Reconsidering the Facts
Reconciling With the Rival
Rewriting the Story

<u>The Hart Sisters</u>
The Road Not Taken
The Road Less Traveled By

About the author

Emily Tudor creates characters and stories about platonic and romantic love for anyone and everyone. She lives in the state of New York and loves listening to music and creating stories. She loves Marvel movies, the song *mirrorball* by Taylor Swift and buying too many books when she already has many to be read at home.

You can find her on Instagram at:
@authoremilytudor
www.authoremilytudor.com